HARD LINES

BLACKSTONE HOUSE
BOOK 1

ELISE NOBLE

Published by Undercover Publishing Limited

v3

ISBN: 978-1-912888-59-7

Edited by Nikki Mentges, NAM Editorial

Cover design by Abigail Sins

www.undercover-publishing.com

www.elise-noble.com

If you're going through hell, keep going.

CHAPTER 1
VIOLET

"Cut!" the director yelled.

Cut what?

My wrists?

The thin thread tethering my sanity to my half-naked body?

Or just the cameras in this…this…soft-core porn movie masquerading as a thriller. *Hidden Intent* had passion, intrigue, and drama, or so my agent had said right before I fired him for getting me into this whole mess. If only I could click my heels together and fly right back to Kansas.

Because right now, I was lying on my back, topless, on a sweaty leather couch, with fifty people watching as I tried to moan in all the right places. Even to my own ears, it sounded less convincing than Dick Van Dyke's cockney accent in *Mary Poppins*.

Kane Sanders, my co-star, removed his hand from under my skirt and stepped back. His grin wasn't as big as his ego, but it was certainly bigger than his dick. A wardrobe assistant leapt forward with a robe for him while I staggered to my feet and fetched my own from the back of a chair, cotton to Kane's silk, a flimsy shield between my body and the horrors around me. Kristen, my assistant, was too busy gawping at Kane's ass to actually assist, and I couldn't totally blame her. It *was* a nice ass. Just a shame about its owner.

Kane flashed me another of his trademark smiles as he strode off set, leaving me confused. Why was he happy? The whole scene had been a disaster from start to finish. Did he have a date later? Or was he merely pleased about the stern word the director would undoubtedly want to have with me?

Speaking of which... David Jackson beckoned in my direction. Too late, I realised the tie from my robe was caught around the chair, and the front gaped open, giving everyone in the vicinity another eyeful. Oh, what did it matter? Soon the whole damn world was going to see my boobs, at least, they would if the movie turned into the box-office hit David assured us it was destined to be. Well, as long as a certain member of the cast got her act together, anyway.

D minus, Violet. Must try harder.

David's minions studiously looked away as I approached, hovering around the periphery of his aura, close enough to hear the gossip but far enough away that if he threw his clipboard again, he'd probably miss.

"You wanted to speak to me?"

He sucked on his front teeth, and I forced the image of Bugs Bunny out of my head because there was nothing even vaguely funny about the situation. Everything was up, Doc.

"Violet, what the hell was that? You're with Kane Sanders —*Kane Sanders*—and you look like you're paying a visit to the gynaecologist instead of dancing the horizontal tango. Six takes, and we'll still have to fix that scene in post-production."

I choked at the mere mention of the word "gynaecologist." My last visit to Dr. Samuelson back home in Oakwood Falls had been over a year ago, and I still remembered every moment in excruciating detail. Bad enough that I'd gone to school with his granddaughter, but as he'd fished around down below with a flashlight, he'd chuckled and cheerfully informed me that he couldn't find the tunnel for the bushes. And did I know that Kathy at the beauty salon had a special on waxing this week? Twenty percent off, or so his wife said.

Okay, maybe the whole Kane ordeal wasn't so bad after all, except David was still staring at me, as were the minions.

"I'm so sorry. With all the people watching us…"

And we weren't actually horizontal. More…haphazard.

David tutted, shaking his head. "You're an actress, Violet. People watch. That's the whole point. And this isn't Little League anymore. *Hidden Intent* might have an eighty-million-dollar budget, but we can't afford to keep reshooting scenes."

Probably because most of that eighty million dollars was going on Kane's fee.

"I'll do better, I promise."

David draped one arm over my shoulders, a fatherly gesture when his words were anything but.

"Look, it's simple. If Kane doesn't do it for you, just block him out and imagine the last man to give you a rabid fucking. That way, we might get home on time tomorrow. Capiche?"

My mouth dropped open, and in the battle to close it again, I felt like a goldfish out of water, panicking as I gasped for air.

"Y-y-yes. Yes, I understand."

Sniggers came from the crowd as David strode off, leaving me behind to contemplate my lies. Firstly, I wasn't sure I *could* do better, and secondly, while I understood the theory, the sum total of my sexual experience hovered dangerously close to zero. In Oakwood Falls, my one drunken fumble in the back of a Toyota Camry had left me stranded in a movie theatre parking lot wearing a ripped dress. In summary: a disaster.

Encouraged by Lauren—my best friend and roommate—some alcohol, and memories of my dad telling me that if I fell off the horse, the best thing to do was get right back on, I'd tried the sex thing again soon after I moved to LA, and I still cringed at the memory of my suitor storming out when I asked, "Is it in yet?" Honestly, I hadn't meant to offend him, but it was dark, and there was a lot of fumbling. Then, when he slammed the door, a chunk of drywall had fallen from the ceiling and broken my toe. After the swelling went down, I'd hoped for third time lucky, but my final foray into the world of dating had resulted in a month-long mistake I'd needed therapy to get over. Except I couldn't afford therapy, so I'd been forced to drink more wine instead.

Shit. I needed help, I needed it fast, and there was only one person I could call. As soon as I got back to my trailer, I picked up the phone.

"Lauren?"

As a romance author, Lauren had offered me many nuggets of wisdom, but so far, I'd struggled to translate them into actions fit for a Hollywood blockbuster. A blockbuster I was way, way out of my depth in. Yes, I'd been in movies before, but only once in a leading role. Most of my acting experience came from "third girl on the left" parts and a short-lived series of infomercials for Diamonesque jewellery.

"So, how was your big day?" Lauren asked. "You had another scene with Kane, right?"

Why did she sound so dreamy?

"I keep telling you, he's just a frat boy stuffed into a designer suit."

"But he looks soooo good in the suit. Tall, dark, handsome, and hung."

"Should I introduce you? You'll soon change your mind about wanting to breathe the same air as him."

"Wish I could visit, Vi, but until I can get another book written, I need to work all the shifts I can."

Lauren might have been an author, but she'd barely penned a word since her last boyfriend dumped her via WhatsApp. Sure, they'd only been together for three months,

4

but she'd fallen hard. Would a phone call really have been that difficult?

"You can be my date for the premiere." If I didn't get fired first.

"Are you serious?"

"There's nobody I'd rather go with. But first, I need more pointers, or the movie's never gonna get finished."

"What happened this time?"

A groan escaped as I dropped onto the couch. Three-quarters of the space in my trailer was set aside for a make-up chair and a two-seater table, with the remainder taken up by a tiny bathroom and a bedroom containing a fold-out couch and a TV. At first, I'd been so excited to see my name on the door, my picture on the movie poster… But now? The longer I spent in LA, the more depressed I got by the layer of dirt that lay beneath the gleaming façade.

"Veronica decided to go for a walk after an argument with Drake—"

"Drake's the boyfriend?"

"Yes, on again, off again." Veronica was my character. A cop. Tough on the outside but broken on the inside, thanks in no small part to Drake's violent temper. "Well, the walk was more of a wild sprint, really." In high-heeled boots. "But it rained, and she got soaked. Then Kelvin found her outside his office and took her in to dry off."

I'd read the script with a mixture of longing and incredulity. What kind of a millionaire found a bedraggled woman slumped in his doorway and invited her up for drinks? That was the stuff of fairy tales, not real life.

"Then? What happened next?"

Lauren's voice hitched with excitement, and for a moment, I envied her. She still believed in the magic, the dream that Mr. Right was out there, waiting around for fate to lend a hand. Me? I knew she was wrong. After all, I'd already found the perfect man, but he wasn't interested.

When I hesitated, Lauren prodded harder. "Hey, don't hold back on me, superstar."

I tried to inject a little enthusiasm into my answer. "Kelvin asked about the bruise on Veronica's cheek, and because it's perfectly normal to discuss your problems with a complete stranger, she told him that her boyfriend drank too much and pushed her into a cupboard."

"People do talk to strangers. Think of confessionals."

"Those are priests, Lauren. Men of God. That's totally different."

"They must hear so much good stuff. Do you think they recognise the voices? I mean, how do they face sweet old Mrs. Robins in church if she's recently confessed to messing around with the gardener?"

"Can we stay on topic here?"

"What about bartenders? When you were pouring drinks, didn't you get weird old guys spilling their dirty secrets?"

"Mostly they just hit on me."

"They must've seen that star quality, babe. Anyhow, last night in the bar, this bald dude told me how he came home and found his neighbour screwing his son on the living room floor. But—get this—daddy was also doing the neighbour, and she'd been cheating on both of them. Then his wife came home, and—"

"Lauren, please?"

"Okay, okay, so where did it go wrong?"

"Well, I managed the crying part, and I suppose the pushing-Kelvin-away part went all right too."

Let's face it, calling Kane an arrogant prick came naturally.

"And…?"

"And then he kissed me. Lauren, he'd eaten fish for lunch. Salmon, I think."

"OMG, you *hate* salmon."

"I know."

"Yeuch! He didn't brush his teeth?"

"He didn't even suck a breath mint. He's Kane Sanders. *Kane Sanders.*" I mimicked David. "Women are supposed to relish the gift of his second-hand sushi."

Lauren gagged. "Okay, kissing aside, what about the rest?"

I pulled a face, even though she couldn't see it. Right now, she was probably lying out by the pool in our apartment complex, catching the evening sun, which sounded more glamorous than it really was. Firstly, it was the end of January. Secondly, the pool had been empty since we moved in, save for some leaves and a few crumpled beer cans, and Lauren only sat outside because our upstairs neighbour liked to do Zumba between six and seven every day, and the ceiling shook alarmingly. But still, I couldn't help wishing I were there with her.

"The rest? Kane tore my top off, and my mind went blank. I forgot everything you told me last time and just stiffened up. David got pissed again, and afterward, he told me I should lie back and visualise the last man to rabidly fuck me."

Lauren spluttered, and I heard a clatter followed by muffled curses. "Shit, sorry, I dropped the phone. No way— he really said that?"

"I only wish I'd misheard. Lauren, what am I supposed to do?" No answer. "Lauren?"

"I'm thinking, okay? I mean, there is the obvious solution."

"A one-way flight to Timbuktu?"

"No, you could pick up a guy for the night and solve this whole problem. With your looks, it'd be easy."

"But I don't want any old guy."

No, I wanted Trent Vickers, the man who'd grown from my childhood crush into a successful lawyer. The problem? He'd always seen me as a little sister. No matter how many hints I dropped about my interest in him, he remained oblivious. When I moved to LA, I'd hoped the distance between us would lessen my feelings, but you know that old saying about absence making the heart grow fonder? Totally true. We were still friends, good friends, but every time we spoke, I longed for more.

"And that's exactly why you need to do this. Remember what we discussed? OTT?"

Ah, yes. Operation Tempt Trent. We'd come up with the name while knocking back margaritas, and *you* try saying the words quickly when you're drunk. After the second pitcher, we'd shortened it to an acronym.

The plan was simple—show Trent that I could be both adventurous and sophisticated. Polished. Independent. Capable. After all, that was the type of girl I'd overheard him telling his friend Colby he wanted. Back in Kansas, I'd been none of those things, but I'd changed. In the two and a half years I'd been away, I'd changed.

"Nothing in OTT mentioned using another man for sex."

"Not using, exactly. He'd get something out of it too. What about that other actor? Lucas? He always seems kind of quiet."

Ah, Lucas Collins. Hollywood B-list, and my partner in crime. Well, the opposite of crime. He played Lance Hosier, Veronica's partner in the SFPD. Lucas was a good guy, friendly, but…he wasn't Trent. And I'd been in love with Trent since I was ten years old. I slumped back on the couch and buried my head in the crook of my elbow.

"Lauren, I can't. Even if I did want to…to *you know*, with Lucas, can you imagine the awkwardness the morning after? We'll have to come up with an alternative plan."

She fell silent, but not for long. Lauren always had an answer for everything. "How about going to one of those cabaret shows? Sure, you wouldn't be doing the deed, but you could writhe around with a man for a while."

"You're seriously suggesting I go to a strip show on my own?"

"Couldn't you take someone with you?"

"I barely know anyone here."

"Mikki the bitch?" Lauren giggled as I made a gagging noise. Mikki was my female co-star. My competition, as the gossip websites kept reminding me, although I'd rather throw myself off the Golden Gate Bridge than aspire to be like her. "Is she still driving you crazy?"

"This morning, she threw a hissy fit because we'd run out of low-fat soya milk. She accused me of drinking it all."

"And did you?"

"Of course not! It's disgusting. No, Kane drank it, but if I told her that, she'd only call me a liar. She thinks the sun shines out of his derrière."

"What about the make-up lady? You get along okay with her."

Get along okay with her? I freaking loved the woman. First, she'd taught me how to put in my contact lenses without blinding myself—David insisted my eyes had to be blue instead of brown—and then she'd worked her magic with scissors and brushes and jars of mystery miracle creams and turned me from a beggar-woman into a bombshell, or at least, that's what Lauren called me when I sent her the first photo. My dark hair shone, and my skin was flawless. But taking Shonda to a strip show? No.

"Shonda's forty-five years old, and she's married."

"Fine. I have a new plan. I'll send you a fun little video. Watch it and give yourself sweet dreams."

"What sort of video?"

"Think of it as instructional."

"You're gonna send me porn?"

"Plenty of women watch it nowadays."

"Lauren…"

But it was no good. She'd hung up, and I was talking to dead air.

And it was time for me to go home. Or rather, back to the rented beach house I was sharing with Kane, Lucas, and Mikki for the duration of production. Why was I sharing a place with two people I hated and one who made me swoon a bit? A good question, and one I'd asked myself many times over the last two weeks. Why had I ever listened to my ex-agent and signed on the dotted line?

Hidden Intent wasn't just a movie, you see. It was David's creative vision, a project billed as Blockbuster versus Big Brother. He'd hired the four of us not only to star in the final product but also to make a twelve-part behind-the-scenes reality show about the process. The whole movie was being filmed in chronological order, and we hadn't even been allowed to read the script before we started. It got revealed to us in small chunks, scene by scene, and each time David brought around those golden envelopes, the cameras were on hand to capture our reactions as we read through our parts. My gasp of horror when I received today's instalment had been all too real, and two hundred thousand people had watched my knees buckle on YouTube, much to David's delight.

So far, the movie had opened with the gruesome murder of Del Swanson, the husband of Mikki's character and the business partner of Kane's. There'd been grief and a funeral. The tears had been followed by an argument as Mariah and Kelvin each accused the other of the dastardly deed. *Mariah and Kelvin*—the scriptwriters thought it would be cute to make each of our characters' names start with the same letter as our own as a way of—to quote David—blurring the lines between fantasy and reality.

"Knock-knock," Kristen called before walking in without waiting for an answer.

I pulled the robe tighter around myself but then thought,

why bother? Thanks to last week's supposedly leaked photos —and I say "supposedly" because I overheard David congratulating Debbie, the publicist, for leaking them— several million people had already seen my ass in the opening shower scene.

Kristen tapped her watch, a bubble-gum-pink model with no numbers—the perfect accessory for someone who arrived late half the time.

"Everything okay?" I asked.

"If you want to ride back with Kane, you need to go. The car's outside. Kane said he'd wait, but Mikki insists they're leaving right this second."

After today's events, I'd rather walk. "What are the other options?"

"You could ride with Lucas. I think he stopped to talk to David."

"Perfect."

"Okay, I'll tell him. Uh, did you know you have your robe on inside out?"

No, but on current form, that didn't surprise me at all.

CHAPTER 2
VIOLET

A camera flashed in the background as Lucas opened the door of the town car for me. *Legs together, Violet.* I'd grown up as a tomboy, always in pants, and the first day on set, I'd made the mistake of climbing out of the car in my typical fashion.

#VioletWearsViolet had trended on Twitter before filming even began.

But today, I managed not to show off my panties despite wearing a floaty skirt. The outfit was part of OTT—Trent liked his girlfriends feminine, or at least, the two I'd seen him with had been wearing fancy dresses and perfect make-up.

"Thanks."

I flashed Lucas a smile, and he walked to his own side of the car. He'd held the door for me on every trip because the driver rarely seemed to bother, but I wasn't sure whether Lucas was a true gentleman or just wanted to make a good impression for the cameras that constantly followed us. I struggled to figure him out. I'd told Lauren he was a good guy, and I was pretty sure that was true, but he mostly kept to himself in the house. Kane hogged the gym, and the kitchen, and the sunlounger on the far side of the pool that caught the last few rays before dusk. If Mikki wasn't hovering around him like one of those pesky flies you always want to swat, she was sprawled on the couch watching a dating show with the volume turned right up. On my second day in the house, I'd asked if she might consider turning it down a notch, and she complied until Kane left the room. Then she'd fixed her eyes on me as she raised the volume to ear-splitting, one brow quirked, daring me to complain.

My response? I'd retreated upstairs. Confrontation made me break out in hives.

Lucas spent most of his free time locked in his room too, which meant we'd barely spoken without a film crew listening in. Who was he, really? I'd watched a few of his movies—okay, every single one of his movies—but all that exercise taught me was that he liked to split his time between risky indies and mainstream projects as he clawed his way up the ladder from obscurity to C-list to B-list. In his latest role, he'd played the Blue Avenger, a comic-book hero intent on cleaning up the world's oceans. I'd googled Lucas too, but until he signed up for *Hidden Intent*, he'd kept a remarkably low profile in terms of his private life.

"You okay?" he asked after he'd slid into the car. "I heard about what David said, and he was way out of line."

A groan escaped my lips before I could stop it. "Is there anyone who doesn't know?"

"Nope." The driver turned to grin at me. "One of the runners put it on our WhatsApp group."

Lucas leaned forward and raised the privacy screen. "Damn ears everywhere. If I'd realised what I was signing up for…"

Hold on, hold *on*… Did that mean I wasn't the only one shocked by this circus?

"They didn't tell you all the details either?"

"Well, I knew it was David Jackson and Kane Sanders,

13

obviously, and the contract talked about the extras, but I guess I just wasn't prepared for how invasive it would feel."

"Oh."

He shifted in his seat to face me. "Oh? What does that mean?"

"Nothing."

"Which means everything. Can I help in any way?"

"Not unless you can turn the clock back eight months so I can un-sign my contract."

Tears threatened, but I sniffed them back. If I arrived at the house with smeared mascara, reports of me crying would be on social media within minutes.

"That bad, huh? What happened to the Hollywood dream?"

It all came tumbling out. My nerves, my total lack of experience, the way I felt as if I were drowning every time the clapperboard snapped shut. Something about the way Lucas looked at me, those baby blues kind but focused, made me want to spill my secrets. At least he wasn't a complete stranger, just slightly mysterious.

"So, for me, it's more like a Hollywood nightmare," I finished up. "How am I meant to get through this? Everyone knows what they're doing except me."

"But the casting director chose you for the part, so you must have stood out. Most girls didn't even get an audition."

"Well, I only got one by accident."

"Huh?"

It was true. I'd kept it quiet, but the only reason my agent received the call was because the casting director's assistant had gotten me, Violet Miller, confused with Violet Müller, a former Victoria's Secret model who rescued puppies in her spare time. Cue many apologies and red faces all around. Out of sympathy, they'd let me read for the part, some weird improv involving apples and a pogo stick that called for me to act scared out of my mind. Scared, I could do. Call it a specialty. And it turned out that David wanted a fresh face, someone new. In his words, someone innocent. He'd seen my audition tape, and the rest was history.

Except it turned out that innocent in David's eyes wasn't the same as my definition.

"There was a small mix-up in the casting process, and I thought I'd signed up for a nice, tame thriller movie plus a documentary."

Kane hadn't even been attached to the movie at that point, and the script had remained a closely guarded secret. I closed my eyes and groaned as I recalled the fateful conversation with Randy Lemieux Jr., my former agent.

"A David Jackson movie?" I'd said. "I'm still not sure…"

His spare chin wobbled as he shook his head in disbelief. "Are you crazy? *Hidden Intent* is a chance in a million. You could hit the big time with this."

"But it's a main part."

"You already played the lead in *Rules of Play*."

True, but *Rules of Play* had been different. I'd thought of the production team on the micro-budget indie movie as family. None of us had much experience—the director had only graduated from university the year before—and we did our own make-up. I choked back a laugh as I recalled the sandwiches I'd made for the crew's lunch each day. I bet David Jackson would expect more than PB&J. At the time of the casting for *Hidden Intent*, *Rules of Play* hadn't even been released, and apart from a small paragraph on IMDB, it had still been flying under the radar.

"I'm not sure I can do the role justice," I'd told Randy. "And David didn't even want me. He wanted Violet Müller."

"Well, I've checked, and she's committed to projects for the rest of the year, so he can't have her. And they're offering two hundred thousand dollars for *Hidden Intent*."

Two *hundred*? Two hundred *thousand* dollars?

That changed everything.

The last time I'd been home to Oakwood Falls, it had rained, and I mean *rained*. A real thunderstorm. When I was a child, I'd loved to stand at my bedroom window and watch the deluge, the trees whipping back and forth in the wind, the flashes of lightning gleaming off rivulets of water rushing along the cinderblock path from the front door. But that day? That day, I'd watched in horror as Mom ran around the house with buckets and a mop.

"The roof's leaking?" I'd asked stupidly, because of course it was.

"Just now and again."

"How long has this been happening? Here, give me the mop."

"A while now, but you shouldn't worry."

Shouldn't worry? How could I not? "I'll call someone to look at it. Billy Johnson's father—is he still a builder?"

"He's already looked at it." The despair in Mom's voice made my heart break. "Patched it up as best he could, but it all needs to be replaced, and I can't run to that."

"How much would it cost?"

"Eight thousand dollars." She saw the look of shock on my face. "The buckets work, Violet. It doesn't normally rain this bad."

True, but Mom was getting older, and the roof was only going to get worse. Plus some of the boards on the front porch were loose, and the whole place needed painting. I'd offered to move home, to help with what I could, but Mom had shaken her head.

"One of us needs to get out and see the world, Violet, and it's not gonna be me. I'll be just fine muddling along here."

I didn't have eight thousand dollars. Most weeks, I barely even had eight dollars after I'd paid the rent and utilities. I ate ramen in the fourth week of every month while I counted down the days to my paycheck, and my fifteen-year-old Honda made horrible noises every time I started the engine.

Hidden Intent was my best chance, my *only* chance of fixing Mom's house up for her retirement.

And secretly, I'd hoped that Trent might be impressed by my new job too.

"Do you think my name would go on the poster?" I asked Randy.

"Sure, sure. You'll be a star, Vi."

A star. If Trent saw me on-screen at the movie theatre in Oakwood Falls, then maybe he'd finally start to realise I was girlfriend material?

"And it's definitely two hundred thousand?" I'd asked Randy, just to check. "You're positive?"

"I've read the contract thoroughly. It's watertight."

Oh, he'd certainly read the contract. Including, I found out later, the clause hidden away in the small print that said I'd be happy to take off my clothes at any given moment. And the part where I agreed to share a house with three strangers for three freaking months. Yes, I know I should have read it better myself, but all I'd been able to think about was getting my mom a new roof, and it was simply a standard contract, Randy had assured me. Nothing special. When I found out the truth, it was too late. I'd already signed. Signed the contract that gave him twenty-five percent of my two hundred thousand dollars.

And the lying swine had acted surprised when I fired him.

The only thing he'd been right about was that the contract was indeed watertight. I'd even consulted a lawyer to check. Not Trent, of course. No way. Because what could be worse than confessing my utter stupidity to the guy I had the hots for?

Nothing.

Right now, my only goal was to survive the next ten weeks and then re-evaluate my poor life choices.

Meanwhile, Lucas burst out laughing.

"A tame thriller movie? From David Jackson? The man

who convinced Velvet Jones to frolic naked halfway up an actual volcano? Didn't you realise he wants *Hidden Intent* to be the next *Basic Instinct*? But dirtier. And with more blood."

Oh, heck. I clenched my legs together just at the thought.

"You're not helping," I said through gritted teeth. "All I want to do is run back to Oakwood Falls and get a job waiting tables. I mean, the thriller part I'm okay with. It's the other stuff. I'm… I'm not exactly experienced in that department."

Lucas gave a low whistle. "Wow. I always thought you seemed surprisingly unenthusiastic. This must be hard for you, especially with the world watching."

"Every time I put a foot wrong, I read about it on Celebgossip.com."

Because I was no longer an unknown. Against all the odds, *Rules of Play* had taken off at the box office, helped by a viral campaign on social media started by the director's roommate, who happened to be some sort of internet marketing guru. In the five weeks since release, the movie had raked in ninety million dollars, and the media was muttering about awards. I still had to pinch myself. Most of the time, I considered it a good day if I managed to put my pants on the right way around in the morning.

The last month had been surreal. I'd earned five thousand dollars for *Rules*, the making of which had been financed by the producer's mother remortgaging her house. A week after filming wrapped, I'd been back behind the bar with Lauren, wiping tables and washing up glasses at the end of the evening like all the other staff. Even after the movie struck gold, I couldn't afford to quit, and until filming for *Hidden Intent* started, I'd had to sign autographs on the sly because the boss got annoyed if I wasted time doing anything but pouring drinks or clearing tables.

"I don't pay you to chat, Violet," he always said, even though the place had gotten undeniably busier once word of me working there spread.

By the time *Rules of Play* hit number one at the box office, I'd read the first scene for *Hidden Intent*, freaked out because it involved me being naked, and suggested to David that since I wasn't quite such a fresh face anymore, perhaps he might like to recast? But he'd just rubbed his hands together.

"No, no, no. This is *perfect*. You're still new to the scene, not typecast, but the publicity you're getting for that horror movie… We couldn't buy it. You and Kane are going to smash this."

So far, the only thing I'd smashed was a coffee mug, which I dropped when Kane's butt double meandered onto the set starkers. That man had no inhibitions. Not that he needed them—his ass could have been sculpted by Michelangelo himself.

What the hell was I doing here?

Lucas nodded his agreement. "Celebgossip.com reports everything. When I ate a cheese sandwich for lunch yesterday, there was a photo on the front page within minutes, and this morning, a fan couriered me a block of cheddar with a lipstick kiss on it."

"Ugh. What did you do?"

Lucas grinned, the first time I'd seen him smile for real. Sure, he smiled on set and looked handsome while he did it, but those emotions never reached his eyes. Now, they twinkled the same clear blue as a summer sky.

"Left it in Kane's trailer with a note. *Dinner tonight?* I signed it from Mikki."

"Are you serious?"

"Yeah. But she'll never eat cheddar. Too many calories."

I snorted, properly snorted, then clapped a hand over my mouth. There might not have been cameras in the car, but did I really have to make that noise in front of Lucas? Who, it seemed, was sweet as well as hot.

"Could you just pretend you didn't hear that?"

"It's good to see you smile for once. Although I can't

19

blame you for being unhappy back in the house. Mikki isn't exactly your biggest fan, is she?"

"You've noticed? I was beginning to think I was imagining it. I mean, she's nice to everyone else."

And what had I ever done to upset her? Nothing that I knew of. When I first walked into the house with Kane and David, she'd given me a sweet smile, verging on sickly, and said we should go out for cocktails. *Cocktails*. I was more of a beer-and-burgers girl, but I'd nodded enthusiastically, only for her to blank me whenever we were alone. And worse, I'd overheard her sniping about me behind my back on more than one occasion.

Violet took my mascara.

Violet borrowed my blow dryer and broke it.

Violet ate the entire tub of cottage cheese; no wonder she's so fat.

It was like being back at school.

"We've all noticed," Lucas said. "Well, maybe not Kane because he only notices himself, but everyone else." He wrapped one arm around my shoulders and gave me a light squeeze. "Nobody believes what she says about you."

Well, that was something, at least. "I don't understand why she hates me so much."

"I heard she wanted your part. All those juicy scenes with Kane that rumour says are coming up."

"Really? She can have it. I'll gladly swap."

Because so far, as the grieving widow of *Hidden Intent*'s first and possibly only murder victim, Mikki had been allowed to keep her clothes on.

"David won't go for that."

Dammit. "Because I'm so good in the love scenes?"

Sarcasm rolled off me, but Lucas only shrugged.

"No, because Mikki's backbiting has the potential to drive up ratings. How many column inches do you think a catfight between the two of you would get?"

I couldn't help groaning, and the little choke at the end

sounded worryingly like a half-sob. How had I gotten into this mess? All I wanted to do was go back home, properly home to Oakwood Falls, where I could scrape by with a boring job, run around with buckets when it rained, and see Trent every single day. But it wasn't an option. I forced myself to think of Mom's house again. Of the new roof, of the swing seat I'd buy for the porch once it was fixed, of watching storms from my bedroom window for many years to come.

Lucas's arm tightened, and I found myself pressed up against his side. Which was kind of nice, even if he wasn't Trent. Nice because it meant he cared, and precious few people in this industry did. Most of the folks I'd come across were only out to get what they could for themselves.

"I don't want any column inches. I just want these three months to end so I never have to see a movie set again."

And in ten years' time, I'd be a footnote on Wikipedia, a subpar actress who quit the business after two features, one of which was terrible.

"Isn't that slightly drastic?" Lucas asked.

"No. No, I don't think so."

"Acting gets easier with time. My first couple of movies felt surreal, but at least I started with the smaller parts and worked my way upward. Going from practically zero to this feeding frenzy is something else."

"Why did *you* sign up for *Hidden Intent*? I mean, I understand why Kane and Mikki got involved, but you were landing a steady stream of parts."

Kane might have been A-list, but his halo had slipped after a drugs scandal last year, and he'd lost the lead in at least one major movie. *Hidden Intent* would cement his status as a household name, this time for the right reasons. Plus, according to their Wikipedia entries, he'd been in the same fraternity as David and I figured bros stuck together. Mikki was a former reality TV star famous for having a nose job live on the internet, so David's freak-show mashup was right up her alley.

"Because David's ideas may be off the wall, but the man knows how to direct. I wanted to see firsthand how he worked and maybe land a lead role off the back of it."

The car began to slow, and I sagged against Lucas as I recognised the shimmering façade of the beach house, its pale pink stucco walls lit by strategically placed spotlights. When I'd first seen the place, I'd been beyond excited at the prospect of living there for three months, right next to the sea amid tropical gardens with a freaking swimming pool—one that actually had water in it—but now my stomach dropped like a lead weight.

"I wish I didn't have to go inside," I whispered.

Lucas held out a hand as, for once, the driver opened the door. "I'll look after you. I promise. Mikki and Kane can only hurt you if you let them."

Another sob threatened to escape, but this time from relief because I had an unexpected ally in the house of horrors. Why was Lucas helping me? I had no idea, but I couldn't afford to turn down the offer. I wiped my sweaty palm on my jeans before reaching out to him, and as our fingers touched, a little of his strength flowed into me.

Ten weeks left. Could I survive them with Lucas's help?

CHAPTER 3
VIOLET

My alarm rang at four thirty the next morning, and despite the early hour, I sprang out of bed. Why? Because it was time to call Trent. Over the past several months, we'd worked out a system. I'd message him the night before to let him know I planned to call, and he'd get up a few minutes early so we had time to chat before he went to the gym. With Kansas two hours ahead, that meant I had to wake at stupid o'clock, but it was worth it to hear Trent's voice.

"Violet?"

"Yes, it's me."

"How are you? How's the movie going?"

"Oh, it's going great." Rule number one, according to Lauren: always stay positive. No man liked a negative Nelly. "I filmed in an office building with Kane yesterday, and tomorrow, I have scenes with Lucas at the police precinct. Except we're only using a real precinct for the outside. For the interior shots, we're using a soundstage. David, the director, knows the owner of a new studio here, and…" Oh heck, I was rambling again. "And we're using that. How's your case going?"

"Cases, plural. I have a full load at the moment. Pop is quite the slave driver."

Trent chuckled, but I heard the tiredness in his voice.

"What about that murder case? Is the trial gonna start soon?"

Not much ever happened in Oakwood Falls, population 2,074. Well, 2,073 since old Mrs. Monterey's heart gave out last week. Trent's father ran the town's law firm and picked up work from nearby Oakwood Ridge too, seeing as he had a reputation for being the smartest attorney in the entire township. A sharp mind and a sharper tongue, Mom had always said. Trent was set to follow in his footsteps, and this would be his first time defending a murder case. He was nervous, I knew he was, and with good reason. I'd been following the story online, and according to Mom, everyone in town knew Tommy Jameson had raped Kaydee Bryant behind the Cartwheel Saloon and then stabbed her with a steak knife afterward. DNA evidence didn't lie, and they'd found the murder weapon in his car, covered in his bloody fingerprints. But Trent said that everyone had the right to a fair trial, and I had to respect him for thinking that way.

"The trial starts in three weeks. They're keeping me busy with the legwork, but Pop hired an extra paralegal to help."

"At least you'll have time for a lunch break. You are eating, right?"

"Your momma still makes us sandwiches every day and brings them to the office."

As she had done since I was a little girl, for Trent's pop and his father before him. My mom had become the Vickerses' housekeeper when I was five years old, and after my dad died when I was twelve, they'd become like our second family.

"I miss Mom's sandwiches. Out here, it's all carrot sticks and celery."

"Are you coming back to visit soon?"

"I'm not sure. The schedule's so busy." Plus Lauren said I should play hard to get. *No man worth having wants a girl who's easy,* she'd told me time and time again.

"How about for my birthday? Five weeks, don't forget. And you know what both of our moms are like—they'll be throwing a party no matter what I say."

A giggle slipped out because every year, we both said we didn't want a fuss, and every year, we got a buffet that fed the entire town, plus cake and usually a band.

"At least you'll only be twenty-eight. Two years until they really push the boat out."

"It can't be worse than my twenty-fifth. I think Mom flew in every relative we have, and I didn't even know who most of them were."

"I'm sure she'll think of a way to outdo herself. A costume party, maybe? Or she could get your old baby pictures out, or—"

"Violet, stop. Please. I'd threaten to emigrate, but she wouldn't believe me because… Well, I have some big news."

My stomach did a backflip. The last time he'd had big news, he ended up spending six months in London on a study placement, and it had taken me another six months after that to pay off my phone bill.

"What news?"

"I bought a piece of land. Bobby Walden decided to sell off six acres to pay for his wife's medical bills, and I got it for a good price."

"Not the field at the bottom of the elephant mountain?"

"Yes, that one."

Officially, the small hill on the outskirts of town was called Norton's Rise, but it had a rock near the top that looked like an elephant, and thirteen-year-old me had given it the nickname after I'd huffed and puffed my way up there with Trent. We'd taken a picnic and his old dog and spent the whole day together, just the two of us, before high school got

25

serious and Trent started hanging out with guys his own age rather than the housekeeper's daughter. And I still remembered what I'd said that day as we sat on a boulder with nothing above us but sky and nothing below us but green.

"One day, I'd love to live here."

"What, on top of a mountain?" Trent had asked.

"No, silly." I pointed to the pasture at the bottom, dotted with trees, the narrow stream along one edge glinting in the sunlight. "Down there. I'd build a big house and buy a pony."

And now Trent had bought the land. Was it fate? Did he remember my words? I almost asked him, but Lauren's voice echoed in my ears: don't seem too keen.

"Are you going to build a house there?" I asked.

"A house, somewhere for my cars, possibly a barn. I already have an architect drawing up the plans."

"I can't wait to see them."

"You'll be the first. Maybe in person? And your mom keeps asking when you'll be back, too. Haven't you called her recently?"

"I've been busy."

Busy avoiding what would undoubtedly turn into an interrogation about my new disaster of a job. She'd been so proud when I told her I'd landed a big role, and I didn't want to admit what a huge error in judgment I'd made. Not to my mom. No, I just wanted to get the job over with and then surprise her with a gang of builders. Thank goodness she didn't know how to use the internet.

"So I noticed. You're a YouTube star now. But you should still speak with her."

Tell me Trent hasn't seen the pictures of my ass. "Okay, I will. I promise."

"I have to go, Vi. Sadly, the work won't do itself."

"Same. I'll call you soon, okay? How about Friday?" The day after tomorrow. I could last that long.

"Friday's good. Break a leg at work."

If only. Because then I could get out of shooting. Hmm, that was a thought… Was there any kind of non-life-threatening injury I could inflict on myself in the next day or so?

"Bye, Trent."

Broken bones healed, right?

I used the bathroom, and I was about to consult WebMD for ideas when I heard Debbie calling. She didn't so much speak as squawk with the voice of a forty-a-day smoker, and I felt an almost insurmountable urge to crawl back under the quilt and bury my head beneath the pillow. It was only six a.m., for Pete's sake. What had I done wrong this time?

The others—Kane, Lucas, Mikki, and David—were already in the living room by the time I threw on a sundress and jogged down the stairs. Great.

"Are there any cameras?" I asked, peering around the doorjamb.

David shook his head. "Not this morning."

That hadn't stopped Mikki from trowelling on a full face of make-up, including false eyelashes, and curling her platinum-blonde hair. Kane hadn't even bothered with a shirt.

"Has there been a change of plan?"

According to the schedule, I didn't have any scenes today, just lines to learn and a three-hour session in the gym.

Debbie clapped her hands together. "This is a change for later in the week. As we all know, it's never too soon to start drumming up publicity, so I've arranged some wonderful opportunities. Mikki and Lucas, you'll be helping out at an animal shelter here in San Francisco on Friday afternoon. They've agreed to name a dog after each of your characters; isn't that wonderful?"

The look on Mikki's face said it was anything but.

"What about Kane and Violet?" she asked.

27

"They'll be flying to LA for a special charity showing of *Rules of Play*."

Upset didn't even begin to cover it. Mikki scowled as if I'd just thrown her favourite curling iron into the swimming pool, and I quickly found myself trying to rectify things.

"Why don't I visit the animal shelter instead? I love dogs."

Debbie might have looked confused if her Botox had allowed it. "But *Rules of Play* is *your* movie."

"Yes, and I've seen it lots of times."

Okay, so I hadn't exactly thought this through.

"Don't be ridiculous, Violet. All those poor little disabled people want to see you. Selfies, autographs, soundbites—you know the drill."

"But—"

"You'll fly down after filming on Saturday. Kane, you'll be wearing Tom Ford, and Violet, Ishmael's sending a selection of dresses for you to choose from." She studied me, her gaze critical. "Actually, we'll ask a stylist to choose. Yes, that's a much better idea."

Even Kane didn't look too thrilled. "I have a table booked at Chess on Saturday night."

"Don't worry—I'll rearrange it. I know the owner."

"I don't mind going to LA," Lucas tried.

"We need Kane for the column inches." Debbie leaned over and patted Kane's hand. "Just try not to snort anything you shouldn't, sweetie."

Kane opened his mouth to retort, but David waded in first.

"Now that's all arranged, we need to get on set. Mikki, Kane, it's the big post-funeral scene today, so think sad thoughts, people. I need tears."

Crying? *I* should have been in this scene because sobbing was my specialty. And when my phone pinged with a message from Lauren after I left the room, I didn't know whether to laugh hysterically or weep. She'd emailed me a whole list of porn videos to watch, everything from a blow job to a clip labelled "double penetration" that made me feel ill without even clicking on it.

"You okay?" Lucas asked from behind me.

I shoved the phone deep into the pocket of my sundress. "Fine."

"Debbie did that on purpose to get a rise out of Mikki."

"Do you think so?"

"Naming a dog after her? Conflict means ratings."

That basic premise underpinned the whole world of showbiz, it seemed.

"In that case, our ratings are gonna be sky high."

CHAPTER 4
VIOLET

L unchtime on Thursday, and I had eight minutes to gulp down a box of vegetarian sushi—no raw fish for me, yuck—in my trailer before Shonda needed to fix my make-up for the next scene. Under the hot studio lights, the darn stuff melted right off my face and left me feeling like a cheap waxwork.

But the day wasn't all bad. Mikki was still upset over the Kane thing, which meant she hadn't spoken to me in over twenty-four hours. And today, I got to wear actual clothes— jeans, a T-shirt, and a bomber jacket. Plus a push-up bra that cut me in half and high-heeled boots that made my feet ache, but I was trying not to think about those.

"Some stuff arrived for you while you were out, hun," Shonda told me as she scurried around with brushes and potions. "The runner left it on the table over there."

I glanced across, chewing quickly so I could swallow my mouthful. "Who are the flowers from?"

"It doesn't say. Probably the card fell off."

I popped a sushi roll into my mouth and meandered over to take a closer look. Nobody had sent me fresh flowers before, and these were roses, a beautiful deep red.

"But they're so pretty. I should send a thank-you note."

"Maybe you have a secret admirer?"

I lifted the bouquet out of its box to smell it, then squealed in pain.

"Ow!"

"What's wrong?"

"There's a thorn."

I dropped the flowers and checked the damage, holding my finger up to the light. A drop of blood the same colour as the petals bubbled out of my skin and plopped onto the table.

"Stay still—I'll bring a tissue."

Shonda wrapped up my finger, pressing hard to staunch the flow. In a way, the thorn didn't surprise me. If ever there was an appropriate metaphor for my life, this was it—pretty on the outside, prickly and painful under the surface.

Lucas walked in as I slumped back into my make-up chair, but his smile soon faded when he saw my face.

"What's up?"

Shonda answered for me. "Someone sent Violet roses, but the florist missed a thorn."

Lucas crouched to pick the bunch up gingerly, careful not to make the same mistake as I had.

"Looks as though the florist missed *all* the thorns. Who sent them?"

"We don't know," I told him.

"Strange. Did anyone else get flowers?"

"No idea."

"I'll ask around. How's your finger?"

I peered under the tissue, and another drop of blood formed, vivid against my fake-tanned skin.

"Well, it's not gushing."

"I'll find a first aid kit."

Why me? The drama was supposed to be on set or possibly in the beach house if David got his way, not in my trailer. That was my sanctuary, the one place I could escape to when I needed space.

"We'd better finish your make-up, hun," Shonda said. "Time is money, or so David keeps telling us, and the costs for this picture must be crazy because of the way he's shooting it. Every other movie I've ever worked on, they filmed all the scenes that took place in one location in a block, but he's bouncing back and forth between them in chronological order. Have they given you any more of the script yet?"

"Nope. There's another reveal in the morning, and I feel ill already."

"He told the crew you're coming back here tomorrow, if it helps."

It did, a little. If we were shooting cop scenes, then I wouldn't have to be naked. Unless David decided to change up the plot and have Lance screw Veronica over his desk. Oh, hell. He wouldn't, would he?

The mere thought almost brought up my lunch. *Calm down, Violet. Breathe.* At least Lucas was enough of a gentleman that he'd use breath mints.

I tried to take my mind off David and his stupid script by thumbing through the letters that had arrived along with the roses. Nothing unusual there, just a handful of requests for signed pictures and an invite to a teenager's birthday party next week. I couldn't go, but I'd write them all back. I always did. Mikki threw her fan mail in the trash while Kane and Lucas let their publicists handle theirs, but I still liked to answer mine personally. It gave me something to do in the evenings while I avoided the gruesome twosome.

The final envelope was typewritten, not the usual longhand scrawl, and I peeled the flap open, curious. A single sheet of paper nestled inside, and I skimmed over it.

Dear Ms. Miller,

Forgive the unorthodox approach, but Randy Lemieux informed my people he's no longer in contact with you, and you're a hard lady to get ahold of. We're currently casting for a remake of The Thing, *and after your performance in* Rules of Play, *you're on the shortlist of people we'd like to talk to. If you'd be interested in discussing this, please call me.*

Racino.

What? *What*? Was this a prank? Racino was one of the best sci-fi directors around, so famous that he didn't bother to use his first name. The king of special effects, they called him. My heart skipped as I read the letter again, more slowly this time, and took in the phone number jotted at the bottom. Racino wanted to talk to *me*?

"I have Band-Aids," Lucas said from the doorway, making me jump. "You okay?"

I waved the letter at him. "Racino wants me to call him about a part in his new movie."

"That's great news." And Lucas did look genuinely happy, which made a pleasant change after Mikki's scowls. "Does this mean you're not quitting showbiz forever now?"

"I don't know. I mean, I only read this two minutes ago, and I don't have an agent, or a lawyer, or even a clue what I might be doing in three months." And the dreamer in me thought back to Trent and the piece of land at the bottom of the elephant mountain. "Part of me wants to go home, but… this is Racino."

"Keep still a second," Shonda said as she patted powder onto my cheeks.

Lucas took my hand in his, stretching out my fingers so he could put a Band-Aid on my cut. His touch was gentle, kind, and when he'd finished sticking me back together, he brought the back of my hand to his lips and kissed it softly.

"All done. You'll have to hide that hand during filming."

"Good thing this jacket has pockets."

Lucas gave me a side-hug. "I'll see you out there."

"Any closer to changing your mind?" Lucas asked in the car on the way back to the beach house.

"Huh?"

I was still coming down from the high of the afternoon's filming, a weirdly euphoric feeling I'd experienced often during *Rules of Play* but which had been missing from this movie until today. The satisfaction of slipping seamlessly into another persona. The spring in my step as I walked away from scene after scene shot in a single take. The warm glow that spread through me when David congratulated me on my performance. I'd begun to feel like an imposter, a con artist with a SAG card, but today had reminded me I really could act.

"Making another movie?" Lucas said. "Racino?"

"I guess it would be rude to ignore him. But do I just phone the number? What if he doesn't answer? Should I leave a message? I'm floundering in the deep end here, in case you hadn't noticed. Randy dealt with everything for this movie, and the part in *Rules* was advertised on the noticeboard at my acting class."

The acting class I'd only attended because Lauren had dragged me along, and she'd only gone because a guy she liked from the bar had signed up. Their relationship lasted a whole two weeks, but I'd kept going to the classes because I'd paid for the full semester in advance. Plus, I'd hoped they'd give me confidence and maybe help me to pick up some pocket money from "extra" gigs. Not once had I ever imagined that I'd land a lead role.

Lucas reached across and gave my hand a comforting

squeeze. "You were perfect today. Everyone who's seen *Rules* says you're a natural, and this afternoon, you proved them right."

"Have you seen it?"

"Twice. Do you want me to ask my agent if she'll help out? Donna can be a bitch, but she always has her clients' backs."

"Would you mind?"

"I'll call her tomorrow. She's probably in the bar by now."

"The bar? Isn't it a bit early for drinking?"

"She has a rule: sober until six. And she always goes to bed by nine because she gets up at five every morning to do some weird yoga shit."

"I'd definitely appreciate her help because this whole industry freaks me out. How do folks stay sane?"

"I've asked that question many times myself. People say it can be lonely at the top, and I used to see celebrities and their entourages and think it couldn't possibly be true. But it is. I'm still a ways down the ladder, but I feel it. The loneliness. It creeps up on you if you're not careful."

"You're not really selling this."

"The secret is to keep a few close friends, people you trust and who trust you back. The rest is just window dressing."

That was the advice I'd needed to hear, and at the moment, I had Trent and Lauren to keep me grounded. Two friends who made me smile and helped to lighten the load. One day, would I be able to add Lucas to that list as well?

CHAPTER 5
VIOLET

On Friday morning, my call to Trent was reduced to five minutes of *How's Kansas? Great. How's San Francisco? Great!* because we had a script reveal to endure before we began filming. Apart from the love scenes, this was the part I hated most, and my heart beat against my ribcage like a studded club as I trudged downstairs. Seven a.m. found us sitting around the oversized dining table in the conservatory overlooking the pool. Mikki and Kane looked as though they were auditioning for *Baywatch*, dressed in a bikini and swim shorts respectively. Mikki might have a floaty blouse on over the top, but it left nothing to the imagination. Lucas had gone for tailored shorts and a linen shirt. Formal compared to Barbie and Ken, but he hadn't bothered to shave, and the smattering of stubble would do everything for David's precious ratings. Debbie would be thrilled too. In fact, she was staring at him so hard that she missed her mouth with her organic mango juice and dribbled it down her chin.

"Cameras, are we ready?" David asked.

"And…rolling."

I smoothed my dress and perched on the edge of one of

the padded leather chairs. Today, I'd erred on the side of demure in the hope that the footage might focus on the others. My hands wouldn't stop twisting in my lap, so I poured a glass of water in an attempt to keep them busy.

"Here." Lucas passed me a handkerchief to clean up the puddle I made.

"Thanks," I mouthed.

David didn't even notice. He was too busy telling his adoring public via live broadcast that the next week of filming was going to be gritty, dramatic, and just a little bit dirty. Great. Debbie passed out the shiny gold envelopes, one for each of us, and they seemed thicker than the last ones. Did that mean worse news?

Mikki tore into her envelope like a starved wolf, slavering over the contents. Kane mugged for the camera, flashing that Hollywood smile as if he were in a toothpaste ad. I had no idea what Lucas did because I screwed my eyes shut as I slid my script out.

"Remember, folks, don't give the plot away," David warned us.

Of course, because people wouldn't pay to see the movie otherwise.

I skimmed the pages frantically, trying to block out Mikki's little gasps and squeals. The men were more stoic, and it wouldn't have surprised me if Kane already knew the contents since he was all buddy-buddy with David. The pair of them probably conspired over beer about which items of clothing I'd remove first.

Mariah monologue; Kelvin and Mariah; Kelvin alone; Veronica, Lance, and Mariah; Veronica, Lance, and Kelvin; tension building… Oh, shit. Veronica and Kelvin alone.

According to the schedule, next Wednesday, Veronica would swing by Kelvin's office to ask some follow-up questions about the death of his business partner. Lance had made the initial visit, but since he was busy attending the autopsy, she decided to go it alone. Except that Kelvin, having recognised her as the girl he'd gotten carried away with on that rainy night, would be more intent on flirting than giving straight answers. And at the end of the meeting, Kelvin was supposed to push Veronica up against the wall and kiss her. Talk about inappropriate. Veronica ought to Taser him for that, but in our world of make-believe, she'd kiss him back instead.

And knowing Kane, the smooch would end with his hand under my dress and probably a few items of clothing missing —my clothing, not his—and Debbie would "leak" the stills to the media. This scene wouldn't be as bad as the one on the couch, but even so, the prospect of being mauled by Kane again left me nauseated.

One more straw on the camel's back.

David began chatting with Mikki, interview-style, and Lucas met my gaze across the table, his clear blue eyes to my fake ones. He raised one eyebrow.

"I'm okay," I mouthed.

But I was lying.

"Kane! Kane! Can I get a picture?"

"Kane! Will you sign my purse?"

With my illustrious co-star at my side, even a simple task like walking through the airport turned into a parade. Kane smiled and waved, pausing to snap selfies with every pretty girl as well as sign the occasional body part. He'd even brought his own Sharpie.

And me? I scuttled along in his shadow, wheeling the little pink case that contained three different dresses and enough make-up to start a new career as an Instagram influencer.

Shonda had shown me what to do with everything, but honestly, my only goal was to avoid poking out my eye with a mascara wand. Back in Kansas, the most I'd worn was a swipe of lip balm. Oh, and I'd bought one of those little compacts from the Spend 'n' Save once, but when I tried using it, I'd looked more like a clown than a siren. My only attempt to dye my brown hair blonde had resulted in an orange disaster of epic proportions, and after I'd spent a whole week's wages from my job working on Delbert Rodwell's ranch to get it fixed, I'd sworn on my split ends that I'd never mess with the colour again.

"Kane! Are you dating Violet Miller?" one guy asked, a reporter rather than a fan.

"Tonight, we're just enjoying an evening out at the movies."

Debbie had instructed us both to be deliberately vague on our relationship status because—you've guessed it— speculation would put us right in the spotlight. My first instinct had been to veto the whole stupid idea, but then I'd spoken to Lauren, and she'd insisted that rumours of Kane's interest would make Trent jealous and me more desirable. So when Kane settled a hand on the small of my back and steered me toward the limo waiting outside, I gritted my teeth and squinted against the camera flashes.

Kane had a home in LA, according to Celebgossip.com, but tonight, we were both staying in a suite at the Black Diamond Hotel. The *same* suite. Separate bedrooms, but the media didn't know that, and ten bucks said Debbie would leak our roommate status to the press.

"Have you stayed in the Diamond Suite before?" Kane asked as we walked into the hotel lobby. A gaggle of reporters was hot on our heels, so he passed my case to the bellhop and then held the door open.

I hadn't even stayed in a hotel before, but I wasn't about to admit that. "No."

"It's okay, as suites go. The beds could be softer, and the baths aren't all that big."

Was Kane serious? When I opened the door to my en-suite, I found a freaking swimming pool. And there was nothing wrong with the bed either. I'd have liked nothing better than to curl up with a room service dinner and binge-watch Netflix for the rest of the evening instead of dressing up to sit through my own movie yet again, but I was under contract and therefore didn't have a choice. So I laid the three dresses the wardrobe lady had picked out for me on the bed and set about making myself presentable. How did other women do it? Hair and make-up took me an hour, and I pulled a muscle zipping up my dress.

We'd never had a premiere for *Rules*. Well, we sort of did, but nobody took pictures of our pizza party at the director's house. Good thing too, because it had spilled out onto the back deck, and after too many beers, one of my co-stars tripped over a stray set of barbecue tongs and we had to take him to the emergency room for stitches.

Tonight, the only drama was on the red carpet the Wish on a Star foundation had set up. Kane turned his magic on the waiting crowds, and although I knew he was an asshole at heart, I had to give him credit for making the fans smile.

"Violet, come over here. Damon wants to meet you."

I turned to see Kane crouching by a young guy in a wheelchair, thirteen or fourteen years old maybe, and he beckoned me in their direction.

"See?" Kane said. "I told you she was pretty when she smiled." Then to me, "Damon wants to be an astronaut when he grows up."

I took in his thin frame, the missing hair, and the oxygen line running under his nose, and in my heart, I wasn't sure he'd ever achieve his dream. But I had to pretend he would.

"Space, huh? When I was little, I had a whole glow-in-the-dark universe stuck to my bedroom ceiling. Every night, I used to lie awake, wondering what was out there."

"Same as me! Then my mom and dad got me a telescope for my birthday so I could look at the sky for real. Did you know there's gonna be a meteor shower next week?"

"No, I didn't know that."

"I have a book about it. Want me to mail it to you?"

The kid wanted to send me a gift?

"There's no need—"

"I'd really like to."

"Okay, uh, sure. That's very kind of you."

I scribbled the address of the beach house in Damon's autograph book, then posed for a picture with him and Kane. My knees cricked, but Kane gave me a hand to get to my feet, slipping one arm around me as he did so. His hand crept lower, and as it hit my ass, I felt the flashbulbs burning into my back. Guess which photo would be on all the gossip sites tomorrow? I almost slapped him away, but at the last second, I realised that would create an even bigger scene. Why did he have to spoil everything?

"Will you get your slimy hand off me?" I whispered.

"No."

No? *No?* "It's not freaking optional."

Rather than respecting my wishes, Kane squeezed. He actually *squeezed*, then waved to the reporters as though nothing had happened.

"You asshole!" I hissed, twisting around so he had no choice but to drop his hand.

He just shrugged and carried on waving.

"Debbie's orders. This is showbiz, baby."

"For the last time, I'm sorry I put my hand on your ass."

41

I stomped into the suite ahead of Kane and threw my purse onto the couch.

"You're a pig."

"Would it help if I said it was a nice ass?"

Really? He thought it was nice? I mean… *Violet! Get ahold of yourself!*

"It would help if you apologised *and meant it*."

Kane just sauntered past me and poured himself a glass of Scotch. The ice cubes clinked as he leaned back against the wet bar, one arm stretched out along the black marble. He'd taken his tie off in the elevator, and if I hadn't spent the last two weeks finding out what an arrogant dick he was, I might have drooled.

"Mikki would have been all over that photo op."

"Well, I'm not Mikki."

"Don't I know it."

"If you wanted a media whore, why didn't you ask David to swap us? I offered to go to the animal sanctuary with Lucas."

"Because, Violet, your star is on the rise while Mikki's more of a comet. Kind of fun to look at and occasionally does something interesting, but when you get up close, there's not much there. For today's task, we needed someone who could connect with the teenagers, and you have the right balance of intrigue, compassion, and looks. Mikki would have made the evening all about her. Drink?" He held out his tumbler. "You look as if you need one."

"I'll make my own."

My fingers shook as I dropped ice into a glass and added tonic with a tiny splash of gin. The last thing I wanted to do was get drunk around Kane, and I already felt sick. This whole industry was a game. Chess mixed with *World of Warcraft*. I was a mere pawn, just figuring out the moves, while Kane was a king. I might have starred in *Rules of Play*, but the irony was that I didn't understand the rules at all.

"You discussed this trip beforehand? With David and Debbie?"

"Of course. Rule number one: always stay one step ahead."

See?

"I'm ten steps behind."

"Rule number two: never admit that you're not one step ahead."

"I give up, okay? I'm not cut out for this."

"Rule number three: never give up."

I growled in frustration and knocked back the whole drink, then poured myself another. More gin this time. At least I didn't have far to crawl to bed.

"Why do you get so uptight around me, anyway?" Kane asked. "Especially in that scene the other day—I understand that you're new, but it was only a bit of skin. The crew's seen it all before."

Oh, there wasn't enough alcohol in the world for me to go there.

"I just felt uncomfortable."

He took a step toward me and stopped close, too close.

"Then how about we practise? You and me. Tonight. Loosen you up some."

Was he serious? Kane Sanders was propositioning me right after I'd called him a pig?

"I don't think so."

He trailed a finger down my jaw, and a little bit of vomit came into my mouth. Kane was familiar with the Hollywood rules, sure, but he clearly didn't understand my "get lost" vibes, and if I'd felt uneasy before, in a room full of people, it was nothing compared to the discomfort I felt right now, alone with Mr. A-List in this fancy hotel suite.

"Nobody would know. Hell, half the world probably thinks we're sleeping together already."

And Kane wanted to confirm their suspicions? What a jerk.

Rather than say something I regretted, or worse, that would either encourage or antagonise him, I set my glass on the bar and backed quickly away. Toward my room. My room that had a sturdy lock on the door.

"Good night, Kane."

Great. Just when I thought my life couldn't get any worse, Kane had gone full-on sleaze. Lauren wasn't going to believe this.

CHAPTER 6
VIOLET

"Kane *what*?" Lauren squealed as I reached the end of my blow-by-blow account of yesterday evening. "Say it again. I think the line's bad."

"You heard. He came on to me."

"That's brilliant!"

My silence said I disagreed.

"Or…not brilliant?"

"Lauren, the man's a womanising slug. He actually expected me to hop into bed with him."

"It might have been okay."

"Okay? I don't want a man who's just okay, and I definitely don't want Kane Sanders."

"At least he wouldn't sell your story."

I picked at the bowlful of fresh fruit from the room service cart. I'd longed to order waffles and bacon, but my soon-to-be-naked-on-camera-again waistline had vetoed that idea.

"But he'd probably tell his friends. And he's so two-faced. He's nice to Mikki when she's around, but yesterday, he said really insulting things about her."

"Hmm, maybe it's time I start throwing darts at my Kane Sanders calendar?"

45

"Save some for me. I have no idea what I'm going to say to him next week."

"You haven't spoken to him yet?"

"Not properly. This morning, he muttered something about catching up with an old buddy, then checked out of the hotel. Said he'd make his own way back to San Francisco."

"Sounds as if he's embarrassed too."

"He's lived through ten years of Hollywood drama, including a cocaine scandal. I don't think he gets embarrassed."

"Well, pretend you don't either. What did he say? Rule two?" Lauren laughed and mimicked Kane. "Never admit that you're not one step ahead."

"Is it too late to emigrate?"

"Hey, it's not all bad."

"How? How is it not all bad?"

"Because I saw Kane Sanders on Twitter with his hand on your ass. Did he squeeze?"

"I don't want to talk about it."

"So he did." Lauren let out a low whistle. "But as I was saying, this is good news. Because if I saw you and Kane on Twitter, I bet you five bucks that Trent did too."

"Oh, heck."

"Sweetie, he's gonna be so jealous. I bet he messages you before lunchtime."

"He already did. Nothing exciting, just asking how yesterday went."

"See? It's working. OTT is working!"

"I still think emigrating is a better idea."

"Ten more weeks, and then you're done. Want to take a girl-trip to somewhere with plentiful tequila afterward?"

"Deal."

On Monday, I didn't have any scenes, but Kane, Mikki, and Lucas did, and I revelled in the relative peace of the house. Eight whole hours alone, but it wasn't long enough, and the others caught me eating salted caramel ice cream in the kitchen when they arrived back.

"Is that full fat?" Mikki asked, peering into my bowl.

"Probably."

"Gross."

My mom had always told me that if I couldn't say anything nice, I shouldn't say anything at all, but Mikki obviously hadn't gotten that memo. I blocked her out and focused on Lucas instead.

"How was filming?" I asked.

"Good. Better than yesterday."

Yesterday while I was still in LA, Mikki had thrown a hissy fit because her make-up artist was off sick, and she didn't like the replacement. So she'd insisted on an alternative, which had delayed everything by an hour and meant the whole crew left in the dark. At least now, I wasn't the only person who disliked her.

"I don't suppose that was difficult."

Lucas put a pile of envelopes and a gift-wrapped box on the counter next to me. "I brought your letters in case you wanted to reply to them this evening."

"Thanks, that's—"

"You actually write them back?" Mikki asked. "That's so cute. What's in the box?"

"Does it look as though I've opened it?"

"I'll take a look for you."

"No!" I snatched the box away, and she pouted. "It's for me, not you."

"Suit yourself. Ishmael already sent me a package today. A necklace and matching earrings. I might wear them when me and Kane go out to Capparo on Thursday."

"What's Capparo?"

"The new restaurant in Pacific Heights. We're going with David and his wife."

Phew. A night of quiet to look forward to. I settled for ignoring Mikki and her gloating while I tore the layers of paper off my gift. Chocolates. Somebody had sent me chocolates, and in an expensive-looking box as well. I untied the ribbon and picked off the little gold sticker that held the lid closed.

"Do you want one?" I asked Mikki. Kill people with kindness, another one of Mom's sayings, and I refused to stoop to Mikki's level of bitchiness.

"Ugh. What are they? Belgian truffles? Do you know how many calories are in those things?"

The label just said *Luxury Truffles*, and in smaller writing underneath, *Handmade by Artisans*. At least it was a nicer surprise than Lucas's block of cheddar.

"No, it doesn't say how many calories."

"Hundreds. Thousands if you eat the whole box."

Well, maybe I would. I'd spent three hours in the gym this morning, and every muscle still ached because of it. I bit into a chocolate, and the sweet taste of cocoa burst on my tongue. Delicious. Then I chewed, and something... something wasn't right. Were Belgian truffles supposed to be crunchy?

I squinted at the half of the chocolate I was still holding, and instead of a smooth filling, little legs poked out at me.

"Are you okay?" Lucas asked.

Instead of answering, I shoved the chair back and ran toward the sink. I got most of the way there before I vomited, and bits of beetle and chocolate and ice cream dripped down the pristine cupboard door, brown against white.

Mikki shrieked, and she didn't stop even when Kane covered her eyes.

"Don't look, babe."

But *he* did, and I didn't miss the expression of disgust on

48

his face. Only Lucas managed sympathy, sidestepping the mess to pour me a glass of water.

"Drink this."

I took a sip and retched again, visions of dead things floating before my eyes. Giddiness washed over me, and Lucas helped me onto a stool before I keeled over.

"Just sit."

"I swallowed a freaking beetle!"

Mikki ran out of the room, and Kane turned his attention to the chocolates.

"I think it was a locust, actually." He picked up another and broke it in half, then another and another. "They all have locusts inside."

"I'm so sorry," Lucas said, lips close to my ear. "If I'd realised…"

"How could you have known?"

I wiped my mouth with a tissue and tried another mouthful of water. This time, it stayed down, and I drained the glass in an attempt to take the taste away. And the feel. The feel of those little legs tickling my tongue and crackling between my teeth.

"Who sent them?" I asked.

Kane flipped the box over. "Who knows? There isn't a card attached. Did you have to puke? It stinks."

"I couldn't help it, okay?"

"When I filmed *Dogs of War* in Cambodia, we ate crispy tarantulas. They're not that bad."

Lucas turned to him. "Stop being a prick, Kane."

"What? I'm just saying she overreacted."

"She didn't. Who expects to find dead bugs in their candy? If you want to be helpful, find a mop."

"Do I look like a maid?"

I thought Lucas was going to say something else, but he bit his bottom lip, took a deep breath, and gave my shoulders a squeeze.

49

"Go get changed, and I'll clean up."

"Changed?"

He pointed at my top, and I groaned out loud when I saw the streaks of second-hand ice cream decorating it. "You shouldn't have to do that. *I'll* clean up."

"Just go and change, Violet."

"Sorry."

"There's nothing to be sorry for." He helped me to my feet and gave me a gentle push toward the doorway. "Go."

I heard Mikki laughing in the living room as I fled up the stairs. Was Kane with her? Were they laughing at me? *Had* I overreacted? Yes, puking was drastic, but I'd never eaten anything so disgusting before, and it all came up before I could stop it.

In the bathroom, I tore off my top and wadded it into the trash can. I never wanted to see it again, let alone wear it. Then I scrubbed at my skin until it was red, but the grubbiness came from the inside, something deeper, not just the beetles but the fact that this little country girl from Kansas didn't belong in the shiny, sparkly world of Hollywood.

A soft knock at the door startled me.

"Who is it?"

"Lucas."

"I'm not dressed."

Half a minute passed, and then the door cracked open. His hand snaked through the gap, holding a T-shirt and a pair of yoga pants.

"Here. Will these do?"

I tugged the clothes on and prepared to face Lucas. This was even more awkward than the Kane situation, but when I peeped around the door, he gave me a kind smile.

"How are you feeling now?"

"Better. Maybe I did overreact."

"I'd probably have puked too."

"No, you wouldn't." I sat on the bed, scrunched up into

the pillows with my knees tucked against my chest. "What kind of sick freak does that? Sends somebody beetles, or locusts, or whatever?" I found a thread of hope and clung to it. "Are you sure they were meant for me? Kane said there wasn't a card."

"They were in your trailer with the fan mail. I'll ask around to see if I can find out who delivered them, but I doubt anyone will remember much, like with the roses."

"You asked about those?"

"Yeah. A brown-haired man in a white van pulled up at the front gates while Jimmy was coming in. You know, Mikki's assistant? Anyhow, Jimmy figured he'd bring them to your trailer since he was headed in that direction."

"He didn't see a logo on the van? A name?"

"Apparently not. I'll have a word with David, see if we can get some security for you."

"Do you really think I need it?"

"You should be able to do your job without worrying."

"I don't even want to be in this house. Not with Kane and Mikki. Do you think David would be furious if I moved out?"

They'd paid me fifty thousand bucks up front, so I could move into a hotel, or rent an apartment, or sleep in the freaking car that they'd made me leave at the studio because an ageing Honda didn't fit in with the ambience at the beach house and Kane had commandeered the garage for his Ferrari and his Porsche.

"It would be a breach of contract, and you know how important David thinks this reality show is."

"But if I came back for his stupid script reveals…"

Lucas switched his voice up an octave in a surprisingly good impression of David. "It's not just the moments on camera, Violet. It's the interaction between my stars off-screen, the clash of souls, the melding of psyches… It all adds depth to the atmosphere, an extra layer, that certain

ELISE NOBLE

something that other productions simply don't have. *Hidden Intent* will be a masterpiece, a—"

"Enough!" A giggle popped out. "I get it. I'm stuck here."

"We're both stuck here." Lucas sat on the edge of the bed, his torso twisted to face me. "But I have an idea."

"Does it involve cameras, chocolate, removal of clothing, or floral arrangements?"

"Nope. It involves the pool house."

"The pool house?"

"It's empty. Why don't you sleep in there for a few nights? Give yourself some space?"

Hmm… That wasn't a bad idea. I'd never been inside the tiny stucco villa at the far end of the backyard, but I'd peered through the windows, and it was furnished. One main room with a couch and a bed, plus a kitchenette and a small bathroom. Even better, it was far enough from Mikki and Kane that I wouldn't be tempted to murder them in their sleep, and technically, it was still at the same address. Sure, it might be against the spirit of the game, but my contract didn't specify that I had to sleep in the main house. I practically knew the small print by heart now.

"But what about you? You'd still be here with the terrible two."

"Don't worry about me. I've spent enough time around their type to know when to ignore them and when to bite back."

"Are you sure?"

"Pick up the stuff you need, and I'll help you to carry it out."

52

CHAPTER 7
VIOLET

I forgot where I was for a moment, but as light streamed in through the filmy drapes that covered the French windows in the pool house, the horrors came flooding back. Chocolate, locusts, and yes, vomit. Oh, heck. I'd never live that down.

What time was it? Ten minutes to five, according to my phone. I'd gotten a whole four hours of sleep, and now I needed to call Trent before I ventured outside to live the Hollywood dream. Or rather, the nightmare.

I hadn't really noticed last night, but the place smelled musty, stale, as if nobody had ventured in there for weeks or even months. The kitchenette was covered in a layer of dust, and a dozen ants had breathed their last in the shower. I rinsed them down the plughole before stepping inside to wash away my bad decisions.

Wishful thinking—it didn't work.

My hair hung wet around my shoulders as I dialled Trent. I'd left my blow dryer in the main house, but it didn't matter because Shonda would do a far better job at taming the mess than I ever could.

"Violet? How's the filming?"

"Fantastic. I had yesterday off because I didn't have any scenes, so I got to sit by the pool and go over my lines. And the weather's so beautiful here." Most of that was true. It was only the first word that was an absolute lie. "How are your cases going?"

"I successfully defended a DUI today. The cops didn't have any definitive proof that my client had indulged in drink or drugs, so it was a slam dunk. I honestly don't know how it got as far as court."

"I saw a documentary the other day that said the entire system is broken."

"Not the entire system, but it certainly has its flaws. But then again, if they fixed all the loopholes, my job would be a whole lot harder. Do you have scenes today?"

"One with a lawyer, ironically. My character and another cop have to interview a murder suspect."

"Need any tips?"

I choked out a laugh. "The scriptwriters wouldn't be happy if I started changing things."

"Well, it needs to be realistic." A pause. A long, uncomfortable pause. "Violet, are you okay? You're quieter than usual."

Damn Trent and his perceptiveness. He'd honed that skill in court, but I hated when he used it on me.

"It's nothing important. Just a gift that a deranged fan sent me yesterday. I guess it upset me a little."

"What kind of gift?"

"Chocolates. Except they had locusts in them."

"Locusts? As in, actual locusts?"

"I accidentally swallowed half of one."

"That's *obscene*. What did the police say?"

"The police? I didn't tell them."

"What? Why not?"

Because between throwing up and moving out, it hadn't

occurred to me. "All I got was the box. There wasn't a card or a note or anything."

"There might have been fingerprints."

"And there might not. The only guarantee was that the story would have found its way onto the internet. 'Violet Miller pukes over infested candy'—I can see the headline now."

"You really should consider reporting it."

"Fine, I will."

"You'll report it?"

"No, I'll consider it."

"Easy, Violet. I'm not the enemy here."

I forced myself to take a calming breath. In on three, out on five, the way the ultra-bendy yoga teacher told me to do when Lauren had insisted we go to a class last year. Thankfully, her health kick hadn't lasted long, only until she'd found out the classmate she liked had a steady girlfriend.

"I know, and I'm sorry. I'm a bit off balance today."

"When you make it back to Oakwood Falls, I'll take you out for a nice relaxing dinner, just you and me. A good steak, or Italian if you prefer. No locusts in sight."

His offer should have been music to my ears. After all, wasn't that what I wanted? Time with Trent? But instead, it brought back memories, and a tear popped out before I could blink it back.

Dinner, just you and me. I'd been waiting for years to hear those words. *Years.* All through high school, the four years Trent spent in Boston studying political science, and his three years at NYU Law. During his final semester, I'd counted down the days until his return to Kansas, but with five weeks to go, he'd called me, full of news.

"I've done it. I've landed a job at White & Sullivan." My silence must have reminded him I didn't live in his world. "They're the biggest law firm in New York, Violet."

He'd what? A job? He was staying in New York?

"B-b-but I thought you were coming back to Oakwood Falls to work for your dad?"

"I will be, but not right now. Pop's still sprightly, and what better way to gain experience than working for one of the best firms in the world?"

"That's…that's *great*." I'd forced the words out. They hadn't wanted to come, and in hindsight, perhaps that was the moment I'd started my acting career. "I'm thrilled for you."

"Next time I come back to Kansas, I'll take you out to celebrate. Pick any restaurant you want. We can head over to Oakwood Ridge with the old gang and make a night of it."

"I miss you," I whispered. It just slipped between my lips before I could think.

"Being away is difficult for me as well, but this is an opportunity I can't afford to pass up. Three of my frat brothers are starting at White & Sullivan too, and we've rented an apartment together in Tribeca. Quite cramped, not like home. How are the horses, anyway?"

"Fine. They're all fine. Everything's fine."

I'd spent the next month mourning the loss of a man I'd never had while mucking out horses in the morning and waitressing at Jet's Diner in the evenings. Then, on day thirty-two, I did the most impulsive thing I'd ever done in my life. It was also the most stupid. I quit both my jobs, kissed a tearful Momma goodbye, and spent all my tip money on an economy ticket to New York.

This was my big moment, my chance to finally tell Trent that I didn't just miss him, I couldn't think or move or breathe without thinking of him. He'd given me his new address, and after getting lost twice, twisting my ankle when I tripped over a loose drain cover, and getting ripped off by a cab driver, I found myself outside his apartment. A small place, he'd said, but it sure looked big to me. Everything looked big. So tall and noisy and busy. Until that day, I'd never seen a skyscraper, and as I walked around the busy streets, I felt like a mouse avoiding Bigfoot.

I heard Trent before I saw him. I'd have recognised his laugh anywhere. My heart picked up its pace, knocking against my ribs like a woodpecker, but as I was about to throw myself at Trent's Italian-leather-clad feet, I realised he wasn't alone.

No, *she* was with him. I'd never found out her name, and I never wanted to, but she was beautiful. Tall, blonde, willowy —everything I wasn't. His arm around her waist and the way he kissed her softly on the lips as he buzzed open the front door left me under no illusion as to the nature of their relationship.

Trent didn't notice me standing there on the sidewalk, a statue among bustling commuters and tourists. I'd turned to stone from the inside out, and I didn't—couldn't—move an inch until a man too busy looking at his phone walked straight into me.

"Hey! Watch it," he snapped.

Ever noticed how nobody in New York smiles? Not one person offered so much as a sympathetic glance as I fled along the street in tears, tugging my suitcase behind me. How on earth could I have been so stupid? Me, Violet Miller, a waitress from Kansas, had actually thought I might stand a chance against all the polished perfection New York had to offer.

A cab nearly ran me down, but before the driver got a chance to yell at me, I jumped into the back seat.

"Can you take me to the airport?"

"Which airport?"

"Any freaking airport!"

His eyes met mine in the mirror, and I saw that hint of panic men get when faced with a crying woman.

"Okay, lady."

If I'd been thinking logically, I'd have caught the first flight home to Kansas, but I'd left my sanity behind on the sidewalk outside Trent's little love nest. Getting as far as possible away from him and *her* seemed the most sensible option. And when I left Oakwood Falls, Mom had told me how proud she was that I was finally spreading my wings and leaving the nest. I couldn't go crawling back with my tail between my legs. *I couldn't.* In my head, I heard my dad's voice too—*When life kicks you in the butt, Vi, stand up taller.*

At JFK, the lady behind the ticket counter silently passed me a tissue. "Where do you want to go, ma'am?"

"California." Two and a half thousand miles away from Trent. That seemed like a reasonable distance. "I want to go to California."

And while Trent had spent two years in New York, I'd stayed on the West Coast. He'd never found out about my foolish visit, and I didn't intend to tell him, but even on the other side of the country, I couldn't get him out of my mind. Lauren knew the details—she had a way of prying information out of everyone—and when Trent had returned to Oakwood Falls alone six months ago, we'd come up with our grand plan. OTT. Violet 2.0. And with my role in *Hidden Intent*, perhaps I could convince Trent I was a successful career woman, not the quiet girl three years his junior who wiped tables after school.

When I didn't accept his invitation right away, he spoke again. "It'll be just like old times."

Just like old times? Oh, no, that was the last thing I wanted. "I can't wait."

"Violet? You don't sound very enthusiastic." A pause, and then for first time ever, Trent sounded slightly uncertain. "Is it because of Kane Sanders?"

"What do you mean?"

"I saw pictures of you out with him at the weekend. You

looked as if you were having a good time, and I wouldn't want to tread on any toes."

Ohmigosh, Lauren had been right! The plan was working! My feet danced a little jig all of their own accord, but then I regained my composure. *Play it cool, Violet.*

"Kane's a friend. A good friend, but he won't mind me going out for dinner with you."

"Then it's a date. Just let me know when you're coming home."

A date.

I floated out of the pool house and along the tiled path to the terrace. Maybe, just maybe, my California adventure would have a happy ending after all? Only nine and a half more weeks to survive, then I could go back home where I belonged and hopefully snag the man I'd wanted for so long as well.

David still found something to grumble about during filming. Apparently, Veronica looked too happy while she and Lance interviewed Mariah, and we had to reshoot parts of that scene. But my secret smile was allowed while we interrogated Kelvin because, by that point, Veronica was struggling to rein in her feelings for the man she absolutely shouldn't have been swapping saliva with.

In her private moments, she agonised over her relationship. Should she leave her boyfriend? She wanted to, but Drake had a temper. I was keeping my fingers crossed that she found her courage. Drake might have been a cop, but so was she, and she knew how to use a gun by all accounts. Would I get an action scene? The next big script reveal was on Thursday, less than two days away, and my butterflies were already back, fluttering madly as I climbed into the car for the trip to the beach house. Lucas wound up the privacy screen and beckoned me closer.

"Wouldn't surprise me if the driver's selling stories to the tabloids," he said, keeping his voice down. "Kane's driver is."

"How do you know?"

"Kane had a phone conversation with his ex on the way back to the house last week, and the next day, the gossip pages knew all about it."

"That thing about custody of the cat?"

"Yeah, and I can see his point there," Lucas said. "What's he supposed to do with it?"

"I guess she didn't realise how allergic she was before she insisted on keeping it."

"Kane doesn't think she's allergic at all. He figures she just doesn't like cat hair on her clothes."

"Listen to us—we're at it now. Gossip, gossip, gossip. Uh, do you know what the outcome was?"

Lucas laughed, and it was infectious. If only all men were so easy to get along with.

"I wouldn't be surprised to find a new pussy back at *casa de pesadillas*."

The house of nightmares.

"Might give Mikki some competition."

"Now who's being the catty one."

"Miaow."

I burst into giggles again, and Lucas slung an arm over my shoulder and chuckled into my hair as I buried my face in the crook of his neck.

"That's better, my sweets. At least you're smiling today. I was getting worried about you."

"It's been a tough couple of weeks."

"I know, but I have news that might help. Donna called me earlier. I didn't want to say anything until after we finished for the day."

"That's your agent?"

Lucas nodded. "She's been in touch with Racino, and he's definitely interested. If you want to explore the project further, she's willing to represent you."

"Really? Did she find out what's involved? I'm still not sure I want to do another movie, but I loved Racino's last one."

"It's a horror movie with otherworldly elements. No romance for your character in this instalment, but you'd still be alive at the end, so there's also potential for a sequel. Plus you wouldn't be locked up in a house with a bunch of miscreants."

"One of the miscreants isn't so bad."

"Kane?"

"No, Mikki. I love her diet tips."

We stared at each other for a beat and then started laughing again. Perhaps some parts of this job weren't so terrible after all.

CHAPTER 8
VIOLET

Nine a.m. on Thursday, and I glanced toward the refrigerator. Was it too early for wine? Because right now, I sure needed a bottle. No, a glass. Just a glass. I absolutely wasn't an alcoholic.

David had decided we'd do today's script reveal in the kitchen at the beach house. Casual. Relaxed. The five of us sitting around like old friends as we nibbled on low-fat croissants and slivers of fresh fruit. At least, Kane and Lucas would be nibbling. Mikki had announced yesterday she was on a new diet where she only drank water until noon, and my churning stomach had made its feelings clear. I'd puked in front of my housemates once, and I didn't want a repeat, thank you very much.

The camera operators set up their equipment, four of them, one to capture each of our reactions in glorious, horrific detail. My look of shock-slash-disgust from the last reveal was already doing the rounds as an internet meme with captions like *That face you make when you realise it wasn't a fart* and *When you see bae for the first time without make-up*.

Shonda had arrived at six with the rest of the crew, so at least I looked the part. Mikki was wearing a sparkly dress better suited to a nightclub, while Kane had agonised over a button-down shirt versus a V-neck sweater. Which would the ladies prefer? When he'd asked us, Mikki suggested he ditch the shirt altogether while I just shrugged. I'd barely been able to dress myself this morning, let alone coordinate somebody else's outfit as well.

"Ready?" Lucas asked, meandering through from the dining area. He'd gone with jeans and a plaid shirt; California does cowboy.

"Don't think I'll ever be ready for one of these horrible little vignettes. Has David dropped any hints?"

Lucas shrugged, but his nose also did that little crinkle I'd noticed on occasion, usually when he wanted to avoid giving me bad news.

"What is it? Tell me. *Please*."

Anything to help me prepare, to temper my reaction while the cameras rolled. Shonda had done her best to assist, caking on enough foundation to hide any blushes, but now I was in danger of melting like a candle under the hot lights the gaffer was directing the technicians to position.

Lucas reached for a croissant, but a member of the crew smacked his hand away.

"Not yet! We need five to make the plate look balanced."

"But I'm hungry."

She pointed in the direction of the refrigerator, and he groaned. "That's full of weird health food and non-fat power shakes."

"Not my problem."

I grabbed his elbow and steered him out of earshot. "Lucas, would you just tell me what's going on?"

"David mentioned that it might be another—"

Clapping from behind made me jerk my head around, and I saw that the man himself had walked in. David looked chipper this morning, one of those men who grew ever more cheerful at others' misfortune as long as he could somehow leverage that misfortune into ratings.

"Everybody ready to go?" He didn't wait for an answer. "Right, let's have Violet next to Kane, Lucas opposite her, and Mikki in the far corner."

Mikki's pout told everyone exactly what she thought of the seating arrangements, but she did as she was told. So did I, and the instant I settled onto the white leather stool, beads of sweat popped out on my back. On Shonda's advice, I'd worn black so the stain wouldn't show, but I could feel the sweat trickling down my spine while my stomach defied gravity to claw its way up my throat.

How bad would this be?

The answer? Bleeping awful. Like, literally. Good thing there was a ten-second delay on the live broadcast. A string of curse words slipped from my lips as Mikki sniggered in the background, and even Kane raised an eyebrow.

"Is this some sort of…" I trailed off. No, of course it wasn't a joke. Getting naked with Kane for a love scene on a sunlounger was totally in keeping with the rest of this awful experience.

During yesterday's filming, Veronica had left her phone at Kelvin's place when she visited with Lance for another follow-up. The ME had found a needle mark in the autopsy. Where did it come from? The toxicology results were still outstanding, but if Del Swanson had been drugged, that could go a ways toward explaining how a big man like him had been overpowered. Kelvin had dodged and weaved, avoiding straight answers but stopping short of asking for a lawyer. For a man who claimed he had nothing to hide, he sure didn't behave that way.

Anyhow, rather than doing the smart thing and asking Lance to go back with her, Veronica had decided to pick the phone up on her way home. But she just couldn't resist asking a few more questions while she was there, and that would be the basis of our next scene. Kelvin would negotiate a deal with her. If she agreed to a repeat of their first encounter, he'd provide answers. Each time she "made him happy," she got to ask another question, with a maximum of three. "Use them wisely," he warned like a debauched genie, except Veronica wouldn't be rubbing a lamp. No, she'd be rubbing… Oh, hell, I didn't even want to think about it. And of course, she didn't know whether Kelvin would actually tell the truth, but since she had this weird attraction to him, she went along with the plan anyway.

And where did this scene take place? Out back, by the pool.

Before I met Kane, I might have been tempted by the offer too, murder suspect or no murder suspect. But the idea of screwing him in broad daylight? I checked my arms to see if any hives had appeared yet.

"What are the questions Veronica asks Kelvin?" Mikki wanted to know.

David beamed because he'd obviously been waiting for somebody to ask precisely that.

"This is the fun part. I thought we'd encourage a little audience participation, so we're going to ask our Twitter fans to make suggestions."

Words deserted me as the others talked. Probably that was for the best because rambling incoherently on tape would only embarrass me further. I noticed Lucas kept glancing in my direction, asking with his eyes whether I was all right. I managed a quick nod, even though I was anything but.

"When do we film this?" I blurted during a lull.

"Mikki and Lucas will film their scenes today," David said. "Then we'll continue with you, Lucas, and Kane. Build-up tomorrow, and the big scenes the day after. Let's keep our fingers crossed for sunshine seeing as we'll be outside."

Twenty-four hours before I was due back on set. Outside.

In freaking February. How far could I get in twenty-four hours? Alaska? Outer Mongolia? Australia?

This promised to be an utter disaster.

Two days. I had two days to prepare for the most embarrassing moment of my life.

"Shonda, I need help."

"Thought you might be in touch. Is this about you bumpin' uglies with Kane?"

"What else?"

"Don't worry, sweetie. I phoned my girls the moment I saw the script this morning. We'll be there in an hour to fix you up."

She ended the call before I could ask who "we" was. More witnesses to my impending humiliation? The situation got worse with every passing minute, but I didn't have time to waste worrying. I needed to get to the gym because the clock was ticking.

An hour later, Kane handed me a bottle of water as I crawled off the treadmill.

"Why are there three women in the living room? One of them is setting up a tent."

"They're beauticians. We don't all have the luxury of a body double."

He looked me up and down. "Don't worry—they can always edit out your love handles in post."

Count to ten, Violet. Don't maim the movie star. "I'll bear that in mind. Would you mind getting out of my way?"

Kane's words echoed around my head as I stumbled toward the living room. Love handles? Did I really have love handles? I'd barely eaten a thing for the past week, and the wardrobe assistant had spent yesterday morning grumbling about having to take my costumes in. Well, she'd be happy tomorrow, seeing as I wouldn't need to wear one for most of the day.

"We're ready," Shonda announced, beaming. "Marsha's gonna do an anti-cellulite wrap to start with."

I'd been on a spa day with Lauren last year, a gift from her parents, and the facial and massage had been kind of relaxing. Shonda's version, not so much. After I'd been slathered in some sort of magic cream and mummified in plastic wrap for an hour, Marsha went at me with a sander. Literally, a sander. Back in Oakwood Falls, the Vickerses' gardener had used a remarkably similar machine on the front gates each year.

"Won't this make my skin red?"

She waved at the tent thing behind us. "Don't worry; we'll spray you the right colour again afterward."

David should've filmed this part for his YouTube channel. *Hidden Intent: Behind the glitz and glamour.* Or maybe I could start my own show as a public service? *Remorse: The Diary of a Lonely Actress.* If I showed all those teenagers dreaming of stardom what Hollywood was truly like, perhaps I could prevent a young girl from going through the same heartache.

"Violet? Are you ready for your bikini wax? We need to take everything off, or the modesty patches won't stick."

"Please, just get it over with."

CHAPTER 9
VIOLET

S ix p.m., and I sat alone in the pool house, beyond exhausted through stress, exertion, and lack of proper food.

At least I looked the part now. Skinny and tanned with glossy hair to catch the sun as Kane screwed me over a freaking lawn chair. Although the script had been hazy on the mechanics of that—David and his fetish for improvisation had struck again.

But the useless script aside, what was I supposed to do? How could I come up with three creative ways to give Kelvin what he wanted? I considered calling Lauren, but I knew what her answer would be. She'd already sent it—six links in an email, each one handpicked for maximum pleasure. Classy as well as filthy, she'd assured me in italics at the bottom. I suppose I should have been thankful for all the effort she'd gone to. I mean, how many girls had a bestie who'd spend hours watching porn for them?

The question was, did I dare to watch it too?

Oh, what choice did I have? It was either that or lie there in the missionary position on Saturday, waiting for the ground to open up and swallow me.

Blushing even though I was alone, I fetched my iPad and settled on one end of the couch. Did I need sound? Probably. I unravelled the wires on my headphones and plugged them in. If I signed up for Racino's movie, I'd be able to afford the latest iPad and wireless headphones too, but right now, I was saving every cent in case I never worked again. *Deep breaths, Violet.* The poolside was empty, the crystal blue of the water rippling in the glow of the submerged spotlights. Thank goodness. If any of my housemates had been in sight, I couldn't have done this.

Okay, here goes…

In the first video, a man played a grand piano as a blonde woman sat on the lid and watched, legs spread wide, one stiletto-clad foot either side of his hands. Gradually, the music slowed, and he abandoned the keys in favour of sliding her dress farther up her legs, all the way up to her… Holy shit! She wasn't wearing any panties! He buried his face in her pussy without hesitation, and she dropped back onto her elbows to give him full access as she writhed under his tongue.

I found myself squirming in the seat, moving in time to the blonde's moans, and when I realised what I was doing, I didn't know whether to be happy or horrified. Because Lauren was right—this was actually kind of hot. But it still didn't help me with the Kane situation because the man was doing all the work. Dammit.

Before I clicked on the next link, I staggered over to the window and pulled the drapes, just in case anyone happened to walk past. The mere thought of somebody seeing me watch a couple do *that*… Okay, so it made my thighs clench, but that didn't mean I wanted it to happen.

A guy in a suit walked into shot, and Lucas popped into my head. What the hell? Trent. *Trent* popped into my head was what I meant. Trent at senior prom, wearing a tuxedo with red suspenders and a matching boutonniere. I blocked out his date, Mandy Richards, because this was my fantasy and she had no place in it, especially after the way she'd laughed when I dropped ice cream on my gown.

On-screen, a brunette in a red sequinned cocktail dress dropped to her knees, eyes level with the guy's crotch. Slim, manicured fingers reached for his zipper and the not-inconsiderable bulge behind it. I'd never watched a woman suck a man's cock before, and when she freed his length and wrapped her lips around it, I found myself strangely curious, in a purely educational way, of course. What did he taste like? She never got to find out because two minutes later, he pulled out, a string of saliva still connecting his cock to her chin, and spurted all over her face. Ick! Did women really enjoy that? I wanted to assume no, but the throbbing between my legs suggested my subconscious disagreed with me. Had someone turned off the AC in here?

Cheese and rice, I'd need to jump into the swimming pool to cool off after this. Should I try watching another scene? My finger clicked on link three of its own accord, and I leaned forward as a couple filled the screen. Flipping heck—had Lauren been secretly talking to David? Because she'd picked out a couple on a sunlounger. He lay on the bottom wearing a pair of camouflage-patterned swim shorts while a bikini-clad woman rubbed her pussy along his crotch. Back and forth. Back and forth. Back and forth. He let out a groan and freed himself, using his other hand to push her bikini bottoms aside so she could lower herself on top. That shouldn't have turned me on as much as it did, but somehow, the two of them staying clothed rather than letting it all hang out ratcheted up the heat by a factor of ten. David should have taken notes.

I leaned forward to get a better look, then screamed as I caught movement in my peripheral vision. Who? What? The iPad went flying, but the headphones stayed firmly in my ears, wire trailing, and Lucas stared down to see the well-endowed couple going at it on the floor. Worse, the sound of their groans filled the pool house, the woman telling Sergeant Salami to thrust harder, harder, *harder*.

Death, take me now.

Lucas set the bottle of wine he was holding on the side table at the end of the couch.

"Shit, I'm sorry. I knocked, but you didn't answer, and... I thought you might need this tonight, but... I'll just leave."

I came to my senses and scrambled to my feet, then snatched up the traitorous tablet and jabbed at the "off" button.

"This isn't what it looks like!"

"Violet, it's nothing to be embarrassed about. Lots of women watch porn nowadays."

"I wasn't doing it for *pleasure*." I swiped at my face as a tear popped out, quickly followed by another. "It's research."

Lucas paused mid-stride, halfway to the door. "For the movie?"

"Of course for the movie." More tears fell, and I slumped back onto the couch. "I have no idea what I'm doing, in case that wasn't obvious already."

"But you're, what, twenty-five? I just assumed..."

Sobs burst out of me now, and I couldn't rein them back. "I lost my virginity in the back of a car, okay? I didn't even like the guy. The second time I had sex, it lasted literally twenty seconds and then the guy left. And the third asshole..." I screwed my eyes shut at the mere memory. "He cheated. Three weeks into our relationship, I walked in on him and some random girl he'd picked up in a club when he was drunk. But apparently, that was fine because he didn't even remember her name."

And when I'd gotten mad at him, somehow *I* was the unreasonable one.

Lucas wrapped me up in his arms and stroked my hair, soothing me with gentle fingers.

"Shhh. I understand. It's okay, I understand."

"Do you? Do you really? Have you ever been utterly humiliated and then had to go to the VD clinic and get tested for *everything*?"

"Well, no, but—"

"Then how can you possibly understand?"

"Why don't I open this wine?"

Lucas got up to find glasses, and I curled into the smallest ball possible. Just when I thought things couldn't get any worse, porn happened.

"Here, drink this." Lucas shoved a glass of white into my hand and dropped onto the couch beside me. "It might help."

"The only thing worse than filming with Kane tomorrow would be filming with Kane and a hangover."

"Maybe just stick with a glass or two."

"Lucas, what am I gonna do? I need to 'make Kelvin happy' three times." I used my fingers to make little air quotes, and wine slopped onto my top. That indignity barely registered.

"What, you want me to give you tips?"

"No! I was asking a rhetorical question." Although… I glanced up through my eyelashes. "Unless you do want to?"

"Shit, Violet. I'm not the man to ask for this."

"Sorry, I'm sorry." I gulped back the remains of the wine, plus a few stray tears that had plopped into the glass. "I'm so sorry."

Lucas swapped his full glass for my empty one and wrapped an arm around my shoulders, pulling me closer until I was nestled into his side. His sweet kiss to my hair made me sigh. Why couldn't Lucas have Kane's part? That way, at least I wouldn't have had the double discomfort of disliking the man I was supposed to be sleeping with.

"I suppose you could go with hand, mouth, and pussy," he whispered. "Build things up."

"You think that would work? Do men like hand jobs?"

"Men like anything that gets them off. And that way, you

could keep your clothes on for part of the time."

I thought back to the video I'd been watching when Lucas walked in. Even my underwear would be better than nothing.

"You think David would go for that?"

"If you play it sexy enough."

A thousand frustrations came out in one long sigh. "And therein lies the problem."

"Violet, you're naturally sexy as hell. You just get nervous."

Really?

"You truly think that?"

I shifted to face him, our bodies mere inches apart. Tonight, he hadn't changed his clothes after he came in, and he was still wearing Lance's suit and tie. So many lines got blurred making this movie.

"Yeah, I truly think that."

A second passed, then another, and another. Neither of us moved, but my pulse raced, my mind alight with possibilities. Should I risk it? If I didn't, I'd forever be Violet-the-Frigid, colder than an ice cube in the Arctic.

So I did. I kissed Lucas. I pressed my lips against his and even tried a little tongue.

And he didn't kiss me back.

Oh hell, oh hell, oh hell.

"Shit, Violet. I didn't mean it in that way."

I shoved away from the couch, running for the door, but he chased me and held it closed.

"Don't go."

Sobs burst from my throat as the evening ended in the total annihilation of my final shred of dignity.

"You told me I was sexy, you asshole. What other way could you mean it?"

"Fuck. I was just trying to make you feel better."

"Well, you failed."

"Violet…" Lucas leaned back and closed his eyes. "Violet,

I'm gay, all right? You're sweet as sugar, and if I was into women, I definitely would, but I'm not."

What? I tried to process his words, and the wine wasn't helping. Gay? Lucas was gay? But...but he *couldn't* be. He'd made romcoms, and my research had unearthed pictures of him with a girl last year. An on/off romance, the media called it.

"But... But... You had a girlfriend."

"Jeanie's a childhood friend who helps out occasionally. She's one of the few people who know my secret, and now you do too."

"But why is it a secret?"

"Because most of my fan base is female. At this point in time, my name alone isn't big enough to land the good roles if I come out of the closet. That's the main reason I took this shitty part—to raise my profile."

Anger welled up inside me on Lucas's behalf. "But that's not fair. I mean, if you can act, and you obviously can, your private life shouldn't matter."

"It shouldn't, but it does."

"That sucks."

"It's just how it is. Someday in the future, I hope we'll reach a point where I can walk down the red carpet with a man on my arm, but we're not there yet."

"Do you have a boyfriend?"

"Not at the moment." He gave me a shy smile, the one that made women swoon. "I haven't been so lucky in love either."

I stepped backward, away from the door. Weirdly, knowing that Lucas's love life was a disaster too offered a sense of relief, and I immediately felt guilty for the thought. But kindred spirits and all that.

"Want another glass of wine?" I asked.

"I wouldn't say no."

A glass turned into the rest of the bottle, and now that

he'd spilled the beans, Lucas was more open than I'd ever seen him. He didn't ask me to keep quiet about his secret, but we both knew I would.

"So, have you ever been with a woman?" I asked, curiosity and alcohol getting the better of me.

"A bunch of them, but it never felt right. I kept thinking I just hadn't met the right girl yet, but one night, I got talking to this guy, and yeah, things happened. It was only casual, but that was the moment I knew."

"I've never felt right with a man. Maybe I'm a lesbian?"

Lucas choked on his wine, and I thumped him on the back until he was able to speak again.

"I doubt that's the reason, Vi. You've only tried three men, and they all sound like pricks."

"You tried more than three women?"

He blushed. He actually blushed. "A lot more. I have the equipment and I know how to use it, but it wouldn't be fair to either of us for me to demonstrate with you."

My cheeks burned too. "I wasn't… I didn't…"

"I know, sweets. Just sayin'." He snapped his fingers. "But I might have a solution to your problem."

"You do? Can you help me disappear to a non-eska… esta…extradition country?"

"Not quite, but how does a night of hot, no-strings sex sound?"

My turn to choke. "What? Who the hell with?"

"I'm not sure exactly, but I know a man who can arrange it."

"Like a pimp?"

"Fuck, no. A businessman. He owns a club, a private one. Above ground, it's perfectly respectable, but there's a dirty little secret in the basement. They call it The Dark. I used to go there back when I was experimenting."

"A sex club? You went to a sex club?"

"There's more to it than sex. Networking, a spa, a gym, a

great restaurant… Okay, basically it's a sex club, yes. People go for the kink."

A little voice in the back of my mind whispered Trent's name. Shouldn't I save myself for him? But then again, what if we finally got together, only for me to embarrass myself totally with my lack of experience in the bedroom? And this was just one night that Lucas was offering, not a deep and meaningful commitment. Couldn't I simply use it as a learning experience the way he had?

"What if somebody recognised me there? What if the paparazzi found out I'd visited a place like that?"

"They won't."

"How can you be sure?"

"Because The Dark was set up for precisely that reason. Members are carefully selected, and most of them have as much to lose as you do if their membership becomes public knowledge."

"The Dark? It isn't a dungeon, is it?"

"It caters to all tastes. But nobody's going to start with the ropes and paddles unless you want them to."

The mere mention of torture made me shudder. "Can I think about this?"

"Sure. But if you want to go before the Kane thing, that only leaves tomorrow night."

"You'd take me?"

"Sure, I'd drive you there." Lucas put his glass down and fished around in his pocket. "Here, take this." He pulled out a rolled-up tie and handed it to me. Dark red silk. "I'll come here at eight tomorrow. If you're wearing this as a blindfold, I'll take you to The Dark. If not, then I'll take you out for dinner instead, and we won't mention the subject again. No awkwardness. How does that sound?"

I nodded, feeling a tad queasy. "Good. It sounds good."

Lucas dipped his head and kissed my flushed cheek. "Try to get some sleep, and I'll see you tomorrow."

CHAPTER 10
VIOLET

Thank goodness for alcohol. If I hadn't passed out, I wouldn't have slept a wink. As it was, I woke from a dream of porn stars doing unmentionable things in a dark, damp dungeon and quickly ran to the bathroom because my stomach was threatening to lose its contents. Again.

I gripped the doorjamb, swaying slightly as yesterday evening's conversation replayed in my mind. Lucas's revelation, and more importantly, his invitation.

Last night while I was under the influence, the idea of visiting a—I could barely even think the words, let alone say them—a *sex club* had seemed almost reasonable. But now? A hysterical giggle burst from my lips, and I glanced around guiltily, even though I knew I was alone.

What was more, Lucas had confessed to visiting the place himself. I'd need all my acting skills to look him in the eye today. What did they do there? Tie up helpless virgins Fifty Shades-style? Have leather-clad brutes do freaky things with whips and chains?

The red tie was draped over one arm of the couch, a dark

slash against the cream leather. I hastily scrunched it up and stuffed it under my pillow.

A sex club? No.

No way.

Absolutely no way.

While Kane and Lucas ate breakfast, I leapt into the first car with Mikki, who was currently refusing to eat a single bite before noon. It was easier to put up with her whining than pretend to Lucas that everything was normal when last night's tête-à-tête had been anything but.

"Aren't you going to the gym this morning?" Mikki asked.

"I don't feel great."

"Well, don't puke near me again. It freaks me out. I have emetophobia."

"You have what?"

"It's a fear of vomiting."

She acted so smug, it took every ounce of effort to stop my eyes from rolling. Did she just look that up on Wikipedia? After all, everybody who was anybody in Hollywood seemed to have some weird quirk or condition, both to ensure special treatment and to gain those oh-so-important column inches. Then they could hire an outrageously expensive lifestyle guru or holistic healer to make it all better and bleat on about that too.

Anyhow, I decided it was easier to humour her than to dispute her claim.

"Don't worry; I already threw everything up today."

She glanced over, a little more interested.

"Are you bulimic?"

I shrugged. "Maybe."

"My friend Magnolia's bulimic, and she has a great therapist. I guess I could get you his number."

"Thanks." I think.

Mikki tapped away at her phone, then went back to staring out of the window. I relished the peace.

Lucas didn't come near me all day, so perhaps he felt as awkward as I did. Instead, I got Kane, and today, he'd eaten onions for lunch. Yuck, yuck, and triple yuck. I was tempted to take a leaf out of my mysterious gift-giver's book and send Kane an anonymous care package—not locusts but toothpaste, mouthwash, breath mints, that sort of thing. But first, I needed to get through the final scene of the day. Kelvin was supposed to back Veronica up against the wall of the elevator in the police precinct and get in close, finishing with a kiss that she returned for a second before pushing him away. The pushing-away part I could manage, no problem. It was the kiss that turned my stomach.

And of course, David noticed.

"What's the problem? You're looking at Kane like he's a diseased slug."

"I, uh…" Kane *was* a diseased slug. "I just…"

To my left, Mikki stuck two fingers in her mouth and made a gagging noise.

David turned to her. "Violet's sick? Do we need a doctor?"

I interrupted before she could tell everyone I had an eating disorder. "I'm fine."

He narrowed his eyes. "You're not pregnant, are you?"

"No! I…" I couldn't admit to being hungover because that would be totally unprofessional. "I think I ate something that disagreed with me."

"Jimmy, check the craft table. How long has the food been sitting out there?"

"Uh…"

I waved a hand. "Honestly, there's no need to do that. It was probably something I made myself."

"You should be more careful. Avoid shellfish and make sure any chicken is cooked right through."

Thanks, Dad. "I will."

"One more take. Do it well, and we're finished for the day. And somebody get a bucket over here."

I held my breath and closed my eyes, imagining Trent in front of me rather than Kane. At least there were no tongues involved today. Ten minutes later, it was over, and I admitted what I'd known inside for a long time: I needed professional help.

I needed professional help, and *fast*.

Back in my trailer, I tried to call Lauren because I figured a romance novelist counted as a sort of professional when it came to sex, but there was no answer, just a cheerful message from her voicemail.

"Hey, it's Lauren. You know what to do."

I did. In truth, there was no need for me to speak with her because I knew exactly what she'd say. *Go for it.* Take Lucas up on his offer and spend the night with a man who could teach me how to fake it.

I closed my eyes for a moment and swallowed because now I felt really, *really* sick. Kristen had disappeared as soon as the cameras stopped rolling, but Shonda bustled in while I was trying not to hyperventilate.

"You okay?" she asked as she packed her bits and pieces away for the day. "Heard you weren't doin' so good."

"I felt a little queasy, but I'm better now."

"One of those stomach bugs?"

"Shonda, could you do me a favour?"

"Sure, hun."

"Do you have a wig I might be able to borrow? A blonde one?"

"What do you need a wig for?"

"I want to meet a friend for dinner tonight, but the media keeps following me everywhere."

Shonda nodded knowingly. "Dinner?"

"That's right."

"Uh-huh. They all say that. Girl, I don't blame you for wanting to spend time with a proper man. Kane Sanders doesn't do it for every woman."

"Really? I thought it was just me who felt that way."

"He's too arrogant for his own good, and someone needs to give that boy a pack of gum."

"You noticed the smell too? Oh my gosh, I thought I was gonna be sick when he kissed me."

"My girl Trina works in the catering truck. I'll ask her to serve him a dish with mint tomorrow."

"She'd do that?"

"Trina owes me for fixin' up her face when she got pimples right before her big anniversary date last month." Shonda nodded. "She'll do mint."

"I think I love you."

Shonda grinned. "You're not like the rest of those big shots. Glad I got you to look after for this shitshow."

"And I'm glad too. Uh, about that wig?"

"I can do better than that. What time are you going out?"

"Eight o'clock."

"Then I'll come over at seven to do your hair and make-up myself. 'Bout time my husband took a turn at cookin' dinner."

I gave her a hug, and after a second, she hugged me back. Shonda was right, this was a total shitshow, but at least now I had one more friend.

Five minutes before eight, and I took one last look at myself in the mirror. Shonda had worked her magic, and now I was blonde. Not quite platinum, but a shade or two darker with lowlights running through the wavy strands. I swished the ends around my shoulders, and they bounced and caught the light. Was it true? Did blondes really have more fun?

My eyes were dark and smoky, my lashes curled by some miracle mascara that Shonda assured me wouldn't run even if

ELISE NOBLE

I went scuba diving. She'd chuckled to herself as she painted my lips too.

"This shade's called Scarlet Harlot, and if you're still wearing any of it when you get home, I'll be disappointed."

"So will I."

Because that would mean I'd failed. Failed to get it on with a man provided expressly for that purpose. And tomorrow, I'd be either humiliated or fired. Possibly even both.

No, I had to do this.

My fingers trembled as I knotted the tie behind my head. Glimmers of light seeped in around the edges of the fabric, but I couldn't see anything except the pale green carpet underfoot. I sank onto the couch, waiting. Three minutes, two minutes, one… Then the door clicked, and I detected the faint aroma of Lucas's cologne. A woodsy scent, part of the image he wanted to project rather than the secret persona he kept hidden away.

I'd sprayed perfume on too, because the real Violet smelled like fear.

"Are you sure about this?" he asked.

"No. Yes." I sucked in a breath. "Honestly? I'm scared."

He helped me to my feet and looped my arm through his. "I promise nothing bad will happen."

"I know, but… Can we just get it over with?"

Lucas pressed a soft kiss to my forehead, and I cursed the universe that things couldn't be different between us. If only he were straight…

"The reporters are hanging around by the front gates, so we'll sneak out along the beach. Give me your shoes."

"I have to keep the blindfold on?"

"Lift it until we get to the car, but you'll need to put it back on for the journey. The club's location must stay a secret."

Sand scrunched between my toes as we snuck out to

82

Lucas's car. He'd parked it by the shore a five-minute walk away. Something low and sporty, and the engine growled when he started it, deep and throaty. This was my last chance to back out, but instead, I gripped the hem of my dress as Lucas fastened my seat belt.

I'd just made either the smartest or the stupidest decision of my life.

CHAPTER 11
VIOLET

Time blurred as we drove. Lucas turned the radio on, and I counted nine songs before the car swung left, trundled down a short slope, reversed, and then stopped.

"Are we here?"

"We are."

"Now what?"

Lucas reached over and took off my blindfold, and I realised we were in an underground parking garage filled with expensive cars. A Ferrari, several Porsches, enough Mercedes and BMWs to start a dealership.

"What type of car is this?" I asked Lucas.

"A Maserati."

"It's yours?"

He nodded. "I asked a friend to drop it off for us tonight. You need to put your shoes back on."

My mouth went dry as I slid my feet into the plain black stilettos, and Lucas climbed out to open my door. Our footsteps echoed as we walked to the elevator in the far corner of the garage, plain silver doors with no indication of what was above.

"Do you want something to eat?" Lucas asked. "The food here is good."

I quickly shook my head. "No, I couldn't stomach anything."

"I figured you'd say that, but I wanted to check."

The reflection in the mirrored wall of the elevator didn't look like Violet from Oakwood Falls. No, the woman staring back at me was a femme fatale, a throwback to old Hollywood in a sleek black dress with cleavage I'd never have dared to show if Shonda hadn't made me. Apparently, she had friends in the wardrobe department too. But under the glamour, I was just a scared little girl from small-town Kansas.

"I'm going to introduce you to an old friend of mine," Lucas said. "Braxton Vale. He owns this place, and he'll take care of you tonight."

"Take care of me as in…"

Lucas's laughter bounced off the walls, which felt as if they were closing in when he pushed the button for the first floor. "I don't know what he has planned, but he's a real ladies' man. Back in college, his nickname was Captain Kitty because of all the pussy he got. Well, until our final year, but the less said about that, the better. Anyhow, women love him."

"Captain Kitty?" My snort was most unladylike. "And what was your nickname?"

"Baloo."

"Dare I ask?"

"Because I'm ticklish."

Oh, really? I ran a finger up his ribs, and he squirmed away from me.

"Wish I hadn't told you now."

The doors slid open, and Lucas led me out into a quiet lobby. Soft music played in the background, something classical, but apart from that, there was no noise other than the *click* of my heels on the polished marble. I'd expected the place to look…well, a bit seedy. A dark little hole with men in leather and possibly a dungeon door. But I could have been in a fancy office building or an upmarket hotel if it weren't for the pair of tuxedo-clad security guards standing on either side of the front door. A chandelier glittered overhead, casting intricate shadows over walls decorated in black-and-grey velvet wallpaper with a fleur-de-lis pattern, and when I glanced to my left, I glimpsed a bar, an island of shiny wood and fancy bottles amid red velvet seating. In front of us, a perfectly made-up brunette standing behind a polished ebony podium smiled at Lucas as we walked over.

"Good evening, Mr. Collins. It's been a while."

"Lovely to see you, Jewel." When he bent to kiss her on the cheek, she blushed. "This is my guest for the evening. We're here to see Braxton."

"He's expecting the two of you." She pressed a button on the podium, and I heard a muffled *click*. "Go straight through."

Lucas pushed on the wall next to her, and a hidden door swung open, leading to a high-ceilinged hallway. Again, not what I'd been expecting. Cream walls stretched ahead of us with paintings hanging at regular intervals, but I got a shock when I paused to study one.

"Brax commissioned those. Every position from the Kama Sutra," Lucas told me. "All sixty-four of them." Just looking at the pictures made me dizzy, and I stumbled before he caught me. "You okay?"

"Do I honestly have to answer that?"

"If you want to leave at any time, just tell Brax, and he'll bring you back."

"Wait! You're not staying?"

"I have a phone interview. Some talk show."

"Tonight? But it's almost nine o'clock."

"Tokyo is sixteen hours ahead—it's afternoon there. And besides, someone has to cover for you at the beach house."

"But—"

"Do you trust me?"

"Yes."

"So you know I wouldn't have brought you here if I thought anything bad would happen." Lucas traced the outline of my mouth with a finger, then pushed up one corner of my lips. "Smile. You might even enjoy it."

"Somehow, I doubt that. But as long as it gets me through tomorrow's…" What had Shonda called it? "Through tomorrow's shitshow, I'll cope."

We reached the end of the hallway, and Lucas knocked on a set of tall double doors made out of swirly wood. Was that walnut? Everything about this place screamed money. Filthy, dirty money.

"That you, Collins?"

Lucas pushed the doors open, and I got my first glimpse of Braxton Vale. I suppose I shouldn't have been surprised that he didn't look like a man who owned a sex club. If I'd seen him in any other situation and been forced to guess, I'd have said he was a lawyer or a banker. Maybe a Silicon Valley entrepreneur. He sat behind a desk that matched the doors, feet propped up on a blotter. When we got closer, I saw that he'd scribbled down a few numbers and doodled a naked lady with her head in a man's lap. Perhaps appearances could be deceptive.

Lucas nodded toward his drawing. "Still haven't grown up, I see?"

"I got bored on a call with Tokyo. Too much waiting around for translators." He pushed his chair back and rose to his feet. "So, this is the lovely Violet."

"Y-y-yes."

I wasn't sure whether to shake Braxton's hand or hide

behind Lucas, but Braxton solved the problem when he walked around the desk and kissed me on the cheek.

"Downstairs, we don't use real names. I think you look like a Fawn. So sweet and nervous." He circled us, and I felt his gaze burning into my ass. "Yes, we'll call you Fawn. Lucas filled me in on your little problem."

Oh, hell. I opened my mouth, but no words came out, and Braxton laughed.

"Don't worry. My whole business is built on secrets, so nobody else will find out." He nodded at Lucas. "Didn't you say you had to leave?"

"Yeah." Lucas squeezed my hand. "Remember, I'm only at the other end of the phone."

"She won't need you," Braxton told him. "I know what I'm doing."

"Captain Kitty, right?" I said.

"Baloo, you're a dead man."

Lucas backed away before Braxton could make good on his threat, the doors closed behind him with a soft *thunk*, and then we were alone. Just me, Braxton, and a whole roomful of my insecurities.

"You look as if you could use a drink."

"Only a small one. I'm still getting over last night's hangover."

Braxton reached into the cupboard behind his desk and retrieved two tumblers and a bottle of Scotch. Once he'd poured us both a generous measure, he settled back into his chair, but this time, he kept his feet on the floor. I swirled the amber liquid. Normally, I didn't touch the hard stuff, but I'd make an exception tonight because sober sex sucked.

"That movie's a real bitch, from what Lucas has told me. I caught one of those YouTube videos earlier. You turned white reading through the last script." He studied me. "Fake tan?"

"Fake everything. I'm in totally the wrong job. I came to California to wait tables, not to star in a movie."

"Isn't it usually the other way around?"

"So they say."

"Mikki Moretz looks like a handful to deal with. Well, two handfuls, but you know what I mean."

I choked on the mouthful of Scotch I'd just taken, and my throat burned. "She can be a little difficult."

"Lucas was right—you're too fucking polite. Sometimes, you have to say what you think. Now, what's your real opinion of Mikki?"

"Uh, I…"

"When you get downstairs, you'll need to tell the man you're with what feels good and what doesn't. He's good, but he's not a mind reader."

"Man? What man? I thought I was going with you?"

"I'll escort you, but I don't mess around with the women in my clubs. Don't shit where you eat, my mother used to tell me. Plus my wife would have something to say about it."

I had to stop drinking because this choking thing wasn't going to end well for me. "You're married? Doesn't your wife mind you running a place like this?"

"Not as long as my dick stays in my pants and the money keeps flowing." He rolled his eyes. "Now look who's being too honest."

"So who am I going to meet?"

"He hasn't arrived yet. Another drink?"

I shook my head. "No, thanks."

"While we're waiting, I need to go over the rules. First, know that I'm making an exception for you to visit tonight. A favour to an old friend. Guests usually aren't allowed into The Dark without their sponsor, but I understand David Jackson is very demanding when it comes to Lucas's time."

"Yes, he is, and thank you."

"I started this place eight years ago. Scandal after scandal was rocking the worlds of business, politics, and showbiz. Kiss-and-tells, irate mistresses, sex tapes, important men being caught with their pants down. So I spotted a gap in the market for a safe place where people like that could let off steam without fear of reprisals, and the club became more successful than I ever imagined."

"How do you ensure there won't be reprisals?"

That was my biggest fear, other than screwing up the sex.

"Strict membership requirements. Every member is vetted, and we only take those who have something to lose." Much as Lucas had said. "The only clothing permitted in The Dark is club robes, all electronics and jewellery are banned, and nobody asks personal questions." Braxton gave me a wolfish grin. "Plus any un-vetted guests have to wear blindfolds."

He meant me, didn't he? "I have to wear a blindfold?"

"I'm afraid so."

"So I won't even see the man I'm supposed to be with?"

"All part of the fun, don't you think?"

Er, no?

What if he was hideous? Or old? Or had a habit of picking his nose like Robby Graham in my high school math class? Could I really let a man touch me all over if I never saw his face?

Then again, Kane was undeniably good-looking but he still made my skin crawl every time he came near me. Perhaps being blindfolded wouldn't matter so much after all? As long as the guy didn't smell. And he'd brushed his teeth.

"I'm not sure about fun."

"I'll ask you that same question later, and I bet you'll give me a different answer."

"Where do I get the blindfold?"

"We have a selection you can choose from in the changing room. Don't worry—we don't reuse them. You can take it home with you as a souvenir. I should also mention our safety code. Any man engaging in penetrative sex with a person other than their regular partner has to wear a condom, and those are supplied too."

"What about the…uh, the room? Will strangers be able to see what I'm doing?"

"If that's your kink. The main bar has seating and a stage, and that's open for everything but the really hard stuff. We have a side room for that. At the rear, there are twelve playrooms, four with viewing windows and eight without. We've booked room twelve for you tonight."

"No window?"

"No window." Braxton smiled, and I felt a pang of jealousy over his wife. Yes, I understood now why Lucas had described him as a ladies' man. Did they have any more friends? "Just think of it as a hotel." His phone vibrated on the desk, and he glanced at the screen. "Your man's here. Time for you to change."

Oh, hell. At his words, the little shreds of confidence I'd been clutching whipped away, my heart raced at a wild sprint, and my feet almost followed it. Until now, this somehow hadn't seemed real, but here I was, ready to ditch everything from my dress to my earrings, blindfold myself, and meet a total stranger for sex.

Had I lost my freaking mind?

Braxton picked up on my fight-or-flight dilemma. "It's not too late to back out."

"Won't he be upset?"

"No."

"Will he find another girl instead?"

"Maybe." Braxton shrugged. "Probably. Do you want to go back to the house of horrors?"

"I can't. Not without doing this first."

"As you wish." Braxton rose again and held out his hand. "Shall we?"

I placed my hand in his, too nauseous to do anything but nod.

The changing room wasn't one of those tiny cubicles you found in department stores, but instead a luxuriously appointed boudoir bigger than the living room in the apartment I shared with Lauren. A rainbow of silk robes hung from a rail, each on a padded hanger, and one wall held a fascinating selection of masks, everything from plain satin to ornate carnival-style creations covered in beads and feathers. What should I choose? A black robe seemed too vampish, while red screamed out for attention. Bubblegum pink was cute, but perhaps too cute. I held a purple robe against myself, but put it back because it was too similar to my name. In the end, I settled on a dusky pink, feminine yet subdued.

Next, I needed to pick out a mask, and many of them were works of art. At first, I was tempted to go for something fancy, but would feathers and jewels be practical for what I was about to do? I rubbed a soft black leather affair between my fingers. Tempting, but too kinky. Then I found the same style in cream with delicate silver beading around the edges, just enough decoration to catch the light. That was the one.

Braxton had told me to leave my belongings on the velvet bench. Somebody would keep them safe and return them to me when I was ready to head back to the beach house. As I placed a hand on the door, I glanced at the little pile, saying goodbye to the old, safe, boring Violet because whatever happened tonight, I wouldn't be the same girl in the morning.

Then I walked into The Dark.

CHAPTER 12
VIOLET

"What should I call him?" I whispered to Braxton.

"Grand. Call him Grand."

"That's his surname?"

"More of a nickname, but Mr. Grand works."

Why did it work? Was he rich? Powerful?

Soft music played, not classical this time, more of an electro beat, intoxicating and insistent. Voices talked softly, and glasses clinked in the background. Then I heard the sharp *crack* of a hand on flesh followed by a moan, and I froze at Braxton's side.

"Don't worry, that's not for you," he whispered. "Keep walking, Fawn."

I lived up to my nickname, all gangly and unsteady as I hung onto his arm. The air smelled of red wine and perfume, but most strongly of sex. I might not have had much experience, but I'd never forget that heady aroma.

The sounds grew quieter, and I could feel the warmth of bodies passing on either side of us. Apart from the occasional "Good to see you, excuse us" from Braxton, nobody talked. Then we came to a halt.

"Ready?"

"I don't think I'll ever be ready."

"If you want to stop at any time, just say so. I'll be here the whole night, and one of the girls will fetch me right away."

I took a deep breath. "Okay, let's do this."

The door opened with a quiet *creak*, and although I couldn't see Grand, I felt him. There was a presence in the room, something tangible that drew me in his direction. Braxton's arm fell away as I took a step forward.

"Grand?"

"Right here."

His voice was deep and husky, the kind of throaty rumble women would pay a buck fifty a minute just to listen to. And also somehow reassuring. Warm. I took another step with my hands stretched out in front of me, then another, and then I hit a wall. A wall of muscle, warm and solid.

"Oops. Sorry."

"I've got you."

A hand brushed my side and came to rest on my hip. A big hand. How tall was he? I couldn't exactly reach out and feel for his head, could I? Boy, this was awkward.

"Grand, meet Fawn," Braxton said. "I'll leave you two to get to know each other."

The door closed, and all I could hear was Grand's steady breathing and the whooshing of blood inside my ears. Now what? Braxton had covered the basics, but nothing could have prepared me for this.

Grand's spare hand found my other hip, and his thumbs rubbed over hipbones that had appeared in the last few weeks since I started my stupid movie-star diet. What was he thinking? Too thin? Too fat? And where should I put my own hands? One was still resting on his chest, and I didn't dare to move.

He didn't move either, and I felt him studying me. Without sight, I couldn't do the same, so I inhaled deeply, trying to compensate. Grand didn't wear cologne like Lucas and Brax. He smelled earthy with a vague hint of spice, as if he'd showered a few hours earlier with a body wash called Spartan or Gladiator or Brutus. And underneath that was the musky scent of man, as if he should be out chopping wood or hunting instead of studying a nervous actress in an upmarket sex club.

"Brax told me I should be careful with you," he murmured. "You look like a porcelain doll."

"But slightly more orange, right?" I laughed, but he didn't. "I won't break."

"I'm not so sure about that."

"Honestly, I'm okay. What do we do now? Should I take off the robe?"

I reached for the tie, but he grabbed my wrist, wrapping his fingers around it.

"Your heart rate must be a hundred and forty." He raised my hand and kissed the spot on my wrist where blood pulsed below the surface. "You're scared."

"I'm not."

Silence.

"Okay, so maybe I'm a little nervous."

"There's no need to feel embarrassed. Everybody's scared of something."

"I'm not very fond of clowns," I blurted. "That's silly, isn't it?"

"Fears can be irrational, but anyone who's read *It* would agree with you."

"What are you scared of?"

"When I was a kid, I hated the dark. Ironic, huh? Come over here and sit."

I thought we'd end up on a bed, but he guided me over to a leather couch instead. A moment later, he swivelled me so I was leaning against the overstuffed arm with my legs over his lap, and then he placed a wine glass in my hand.

95

"This is red, but I can have them bring white if you prefer."

"Red's fine. But why are we sitting here?" I recalled the paintings that lined the hallway leading to Braxton's office. "Is this some weird position from the Kama Sutra?"

Grand's chest vibrated as he chuckled. "That's Brax's thing, not mine. No, I thought we'd talk."

"Talk? But I'm here to—"

"Shh." He put a finger to my lips. "You're not the sort of girl who drops her panties and bends over the nearest padded bench." He clinked a glass against mine. "Tell me about yourself, Fawn. This is your first time here?"

"How did you guess?"

"If you don't stop biting your lip, you're gonna chew right through it. So, how did you end up in Braxton Vale's debauched playground?"

"You really don't want to know."

One big hand rested on my thigh, but it didn't feel sleazy. More…comforting.

"If I don't know what's broken, I can't help you to fix it."

I couldn't tell him the whole story, that I needed to fake sex with Hollywood's biggest dick tomorrow—metaphorically speaking, not literally—but sitting here in the dark with a man whose path I'd never cross again, I spilled a few of the secrets I'd only ever told Lauren and hinted at with Lucas.

A confession.

"My first time was three weeks after my eighteenth birthday. I'd been dating the guy for five months, and he'd convinced me that I meant something. We even went to prom together. One night, he took me to watch a romcom, and I guess he figured I owed him for that because when we got back to his car, he helped me into the back seat rather than the front." I screwed my eyes shut under the mask. "I wish I'd never met him."

"He forced himself on you?"

"I didn't say no, but I should have. Once he'd gotten what he wanted, he left me right there in the parking lot."

Grand's grip on my leg tightened. "I'm sorry that happened."

"You have nothing to be sorry for."

"So that's why you're here with me tonight? Reparations by proxy?"

"That wasn't my only disastrous attempt. There were two more. People say sex is supposed to be some magical, pleasurable experience." And by "people," I meant Lauren. "And I really want to believe that, but deep down, I'm struggling. I just want one night with a man who isn't a complete asshole."

Another laugh. "And Brax thought that was me? Most people would disagree."

"Are you saying you *are* an asshole?"

"I'll keep it under wraps for tonight. What else went wrong for you?"

"Ah, yes. Number two and the micro-penis."

Grand spluttered. "Lucky that landed back in the glass."

"The size wasn't so much the problem, more his reaction when I inadvertently drew attention to it." Lauren had dated a smaller guy once, and she said he'd definitely made up for it with technique. "Let's just say it didn't end well."

"And number three?"

"I thought it was good for him, but I guess it wasn't because he cheated on me after less than a month."

"And it wasn't good for you?"

Ugh, no. "He'd hammer away like a jackrabbit for a minute or two, then just lie there like a side of beef."

"Good to know the bar isn't very high. I might even come out on top."

"It wouldn't be hard."

"If it isn't, we have a problem."

A beat passed, and then I giggled. That was the last thing I'd expected to be doing tonight, but I couldn't help it.

"This is weird, don't you think?"

"Not as weird as what's going on out there, trust me."

"Do you ever join in with that?"

"Not my thing."

"So why do you come here?"

Grand reached behind me to put his wine glass on a side table, and then rested his free hand around my waist. A whole minute of silence followed, and I thought he wasn't going to answer, but finally, he spoke.

"Because I don't do relationships, and this is the easiest way to avoid them."

"Me neither. Except…"

"Except?"

"Except there's this guy I like. I grew up with him, and one day, I hope he'll look at me rather than straight through me."

"Nobody could look straight through you, Fawn. You could stop traffic with that mouth. I bet if you took the mask off, you'd cause a pile-up."

"But I can't take it off in here."

"No, you can't."

I stiffened as his lips whispered along my jawline, as soft as a butterfly's wings, if butterflies breathed fire. Grand had a beard, not a long bushy one, but more than a few days' growth, and it tickled my skin.

"Okay?" he asked, and I nodded, surprised to find that I actually was.

He might have been a stranger, but he didn't come across as the asshole he claimed to be, and from the way my nether regions were throbbing, they didn't care what he was or wasn't so long as he kept doing what he was doing.

"Don't stop."

The tip of his tongue followed the same path as his lips,

and he leaned in closer to nibble on my earlobe. He'd barely touched me so far, and already, he'd come closer to getting me off than numbers one, two, and three combined.

And then he kissed me. Softly at first, the merest brush of his lips against mine. Little puffs of our breath mingled, and I wrapped my arms around him awkwardly because I wanted to be closer. He was even bigger than I'd first thought. Was that where the nickname came from? His size? It had to be. Grand's arms, his chest, his back, they were all solid, muscles upon muscles, but rather than feeling intimidated, I felt safe.

He licked along the seam of my lips, and I yielded, beyond relieved when he didn't taste of fish or onions or Kane. No, Grand had been using minty-fresh toothpaste, although that was overlaid with the red wine we'd been drinking.

As I shifted position to deepen the kiss, something jerked against one ass cheek. Was that…? Holy hell, it was, and safe to say, Grand was no number two.

"You're so pretty like this," he murmured. "Lipstick all smeared. You don't want to know where else I'm picturing that mouth."

"I think… I think that maybe I do."

His answering groan sent a flash of heat through my veins, but before I could either melt at his feet or freak out, he nuzzled my neck.

"Straddle me," he whispered. "I want to see more of you."

"Isn't this a bit unfair? That you get to see me, but I can't see you?"

"Maybe it is. But you get to feel."

CHAPTER 13
VIOLET

I got to feel? How could a girl pass up an open invitation like that? I started at the top, running my fingers through longish hair, messy rather than stylish. What colour was it? In my head, I pictured Grand as dark, much like the club itself, but he could just as easily have been blond. My thumbs brushed over faint lines on his forehead. Stress or age? He didn't sound old, but he obviously had experience.

Gently, I cupped his cheeks in my palms and leaned forward to kiss him again before I went any further. Already, it felt normal. A little too right. Trent popped into my head, dragging guilt and regret along with him because he was the man I'd wanted to do this with. But I couldn't let him overshadow tonight. A mysterious stranger was doing me a big favour—possibly even a huge favour—and I needed to take advantage of him while he took advantage of me.

Grand slid his hands under my arms and wrapped his strong fingers over my shoulders, tilting me back so my chest arched forward. The robe fell open, and my nipples hardened under his gaze. I'd always hated my breasts. They were too big and awkward, and I'd had to put up with lecherous stares and "she'll knock herself out if she runs" jokes my whole life. But when Grand sucked on one hardened tip, a zap of electricity shot straight between my legs, and I discovered a belated appreciation for my most hated asset.

"You're beautiful, Fawn."

Such a simple declaration, but one that left me speechless. "Uh…"

Grand chuckled. "You don't need to say anything. Just stating a fact."

"But you can't see my face."

"Beauty comes from within."

I gripped his biceps as he laved me with his skilful tongue, and my skin wasn't the only thing getting damp. When Grand caught me by surprise and ran a finger between my legs, a horrible squelching noise escaped, and I wanted to die of embarrassment.

"Sorry," I muttered.

"Why are you sorry? That's hot as fuck."

"It is?"

He didn't answer, just picked me up effortlessly and walked across the room in smooth strides. Then I was on a bed, the satin sheets cool beneath my back. Worry battled with excitement. I'd thought I'd feel dirty at this moment, cheap, but instead, a delicious sense of anticipation built, making every nerve ending tingle.

Then Grand surprised me again because the next thing I felt was his tongue, right *there*. Lauren had bought me a fancy vibrator with six speed settings for Christmas last year, the king of sex toys, she called it, but Grand blew it out of the water. I gripped the sheets as he licked and sucked, and when he slid a finger inside and stroked, I was gone.

To my own ears, I sounded like a dying cat, but Grand didn't miss a beat, just crawled forward to kiss me. I could taste myself on his lips, and it wasn't as disgusting as I'd imagined.

"You look like an angel when you come," he said, smoothing out my hair.

Except it wasn't my real hair, and I found myself wanting to tell him that I wasn't blonde, I was brunette, and my name wasn't Fawn, it was Violet. But I couldn't. Nor could I tear off the horrible wig, which was starting to feel sweaty and more than a bit itchy.

But I soon forgot about my hair and also my name when he leaned into me, and I felt his cock pressing into my stomach, a rod of granite that made me gulp.

"Do you want more?" he asked.

I quickly nodded. "I want whatever you're offering."

He shifted to the side, and I heard a drawer open and close, followed by the rip of foil. Would it be fourth time lucky? Oh, who was I kidding? This was the sexual equivalent of winning the lottery.

Grand nudged his cock between my legs, and slowly, oh so slowly, he pushed inside.

"Fuck, you're tight."

"Fuck, you're big." I rarely used the f-word, but his dirty mouth brought out the worst in me.

It must have taken a full minute before his hair tickled my skin. I was totally bare down there—Shonda's friend had taken everything off yesterday, but at least the blotchiness had faded now.

"You have the prettiest pussy, Fawn. Juicy pink lips and that little clit standing to attention." He slid out halfway, then filled me again slowly. In perfect control. "I can't wait to feel you clench around my dick."

My muscles twitched all of their own accord, and Grand let out a low groan.

"Yeah, just like that. Are you still okay?"

"Mm-hmm."

"Nothing hurts?"

"No."

HARD LINES

Now Grand began to move, and once I'd gotten used to his size, my own hips began bucking back at him, pleading for him to increase the pace.

But he didn't. Instead, he slowed down and kissed me, ravished me, took my breath away.

"More," I begged. "Please, more."

"There's no hurry."

"But…"

"But what?"

Grand ghosted a finger down my side, adding another layer of sensation. I felt him watching me. At that moment, I was the centre of his universe, and I loved the way that made me feel.

"But…nothing."

He sped up infinitesimally, and a ripple started inside my belly. A ripple that turned into a tsunami and flung me gasping against his chest when I tumbled over the crest. Grand soon followed me with a quiet grunt, and heat spread through me, his and mine.

Okay, I owed Lauren an apology. She was definitely right about the magic.

Grand rolled to the side, the mattress dipping, and I felt him watching me. The intensity of his gaze was a tangible thing, and I squeezed my legs together, suddenly self-conscious, but he started with the kisses again, all the way from my lips to my toes. Who knew my feet were quite so sensitive? I tangled my fingers in his hair, but I could already sense the sand slipping through the hourglass.

"What time is it?" I asked.

A pause. He must have looked at a clock because I knew he wasn't wearing a watch.

"Half past eleven."

"How long do we have left?"

"As long as you want. I don't have to get up in the morning."

But I did. I had to get up and do vomit-inducing things to Kane beside the pool, and right now, I still didn't know exactly what those were. So, even though I wanted to fall into a blissful sleep right then and there, I forced myself to think of work.

"Can I try some stuff?"

Grand brushed stray strands of hair away from my face and tucked them behind my ears. "What sort of stuff?"

What had the script said? "Making you happy."

"Fawn, you don't even have to ask that."

"But I'm not sure… I don't know…"

"You want me to show you?"

"Please?"

He lifted me up again, effortlessly it seemed, and this time, I found myself kneeling on a leather chaise longue, nestled between Grand's massive thighs as he reclined against the back. Time for a lesson in the dark art of satisfying a man, and I hungered to be the best student ever.

"Let's start with your hands. The head of a man's cock is the most sensitive part, so go easy around there and be careful with your fingernails."

Oh, this wasn't weird in the slightest. Being given sex education by a man I'd never met and who may or may not look like the Incredible Hulk, and all after he'd gifted me the most mind-blowing experience of my life.

He squirted something cold into my palm, then wrapped one hand over mine and guided it to his shaft, already hard again despite its earlier exertions. It was the first time I'd touched a cock in the flesh. The giant dildo Lauren had gifted me as a joke after the micro-penis guy didn't count.

"Like this," Grand instructed, demonstrating how to vary the pressure and the rhythm. His breathing quickened, and I couldn't help smiling because I was doing that to him. *Me.*

"I want to try with my mouth."

"Lick it, kiss it, suck it like a fucking lollipop, but watch your teeth."

"Will the lube taste icky?"

"It's strawberry flavoured."

I shifted backward, ass sticking in the air, and leaned forward on my elbows. I could only fit the tip of Grand into my mouth, and he didn't push for more. No, that was me. *I* wanted more. I'd always thought this kind of behaviour would feel degrading, but tonight, all I felt was power. Power as Grand let fly with a stream of filthy words. Power as his legs began to tremble. And power as he exploded into the back of my throat and I swallowed every last drop of salty cum.

What. A. Rush.

As for Grand, he just lay back, breathing hard, and I liked to imagine that he was smiling.

"Fuck, Fawn. You swallowed. I thought you'd be a spitter."

"Mom always told me that spitting was unladylike."

"Would she find it odd if I sent a bouquet?"

I giggled. "Definitely."

"Just as well—I'm not a hearts-and-flowers kind of guy."

Really? A good thing too, because if he were, I might have been in big trouble. Grand was any woman's fantasy. But with tonight's boundaries firmly in place and him being a fuck-and-forget type of guy, I geared myself up for one last lesson.

"Before I go, can I do the cowgirl thing?"

Lauren had told me about it, and if I had to make Kane happy on a sunlounger, surely that was the best way?

"You want to ride me?"

I nodded.

"Give the little dude a few minutes to recover."

"There's nothing little about him."

Grand chuckled, and the chaise shifted as he got up. "Do you want a drink? Something to eat?"

"It must be after midnight."

"The Dark doesn't follow regular office hours."

I was hungry now, and I hadn't eaten since breakfast. Probably I wouldn't feel like eating much tomorrow either.

"Maybe I could use a snack?"

Grand left me for a moment, and I heard him speaking softly, presumably into a phone, but I couldn't make out the words. When he returned, he pressed a cool glass into my hands.

"Water. You need to stay hydrated. Someone will bring food in a minute."

"If a server's coming, I should get dressed. Did you see where my robe ended up?"

"Babe, there was a woman taking it up the ass in the main room when I walked through. Believe me, nobody here is concerned about seeing your breasts."

Up the ass? Freaking heck.

"Are you gonna wear a robe?"

"They make me feel like a girl. Or Hugh Hefner."

"That's a no?"

"It's a no."

"Don't you think this is weird? Two strangers sitting naked in a room waiting for dinner to be delivered? Or do you do it all the time?"

He didn't answer right away. Probably wondering whether to admit to how strange he really was.

"I don't make a habit of it."

"Coming here?"

"Eating dinner here." He took the glass out of my hand and pulled me to my feet. Discussion over. "Let's head back to the couch."

"Is this room big?"

"Big enough."

"What else is in here? Is there a torture rack in one corner?"

"You're acquainted with most of the furniture. There's also a drinks cabinet, a table, and a chest of drawers with toys."

"I take it we're not talking My Little Pony?"

"Whips, floggers, canes. Butt plugs. Cuffs. Feathers. A whole bunch of stuff that vibrates."

I stepped forward, feeling my way, and Grand guided me in the right direction. The top drawer slid out silently, and I felt inside. My fingers landed on something long and slim. Leather. A riding crop? I pulled it out and smacked it against my palm, aware that I probably looked like an idiot, but beyond caring.

"Do you use this stuff?"

"Not with you." A pause. "Not often."

My first thought was *thank goodness*, and then *I wonder what it's like*, quickly followed by *Violet, you've lost your damn mind*.

Fortunately, the sound of the door opening stopped me from thinking any further, and china clinked as somebody put a tray down on the table. When the door closed again, Grand led me over to the couch.

"I just ordered a dessert platter and champagne. I hope you like chocolate."

"As long as it doesn't have locusts in it."

"Locusts?"

Oops. Grand definitely didn't need to know about the mess at the beach house. I forced out a giggle.

"Never mind, it was only a joke. I love chocolate."

And I loved it even more when I was curled up on Grand's lap, resting my head against his chest while he fed me delicious mouthfuls of cake and mousse and ice cream and whispered sweet but smutty compliments that made me blush.

The food gave me another burst of energy, and when

Grand carried me back to the bed, I said to hell with my inhibitions as I straddled him. I'd never get this chance again, the freedom to experiment and play and *feel* without any awkwardness the morning after, and I intended to make the most of it.

Grand's abs reminded me of a mountain range as I worked my tongue across the peaks and valleys. Every part of him was sculpted. Why did he have these muscles? From what Braxton had said, The Dark catered mainly to politicians and businessmen, and I couldn't imagine them spending that much time in the gym only to hide the good bits under a suit all day. What if Grand was a sportsman? A football player, maybe? Those guys earned enough to afford the fees, which were undoubtedly exorbitant. I longed to ask Grand more about himself, but Braxton had said no personal questions, and I suppose that worked both ways because I didn't want to discuss my occupation either.

So I concentrated on the task at hand: studying Grand with my hands and tongue. And when I'd committed every inch of him to memory, I lowered myself onto my favourite part of his anatomy, threw my head back, and rode him as he bucked like a prize stallion. Gone was the gentleman from earlier, and gone were Kansas Violet and the last scraps of her moral code. I moaned my release as I came and then collapsed, spent.

"You're nothing like I expected," I murmured as I lay on Grand's chest, his cock still twitching inside me.

"I could say the same about you. You look so fragile, but inside, there's a wild succubus just begging to escape."

"I'm not sure whether that's a compliment or not."

"Tonight, it's a compliment."

He kissed me, wringing every last ounce of pleasure out of me with his mouth, and he didn't back off until my lips burned from his beard. I'd need every bit of Shonda's expertise to cover up the redness tomorrow. No, today. There were only a few hours left until I was due on set.

"I have to go," I whispered.

Grand moved in for one last kiss, a furious clash of tongues and teeth, but this time as he pulled away, he knocked my mask. He reached to straighten it, but as he did so, I caught a glimpse of his wrist. Tanned skin, a smattering of dark hair, and on the inside, a tattoo. 10/10. Ten out of ten.

Wrong.

I'd give him an eleven.

CHAPTER 14
VIOLET

"What happened to you last night, hun?" Shonda asked as she opened her box of tricks in the spare bedroom, where the crew had installed mirrors and a make-up chair. "You look as if you got two black eyes."

Who cared? It was worth it.

"I didn't get much sleep."

"Your date decided to have himself a little fun after dinner?"

Could I go any redder? "Something like that."

"Well, don't you worry. Shonda's gonna fix you right up. Just sit back, relax, and think of your hot man."

I'd thought of little else since I woke up after three hours of sleep. The car journey had passed in a blur, although I vaguely remembered Braxton asking me one question: did I have fun? I'd had to admit that I did. Then I recalled him carrying me along the beach and handing me over to Lucas somewhere near the pool house. Beyond that? Nothing. And I hadn't seen Lucas yet this morning because he had an interview with one of the East Coast TV networks.

As for the second part of Shonda's instruction—relax—I

didn't have a hope. Between what I'd done with Grand and what I was about to do with Kane, my mind was churning like a possessed washing machine.

Then my phone vibrated in my lap.

Lauren: Sorry I missed your call. Was it important?

Me: Sort of. I need to talk to you.

Lauren: Home all morning. Think I'm finally getting over that writer's block.

Me: Great! Will call in a min… xx

Because I wasn't about to have this conversation over text. What if somebody picked up my phone by accident? Or worse, screenshotted my words and sent them to a reporter? Their grubby little checkbooks would be itching for a story as juicy as this one.

The instant Shonda finished, I excused myself to my en-suite in the main house. I didn't want to publicise where I was really sleeping because David would undoubtedly give a lecture about team spirit and tell me the pool house was off-limits. In the bathroom, I locked the door and quickly checked my face in the mirror. Shonda truly was a miracle worker—there wasn't a hint of stubble burn or dark circles in sight.

"Lauren?"

"Is everything okay? It's your big scene with Kane today, right?"

Even though I didn't speak to Lauren every day, I still kept her updated. She was my anchor to the real world.

"Yes, but that's not why I'm calling. You're not gonna believe this…"

I filled her in on my trip to The Dark, leaving out Lucas's involvement and any names. At the end of my story, she gave a low whistle.

"Are you serious? You're not kidding around?"

"Cross my heart."

"Wow. That just doesn't sound like a thing you'd do. Me, possibly, but not you."

That was true. When writing her romance novels, Lauren believed in the power of in-person research.

"This whole situation has me losing my mind. I guess when you're living in a pressure cooker, every so often, something's gonna blow."

"Like you, you mean? Did you swallow?"

"Lauren!" How could she ask that? "Uh, I did."

"Good girl. This is *great*—not only are you all ready for Kane today, but I bet Trent's gonna be impressed when you finally get it on with him too."

"Trent. Yes. Absolutely."

The truth was, I'd barely given Trent a thought this morning, and I was ashamed for not feeling guiltier about that.

"Maybe on his birthday? Are you going back to Kansas for that?"

I'd checked the schedule, and according to the production team, I'd have a window of twenty-four hours to get home to Oakwood Falls if I flew out right after a magazine interview in the morning.

"I'm planning to, but I haven't confirmed yet."

"Perfect. Leave him hanging. He's been doing that to you for enough years."

"But he didn't even know how I felt."

"You think? Vi, he knew. He just wanted to have his cake and eat it too. But now *you* have all the power. If he wants to be Mr. Violet Miller, he'll have to work for the pleasure."

By lunchtime, I'd had two messages from Trent, one asking how I was and the other reminding me of his birthday dinner, both of which I ignored, as per Lauren's instructions. I'd also had pea-and-mint risotto balls followed by mint choc chip ice cream. Shonda's friend Trina, the chef, had brought them over personally and assured me she'd taken the same to Kane. And Trina turned out to be a big fan of *Rules*—she'd watched it a half-dozen times, so I signed her an autograph.

"You're looking cheerful," David said. "What's wrong?"

"Why would something be wrong?"

"Because I thought you were gonna faint when we did the script reveal for today. We even had a first-aider on standby."

"Well, I'm fine. I've been practising." David had a coughing fit, and I hastily added, "My lines. I've been practising my lines."

David walked off as Kristen ambled over, eating her second bowl of ice cream. I'd given up asking her to do anything because she just ignored me anyway.

"We thought you'd 'practise your lines' with Kane in LA." She used the hand with the spoon to do finger quotes, then cursed as green glop dripped onto one of her jewelled flip-flops. "But he said you didn't."

"I'm not interested in Kane."

A giggle. "You're weird."

I was, just not in the way she thought. "Thanks for your observation. Could you find my robe before we start shooting?"

"Sure."

She meandered off toward the beach, and I knew she wouldn't. Fortunately, I had a worn-only-once dusky-pink silk robe in the pool house. I'd found it on the couch when I woke up, along with my mask. An extra gift from Braxton, it seemed.

And I had a half hour left before I needed to wear it. Just enough time to run through my lines once more with Lucas, and I found him sitting down by the beach, not that we could see the sand anymore because the production team had erected screens along the edge of the property to hide us from any prying lenses. Thank goodness. The production team had posted a security guard by the walkway to the beach, but it would only have taken one reporter in a boat for my butt to be front and centre on the internet tomorrow.

I waved my script at Lucas. "Would you mind…?"

He waved at the seat beside him. "Go for it."

"First, I need to thank you. For last night."

"I'm just happy to see you smiling."

"I'm exhausted."

"He wore you out?"

Heat crept up my cheeks as I nodded. "In a good way. Do you know who the guy was?"

"I left that to Brax. You're prepared for today?"

"As ready as I'll ever be."

"I'm glad— What the…?"

We both jolted upright as a shriek came from the house, followed by shouting and the sound of running feet. Something small, white, and furry dashed past, leapt at the security screens in a desperate bid for freedom, and then slid down the smooth surface when it didn't quite get high enough.

A kitten. It was a tiny white kitten, and it looked terrified.

Kane's assistant skidded to a halt alongside us. "Where'd it go?" she gasped. "Have you seen it?"

"The kitten?"

"Yes, the— There it is!"

She dove forward, arms outstretched, only for Lucas to haul her back.

"Don't. You'll scare it."

"Mikki already did that."

Guess that explained the shriek. Rather than trying to grab the kitten's collar, I broke off a stem of ornamental grass with a fluffy head and batted it on the ground. Our cat at home might have been twelve years old now, but she still liked to pounce on things, and I hoped this little furball had the same instincts.

Aw, the kitten was so cute. A couple of pounces, and it rubbed against my leg, pausing long enough for me to hook a finger under its sparkly blue collar just before Kane appeared.

"Is that custody-cat?" Lucas asked.

"It was either here or the shelter."

"Let me guess which option Mikki would prefer."

"She wanted to put him in an Uber. He hissed at her, so she threw a glass of water at him, and then he jumped out the window. I didn't even realise he could get that high."

"Perhaps we could put Mikki in an Uber instead?" I suggested. "I'd chip in." The kitten didn't seem to mind when I picked him up, and I quickly realised there was a slight problem with his choice of attire. "Uh, you know he's a she, right?"

"Huh?"

"The kitten. He's actually a she. What's she called?"

I'd never seen Kane look embarrassed before, but no amount of acting skills could hide his blush. "Lord Fluffingham. I didn't pick the name, obviously. Or the cat. And the breeder definitely said it was male."

Lucas burst out laughing. "Well, it seems as if you have one female in your life who isn't gonna roll over when you snap your fingers."

"Make that two," I added. "Do you have somewhere to put Fluffy here while we work? Food? Toys? A litter tray?"

"My ex sent a bunch of stuff. How much does a cat eat?"

Much as I disliked Kane, I couldn't see the kitten suffer. As if she understood, she gave me a lick with her sandpapery tongue to say thank you.

"Come on, let's go and read the instructions on the package, why don't we?"

"Uh, thanks." He held out his arms for the cat. "Guess I'd better take her."

Luckily, I had a good memory for lines, and they were pretty much stuck in my head by the time I'd changed into the fancy underwear, blouse, and slacks Veronica wore to work. Kane was ready too, reclining on a sunlounger in a linen shirt, tailored shorts, and boat shoes. In that outfit, he reminded me a little of Trent, which could only be a good thing.

And after a briefing from David, we were ready to roll.

"Okay…action."

"I haven't moved your phone," Kelvin said. "It's still on the table. I figured you'd be back to pick it up.

I gave a nervous smile, avoiding eye contact. "Expecting company?"

"Yes, and now it's here."

We made it through the first scene without a hitch, but I saw the tension in the crew's faces as we prepared for my big test. I couldn't blame them for being apprehensive because for every butterfly they felt, I had a bald eagle flapping in my belly.

Hands. I followed Lucas's advice and went for the hands first. A subtle reach, a lot of innuendo, and I only ended up with my shirt undone. Then I reached down toward Kelvin's crotch. Was I supposed to touch it? How much did David want to show? Oh, screw it. I gave Kelvin a good grope, but it didn't feel right. It didn't feel like Grand. Had he…? Had he…?

"Cut!"

Ohmigosh! He *had*. There was something extra stuffed in there. Cotton balls? Tissue? Some kind of specially made padding?

Keep a straight face, Violet.

"I need to visit the bathroom. Excuse me."

For the second time that day, I dashed to my sanctuary, only this time it was to laugh.

One down, two to go.

Kane didn't say a word before we started the next scene with Veronica's first question. Thankfully, David had picked out tame ideas. Suggestions on Twitter had included asking Kelvin whether he believed in extraterrestrials and trying to find out whether he'd ever had a three-way.

"If you didn't kill Del Swanson, who did?"

"Mariah Swanson's the obvious answer."

"Tell me something I don't know."

"Are you aware that Del had a mistress?"

Veronica tried to conceal her surprise because so far, nothing in the police's investigation had suggested the existence of another woman.

"Go on."

"He's been screwing around with her for months, and there's also the Russian he ripped off with a property deal. Remember the beach house he sold last year? It was structurally unsound. The whole thing needed to be knocked down and rebuilt, but he bribed the surveyor. The Russian was pissed. I mean, really *pissed*."

"What are their names?"

"That, Veronica, is another question. Two, actually."

"Look, I'm trying to help you here."

"You're enjoying this game. Admit it."

Veronica obviously was, because she put on the groupie stare. I'd copied it off the girls who'd been hanging over the barrier at the movie screening last weekend, screaming Kane's name. Then Veronica yanked off his pants, and his boxers, leaving Kelvin in a tiny flesh-coloured cock sock. Emphasis on the tiny.

She knelt on the sunlounger between his legs, much like I'd done with Grand.

"I want names *and* addresses."

"Suck up enough, and you'll get them."

"Cut!"

Another scene in the bag, barring the close-ups David wanted to do at the end, and I was ready for the next challenge. The big one. Bring it on.

The cameras rolled, and Veronica got her addresses, then asked her next question.

"If you were going to commit a murder, how would you do it?"

"You know the drill, Detective."

"You're sick, you know that?"

"And you're playing along because behind that badge, you're just as warped as me."

"I'm not, I—"

Well, there goes Veronica's shirt. Kelvin tore it open, and buttons scattered all over the terrace. Next, he tossed her badge onto the table.

"Forget work for five minutes."

"Only five minutes?" Grand had taken much, much longer.

"It was a figure of speech."

My slacks disappeared next, tugged off in one smooth move by Kelvin-slash-Kane. He'd definitely done that before.

"Poison," he told Veronica. "I'd use poison. It's harder to establish a timeline that way."

While I ground away on top of him, I closed my eyes and thought of Grand. The way I'd ridden him until he groaned. The way he'd gripped my thighs and squeezed my breasts together. The way he'd shuddered underneath me when he…

"Cut! Easy, Violet. We're not making a porno."

Whoops. When I opened my eyes, even Kane looked shocked.

"Nice," he said, out of earshot of the film crew. "You've upped your game today. What changed?"

Everything had changed. I'd never felt as powerful as I did in playroom twelve with Grand, and today, I'd experienced that rush again. I flashed Kane a grin and shrugged.

"Just settling into the role."

CHAPTER 15
VIOLET

"Let me get that for you, ma'am."

The sandy-haired man in the security guard uniform pulled open the door to my trailer as I approached, and he carried on crunching a hard candy as I juggled my purse and my script and my coffee. After taking yesterday off, we were back at the studio again today. Bright and early on a Monday morning.

"Oh, thanks. Are you new here?"

"Second week on the job, ma'am. I was over on the gate, but I've just been reassigned here."

"Violet. Call me Violet."

I held out my hand for him to shake.

"Elton, ma'am."

"Nice to meet you, Elton."

"Candy?" He held out a package.

"No, thank you."

Lucas followed me inside with breakfast. Fruit. After Saturday's accomplishments, I felt that I deserved a donut, but I'd spent an hour in the gym this morning accompanied by Debbie and a camera crew, and I didn't want to undo the good work.

"You're popular," he said as I walked into my living area. "This stack of letters must be an inch thick, and you have more flowers."

"Any thorns?"

"I think these are lilies."

He was right. A bunch of white calla lilies in a pale pink vase. They reminded me of the bouquet on my father's casket, and I wasn't sure whether I liked them or not.

"Is there a card?"

"No card. But…oh, shit."

"What?"

"One of these envelopes is unsealed, and some dude's sent you dick pics."

I grabbed the doorjamb and peered around the edge to see Lucas studying an eight-by-ten glossy.

"The guy could have tidied up first," he said, holding out the photo. "And if this was my cock, I wouldn't be hanging it out there for the world to see."

"Are there any more?"

Lucas passed me a close-up of two hairy walnuts.

"Eeuw!"

"Hey, you know you've made it when people start sending you pictures of body parts."

"Do you get tit pics?"

"All the time. Wanna swap?"

"I'm not into—" My phone vibrated, and I checked the screen. *Trent calling*. Oh, heck. I'd meant to message him back yesterday and totally forgotten. "I need to take this."

"See you later."

Lucas grabbed his coffee and a banana, and when the door closed behind him, I tapped the screen to answer.

"I hope I'm not calling at a bad time."

"No, no, it's fine. I'm going into make-up in a few minutes, but I can talk until then. How are things in Oakwood Falls?"

"The same as usual. You know nothing ever changes here."

"How's Mom?"

"You still haven't spoken with her?"

No, I hadn't, and the guilt was strong, but I knew she'd pick up on my misery right away. Well, until this weekend, she would have. Today, I felt…surprisingly okay. "I've been busy."

"Seems like it. Rumour has it you've been spending time with your co-star."

"Which one?"

"You don't know?"

Damn David Jackson and his media manipulation. Lauren's make-Trent-jealous plan had worked, but now that he'd asked me out on a date, I needed the paparazzi to back off. If their interference jeopardised my future with Trent, all our work would be a waste of time.

"I haven't been spending time with either of them, and I've been trying to avoid the gossip."

"They say you're dating Kane Sanders."

"There's nothing going on between Kane and me." A change of subject was in order. "How's the house coming along?"

"Good, good. I'm using Lester Bronstein to draw up the plans. Five bedrooms, a three-car garage, and a big back deck that overlooks the paddocks."

"Paddocks? You don't even like horses."

"But you do."

Wait. What was he saying? That he was fencing paddocks at his new home, my dream home, for me?

"I don't understand."

"When you were little, you always wanted a horse. Now you'll have somewhere to keep it when you come back home. You are coming back home, aren't you? I realise you've been noncommittal, Violet, but the last time we spoke, you were homesick."

"How do you know that? I never said so."

"No, but I heard it in your voice. And I understand because I felt that way too when I was in New York. I always thought I'd love the city, but there's nothing like Mom's home cooking and the neighbours dropping by after church. In a small town, everyone interacts. New York was nine million people all doing their own thing, each one out for themselves."

California was the same, only sunnier. But things with Trent finally felt as though they were going my way. Lauren's plan had worked so far, and I just needed to stick with it for a few more weeks to be sure.

"Of course I want to come home. But not yet. I'm being considered for another movie role."

"Another role? But I thought you fired your agent?"

"I have a new one."

"Well, that's great. But are you sure it's what you want?"

"Hollywood's growing on me." Kind of. The trailer door opened and closed, and Shonda called my name from the other room. "Gotta go. I'll speak to you later in the week."

"Bye, Violet. I've never told you this before, and I should have—I miss you."

"See you soon, Trent."

Elated didn't even begin to cover it. No, really. It didn't. By rights, I should have jumped straight onto the internet to book a plane ticket home, but instead, my headspace was split between Trent, work, and…okay, Grand. I couldn't stop thinking about him, which was why my panties had been damp for the past two and a half days. And also the reason I'd barely slept last night and why I was wondering exactly how much it cost to become a member of The Dark.

"Good job today, Violet."

David's words echoed in my ears as I walked back to my trailer with Lucas. Once I'd changed my shoes, we could head back to the beach house for the evening. Kane and Mikki were going out to a club, so at least we'd have peace. Blissful peace. Wardrobe had made me wear high-heeled pumps a size too small today because the colour worked, and I had a blister on one toe. The second I got inside, I kicked the darn things off, and they hit the wall with a satisfying *thump-thump*.

"You still want to bring all your letters home?" Lucas asked.

"Why not? I'll reply to as many as I can, and we can ceremoniously burn the nasty ones."

"So you want to grill tonight?"

"Are you cooking?"

"I can do steak or chicken, as long as you don't mind a few burnt bits. Hey, weren't these flowers white this morning?"

I finished tying my tennis shoes and went to look. Sure enough, the lilies had taken on a reddish tinge.

"What happened to them?"

Lucas lifted the flowers out of the vase, and dark red liquid dripped onto the cream carpet.

"What's that?" A tentacle of fear wound around my gut. "Lucas, what *is* that?"

He leaned forward and sniffed.

"Fuck."

"Lucas?"

"I think it's blood."

CHAPTER 16
VIOLET

"Why is someone doing this?"

Lucas hugged me tighter as the car sped toward the beach house.

"I don't know, sweets, but the police are involved now. They might find fingerprints."

David had called them after a hasty conference with Debbie and a representative from the legal team. Debbie had been beside herself, flipping and flopping between keeping the whole issue under wraps or using it for extra publicity. In the end, she'd rushed off to her yoga class, citing stress, and decided to sleep on the problem.

"I bet he wore gloves. I mean, if I'd left a blood-filled vase in somebody's trailer, I would have taken precautions. And if he was posing as a cleaner, nobody would have batted an eyelid if he'd worn a pair of those yellow rubber ones."

The police had taken the contents of the vase off for further examination, but while they waited for the results, they'd begun questioning people. Elton had seen a brown-haired man carrying a bucket walking away from my trailer as he arrived for his shift at eight, but when David hauled in the head of the studio's janitorial team, she said that Rosa had been scheduled to clean my trailer today at eleven. Rosa hadn't answered her phone when the supervisor called, but we had no reason to disbelieve the story. Which left us with our mysterious early-morning visitor.

"It could just be a sick joke," Lucas said.

"Do you really believe that? First the roses, then the chocolates, and now this? It doesn't feel like a joke."

The coppery tang of the blood was still fresh in my nostrils. The cops said they'd hurry through the testing on the vase—probably due to the threat of bad publicity from Debbie—but my gut told me what it contained.

"David promised he'd tighten up our security, and he already had the studio reassign that Elton guy to patrol our area. At least the production team is taking it seriously."

"Every time I think this job's getting better, that maybe the whole acting gig isn't so bad, something else awful happens."

"I promise not all movies are as bad as this one. David's basically taken everything that happens on a normal set and put his own spin on it. Have you thought any more about Racino's message?"

"I've thought about it, but I haven't made any decisions. He wants me to read for the part."

"It can't hurt to audition. You should at least meet with him."

"You're right. Of course you're right." Would it be weird to ask him for an autograph? "I'm just so, so tempted to head back home after this. Not to LA, but to my real home in Kansas. There's this guy I've liked for ages, and I'm beginning to hope he likes me too."

"He's crazy if he doesn't."

"I'm just not sure. I've been dropping hints for years, and he ignored them."

"Vi, you're on top of the world right now as well as being unbelievably beautiful. Believe me, if I was straight, I'd definitely have made a move."

"Uh, thanks? I think."

"Don't worry. I'll look out for you. We'll all look out for you."

I stared at him.

"Okay, maybe not Mikki. Want me to stay in the pool house with you tonight? I can sleep on the couch."

"I'll be all right."

"Make sure you lock the door. Are you sure you wouldn't prefer to sleep in the main house?"

"Not with Mikki around. I'd rather deal with the vague chance of a freak turning up than the absolute certainty that Mikki will be a bitch."

There was a wall around the property, and the privacy screens were still in place. A stranger couldn't simply walk in.

"Keep your phone to hand," Lucas instructed.

"I will; I promise."

Three days passed, and by Friday, I'd begun to think that perhaps we'd overreacted. Nothing scary had happened apart from me accidentally catching Kane going at it with a *very* flexible blonde in his trailer. The door had been cracked open, and it swung the rest of the way when I knocked, so… Yes, I'd needed bleach to wash out my eyes.

The liquid in the vase turned out to be pig blood mixed with water and red food colouring, and one of the detectives told me that I wasn't the only person to have weird things sent to me. One poor, nameless actress had received cupcakes with razor blades baked into them several months ago. That little story made me crave salad because at least you knew where you were with vegetables.

Elton had stationed himself outside my trailer in a lawn chair, and he smiled around a mouthful of burrito as I walked past with Lucas. Elton was always eating. He'd confided the other day that he had one of those metabolisms that meant he could never put on weight, and I was more than a little jealous.

"Good afternoon, ma'am. How are you?"

No matter how many times I'd told him to call me Violet, he still hadn't managed it.

"We're filming some of the interior scenes today, so nothing too taxing. Are things going all right with you?"

"Not so bad. My little girl woke up with a sore throat this morning, but my wife's taking care of her." He chuckled. "Probably all of that talking she does—my daughter, not my wife. Three years old, and we never get a moment's peace."

"Bet you come to work for a break, huh?"

"Indeed I do, ma'am."

I only wished I could say the same. I spent my spare moments speaking with Lauren, finessing the details of my future. Trent had begun messaging me several times a day, so I constantly had to think up smart and witty replies as well as mulling over the possibility of working with Racino. I'd said yes to an audition, but beyond that…

"You should do the new movie," Lauren had told me last night as I lay in bed in the pool house. "Trent will wait. You've been pussyfooting around each other for a decade now—a few extra months won't make much difference."

"But I miss him, and I hardly even have time to visit."

"Why can't he visit you?"

"He has a job. A career."

"And what do you have? A freaking hobby? You're not sitting around scrapbooking, Vi. Things have changed. When we started with this plan, your ambition was to be a housewife and raise two-point-four kids, right? Is that still what you want to do?"

"I guess. I mean, I think so. Yes."

"Violet…"

I screwed my eyes shut. "Lauren, I can't stop thinking about him."

"Who? Trent?"

"No. Grand." Just saying his name sent a shiver through me. "In the daytime, I can focus, but not at night. I relive that evening every time I close my eyes, and I've barely slept. Everything's so confusing."

Lauren's dirty laugh didn't help. "That must have been some night he gave you."

"It was. But it wasn't only the sex. He made me feel special, as if I was the only person who mattered."

"And Trent's never done that?"

No, he never had. After my mistake in the movie theatre parking lot, Trent had been the person I'd called. I didn't have money for a cab, it was too far to walk, and no way could I tell Mom. And Trent had come to pick me up right away. But while I was sobbing in the passenger seat of his Mercedes, curled into a ball with his jacket wrapped around me, his phone had rung. I'd been broken, and he'd left me there alone while he took the damn call.

"I should get some rest."

Lauren didn't press for an answer to her question. She already knew. "Good luck."

Now, fifteen hours later, I yawned as Lucas held open the door to my trailer. I'd lain awake for most of the night, considering my options with Grand. Had I lost my mind? Probably.

"Lucas?"

"Yeah?"

"I was wondering… How much does it cost to become a member of The Dark?"

He dropped our lunch bags on the table and turned to stare at me. "You're not seriously thinking of joining?"

"Just curious."

"Three hundred thousand a year to walk through the door

of Nyx—that's the official name of the club—and the last time Brax mentioned it, the waiting list was four years long."

"Oh. You pay that even though you hardly go?"

"I get a special rate because Brax is a friend, and I only use the dining room and the gym now. What's up, Vi? You can talk to me, you know that."

"The guy I met there… It's stupid."

"You can't get him out of your mind?"

"Told you it was stupid. I don't even know his real name."

Lucas took me gently by the shoulders. "There are only two reasons a man goes to a club like that alone. One, because he's cheating and he doesn't want his partner to know, or two, because he doesn't want any emotional entanglements. Okay, three reasons—he could have some weird kink, but Brax wouldn't have let him near you if that were the case."

"It's the second one. He told me."

"Well, there you go."

"He called himself Grand. Do you know him?"

"Sorry, sweets, but even if I did, I couldn't give you any information. Against the rules."

Pull yourself together, Violet. "Forget I asked." My eyes prickled, and I pulled away from Lucas. "I just need to use the bathroom."

Before he could say anything, I hurried into the living area and closed the door, then leaned against it as I blinked back tears. I shouldn't have said anything because the idea of me finding Grand wasn't only dumb, it was insane. And expensive. Three hundred thousand bucks? That was nearly forty new roofs.

I wanted to curl up on the couch and cry, but somebody had spilled something on it. Did I do that? I bent to take a closer look. Something white. I reached out and scooped up a glob on my finger. What was it? Lemon-and-lime frosting from the cupcake I'd eaten for breakfast? Yes, I ate a cupcake for breakfast. I'd cracked, okay? Mikki had been hangry this morning, stomping around the kitchen and bitching that the kitten had scratched her new purse, so I'd skipped breakfast at the beach house. And when I arrived on set, Jimmy had been walking past with a tray of cupcakes. He said they were for Mikki, so she was totally lying about her diet, but he let me steal one, and they were delicious. Absent-mindedly, I stuck out my tongue for another taste. Which bakery had Jimmy visited? I'd have to ask him, and maybe I could send Kristen to pick up half a dozen for me. She didn't seem to do much else.

A second passed. Then two.

No. No way. It couldn't be.

Bile rose in my throat as I ran to the bathroom and threw up, scrubbing at my hands and mouth with toilet paper as I retched.

Because I'd only come across that taste once before, and recently.

Where?

In playroom number twelve with Grand.

CHAPTER 17
VIOLET

"Violet? What's wrong?" Lucas burst in behind me and pulled my hair back as I puked.

Well, wasn't this just déjà vu? I managed to wave a hand, pointing in the direction of the couch, and Lucas retreated.

"What the…?"

I turned to see him on his hands and knees, and the look of disgust on his face told me that firstly, he knew exactly what the blob was, and secondly, he was as shocked as I was to see it there.

Two seconds later, he was on the phone.

"David, get over here… No, now… Because some asshole jerked off in Violet's trailer and shot his load all over her couch."

Hearing him put it into words made me heave again, but Lucas was on hand with a hug.

"It's okay, Vi."

But it wasn't. A stranger had invaded my little sanctuary from the outside world and tainted it. No matter who came over to offer words of sympathy or how many empty promises the police made, a sliver of fear was wedged inside me now, so deep I might never work it free. I was still shaking twenty minutes later as David chewed out Elton for not doing his job properly. A small audience of nosy ghouls had gathered to watch.

"I don't pay you to get lunch, I pay you to keep the place safe, and you let a pervert walk right into Violet's space."

"I'm s-s-sorry."

Technically, David didn't pay Elton at all, and no matter how bad my day had been, I couldn't stand by and watch the poor man get mistreated.

"David, he has to eat."

"Then he can bring a sandwich."

"But what if he needs to use the bathroom? Someone could still slip by."

"She's right," Lucas said, turning to David. "Violet needs better security."

"I'll hire an extra guy."

"Not just an extra guy. A bodyguard, not a mall cop with a burrito habit."

"Lucas!" I hissed. I appreciated him sticking up for me, but his words weren't very tactful, and Elton was looking at his feet.

"I'm not sure the budget will stretch to that," David said.

"Well, make it stretch. Swap the bodyguard for Kristen. She spends most of her time mooning over Kane, anyway."

"I'll see what I can do."

Support came from an unexpected source.

"Violet does need security, buddy," Kane said. "We've had three incidents now, and they're only escalating."

"Four," Lucas told him.

"Four?"

"There was another bunch of flowers before the chocolates. Roses full of thorns."

Kane and Lucas both stared at David, who fidgeted and took a step backward.

"Without proper security, you can't ask Violet to do all the extracurricular activities you have planned," Lucas told him. "No nightclub visits, no cosy dinners, no charity shindigs."

Hmm. On second thought, perhaps I should take my chances with the weird freak?

"Okay, okay." David threw his hands up. "I'll arrange something."

"What about me?" Mikki wailed. Where had she come from? "I need a bodyguard too."

"No, you don't." Kane rolled his eyes. "Besides, if you get a stalker, think of the boost it'll give to your social media pages. You can post all about it."

"Wow, I guess that could work. Has anyone seen Debbie?"

That was it. I needed air.

And as I backed out of the crowd, dragging Lucas along with me, I wondered what fresh hell tomorrow would bring.

"Violet, meet Dawson."

I glanced up from my new couch as David jerked his thumb at the man behind him. And up, and up. Beside me, Lucas did the same thing. Dawson was over six feet tall, and he made David look like a Lego man.

"Dawson's your new bodyguard. He'll be with you whenever you're not at the beach house until the police get to the bottom of our little problem."

"Uh, hi."

He didn't say a word, not even "hello." Nor did he smile. Dawson was dark. Short dark hair, dark sunglasses, and a dark aura. And hard. Hard from his smooth, chiselled jaw to his solid chest to his… *No, don't look, Violet.*

I'd seen big men before—Hank Mathison, who ran the feed store back in Oakwood Falls, was six feet three and built like a horse from lifting sacks of grain all day—but Dawson wasn't just big; he was two hundred pounds of muscle barely contained in a suit. I half expected him to flex and burst out of it like a cartoon character. Beside him, I felt like Thumbelina.

David gave a nervous laugh. "Okay, I'll just leave you to it. Back on set in half an hour, Violet."

Even after he left, the trailer was still too small for the three of us. Dawson's presence expanded into every corner, turning it into a shoe box. Lucas must have been feeling it too, because he sidled toward the door.

"I'll get coffee. Dawson? Do you want anything?"

He shook his head, and Lucas hurried out. I did catch him turn to check out Dawson's ass, though. I also saw him smile.

Dawson stayed by the door, watching me as if I were an amoeba under a microscope. Or maybe a microbe or some sort of virus because he didn't seem happy to see me.

"So…" I started, and he raised an eyebrow. "Have you been doing this long?"

"Celebrity bodyguard? About twenty minutes."

His words were clipped, almost annoyed, but shouldn't I have been the unhappy one? David had hired me an amateur. Well, thanks a lot. I should have known that his budget would be more important than my life.

"How does this work?"

"Simple. You carry on with your life, and I'm in the background. But if I tell you to do something, you do it. Turn, crouch, run—no hesitation."

"Okay."

"Other than that, just forget I'm here."

Oh, sure. Just forget. The same way those deer with the funny horns could sit by a watering hole and forget the lion watching from the other side.

"I'll try."

But like with so many things I attempted, I'd definitely fail.

Dawson kept out of the way while we were filming, leaving me with the odd sensation of feeling more relaxed on set than off it. Why was I so tense? Literally all he'd done was stand there. Including when Mikki had attempted to flirt with him, which was amusing because he'd given her monosyllabic answers while she batted her eyelashes and twirled her hair, and she had no idea how to react to that. In the end, she squeezed his arm and backed off to regroup, and once she'd disappeared, he glanced down at the spot she'd touched and his lip curled just a little. No, he didn't like her either.

"That man is fine," Lucas murmured to me in between takes. "Did you get a look at his ass?"

"Not yet. He's always behind me."

"I bet he's straight. The good ones always are."

"Don't you find him intimidating?"

"Yeah, but I like that. Don't you?"

"No. He makes me want to crawl under a rock."

But when he came close, my nipples stood to attention, and I didn't quite understand why. Some weird, primal reaction? Or perhaps fear? Dawson was a paradox. He scared me, but hopefully he'd scare my stalker too, which meant that despite what he'd said about this being his first security job, I did feel safer with him around.

Debbie teetered up on her ridiculously high heels, iPad in hand, and I stifled a groan. What now?

"I have great news for you. Since it's Sunday tomorrow, you get a day off."

"An actual day off?"

There had to be a catch. There was always a catch.

"Yes, on the beach. You're going surfing with Kane."

See? Lucas sniggered beside me, and I elbowed him in the ribs. This wasn't funny.

135

"That isn't a day off, and I don't know how to surf."

"Kane does, and he'll teach you."

"What if I don't want to go?"

Debbie's mouth set into a thin, pearly-pink line. She might have looked like a sun-damaged Stepford Wife, but underneath the polished veneer, she was the Terminator.

"I must remind you that your contract says your time is ours for the next eight weeks, so whether you want to go or not, you'll be sunbathing in a bikini tomorrow morning at ten."

Sunbathing? It was still freaking February. I'd probably get hypothermia.

"Why can't Mikki go? This is exactly her sort of thing."

"Because Mikki's volunteering at a homeless shelter, and no, you're not swapping." She saw David in the distance and waved. "Toodles. Kristen will bring you a choice of bikinis."

Despite Lucas trying his best to get rid of her, I still had Kristen as well as Dawson. And now, it seemed, I had swimwear too.

If I'd thought the trailer seemed small with Lucas and Dawson in it, the car felt positively suffocating. Dawson had removed his sunglasses as he climbed into the front passenger seat, and every so often, I saw him watching me in the rear-view mirror. His eyes were as dark and hard as the rest of him.

"Stop laughing," I told Lucas. "You're not the one who has to strip off most of your clothes on the beach in front of every reporter on the West Coast. I bet Debbie's even laid out a buffet for them."

Pizza slices, cupcakes, and a large helping of mortification à la Violet. Deckchairs, beach towels, and the perfect position to capture every mistake.

"If it's any consolation, Mikki's furious about the homeless shelter. I heard her muttering about inoculations and hand sanitiser."

"I'd like to sanitise Debbie."

Was I imagining it, or did Dawson just smirk?

"She does this shit deliberately to create conflict. Rumour says she gets paid a bonus for every mention *Hidden Intent* gets on social media, and I heard she put a down payment on a new condo last month."

I put my head in my hands. "These next eight weeks are gonna be hell. What does she have you doing?"

"I'm throwing the first pitch at an all-female baseball match. Can Kane even surf?"

"Yes, I googled. But I know him. He'll leave me floundering in the shallows while he rides the big waves. I'll probably knock myself out with my surfboard. Or break a limb. Or drown. Or get—"

"I know a guy," Dawson said from the front, turning to look at us for the first time.

Lucas and I both stared.

"Sorry?"

"I know a guy who surfs. If you want, I can ask him to help."

"Really? You'd do that?"

At this moment, I'd take assistance from anyone.

A shrug. "If I have to jump in and save you, I might get my gun wet."

"You carry a gun?"

Dawson simply held my gaze for another second and then put his sunglasses back on. Conversation over.

CHAPTER 18
VIOLET

I *f I close my eyes and keep really still, maybe they'll all go away.*

It was a good plan until a wave washed over my head and left me spluttering. Of course, the reporters caught that on camera, as well as the other eleven times I'd fallen off my freaking surfboard so far. As predicted, Kane had made a half-hearted attempt to teach me, then given up, and Dawson's friend was nowhere to be seen. I tried to crawl back to my towel, but Debbie flicked her hand, telling me to go out to sea and embarrass myself. Again.

In the distance, Kane crested a wave and stood up, slicking his hair back with one hand into that artfully dishevelled look he'd perfected over the years. And me? I'd managed the dishevelled part, but "artful" still eluded me. One of my boobs threatened to pop out of the ridiculously tiny bikini I'd been given to wear—*all* the options Kristen brought had verged on indecent—and I tucked it back in. Drowning actually seemed like an attractive option right now.

Debbie had picked up her phone, but I bet she'd still notice if I tried to sneak off. She'd also had someone bring a cocktail to her sunlounger, and her leathery legs stuck out from under a kaftan as she watched me with her beady little hawk eyes. Behind her, Dawson appeared supremely uncomfortable in his suit. He hadn't even taken his jacket off, and his deckchair looked as if it was about to collapse.

The sun passed behind a puff of cloud, and I shivered. Goosebumps popped up. I'd always felt the cold, and this really wasn't swimsuit weather unless you were a fifty-something publicist with a condo to buy.

On the plus side, as long as I was soaking wet, at least the paparazzi couldn't tell I was crying.

"Violet Miller?"

I glanced up from my seat in the sand to find a blond guy in a wetsuit staring down at me.

"Why? Do you want an autograph? Because I don't have a pen."

I mean, where the heck would I put it?

He held out a hand. "Zach Torres. Dawson said you needed help."

I did. In every possible way. This was Dawson's friend? I glanced over at my bodyguard, but other than giving me a brief nod, he didn't change his expression. Debbie looked… quizzical. Probably she'd have looked puzzled if her forehead weren't frozen in place.

I put my hand into Zach's, and he pulled me to my feet.

"Please tell me you know how to surf," I said.

"I'm a pro on the World Surf Tour."

Was he serious? He seemed serious, and there was a list of sponsors on his wetsuit. Hallelujah! Bells rang and confetti exploded all around. Now I knew what it felt like to win the lottery.

"Would it be weird if I kissed your feet?"

Zach brushed his hair out of his eyes and laughed. "No need for that. How's the surfing going?"

"The photographers have a great choice of pictures for

their bloopers gallery, and I managed to swallow some sand. Plus there'll be a critique of my ass, probably with a comparison chart that involves several minor planets, and at least one comment about me being well-insulated."

He grimaced. "Sorry about that. I would've gotten here sooner, but my flight was delayed."

"Hold on; you flew in for this?"

"Owed Big D a favour."

Big D? Dawson? Yes, that fit, and now I owed him a favour too. And the dirty part of me couldn't help wondering exactly how big the D was.

Enough, Violet! That visit to The Dark had awakened a filthy side I didn't realise I possessed. I shook my head to clear those thoughts as Zach grabbed a surfboard and laid it down on the sand.

Hmm. "Yours is bigger than mine."

"You have a fish, and I have a longboard."

"I'm going to pretend I understood what you just said there."

"Yours is a better size for a beginner."

Over the next half hour, Zach taught me about the deck and fins and rails, where to lie, how to paddle and, most importantly, how to stand up, all in the shallows. Luckily, the reporters wanted to keep their feet dry.

"Ready to get properly wet again?" he asked.

"No."

"We'll catch a few small waves to start with, just on our bellies. Look for the white tops, remember?"

On my final ride to shore, I managed to stand up for a whole ten seconds, albeit partly in a crouch, but when I wiped out, I was laughing. Zach arrived next to me like the champion he was, shaking water out of his hair, and a female photographer on the beach stared so hard she almost forgot to take pictures.

"I can't thank you enough for this."

"You're a natural."

"And you're charming." I nodded toward the reporters on the beach. "But I know which pictures will make the papers tomorrow."

Zach had the zipper on his wetsuit halfway undone, but now he pulled it up again.

"How confident are you feeling?"

"Why?"

"Just answer."

"From the way you're looking at me, I think a more appropriate question would be how stupid am I feeling?"

"Get in the water, Violet."

He grabbed the longboard and waded out beside me until we were waist deep. Whatever Zach had planned, I was rapidly getting cold feet. Literally. The sun was going down, and with no wetsuit, the shivers had set in. My toes were freaking blue.

"I need to get out."

"No, you need to get on."

"On what?"

"My board. Get on my board." Zach lifted me from my waist, and I landed with a *splat*. "Move forward a bit."

"I can't ride this on my own." A squeal escaped from my throat. "The front's sinking."

He yanked my legs apart and landed between them, chest on my ass, and muttered something that sounded suspiciously like, "He's gonna kill me."

"Sorry, what?"

"Nothing. Now paddle."

I paddled. I paddled until I thought my arms were going to fall off, farther out to sea than I'd ever been before, and when Zach launched us onto a wave, I was panting harder than an out-of-shape porn star.

"Smile," he shouted in my ear, then lifted me to my feet. "We're on camera."

What a rush! I squealed like a kid as Zach kept me steady with an arm around my waist. How did he stay upright? He even managed to wave while we glided onto the beach, and as I staggered toward my towel, he stayed right alongside.

"How do you know Zach Torres, Violet?" a reporter yelled.

"Old friends," he called back on my behalf.

"Is something going on between you two?"

"Does it matter?" He flashed them a perfect smile. "You'll print whatever you want, anyway."

I wrapped a towel tightly around myself as Kane appeared in board shorts. Debbie had tried to insist on Speedos, but Kane refused, citing a sponsorship deal. Secretly, I suspected he just didn't want to risk the padding falling out. At least his timely distraction gave me a moment to speak to Zach.

"Thank you for today. I mean, you don't even know me, and you gave up your time to help."

"No problem."

I gave him an awkward, slightly damp hug. "Well, goodbye."

"For now. I have a feeling we'll be seeing each other again."

Before I could tell him no, no, surfing definitely wasn't the sport for me, Debbie strode over with a reporter in tow. She seemed to know him, and by "know him," I meant he'd be sponsoring a window or two in her condo.

"I promised Simon a short exclusive about *Hidden Intent*. Kane! Would you come over here for a minute?"

By the time we finished, Zach had disappeared. Only Dawson was left, arms folded and biceps bulging. A muscle ticced in his jaw as he stopped beside me.

"Are you done?"

Debbie patted him on the arm. "All finished, sweetie. It's been a good day."

"Debatable."

"You should have worn shorts."

"And put my gun where?"

"You're just here for show, Dawkins. This isn't the Wild West." She turned and headed for her car. "Toodles."

"Sorry," I muttered. "She's always like that."

He shrugged a quarter inch. "As long as I'm getting paid."

"I value your services. Really. Someone's out there watching me, and it gives me the creeps. And thank you for asking Zach to help me. I can't believe he flew in specially."

"Just doing my job."

He wasn't. It was more than that, even if Dawson didn't want to admit it. Or even talk to me. We rode back in silence, broken only by Kane talking to one of his stylists on the phone. Apparently, the sand had played havoc with his complexion and he needed his nails buffed. I imagined Dawson rolling his eyes behind the sunglasses.

"You don't need to come in," I said when we got to the house. "I'll be fine inside with the others."

"My contract says I have to see you to the door."

And see me to the door, he did. Kane marched through, and Dawson reached out and caught the handle before the door slammed in my face. As he did so, his sleeve rode up, revealing a fancy watch on a tanned wrist. Not a ubiquitous Rolex, but something with gauges and dials, a shiny confusion of information. And peeping out from under the leather strap was a tattoo.

10/10

Ten out of ten, but I'd give him an eleven.

Holy fuck. It took all of my acting skills to keep my face blank and walk through the door without collapsing.

"Good night, Violet."

"Good night."

Could it be…? What were the chances of two well-muscled men in the San Francisco Bay Area having the exact same tattoo on the same wrist? I hadn't recognised the voice, but then again, Dawson had hardly spoken, and most of the time, he sounded irritated. Did he hate working the celeb detail? I couldn't blame him for that because I hated it too. Were there any other clues? The aroma of man had been covered up by cologne, but he couldn't hide the pheromones. I glanced down at my chest and grimaced. My nipples didn't lie.

Had I accidentally found Grand?

CHAPTER 19
DAWSON

"What the fuck were you playing at?" Dawson growled. "I'm gonna kill you."

Zach popped the top on a beer and tossed another in Dawson's direction. He caught it without looking and pulled the cap off the bottle with his teeth, just because he could.

"You asked me to teach her to surf."

"Yeah, but I didn't ask you to screw her on a surfboard."

"I did it to help her. Which picture do you think everyone's gonna look at tomorrow? Violet Miller wiping out like a klutz, or Violet Miller riding the waves with Zach Torres? I can just see the headlines now… America's sweetheart and the king of surf."

America's sweetheart.

Violet Miller.

Fawn.

Fuck. Of all the clients in all the world, Dawson had been assigned to her. And the irony? His new job was her fault.

Until that night in The Dark, he'd been happy. Well, not happy, exactly, but as long as he hadn't thought about

145

anything but eating, breathing, shooting, and occasionally sleeping, he'd been able to live with himself.

Then Fawn had come along with all her sweetness and… no, he couldn't say wide-eyed innocence because those soft brown eyes had been hidden away, but he'd imagined her that way. And she'd made him re-evaluate. Wonder if maybe there was more to life than working as a mercenary, living out of a duffel bag in some godforsaken flea-pit while people tried to kill him. If there was more to life than merely existing.

That was why he'd finally called up an old buddy from the teams and accepted his job offer. Executive protection, contract-to-contract, see how they got on. He'd never thought babysitting celebrities would be his thing, but then he'd walked into Violet Miller's trailer and seen that mouth again.

Plump little lips, pale pink now rather than vampish red, her lipstick shiny and tidy rather than smeared all over her cheeks and his cock. The faint smell of her fancy perfume had drifted across, and he'd hardened instantly. Dawson had almost quit on the spot. How could he protect a woman when he couldn't even think straight around her? But then he'd considered the alternative, that some other asshole would be spending every waking hour walking in her shadow, and decided that sticking around would be the lesser of two evils.

And worse, she was having problems at work. A nuisance at best, a stalker at worst. Blood-filled flowers? Chocolate-coated locusts? Overseas, Dawson had eaten them deep-fried and sprinkled in chilli powder, but nobody had ever sent them to his workplace in a fancy box. Those gifts, they'd been unpleasant but not dangerous. The cum on her couch? A whole different story. If a man could get close enough to jerk off, then he could get close enough to put a knife through her chest.

And that meant Dawson was Violet's new bodyguard, whether he wanted to be or not. He just had to keep his head while the cops did their job and avoid doing anything stupid.

Such as inviting her to join him for a carpet picnic, for example. He didn't even know why he'd done that. Usually, he showed up at The Dark, got his kicks, and went home again. Never before had he ordered food and fed a girl three kinds of dessert.

What was wrong with him?

"Earth to Dawson. You want me to order pizza?"

He came to his senses and glared at Zach. "Pull a stunt like that again, and you'll be surfing down the River Styx."

"I get it; she's pretty. You don't need to act like a gorilla."

"She's vulnerable. That's why I'm acting like a… I'm not a fucking gorilla."

"You want jalapeños or just pepperoni?"

Zach had known Dawson for too long to take shit from him. Nearly ten years now. They'd been friends through the worst times of their lives, even if they didn't get the chance to see each other so often anymore.

"Both. Where's Brax tonight, anyway?"

"New York. Carissa made him fly back for some benefit."

Dawson took a seat on the leather couch. "I'm surprised he went."

"He didn't sound as though he wanted to."

"The guy's whipped."

"I've given up trying to second-guess what's going on there. Still, at least we get to borrow his apartment. Nice place he ended up with."

It was. Three bedrooms, three bathrooms, top floor with a view of the ocean. These penthouses sold for seven figures, and Brax hardly ever stayed there. If Dawson were a betting man, he'd put money on the place being Carissa's choice. Brax would have picked a house on the beach, not an ivory tower.

When Dawson first arrived in California, he'd stayed with Jefferson, an old friend and now his boss. But Jeff's wife had just popped out another kid to go with their twins, and

147

nobody in that house was getting much sleep at the moment. Jeff did his share of the chores and then escaped to the office for a break.

"Are you staying here for long?" Dawson asked Zach.

"I'm flying back to Mexico tomorrow. One of my sponsors wants me for a photoshoot."

"Need a ride to the airport?"

"Nah, I'll catch a few waves before I go." Zach settled into an armchair. None of the furnishings were particularly comfortable. "So, what's the story with you and this actress?"

"There's no story."

"Dude, I was watching you on the beach today. You didn't take your eyes off her."

"Because that's my job."

"And why did you call me?"

"She's had a rough time lately. The movie director's exploiting her, and you saw Kane Sanders at the beach today. If they gave out Oscars for being a self-absorbed asshole, he'd win hands-down."

The jury was still out on the other guy. Lucas. Violet seemed to like him, but Dawson twitched every time he touched her. Just a brush of his hand here and a nudge of his thigh there, but she leaned toward him as if she wanted more. Dawson didn't get it. If she was into Lucas, why had she gone to The Dark?

"That's it?" Zach asked. "You just feel sorry for her?"

"That's it. I've only known her for a day, but it's easy to see that she doesn't fit in with the rest of the movie people. They haven't corrupted her yet."

"What, you want to keep her pure or something?"

Not pure, exactly.

"She's got a clean soul in a world of filth."

And Dawson's soul was as dark as they came, twisted and broken. Violet was a summer's day to his winter night.

There could never be a repeat of the evening they'd shared

together, but he still wanted to protect her, not only from the stalker but from the whole damn world. She deserved happiness, and although Dawson couldn't be the one to give it to her, he'd keep her safe until she found it for herself.

Just not with Zach. Dawson knew for certain that Zach made full use of all the toys available in The Dark. He'd take Violet and break all her petals off.

"Okay, pizza's ordered," Zach said. "Don't go getting philosophical on me."

"No danger of that."

"More beer?"

"Why not?"

CHAPTER 20
VIOLET

L ast week when David yelled "cut" for the final time each day, I could walk off set and relax a little. Not anymore. With Dawson constantly hovering three paces behind me, leaving me wrapped in a cloud of pheromones with permanently damp panties, I had to keep acting my little heart out until I got back to the beach house. It was exhausting.

By Friday, my head was about to explode. I had a thousand lines that I needed to memorise all spinning around in my brain, Trent was texting me ten times a day, and yesterday, I might have mentioned to Lauren that I'd accidentally slept with my bodyguard and now she kept emailing me pictures of hot men with guns.

I couldn't take much more of this.

"You seem tense," Lucas said as the car drove out through the studio gates.

No shit, Sherlock.

"The past several days have been busy."

"I thought you were happier with the script this week?"

Definitely. And so was Mikki. Yesterday and today had

called for Mariah to flirt with Kelvin, and she'd sure put plenty of effort into that.

"I am. How did your interview go?"

This morning, a vlogger that apparently everyone but I had heard of interviewed the four of us plus David for his YouTube channel, all individually. He'd be releasing one clip each Monday for the next five weeks.

"Same old, same old. How was yours?"

"He asked me what my favourite thing about working on the movie was, and I literally couldn't think of an answer."

"So what did you say?"

"In the end, I told him I liked the filter coffee from the craft table, and he thought I was joking. Said I had a great sense of humour."

Lucas chuckled and wrapped an arm around my shoulders. I glanced at the rear-view mirror, but Dawson had his sunglasses on again, so I had no idea whether he'd noticed or not. *I* needed to start wearing sunglasses. Right now, he had an unfair advantage.

"That's good. Everyone likes a sense of humour."

"I haven't found anything funny since I got to San Francisco."

"Not even Mikki's tan? She gets more orange every day. I overheard the continuity lady complaining about it earlier."

"I suppose there *is* that."

"So, the script. Do you have any clue who did it yet?"

"Nope." Truthfully, I'd been too frazzled to even consider who the killer might be. "Mariah's the obvious answer, which is why I don't think it's her. David might put in a twist and make Kelvin the culprit, but I'm waiting for some unknown third party to pop up."

"Scott Lowes is gonna make a cameo."

"Really?" He was so A-list he kicked Kane down to S or T. "Who told you?"

"A mutual friend who knows Scott. I reckon that'll be another one of David's surprises."

"Do you think he might be the killer?"

"Who knows? He usually plays the good guy, but I heard he's worried about getting typecast. We haven't met Veronica's mysterious boyfriend yet, don't forget. From the hints everyone's been dropping, he sounds like a prick, and he won't be happy if he finds out she's cheating with Kelvin."

"I don't like Veronica much at the moment. Is that a bad thing to say?"

"This whole script-reveal bullshit makes it hard for us to know how to play our own characters."

"I guess it makes it more realistic when we react to other people."

Lucas gently squeezed the back of my neck with warm fingers. "You're still tense."

I dropped my voice to a murmur. "Can we discuss this when we get back to the house?"

"Are you worried about the driver and Mr. Hot but Grumpy listening in?" He reached out and closed the privacy screen. "There. Problem solved."

No, it really wasn't. Because now Dawson would be wondering what the heck I was doing back here with Lucas, and I didn't know whether he'd be hurt or angry or indifferent. None of those options were good.

"Can you open that again?"

Lucas kept his hand over the button. "Not until you tell me what's going on."

Oh, heck. He'd find out eventually, wouldn't he? There were still seven weeks to go on the movie, and if Dawson stuck around for even half of those… I was in trouble.

"It's him."

"Who's who?"

"My bodyguard. He's the man I met at The Dark, I'm sure of it."

Lucas's eyes went wide. A second passed, then another, and he doubled over laughing until I thumped him in the chest.

"Ow."

"It's not funny."

"Vi, it's brilliant. You said you wanted to meet him again, didn't you? Wait—how do you know it's him?"

"He has a tattoo on his wrist. The blindfold slipped for a moment, and I saw it."

"Well, you were right about him being tasty. I'd do him."

"Lucas! We can't keep talking about him that way. He's not some nameless, faceless guy anymore. And what if he realises who I am?"

"Don't worry; he's bound by the rules of the club. He can't talk about you or any of the other women."

I chewed at my bottom lip and a piece of skin came away, leaving it raw. "It's not only that."

"What do you mean?"

I pointed at my nipples with both hands, and sure enough, they were clearly visible through my shirt. "This happens whenever he's around. It's getting embarrassing."

"Can't you…I don't know… Can't you tape them down or something?"

"You're smirking."

"Sorry. I'm sorry. It's just… Shit. I never pictured you going for the strong, silent type."

"He was quite talkative in the club. Have you ever seen him there before?"

"No, and I'd definitely remember. Look, he probably won't recognise you. Even I barely recognised you that night, and I doubt he was paying much attention to your face, anyway."

"Lucas!"

"It's true. All you have to do is act casual around him, and he'll never know."

"You really think so?"

"Yeah, I do. How about I give you a shoulder rub when we get back? I'm the king of shoulder rubs. Before I got into acting, I worked as a massage therapist."

"In LA?"

"At a spa in Hollywood, and not the seedy kind."

I'd only ever had one massage, courtesy of Lauren's mom, and I'd certainly slept well afterward.

"I wouldn't say no."

"We'll grab a bottle of wine when we get in and head out to the pool house. Mikki and Kane can watch reality TV together and compare make-up."

Although Kane had been spending a lot of time with Fluffy over the last few days. She liked to curl up on his lap, and her presence meant Mikki gave him a wide berth.

"Did Kane get lash extensions today? I'm sure his eyelashes looked longer."

"Sweets, I do believe you're right."

Lucas hadn't been kidding about his abilities. Later, as he dug his thumbs into my shoulders and chatted about his experiences in Hollywood, the good and the bad, I realised that the old saying was true. Every cloud had a silver lining. Mine was more nickel-plated, but I'd made a new friend.

Of course, if I'd realised what a storm was to come, I'd have traded the pool house for a tornado shelter, but at that moment, the sky was merely overcast. So I sighed, forced myself to relax, and let Lucas's magic hands take my worries away.

CHAPTER 21
DAWSON

D awson blocked out the sounds of the girl moaning behind him and knocked back the rest of his Scotch. He'd pay for this tomorrow.

"Another?" the bartender asked.

"Why not?"

Thanks to Brax, his tab at Nyx was larger than his capacity for alcohol.

A middle-aged guy Dawson recognised as a politician helped a thin blonde wearing an ornate blindfold onto the stool beside him and nodded in his direction. Somebody had a new toy. Dawson raised a hand in greeting, but he didn't want to talk. Not tonight.

Perhaps he should have gone someplace different? A sports bar or a shitty dive where he could pick a fight and get rid of the frustration that had been building inside him for the whole of this week. Tonight had been the final straw, when the pretty boy had put his hands all over Violet and then rolled up the privacy screen. They'd been smiling and laughing as they walked into the fancy beachside villa. Wine and dinner had both been mentioned, and they were sharing a house, for fuck's sake. Dawson felt around his mouth with his tongue. He'd gritted his teeth so hard he thought he might have cracked a molar.

The bartender slid another glass of amber liquid toward him with a smile, but he didn't return it and spun his stool around instead. On the stage, a young brunette was bent forward over a flogging bench, her tits squashed against the padded burgundy leather and her eyes hidden by a black leather mask. She squealed and whimpered as the cat-o'-nine-tails connected, leaving red lines on her creamy skin. Dawson glanced downward. Nothing. Not even a twitch. Seemed half-naked women didn't do it for him anymore, just clothed ones. He'd had a semi all week from staring at Violet's ass.

"Hi, Grand. How are you tonight? Can I get you anything?"

A soft hand touched his shoulder, and he turned to see Floss, one of the club girls. They were easy to tell apart from the clients because they wore lingerie rather than robes. He'd never worked out whether she got her name from her light pink hair, her scrupulous dental hygiene, or the fact that she always wore a thong.

Brax employed a bunch of girls as hostesses to entertain the single men, and yeah…they weren't just hostesses. With Floss, pretty much anything went, and if she faked it, she'd give Violet a run in the acting stakes.

Tonight, she could be precisely what Dawson needed to get over this crazy obsession with a woman he couldn't have. Violet had been aloof with him all week, which left him under no illusion as to where he stood. Leading ladies didn't screw around with the hired help.

Just their co-stars.

"Yeah, you can join me for a drink."

Floss flashed him a perfect white smile. "Only a drink?"

"Maybe more."

"Want me to reserve a room?"

The sixty-four-thousand-dollar question. Quite literally,

for some of the members, but not Dawson. Brax had given him free access to Nyx, including its basement playground, after his life fell apart six and a half years ago, although it had taken him another year after that to set foot in the place. The shrink the Navy had sent him to said that time healed, but she'd lied. Dawson had just gotten better at burying the pain.

A woman could help with that. A warm body to sink his dick into for an hour, a momentary distraction from the world outside. Did he feel guilty for using a girl that way? Not really. Brax paid the hostesses very well, and they were only here because they wanted to be.

"Yeah, book one of the private rooms."

Floss beckoned to a besuited man in the corner, and when he came over, she murmured a few words.

"Room seven," he said. "Ten minutes. We need to refresh after the last couple."

The guy was the duty manager. There were three—two male, one female—and they rotated so someone was always there to look after the stock levels, direct the housekeepers, and resolve any issues. Apart from the sex, the place ran like a high-end hotel. Hell, there was even a spa upstairs. Brax had built quite an empire.

Floss perched on Dawson's lap while they waited, drinking something pink with fruit on a stick. She popped a cherry into her mouth as she reached into his lap.

"Let me taste you tonight."

A statement rather than a question, which was good because Dawson didn't have an answer, and he didn't want to chat either. Instead, he kissed Floss's neck, but he was just going through the motions. Sex by numbers. He hadn't felt this disinterested in a woman since Bryony died, and he'd abstained for eleven months after that.

Out of the corner of his eye, Dawson watched the scene on the stage. The brunette was getting fucked from behind by a man old enough to be her father, letting out little gasps every time he hit home. Definitely faking. But her sugar daddy was undoubtedly compensating her well. Dawson had glimpsed them eating in the restaurant upstairs when he arrived, and she'd been a walking ad for Harry Winston. Every woman had a price. He hadn't worked out Violet's yet, and even if he did, it was unlikely he could afford it.

Floss had been stroking his thigh, but now she rose gracefully to her feet.

"Ready to go?"

On previous visits, he hadn't been interested in small talk either, and she clearly remembered that.

"After you."

She was pretty, and she obviously kept in shape. Her bra and panties matched her hair, so sweet it was saccharine, and her hips swayed as she led the way.

In playroom seven, Dawson lay back on the couch and allowed Floss to untie his robe. Once she'd gotten comfortable on a cushion, she looked up from her kneeling position.

"You okay, Grand?"

He shrugged, and after a momentary hesitation, she took his cock in her mouth, all the way, which wasn't the feat it usually was because the damn thing was soft. In desperation, he closed his eyes, imagining it was Violet and not Floss who was fondling his balls, Violet and not Floss whose throat he was fucking. He began to stiffen, but with the change came the realisation that he was a total idiot.

"Stop!"

Floss paused mid-slurp, her eyes wide.

"It's not you; it's me."

She released him with a quiet *pop* and rocked back on her heels, one perfectly plucked eyebrow raised.

"There's someone else. Another woman."

"Why does it feel like you're apologising to me for cheating with your girlfriend?"

"She's not my girlfriend."

"But you want her to be?"

He closed his eyes again, except this time, Bryony was staring at him, and she looked pissed. Not because he was with another woman—they'd always said that if anything happened to the other, they should move on—but because he was with the wrong woman.

"I don't know. I'm not the right man for her, but I can't get her out of my head."

Floss sat on the other end of the couch, facing him with one leg dangling off the side. "How can you be sure of that? Have you talked to her about it?"

"No."

She stopped short of saying "duh," Dawson suspected, but her face gave away her thoughts.

"Well, perhaps you should?"

"It's complicated."

"They all say that."

"You get many men discussing the failings in their personal lives with you?"

"More than you'd suspect." She twirled a lock of hair around her pinkie. "Hey, I just have one of those faces that makes people want to talk."

"She's sort of my boss." He took a deep breath. "I met her here, but she was blindfolded."

"Somebody else's guest?"

He shook his head. "Like I said, it's complicated. And I don't think she knows that I know who she is."

"I have a master's degree in psychology, and it's obvious you're hung up on her."

"You went to college?"

"Don't look so surprised. Do you know how much an actual guidance counsellor gets paid? Not even peanuts." She gave a mischievous smile. "Besides, this is more fun."

"Except tonight, huh?"

"Don't worry about it. Honestly? My jaw still aches from the guy before you. It's good to have a break. Look, you should talk to her. Women aren't all mind readers, and she might feel the same way."

"I doubt that. I dropped her off at her house tonight with another man."

"Okay, that *is* complicated. But drowning your sorrows here isn't the answer. If you really like her, then you need to prove that you're the better option."

Easier said than done. Dawson had nothing to offer Violet. No fame, no fortune, not even a damn house. He was nothing but a washed-up ex-SEAL who'd gotten kicked out of the Navy and then taken on jobs he didn't even want to think about to pay off the remainder of his debt. Deep down, he didn't believe that he *was* the better option.

CHAPTER 22
VIOLET

"Someone's been in my trailer!"

Mikki ran out shrieking, right as a trio of reporters on a set tour meandered past. Bad timing or perfect timing? They all pricked their ears as she burst into tears.

Dawson had tucked me behind him when the noise started, so I was safe.

"What happened?" he asked.

I peered around his arm in time to see her extend a shaking finger.

"There's a l-l-letter."

"Where?"

"On the table."

Dawson turned to me. "Stay here."

"No way. Wherever you're going, I'm going too."

He was wearing his favourite pair of Ray-Bans again, but I felt his eyes roll. Still, he acquiesced.

"Stay close."

Inside, Mikki's trailer was bigger than mine, but it didn't feel that way because of all the mess. Make-up, accessories, and low-fat snacks littered every surface. Acai berry bites.

161

Dangly earrings. Chateau Miel's ChaCha cream, whatever that was. In the middle of the table, someone had cleared a spot big enough to fit a standard sheet of paper with the words "DIE BITCH" pasted on it in cut-out letters. Just looking at it gave me the shivers.

"This keeps getting worse," I whispered.

I jumped as Dawson squeezed my arm. Apart from manhandling me into position outside, that was the first time he'd touched me since we'd met in The Dark.

"Not gonna let anything happen to you, Violet."

"Do you think it's the same person?"

"Don't know."

He snapped a few pictures on his phone and then called David.

"You need to get over to Mikki's trailer and do damage control."

David was still spouting frantic questions when Dawson hung up.

"Aren't you going to answer him?"

"I'll speak to him when he gets here. You okay?"

"Not really."

"Your boyfriend's probably outside by now."

"My what?" Did he mean Lucas? "I don't have—"

But Dawson was already in the doorway, gripping my wrist to make sure I stayed behind him. Mikki hadn't wasted any time. She was laying into Elton with the media hanging onto her every word.

"You call yourself a security guard? You let someone sneak right past you. What did you do? Go for coffee?"

"N-n-no. I haven't moved." He waved at his lawn chair, stationed between my trailer and Mikki's.

"Then you must have fallen asleep on the job."

"But I didn't. I swear nobody's gone inside since you came out an hour ago."

"So what are you saying? You think I put it there?"

Now Elton was stuck between a rock and a reality TV star. He couldn't admit to missing an intruder without risking his job, but if he accused Mikki of lying, she'd probably have him fired anyway.

"The window's open around the back," Dawson said.

"So?" Mikki folded her arms. "It was stuffy."

Good grief, did he have to spell it out?

"Someone could have climbed through the window," I told her, and Elton shot me a grateful glance.

"Why was nobody watching?"

"Because Elton can't be in two places at once."

David rode up with Debbie on a golf cart. Judging by the way she wobbled in her pumps, I suspected she'd had a liquid lunch.

"What's the problem here? And why did you hang up on me?" he asked Dawson.

"Sorry about that. Patchy service."

"Somebody left a threatening note in Mikki's trailer," I told David. "You need to call the police again."

The reporters' heads were swivelling back and forth as if they were at a three-way tennis match. Bet they didn't think they'd get much of a story when they agreed to visit. Zach might have guessed right when he predicted which of the surfing photos would make the gossip pages, but I knew for certain which story they'd be leading with tomorrow.

No doubt Mikki did too.

"Some psycho wants me dead," she wailed. "I need a bodyguard."

"Could you watch both of them?" David suggested to Dawson.

"It doesn't work like that. I can't do my job properly if I'm trying to focus on more than one principal. Why don't you get the cops to look into this in the first instance?" He steered David into Mikki's trailer, out of earshot of the reporters. "Have they made any progress on the other incidents yet?"

"They didn't find any fingerprints, and the DNA results aren't back yet. One of the electricians thinks he saw our mystery cleaner heading for the admin building, but we don't know where he went after that." David glanced back to the huddle outside the trailer. Debbie had her arm around Mikki's shoulders, although I wasn't sure whether she was comforting her or just trying to stay upright. "Guess I'd better increase the security again. Any other newbies I can get a discount on?" he asked Dawson.

"Wait—you got me a cut-rate bodyguard?" I asked.

Yes, Dawson had told me I was his first client, but I didn't realise David had completely cheaped out on my safety.

"It was only a few plants and some horny freak. Stalkers rarely hurt the people they're targeting."

"Says who?"

"I googled it."

For heaven's sake. And now Dawson was looking at his feet because I'd opened my mouth without thinking and basically accused him of not being good enough at his job.

"Dawson, I'm sorry. I didn't mean—"

"It's fine." His tone said the opposite. "David, I need to get Violet home. Why don't you call Jefferson and see if he has anyone else available? If he doesn't, I'm sure he can recommend someone."

David's phone rang, and Debbie called out to him. He glanced in one direction and then the other, torn.

"What if questions come up about Violet's stalker?" he asked.

"Make sure they don't. Violet would rather avoid the world gossiping about that. Let Mikki have her moment in the spotlight if she wants it so badly."

Dawson marched me outside before I could say another word, heading toward the car.

"What if I'd wanted to stay?" I asked.

"You didn't."

"True, but I prefer to make my own decisions."

"Noted."

"Did anyone ever tell you that you're impossible?"

"More than once. If you want your boyfriend to come with us, you'd better call him."

I sent a text to Lucas. We were at the town car now, and Dawson bundled me into the back. I thought he'd get in the front while we waited for the driver, but he sat next to me instead.

"I tried to tell you before. Lucas isn't my boyfriend."

"The pair of you seem awful cosy for two people who aren't doing the nasty with each other."

My fingers quivered, but I forced myself not to slap him. "How dare you? He's just a friend."

The door opened, and Dawson's hand flew to his side, toward the gun I knew he kept under his jacket. I'd glimpsed it on occasion when I absolutely wasn't looking at his chest. But it was only Lucas standing there.

"Hey, I was right behind you. Room for one more?"

He didn't wait for an answer, just shoved me over so I was squeezed up against Dawson's massive thigh. I swallowed a sigh.

"Sure."

"Go on, what happened with the drama queen?"

"Someone left Mikki a horrible note."

"Saying what? Did you see it?"

"'Die bitch.'"

Lucas gave a low whistle. "Nice. Was it written in blood?"

"No, little cut-out letters. Dawson has pictures if you really want to look."

Lucas held out his hand, and Dawson glowered as he handed his phone over. I could practically smell the testosterone filling the air. Where was the driver? I needed to go home and escape to the pool house, preferably with a glass of wine. No, make that a bottle.

"This is all very theatrical," Lucas said. "Weird. Whoever sent it reads *Cosmo*."

I peered down at the screen. "How do you know?"

Lucas zoomed in on the letter H. "If you look real close, you can see Jay Morley in the background. Number one in the America's Hottest Bachelors feature last month. Our mystery letter writer clipped the H from 'Hottest.'"

"Are you sure?"

"Sweets, I read that article twice."

Dawson leaned across me, and I sucked in my chest to avoid my breasts squashing against him. Then inhaled again because what would he do if they did?

The answer was nothing. He remained totally professional as he squinted at the multicoloured letters. The pinks and greens and yellows made the note seem almost cheerful.

"Those look like acai berries behind the D, and Mikki's trailer was full of that shit."

"Hold on, hold on." I shoved Dawson back so I could breathe properly again. "What are we saying? That Mikki wrote the letter herself?"

"I think 'wrote' is a strong term," Lucas said.

"Okay, pasted. Wow—you really think she'd do that?"

"What would a normal reaction be if you'd just received a threat? Surely a girl would lose colour or vomit the way you did."

"Thanks for reminding me."

"Whereas Mikki's out there giving interviews and checking the photographers are getting her good side."

"She did cry at first."

"Violet, she's an actress."

"Wouldn't surprise me if she did it," Dawson said. "That woman's trouble. First thing she did was try to get a guy fired, then she demanded her own bodyguard."

"She already asked for one before you came, and David said no."

I ticked off points in my mind. Did Mikki have a jealous streak? Yes. Did she read *Cosmopolitan*? Yes. Was she so obsessed with publicity that she'd fake her own stalker? I very much suspected the answer was yes.

"I'm so, so sick of this movie." I laid my head back against the seat and tried to ignore Dawson's body heat. "It's like being back in kindergarten. Do you think we should say anything? To David? Or the police?"

Lucas shook his head. "No, I think we should stay out of this."

"Dawson?"

"I concur."

Well, at least they agreed on something for once.

CHAPTER 23
DAWSON

W as Mikki enough of an attention whore to send that letter to herself? Dawson had tried to avoid the woman, but from the little he'd seen, the answer had to be yes.

He fired off a quick text to his boss as the driver fought through rush-hour traffic.

Dawson: David Jackson might call with a request for a second bodyguard. Trust me, buddy, you do NOT want this job.

Dawson wouldn't wish the crazy bitch on any of his colleagues. There were enough second-rate agencies out there, ones who hired big guys with tattoos because they looked intimidating rather than hand-picking former special forces members for their skills. Let one of *them* put up with Mikki. Unfortunately, Jefferson Adams had named his company after himself, which meant Adams Security appeared at the top of every listing and got more than its fair share of time-wasters calling. David Jackson didn't entirely fit into that category, but his idea of what proper security entailed and the actual requirements were poles apart.

When Jeff first outlined the job spec, Dawson had resented being hired for show, but then he'd thought of his bank balance. "Just sit back and take the money," Jeff said, and Dawson had planned to do exactly that until he met Violet.

Ah, Violet. She wasn't the type to kick up a fuss, and even though she hadn't received any more gifts, she was still on edge. Scared. Mikki Moretz, on the other hand… Yeah, much as Dawson disliked Lucas, he had to agree with the man's suspicions. But one thing still niggled at him.

At the beach house, he held the car door open for Violet and then hung back a few feet so she couldn't hear him speak.

"I have a question," he said to Lucas.

"Yes?"

"Why did you check out the hottest-bachelor article?"

Why even pick up a copy of *Cosmopolitan* unless he was hunting for appropriate letters to paste onto a piece of paper? Lucas paled under his fake tan. Everyone on the damn movie set was that colour.

"I was checking to see whether I was in it."

"And that meant you had to read it twice?"

"Fuck."

Dawson waited while Lucas battled with himself, keeping an eye on Violet and her surroundings as she fit a key into the lock on the front door. This was one weird setup they had here.

"You look like a man who knows how to keep a secret."

Dawson nodded. Before the incident that ended his career, he'd had a Top Secret security clearance. His head was filled with so many classified briefings and details of covert missions and visions of dead bodies and hushed-up reports that sometimes, there was barely any room for his own thoughts. And then there was The Dark. If the good people of California knew their governor enjoyed spanking eighteen-year-old blondes in his spare time, they might consider voting for the other guy.

"Yeah, I do."

"And I also know you like Violet."

How? Dawson had been careful to keep his distance, or as much distance as a bodyguard could keep from his principal. Every word he said to her—with the exception of his impulsive offer to invite Zach surfing—had been carefully thought out in order to come across as neutral.

He only shrugged, and Lucas smirked, the asshole. But his expression quickly grew serious again.

"I bat for the other team, but if word of that got out right now, it could sink my career. Just know that my goal is the same as yours: to keep Violet safe."

Hold on—Lucas was gay? Then what was with all the touching? Those little smiles he gave Violet when he thought nobody was watching? And she seemed to like him too.

"Really?"

"I'm not going to make that up."

"Does Violet know?"

"Yes, but nobody else here does, and I'd appreciate it staying that way."

"I'll keep my mouth shut."

"Look, I think we've gotten off on the wrong foot. I'm not the competition. If you're truly interested in Violet, you want to watch out for a guy called Trent. He's from her hometown, and she's had a crush on him since she was a teenager."

"Why are you telling me this?"

"I've never met the man, but he basically ignored her until she started making movies, and now he's texting her ten times a day. Yes, that makes her happy, but I believe she deserves a man who wants *her*, not her fame."

"And you think—"

"Lucas!"

Violet's voice held a hint of panic, and all other thoughts flew out of Dawson's mind as he ran after Lucas. He'd never been inside the beach house before. The cavernous hallway was decorated in pale peach with white leather couches on either side of the door, a showpiece instead of a home.

Abstract art rather than family photos hung on the walls. At the far end, Violet stood in front of an ornately carved wooden table, staring at a pile of letters and two boxes.

"Vi?" Lucas called. "What's wrong?"

"I have two packages."

Dawson hated the tremor in her voice. Hated that when she received an unexpected gift, she was sad rather than happy. Hated the man who thought it was fair game to torment a woman just because she was in the public eye.

"Does it say who they're from?"

Lucas stood on one side of Violet while Dawson stood on the other. She glanced up, surprised to see him there, but she didn't say anything.

"No, there's nothing."

"Want me to open them?"

"Would you?"

One of the packages was flat and thin. A USPS shipping box, and something heavy moved around when Lucas shook it. The other was larger, about the size of the funeral urns Dawson had left in Brax's LA apartment for safekeeping.

Four piles of envelopes lay next to the boxes, one for each occupant of the house. Dawson picked up Violet's pile and thumbed through it. Most of the letters were just addressed to "Violet Miller, San Francisco." Somebody in the postal service had obviously worked out where she was staying.

"Which one first?" Lucas asked.

"Uh… Eeny, meeny, miny, moe… That one."

Violet pointed to the flat box, and Dawson didn't miss the way her jaw clenched as Lucas tore open the flap.

"Looks like a book. Are you into astronomy?"

"Astronomy?" All the tension leaked out of her. "Like, the stars? When I was in LA with Kane, we met this kid in a wheelchair, and he said he was going to send me a book, but he was sick, and I never thought for a minute…"

Lucas wrapped an arm around her, and this time, the red

171

mist that had plagued Dawson for the past couple of weeks didn't materialise. Seemed he'd misjudged the man.

"Sometimes, people send us nice stuff. I had one lady who sent me peppermint patties every week for a year."

"That's sweet."

"At first it was, but I ended up with boxes and boxes of the things, and now I can't stand the sight of them."

Violet giggled, and Dawson caught himself in a smile. Better lose that quick. Impassive was the name of the game.

"Why did she stop?" Violet asked.

"She wrote a really long letter, apologising and telling me she'd moved on to Connor Lowes."

"Dumped for Hollywood's bad boy?"

"I needed months of therapy to get over it." Lucas picked up the other box. "Shall we do this?"

The brown paper had THIS WAY UP written all over it, and Lucas peeled it open from the top down. Hell. It was another plant, this time in a terracotta pot within a pale-pink plastic-fronted box. Someone had stuck a teddy bear on a stick into the soil, one of those schmaltzy Valentine's gifts carrying a little sign that read *I Give You My Heart*.

"Is that a Venus flytrap?" Lucas asked.

It was. Dawson had even seen them in the wild a few years back while crawling through a bog in some desolate corner of North Carolina. What fucking weirdo sent a carnivorous plant to a lady as a gift?

Violet seemed to be thinking along the same lines. "I don't like it."

"Is there a card?" Dawson asked.

Lucas took the plant out of the box and set it on the table. "Nothing. No card, no note. Only that." He pointed at the teddy bear's message. "Reckon it's from the same person as the others?"

"Don't know." Dawson picked up the ripped paper. "But

whoever sent it, they had the full address rather than just writing the name of the city and hoping it got here."

"So they know where I'm staying?" Violet shuddered.

Lucas's arm tightened. "There's nothing threatening about this one, not like the others. No thorns, no blood."

"Apart from it being a flesh-eating plant."

"Maybe the person who sent it just has incredibly bad taste? Or he thought you might appreciate a quirky gift? According to *Cosmo*, roses are so last year."

Lucas might have put stock in a glossy magazine, but Dawson didn't. And there was something wrong with this picture. The pot. Why did such a small plant need such a big pot? Violet stepped back as Dawson upended the thing, then shrieked as a dark, bloody lump hit the pale wood table with a soft *thunk*.

"What the hell…?" Lucas started.

Dawson had grown up in rural Ohio, where hunting dinner and skinning it for the pot was a way of life. Even with bits of soil stuck all over it, he recognised what he saw.

Violet's stalker had, quite literally, given her his heart.

"Breathe," Lucas said, rubbing her back. "Do you need to run to the bathroom?"

She gulped in air, then steadied herself. "I don't think so. Meat? He sent me meat?"

"It's a heart," Dawson told her.

"What kind of a heart?" Her voice rose to a squeak. "A human heart?"

"I doubt it. A deer, maybe." Their hearts looked similar to a person's but tended to be more muscular because deer were active much of the time. "Or a dog."

"A *dog*?"

"Come and sit down." Lucas led her over to the nearest couch. "We'll sort it out."

"How? There's a dead…*thing* on the freaking table."

For the second time that day, Dawson dialled David and

told him his presence was required. The police too. He almost suggested they should stop investigating Mikki's bullshit and look into the real problem, but he couldn't risk Jeff's reputation by being rude to a client. In hindsight, he should have said it anyway, because when Mikki arrived at the house, hot on David's heels and trailed by her assistant, she behaved exactly like the bitch she was.

"What's your problem?" she hissed at Violet. "I got a letter, so you thought you'd upstage me?"

"Huh? I don't understand what you mean."

"I mean that I got threatened today, and right away, you received another plant."

"Wait a minute… Are you suggesting that I sent this to *myself*?"

"You have to admit, the timing's convenient."

"When exactly is Violet supposed to have bought it?" Lucas asked. "We came straight here from the studio."

"You're probably covering for her. Don't think I haven't noticed you following her around like a lovesick puppy."

Lucas spun away with an exasperated sigh. Poor guy couldn't deny it without giving away his secret. And this, *this*, was why Dawson preferred his women anonymous and blindfolded. Mikki wasn't just difficult to deal with, she was impossible.

"Strange how your mind went straight to the most underhanded option," Dawson said to her. "Have you had practice at faking stalkers?"

Mikki's claws came out, extended in his direction. "Oh, another member of Team Violet. Do you want to get into her panties too?"

The words "already did that" hovered on the tip of his tongue, but he bit them back. "Just saying it how I see it."

"She may act all cutesy, but she's only some redneck from Hicksville. I don't understand why everyone fawns over her. She's nothing special."

Fuck, this woman made it hard to keep a poker face. "Deflection. Nice. So if I headed up to your room right now, I wouldn't find a copy of *Cosmopolitan* with a bunch of letters cut out?"

Mikki huffed and spun on her heel, blonde hair flying. "I hate you. This movie's a damn joke."

Her assistant held out a bag of candy. "Jolly Rancher?"

"How do you keep your cool around that woman?"

"Used to it now, buddy."

CHAPTER 24
VIOLET

A long with everyone else in the hallway, I froze in stunned silence after Mikki had her meltdown and stormed off. Finally, after what seemed like an hour, David came to life.

"Tell me someone got that on film."

A guy standing in the corner with a handheld camera nodded. "Yup. Got the whole thing."

Oh, hell. At this rate, the off-screen drama would have more of a plot than *Hidden Intent* and probably more viewers too. Yes, I'd signed a contract, but I didn't sign up for this. Lucas headed for the kitchen, and I was right behind him with Dawson following. Didn't David care how I felt? No, of course not. All he cared about was his precious ratings.

"Wait!" David grabbed at Lucas's arm, but Lucas shook him off. "You can't just walk out."

"Watch me."

I scurried past him. "No, watch *us*."

I didn't stop until I reached the pool house, except my hands were shaking too much to unlock the door. Gentle hands took the key from me, and I thought at first they belonged to Lucas, then realised it was Dawson at my side.

"You don't have to stay," I told him. "It's us who signed up to have our lives splashed all over the internet, not you."

"No, but I signed up to protect you, which includes shielding you from that crowd." He jerked his thumb toward the house. "Is it like this every night?"

"It's not usually quite so bad."

"Probably Mikki's time of the month," Lucas said, walking inside ahead of us. "Do you have any wine in here?"

"No, there's no wine." I'd looked for a bottle myself the other night, but the cupboards were bare. "I actually think I need something stronger."

"Want me to get the gin from the kitchen? I could sneak in while David's busy telling the SFPD how to investigate."

"I don't want to put you to any trouble."

"Sweets, it would be for me as much as for you. Dawson?"

"I don't drink while I'm working."

"Aren't you off duty now?"

"No, I'm…not."

Dawson trailed off, and I turned to see what was wrong. He was looking at something beyond me, and when I followed his gaze… Oh, sugar honey iced tea. The leather mask. I'd left the damn mask out on the table, and now he was looking straight at it.

"Back in a minute," Lucas said, far too cheerfully considering I wanted to die a quick death.

The door closed behind him, and my blood drained to my feet. *Drip, drip, drip.* I could almost feel it falling through my veins, taking the last of my composure with it.

Dawson knew. He knew who I was. Should I admit that I also knew who *he* was? Or pretend to be living in ignorant bliss?

He raised one eyebrow, and I sank onto the couch and buried my head in my hands.

"I'm sorry," I blurted. So much for the ignorant-bliss idea. "I should have said something, but I didn't know what to say, and then more time passed, and ohmigosh, you've seen me naked."

"Violet, I already knew."

I tilted my head sideways so I could see him. "What? How?"

"I spent too much time kissing those lips not to recognise them."

"Then why didn't *you* say anything?"

"Because we both have jobs to do, and I didn't want to make things awkward." Oh, good plan. Excellent. Because things were totally not awkward now. "It was just a one-night thing, right?"

"One night. Yes. Absolutely."

"Is this going to cause a problem between us?"

"A problem? No, no problem. I mean, we're both professionals and David hired us and I have to act and you're just here to keep me safe and the fact that I know what your cock tastes like makes zero difference to the situation." Horrified, I clapped my hands over my mouth. "I didn't mean to say that last part. Could you forget I said that? I can't think straight at the moment."

"Already forgotten." Dawson looked around. "Have you been sleeping in here?"

"Mikki and Kane were mean to me after the chocolates arrived." Good grief, now I sounded like a third-grader. "Anyhow, I decided to move out to get some peace."

"You shouldn't be on your own."

"Honestly, it's fine. I keep the door locked, I have my phone, and Lucas meets me outside in the mornings with breakfast."

"You'd be safer in the house."

"No, I wouldn't. Mikki would probably shave off my eyebrows while I slept."

"In case you didn't notice, somebody mailed you a fucking heart today."

Now wasn't the time for Dawson to turn into a control freak, not when I wanted to knock myself out with alcohol and bury myself under the quilt.

"I could hardly miss it. But whoever it was didn't come to the house, and there are so many reporters out the front that if someone tried to break in, we'd get three thousand photos of the suspect."

"Do you have my number?"

"No."

He picked up my purse, and before I could stop him, he'd rooted through the contents and pulled out my cell.

"Hey! That's private."

"It's not the first time I've seen a tampon, Violet." He dropped the phone into my lap. "Enter your PIN."

I was tempted to refuse, but he'd probably use his secret superpowers and figure it out anyway. Besides, I sort of wanted his number, just in case.

"Here." I passed it back. "What happened to Mr. Grand? You were nice when we were in The Dark. Kind. Sweet."

One of his hands wrapped around the back of my neck, and he tilted my head back to look at him, but all I could see was my reflection in his sunglasses. He must have realised because he pushed them up on top of his head. Those dark eyes locked on mine, and for a brief second, I glimpsed the whirlpool of emotions he usually kept hidden.

"Violet. Fawn…" He traced one finger around my lips, and it left a trail of fire in its wake. "It's better for both of us if you don't find out."

CHAPTER 25
VIOLET

Both of us had jobs to do, Dawson said. Well, it wasn't easy to do mine when I could feel his eyes burning into me. Just in case I hadn't noticed, Lucas helpfully gave me a nudge as we walked back to our trailers at lunchtime.

"Your man's checking you out again."

"He's not my man."

I'd filled Lucas in when he returned with the gin last night. Dawson had left the instant Lucas stepped in the door, citing an urgent need to go to the gym. Lucas had merely grinned and muttered something about thigh muscles before he proceeded to get me drunk. I'd spilled *everything*, both gin and secrets. Now I had a headache to go with the throbbing itch between my thighs, and things weren't just awkward, they were… Was there a word for more awkward than awkward? Because this was it. Uber-awkward.

Oh, and did I mention Mikki was pissed because David wouldn't get her a bodyguard? Well, she was. Apparently, that was Dawson's fault and, by extension, mine as well. Still, I actually preferred it when she didn't talk to me, so it wasn't all bad.

Dawson reached past and held the door open, and a spark shot through me as his hand brushed against mine. A buzz. A vibration. Uh, no, actually the vibration was coming from my phone.

Trent: I know how busy you've been lately, so I thought I'd surprise you. Want to join me for dinner tonight?

Me: I'm in San Francisco.

Trent: So am I. Right outside the studio.

Ohmigosh. Trent was *here*? What the heck? I couldn't decide whether to dance with joy or freak out or run a hundred miles because I wasn't ready for this. When he'd initially suggested dinner, I thought I'd have weeks to prepare, but now it looked as if I had roughly five hours.

"What's up?" Lucas asked. "Your eyes have gone all bulgy."

"Trent." I passed the phone over for him to read. "What should I do?"

Lucas glanced across at Dawson, standing beside the door, and I realised this problem had the potential to get much, much worse. How could I deal with both of them in the same space? The man I wanted to sleep with and the man I had slept with. Uber-awkward didn't even begin to cover it.

Before I came up with a reply, Lucas took over. "I'll call Debbie and set up a tour. You can't just leave Trent waiting outside."

No, of course I couldn't. I frantically catalogued the scenes we had left to shoot today, beyond relieved that I got to keep my clothes on in all of them.

"Do you think Debbie will mind?"

"Who cares if she does? At least it'll keep her from meddling with anybody else for five minutes."

"Okay, and if you do that, I'll call Trent."

Goodness only knew what I was going to say to him.

By the time Debbie had arranged a visitor's pass for Trent and sent someone to pick him up from the gates, we only had time for the briefest of conversations before I had to get back on set. A kiss on the cheek, a promise to catch up properly later, and Veronica was back in the pretend interview room at the mocked-up police precinct with Mariah to ask more questions. Today's scene didn't require much acting; the animosity between Mikki and me was very real. By the end of the day, I was utterly drained while David positively oozed praise.

"Great work, ladies. Good to see last night's little hiccup didn't affect your ability to work together."

Mikki beamed at him, the queen of false sincerity. "I'm always professional on set, David. Did you see how many views we got on YouTube? Debbie said it was our best day ever."

"She did mention it—nice job. Violet, I understand Debbie has arranged something for you and your visitor this evening. Obviously, we can't keep you locked up, but it's important for our plans that the public doesn't suspect you're in a relationship. We need to keep that mystique around you and Kane until after release day."

Another two months after filming ended? Yes, they were rushing *Hidden Intent* through post-production, but I hated the hold it had over my life.

"There's nothing about that in the contract."

"Clause seventeen point two clearly states that all members of the cast will promote the movie as deemed appropriate."

"But my private life is my own business."

"I can run it by legal if you want? And don't forget, people in this industry talk. You want to be known as a team player, don't you?"

"I guess."

He patted me on the arm, giving Mikki a run for her money in the fake stakes. "Excellent. Look, here comes Debbie with your friend."

She was hanging onto Trent's arm, wobbling on her heels as usual. Why did she insist on wearing five-inch pumps when she couldn't walk straight in them? Was it just so that she had an excuse to lean on any man twenty years her junior?

"Ah, Violet. Love your shoes." Liar. I was wearing ballet pumps from Target. "Everything's arranged—I've booked a table for you and Trent at a lovely little Italian place up the coast. Very picturesque. Peaceful too."

"And Debbie organised a car for us so we can talk on the trip. Isn't that great, darling? We have so much to catch up on."

Darling? Trent had never called me "darling" before. Somehow, I'd imagined it would sound much sweeter than it did.

"Don't forget to let Dawson know when you're leaving," she said.

"Dawson?"

"Well, of course. Somebody's been making threats against you, and it's important we keep you safe." Seriously? Debbie wanted me to take another man on what was essentially a date? Had she been speaking with David? Were they determined to screw me over in every way possible? "Don't worry, I've explained everything to Trent here."

"You should have told me the whole story," he said.

Okay, so I might have glossed over the more recent problems.

"I didn't want to worry you, not when I know how busy

you've been at work. And we'll be fine eating dinner without Dawson tonight."

Trent peeled away Debbie's arm and came to my side instead. Score one to me.

"Violet, Debbie's right. Nothing's more important than your safety, so of course you should bring your bodyguard. He can wait in the bar."

I didn't have time to change, but Shonda touched up my face before I rushed out to the limo with Dawson beside me. Trent was waiting by the open door, chatting with the driver.

"Hey, Violet. Did you know Carl here wants to be a lawyer? I've been giving him some pointers."

Carl wasn't our usual driver, and this wasn't our usual car. "We've never met before."

Trent clapped him on the back. "Good luck with the studies."

"Thanks, man."

The privacy screen was already up when I climbed into the back, but I felt the suspension dip and knew Dawson had gotten in too. We still hadn't spoken properly about what happened last night. I'd hoped to clear the air this evening, but Trent's ill-timed visit had put an end to that idea.

Immediately after I'd had that thought, I chided myself for being so ungrateful. Trent had flown all the way here to take me out for the evening, and it wasn't his fault I'd made a huge mistake at the pool house. Why hadn't I put that damn blindfold away? The whole morning, I'd tried to convince myself it was an oversight, but deep down, I knew the truth. I'd liked having the reminder of that night with Dawson right beside me.

I breathed in deeply on a count of three and then exhaled,

counting to ten, letting my problems flow away. Or at least, that was the theory. Lauren said her ex-yoga coach swore it worked, but all I felt was an unbearable need to sneeze.

Trent passed me his handkerchief.

"Allergies? The air doesn't seem so clean here."

"I've gotten used to it now. It's better than LA."

"And New York too."

"Was that why you went back to Oakwood Falls?"

"One of the reasons. I just decided it was time. At first, it was a novelty being able to grab a meal at three o'clock in the morning, but when I took a step back, I realised that the only reason I was out at that time was because I worked so many hours. And it was always noisy. There came the point when I craved peace."

"I can understand that. When I first moved to LA, I shared this tiny apartment above a Chinese restaurant, and there was always traffic outside. Smelled bad too, but we got a discount on the food."

"Did I tell you that Linda Berger opened up a new burger joint? Kind of appropriate, given her name."

"I don't suppose Betty at the diner's too happy about that."

"That's an understatement. The town is split in two over it. Half the people are staying loyal to Betty, but then you've got the others who say Betty's prices are too high and Linda's food tastes better."

"Probably doesn't hurt that Linda's real pretty too."

"Linda's not a patch on you."

My cheeks heated as Trent tucked my hair behind my ears. It would have been a sweet moment if it hadn't reminded me of the time Dawson had done exactly the same thing. Suddenly I was back in The Dark, being fed chocolate mousse while he whispered his dirty words.

Dammit, Violet. I needed to focus on my goal. Trent was my goal.

"Really? You think I'm pretty?"

"It's amazing what you can do with make-up and a curling iron."

The warmth that had blossomed in my chest chilled rapidly.

"So you don't think I'm pretty without make-up?"

"Yes, yes, of course you're pretty all the time. I'm just saying that a touch of mascara makes you even prettier." He twisted in his seat and ran a cool finger down my cheek. "See? Your skin's so delicate, like a perfect cherry blossom. Speaking of cherries, Maria Helman broke a tooth on a cherry pit the other day, and she wanted to hire us to sue the Spend 'n' Save."

"Did you take the case?"

"I told her she'd be wasting her money. Everyone knows that cherries have pits in them. She should have been more careful."

We chatted about life back in Oakwood Falls, or rather, the various legal woes that had befallen its citizens. Years had passed since I'd spent this much time with Trent, and New York had changed him. He'd become more talkative, more… No, I didn't want to say arrogant. More confident.

A short while later, the car slowed, and we turned into the parking lot of Papa Antonio's. When Debbie had said it was picturesque, she meant it looked like a converted crab shack. Carl slotted the limo in next to a pickup, and Trent stared out of the window.

"This isn't quite what I had in mind."

"Knowing Debbie, it doesn't surprise me."

She wanted to keep my date with Trent out of the gossip columns, and what better way than to send us to a dive in the middle of freaking nowhere?

"Do you want to go someplace else?" Trent asked.

"No, this is fine." Far easier to brave the menu here than

face the wrath of David tomorrow. "I'm sure the food's great."

Inside, a young waitress showed us to a table right at the back, half-hidden by a potted plant. Another of David's requests? From my spot against the wall, I saw Dawson take a seat at the bar, watching the door. Always looking out for me.

"Here are your menus. Sorry, but we've run out of the chicken parmigiana. And clams. And fettuccine."

Trent rolled his eyes as she walked off. "Well, that wouldn't have happened in New York."

It seemed a lot of things would have been different in New York from the way he talked. The service would have been better. The beer would have been imported from Italy. The chairs would have been more comfortable. By the time the appetisers came out, I was wondering why he hadn't just stayed there.

"Do you think you'll go back? To New York, I mean."

"Pop's not getting any younger, and…and he had a heart scare. He doesn't want people to know in case they think he's not up to the job anymore."

"I'm so sorry."

Trent shrugged. "We all knew I'd return to take over the firm someday."

"I guess I'm a little surprised you didn't meet a girl and stay in the big city."

"There was nobody serious, and Oakwood Falls is home. It'll always be home. When are you coming back?"

Dawson walked to the door, and I gripped my napkin. What had he spotted? Was there a problem? He disappeared for a few moments, but I relaxed when he returned with Carl.

"Back?"

"Back home. You said at the start of filming you were planning to come home afterward?"

"Maybe. Remember that possible movie role I mentioned before? I have an audition next week." Racino had confirmed it, and David had given me a morning off to fly to LA. "It's a bigger production. More my style than *Hidden Intent*."

I'd watched the original version of *The Thing* late one night with Lucas, a bottle of wine, and a big bowl of popcorn, and it had creeped me out. Not as much as sex scenes with Kane did, but I'd still shuddered.

"But, Violet, you've sounded so unhappy lately. I know you've been trying to hide it, but you forget how long we've been friends."

"I hated filming the scenes at the start of the movie, but I'm beginning to get into my stride now."

And I was. Playing detective with Lucas was fun, even if we didn't yet know who the murderer was.

"What about those nasty gifts you received? Have they stopped?"

"No, but that's why I have Dawson."

"Oh." Trent's mouth set in a thin line. "So, Oakwood Falls isn't good enough for you now?"

"That's not it at all. It's just… I don't know… I feel like this is my chance to make something of my life. I don't want to be waiting on tables and mucking out horses when I'm sixty."

"You know there's always a job for you at the law firm."

"There is?"

"Of course. Now that I'm gearing up to run the firm, I could use a personal assistant." He reached across and took my hands in his. "I can't think of anyone I'd rather have at my side."

Six months ago, I'd have melted quicker than the skinny candle sputtering away between us at those words, but if New York had changed Trent, then San Francisco had changed me. Lucas had taught me I could have fun with a guy, and Dawson had shown me how to burn from the inside out. I looked down at my hands in Trent's. There was no spark. Not even a small one.

I'd spent years putting him on a pedestal, and back in Oakwood Falls, he'd been the most eligible bachelor around. But out in the big, wide world? There was so much more choice. Did I really want to spend my life sorting Trent's mail and picking up his dry-cleaning? Honestly? No. I had a career now. Didn't he realise that? It seemed not, and I had to admit that annoyed me a bit.

"I had no idea."

I had no idea about anything anymore. Beyond Trent, an old guy set plates down in front of Dawson and Carl, and the three of them began chatting. I could hear the low hum of conversation. So Dawson did talk, it seemed, just not to me.

"Violet, we were meant to be together. It took a while for me to realise that, but my time away showed me that the world couldn't offer me a better life than I already had back home. Why do you think I bought that piece of land?"

"Because it's scenic?"

"Because you once said you wanted to live there."

"You remember that?"

"I remember every conversation we had over the years. Such as the time you convinced me that a big brown mare was sweet as pie, and when I turned around, she bit me on the behind. What was her name? Lucifer?"

"Lucinda." Yes, I remembered that day well. She'd taken the seat out of Trent's pants, and I hadn't known where to look. He'd been wearing paisley boxers. "And I seem to recall that soon after the horse incident, you persuaded me that our old school principal wouldn't notice if we took an apple or two from his orchard, and he sent his dog after us."

That had been a wild run. Trent had hauled me over the wall just in time. Luckily, it had been dark, so Mr. Melville didn't realise it was us.

"I still have nightmares about those fangs. Then there was the time you ran out of gas on the road back from Concordia, and I had to rescue you at three o'clock in the morning…"

"I was so scared! Something kept howling in the distance, and I had no idea whether it was the wind or a coyote."

Just like that, we were back to the old Trent and Violet. This was the man I'd missed like crazy when he went away, not slick New York Trent with his expensive suits and fancy menus. And it seemed he'd missed me too.

But the question was, did I want to go right back to Oakwood Falls and abandon this little niche I was carving out for myself on the West Coast? Sure, it would be the easy option, and Trent was basically offering me my dream. But I wasn't the same girl who'd left Kansas two and a half years ago, and I realised that now.

All too soon, the time came to leave. Trent took care of the check while I insisted on covering the tip, and Dawson held the door open as we all trooped out. Then it happened. He touched me. Not his usual manhandling, but a soft palm above my ass that sent my lower back into a spasm. Just as quickly, it was gone.

In the car, Trent held me close and talked about our future, or at least his vision of it. A home we designed ourselves. Him taking over his pop's firm. Us both being close enough to see our folks every day. And when we reached civilisation again, the streetlights twinkling down at us, he kissed me.

So many times, I'd imagined that kiss. In my dreams, angels had played tiny harps while fireworks went off and doves fluttered overhead. Well, not really, but you get my drift. I'd imagined spectacular. What I got was…nice.

A few sighs, a little tongue… Nice.

When Dawson kissed me, I'd gotten an earthquake and a nuclear bomb. Destructive. He'd ruined me for all other men. Even that palm on my back had somehow been more sensual.

Could I live with nice?

What I wanted was a man with Trent's thoughtfulness, Lucas's sweetness and sense of humour, and Grand's magic cock.

Did that man even exist? Could Trent ever become him? Did sex ever build up from okay to amazing over time, or did it all go rapidly downhill until two years later, the only thing that mattered was how well I could fake an orgasm?

Trent didn't share my reservations. "Say you'll come back to Oakwood Falls, Violet."

"I can't make that promise, but I will think real carefully about it."

"Will you visit for my birthday?"

"Yes, I'll visit for your birthday."

CHAPTER 26
VIOLET

"Dawson, we need to talk. And don't tell me that you don't know how, because I saw you chatting with Carl earlier."

With Trent safely ensconced in his hotel room, Carl had driven us back to the beach house. Only Mikki's window still had a light on.

"It's late."

"I don't care."

"I need to get up at five to work out."

"So skip a day. Your muscles are massive already." I leaned down to the driver's window. "Carl, Dawson needs to check security at the house. He'll take a cab home."

Carl looked to Dawson, who shrugged. "She's the boss."

In the pool house, I perched on the bed while Dawson hovered by the door, no doubt plotting his escape, but I'd had enough. Enough of this tension between us, which had only ratcheted up since we found each other out.

"If we hadn't spent that night together at The Dark, would you still be acting like this?" I asked.

"Like what?"

"All silent and moody. We spend half our days together, but we barely speak."

"What do you want me to say?"

"I don't know. Something other than 'stay there' or 'keep moving'? You're a freaking cyborg."

Silence.

"And stop inching toward the damn door."

"I don't like getting close to people."

"We're ten feet apart!"

"That's not what I meant."

"Then you're gonna have to enlighten me."

"I go to The Dark for a reason. The women who work there have one job, they do it well, and at the end of the night, I can walk out of there with no expectations on either side. Then you came along, and you weren't like the other girls."

"Then why did you…you know?"

He laughed, only there was no mirth in it. "A favour to Brax."

"You know Brax?"

"We go way back."

Well, at least that answered one of my questions.

"But that night, you were totally different. Friendly. Fun." Unbelievably sexy.

"Because I thought I'd never see you again."

"How does that make a difference?"

He walked toward me, closing the distance, and I cursed myself for leaning into his hand when he cupped my cheek. It was an automatic response.

"You're the kind of girl I could start to like too much, Violet."

"What does that mean? Why is it a problem? I-I feel this weird pull whenever I'm around you." I pressed my hand over his. "My insides have gone all funny."

"I meant what I said. I don't do relationships."

"Why not?"

His voice dropped to a whisper. "Because if I get too close to someone, it hurts like fuck when I lose them."

He tugged his hand away and headed to the door, yanking it open as if it had personally offended him.

"Don't leave. Please."

"I have to." He paused, then turned to look at me. "But I'll try to act less like a cyborg, okay? That's all I can offer."

CHAPTER 27
VIOLET

"A party? You're kidding?"

My "you're kidding?" was eclipsed by Mikki's shriek of delight, which was even louder than the screech she'd let out ten minutes ago when David had told us that Scott Lowes would be joining the cast as Veronica's abusive boyfriend. Lucas had been right about him playing the bad guy.

"I thought a cast-and-crew get-together on Friday would help everyone to bond." David turned to the camera. "And I'm certain your fans will love finding out what you get up to out-of-hours."

Sure, I bet they'd be fascinated to know that Mikki spent her evenings simultaneously glued to the internet and the TV, searching for mentions of herself, while Kane broke all the rules and snuck his hook-ups into the house because he couldn't go longer than three days without getting his rocks off.

"Who's invited?" Lucas asked.

"Everyone who's working on the movie plus a few special guests." David hammed it up, winking to our YouTube viewers. "Don't get too wild, guys."

There was little danger of me doing that.

"Just when I think it can't get any worse…"

"It does," Lucas finished for me.

We were stuck in traffic. An accident on the freeway, according to our driver. We'd switched back to the regular guy, not Carl.

"I wasn't even a fan of birthday parties when I was growing up. I didn't have that many friends in school, so Mom used to invite the neighbours, and they'd rehash my entire childhood."

"At least there's no danger of that at David's get-together, seeing as we're only allowed one guest each."

"Who are you going to invite?"

"Probably Jeanie. Got to keep up appearances," he added, quiet enough that the driver and Dawson couldn't hear. "How about you? Trent?"

I shook my head.

"Still not sure what to do?"

I'd filled Lucas in on the details of our trip to the restaurant three days ago, including my discussion with Dawson afterward.

Dawson, to his credit, had tried to keep his word. Yesterday and the day before, he'd eaten lunch with Lucas and me rather than sitting outside with Elton, plus he'd spoken several whole sentences and he even took his sunglasses off occasionally. And through all of it, that crazy current ran between us, leaving my body buzzing.

"Trent keeps messaging, but…"

"But?"

"When I stood back and thought about it, I realised I don't

have the same sense of anticipation that I used to get. At one time, hearing from him was the highlight of my day, but now replying is just one more thing on my to-do list."

"That's only natural as a relationship progresses. Or so I've heard."

"*Cosmo* again?"

He nodded.

"But we're not even in a relationship yet. And I'm not sure I want to spend the rest of my life living in Kansas. Yes, I'd like to go home more often because I miss Mom, but I also want to travel. Maybe visit Marrakech or the West Indies. Or Europe."

"Did you watch more travel documentaries last night?"

"I still can't sleep."

"Not sure life's gonna get any easier in the short term, sweets."

Didn't I know it?

"More champagne, ma'am?"

"No, thank you."

With cameras following our every move, I couldn't afford to do anything stupid tonight, plus I had to fly to LA tomorrow for my audition with Racino. Mikki, on the other hand, had no such qualms.

"She knows Scott Lowes is married, right?" I asked Lucas.

"I don't think she cares."

"Should we rescue him?"

"I almost feel as if it's our duty."

"Poor bastard," Dawson muttered from beside me.

Lucas tightened his grip on Jeanie's arm. She'd turned out to be a petite brunette who worked as a doctor in

Pennsylvania, and she seemed a lot more comfortable with the situation than I was. When I mentioned that, she just said nothing could be as bad as a Saturday night in the ER.

I'd brought Lauren as my "date," but ten minutes into the party, she'd spotted a literary agent drinking bubbly with Debbie in the living room and gotten all excited. After they'd chatted, I'd left her talking to an actor friend of Kane's, and when I say "talking to," I mean "flirting with." I'd taken my leave because nobody wanted to be a third wheel. Honestly, I was thrilled to see her enjoying herself. At least one of us was.

"Thought we should introduce ourselves," Lucas said to Scott. "We don't want to be antisocial."

Scott peeled Mikki's fingers away from his arm. His relief was palpable as he reached out to shake Lucas's hand, a sharp contrast to Mikki's reaction. She flounced off in a huff.

"You're a lifesaver," Scott said. "I had no idea how to get rid of her. Lucas Collins, right?"

"For my sins. And this is my friend Jeanie, plus Violet Miller and Dawson."

Cue much handshaking, then Scott motioned between Dawson and me.

"You're together?"

"Oh, no, no, no. Dawson is my bodyguard."

"You're having security issues?"

"I received some disturbing packages."

"That shit's an occupational hazard. I had a naked woman show up in my hotel room last month. Unfortunately, my wife saw her first, and I'm not sure who screamed the loudest."

Lucas chuckled. "I'm surprised David didn't ask you to move in here with us."

"He did suggest it, but I told him in no uncertain terms that wouldn't be happening. Two weeks with Blondie there?" Scott glanced sideways to where Mikki was cosying up to some male model David had invited. "My wife would've nailed my balls to the headboard."

"What made you get involved with the project?" I asked.

"David promised me I'd be playing an interesting character, and he seems to have kept his end of the bargain. Plus it's only a couple of weeks out of my schedule."

"I thought you were only here for this week?"

"No, I'm coming back again later. Are you guys not meant to know that?"

Lucas grinned. "Trust me, we need all the information we can get. David isn't particularly forthcoming."

"You really haven't been told who the killer is yet?"

"Nope. Personally, I'm still waiting for the spaceship to arrive."

"Or Bigfoot," I said. "We're not even sure David knows the ending. Half of the crew thinks the scriptwriters haven't decided yet. Did you get any clues?"

"Sorry. All I have is the dates I'm needed for filming." He glanced at his watch. "Think I can get away with leaving yet?"

"Have you seen David?"

"Briefly." Scott sighed. "I suppose I should stick around for another half hour."

"Feel free to hang with us."

"Safety in numbers?"

"Something like that."

By the time Scott Lowes left, I'd made small talk with a hundred people whose names I'd never remember, and the first floor of the house was standing room only. I spotted Elton turning a handful of people away from the stairs and thanked my lucky stars they couldn't get into my bedroom. I'd had to move my stuff out of the pool house as, technically, I wasn't supposed to be using it, and now my little sanctuary was full of coolers overflowing with champagne and other assorted alcohol.

"We need a cellar," I said to Lucas. "Or a tornado shelter. Somewhere we can hide out until this is over. Why are there so many people?"

"I think folks keep bringing friends."

"Can't we sit on the beach?" Lauren asked.

"Too many reporters."

Dawson pressed against me as a group of drunk revellers pushed past. "The assholes running this show don't know shit about security." He thought for a second. "But I have an idea."

Ten minutes later, we'd stolen the cushions off the pair of sunloungers, Lucas had grabbed a crate of beer, Lauren had found two bottles of wine, and Dawson had shoved open a door hidden away behind a hibiscus bush. Steps led down into darkness.

"What is this place?" I whispered.

"The pump room for the pool. Nobody wants the ugly machinery at ground level. I found it when I checked the grounds."

The space was narrow and slightly chilly, but it didn't have any drunk people—or worse, Mikki—and so to me, it was a tiny corner of heaven. I dropped my cushion onto the dusty floor, and Jeanie did the same with hers.

"Honey, you take me to all the best places," she deadpanned.

Lucas popped the top on a bottle of beer and held it out. "Champagne, my darling?"

"Don't mind if I do." She giggled, a tinkly sound that bounced off the walls. "Did I get the British accent right?"

The two of them settled on her cushion, leaving Lauren and Dawson to share mine. Being squashed next to him felt awkward, but anything was better than the chaos outside.

"Violet, you want a beer?"

"Thanks." I took the bottle from Lucas and sucked half of

it down right away. A little something to take the edge off, to numb myself from the feeling of Dawson being right *there*.

"Normally at this point, I'd suggest a drinking game," Lauren said.

Dawson shook his head. Party pooper.

Jeanie's giggle came again. "It's like being back in high school, don't you think? Hiding away in some nasty little space where the grown-ups can't see you. We have the alcohol; now all we need is a horror movie."

Lucas slung an arm across her shoulders. "Do you remember that night in Josh Burnett's tree house? When he drank half a keg, then the guy with the chainsaw jumped out and he peed himself?"

"That was so gross!"

I rummaged around in the tiny purse I'd been clutching like a security blanket for the whole evening. "Actually, I have a horror movie on my phone. I downloaded it to watch on the flight tomorrow. You know, for research? The screen's small, but…"

"Let's watch it," Lauren said. "Unless we want to be front and centre in the real-life horror movie happening out there instead. Violet told me this gig was a catastrophe, but I didn't believe her until I got here. Who knew Kane Sanders was such an asshole?"

Lauren had been so excited when I introduced them earlier, and Kane had been his usual slimy-side-of-charming self. Then, when she went to the bathroom ten minutes later, Lauren had overheard him talking to David about "Violet and her chubby sidekick."

"Did I tell you he stuffs his underwear for close-ups?"

"Plenty of times, but I'll never get tired of hearing it." She leaned close enough to whisper right into my ear. "Not like Mr. Bodyguard. He's super hot, and I'll bet he has the equipment to match."

"Shh!"

"Well, does he?"

"Yes, okay. Yes."

We'd had a quiet chat when Lauren first arrived, or at least as quiet as we could get with the DJ rattling the windows. Lauren's verdict? She'd sighed when I told her about Trent and the house, but when I mentioned his suggestion that I become his PA, her mouth had dropped open.

"He seriously wants you to give up your career and be his damned secretary?"

"I never wanted this career, Lauren."

"No, but now you have it, and people love you. Don't you read the papers?"

"I try to avoid them."

"Maybe you should take a look? Everyone likes that you're real when so much of Hollywood is fake. That you go wide-eyed and green in those script reveals. That you sometimes put your foot in your mouth in interviews. That you don't cake on ten tons of make-up just to eat lunch."

"So you think I should make another movie?"

"I think you should make a lot more movies."

"But what about Trent?"

"If he loves you, he'll support you. And if you end up making a million bucks a movie, why can't he move here to live with you?"

"Because he has a law firm to run, and there are other employees, and his dad…"

"It's only a two-bit firm in Kansas. He could hire another attorney to help. Look, I'm just saying that if he wanted to be with you enough, there would be some give and take."

"But being with Trent was always my dream."

"You're allowed to change your mind. When I was little, I always wanted a cottage by the sea. Someday, I might even get one although, granted, that seems unlikely since I can't even afford milk this week. But if I win the lotto, then screw the cottage—I'll buy a big fancy beach house like this one instead. And speaking of big, what's happening with the bodyguard? He is one prime specimen."

"Nothing's happening."

"Really? Nothing?"

"Zero. Zilch."

Lauren had glanced toward my bedroom door. Dawson was waiting outside, and I only hoped he couldn't hear our conversation.

"So you wouldn't mind if I...you know?" *What?* Before I could stutter an answer, she burst out laughing. "Your face when I said that! You like him."

My cheeks burned. "I guess I do, but it's all kinds of awkward. And could you keep your voice down?"

"You two are so cute together."

"We're not together."

"If you get married, can I be a bridesmaid?"

"Shut up, Lauren." I headed for the door. "I need more wine."

And now Lauren shuffled sideways on our cushion, pushing me into Dawson. I glared at her, but she studiously focused on Lucas. Tomorrow, I'd put an ad in *Variety* magazine. *Violet Miller has an opening for a new best friend.*

"So, a horror movie?" Lucas asked.

I glanced at the door. "What if somebody notices we're gone?"

"They won't. Not now, not when everyone's been drinking for three hours. E.T. could turn up wearing a top hat and a tutu and Mikki would only invite him to dance."

After all the stresses of the last few weeks, it was oddly pleasant to do something so simple, just the five of us clustered around a tiny screen, jumping out of our skin every few minutes. Well, Dawson didn't jump. Dawson was a freaking rock. Lauren passed me a bottle of wine, and I swigged from it and then passed it back, pretending I was one of the cool kids in high school when in reality, I'd spent most of my time in the library.

"Cold?" Dawson whispered in my ear.

"A little."

"You have goosebumps." He took off his jacket and wrapped it around me, and when I snuggled against him, he didn't move away as I thought he would. That heated me up to boiling point, but I still wasn't giving the jacket back. It smelled of him—a hint of cologne and that earthy, rugged musk that was all Dawson.

I cut my eyes to Lucas and Jeanie, and Jeanie was sitting between Lucas's legs with his arms wrapped around her, the two of them acting like the old friends they were. Comfortable. Not like me. Every one of my nerve endings was jangling.

"You feel tense," Dawson murmured.

"I'm fine." More wine, that was what I needed. I grabbed the bottle out of Lauren's hands and took a good swallow. "I'd rather act in a scary movie than watch it."

When you knew the monster was made out of latex and polystyrene, how could it be terrifying?

Dawson's arm slid under the jacket. Slowly, tentatively, as if he knew it shouldn't be there but he'd decided to try his luck anyway. His hand came to rest on my hipbone, but it didn't stay still. His thumb stroked, stroked, stroked, and every touch sent a lightning bolt straight between my legs.

This was what had been missing with Trent. The visceral reaction that made me lose my mind. And the more I mulled over Lauren's words, the more they resonated. Why should I be the one to give up everything? Being part of the acting world was like riding a roller coaster between heaven and hell, but it was still my career. For Trent to just assume it was a passing fancy, a temporary blip before I got a "proper" job, irked me.

Then I thought of Dawson. Much as it scared me to admit it, he already had a piece of my heart. The only question was, would he take the rest of it as well?

CHAPTER 28
DAWSON

Dawson had parked his car in a public lot a short distance along the shore from the beach house, and when he'd finally left the party last night, it was too late to drive back to Brax's place, so he just caught a couple of hours' sleep in the back seat. When the sun rose, he grabbed the travel bag that lived in the trunk and jogged back along the sand to borrow Lucas's bathroom.

Jeanie and Lauren had bunked in Violet's room, Jeanie on the couch and Lauren sharing the bed, and when Dawson had picked his way through the debris left from the celebration and tiptoed upstairs, their door was still closed.

Should he wake Violet right away? She'd drunk more wine than she should have last night, and without Lucas's help, she'd never have made it to bed. Fuck. He shouldn't have let her get into that state, and he wouldn't have if he'd realised she was such a lightweight, but when she'd been sitting there on the cushion, curled into his side, there hadn't been any of the telltale signs. No wobbly steps, no slurred words.

Dawson swore under his breath. He'd wanted to be the one to carry her upstairs last night, but he was in an impossible situation. Not only was she his principal, but he'd also vowed never to get involved with another woman after his fiancée died. Nearly six years might have passed, but the pain was still raw, an agony that lived in his heart and pulsed through him with every beat.

Except last night, with Violet pressed up against him, that pain hadn't felt quite so sharp.

Fifteen minutes later, Dawson was showered and dressed in his spare suit. He owned two, and he hated both of them. The fabric stretched and pulled, too tight in all the wrong places, and he couldn't move the way he wanted to. Brax's finances might have run to made-to-measure, but Dawson was an off-the-rack guy.

"Lucas, could you do me a favour and wake Violet and Lauren? They're both flying to LA this morning."

"Can't you do it? I'm still asleep."

"Don't think the girls would thank me if I walked right in."

"Really? I think Violet's vagina would throw a party. Besides, you've seen everything there is to see, haven't you?"

Dawson's insides lurched. "She told you?"

"Who do you think took her to The Dark in the first place?"

"That was you?"

"I know Brax from college."

"Fuck." Dawson dropped onto the couch by the window as Lucas shuffled up to a sitting position. "That night was a mistake."

"A mistake because she found out who you were?"

"Yes. No." Dawson shook his head, but the confusion didn't subside. "A mistake because…because I like her."

Lucas started laughing, but Dawson didn't see the funny side. He scowled, which only made Lucas laugh harder.

"What's the problem? You like her, and she likes you."

"It's not that simple. I'm her bodyguard."

"So? You wouldn't be the first to screw around with a client. I've seen it plenty of times in this business. But if you plan on making a move, I'd do it soon. Right now, she's wavering on Trent, but he's asked her to move back to Kansas and live with him, and if he keeps pushing, she might just do that. He wants to build them a fancy house. Even bought a piece of land."

"I can't offer her anything like that. Hell, I've never even owned an apartment."

The right thing to do, the noble thing, would be to let Violet go to the better man. A man who could offer her a stable future. A man who had more to his name than an eight-year-old Camaro, two cheap suits, and a hefty gun collection.

But the selfish part of him couldn't quite let her go.

When he'd handed her over to Brax in The Dark, what he'd really wanted to do was walk right out of there with her in his arms. Find a little place, a cabin on a lake, where he could spend his days swimming and fishing and his nights making love to an angel. And last night, she'd felt so good in his arms. So right. He'd been hard as a rock the entire time, and relief had only come after he'd jacked off into a Kleenex when he got back to his car, like a horny fucking teenager.

Violet Miller would be the death of him, but at least his demise would be pleasurable.

Lucas shrugged and rolled out of bed in his boxer shorts. "I don't think Violet cares about material things. In some ways, she's not suited to this life at all, but she's also the breath of fresh air that Hollywood needs."

"I have a lot to think about."

"Well, think quickly. I'll go wake her up."

"How are you feeling?" Dawson asked, although the answer was already evident from Violet's sickly colour and the way she squinted in the light on the upstairs landing.

"Like I swallowed a cactus. Everything hurts, even my teeth and my fingernails. How is that possible?"

"You don't drink often?"

"Nope. And I'm never touching alcohol again." She screwed her eyes shut. "This is the most important audition of my life, and I'm basically a zombie. What's the point in me bothering to go?"

Beside her, Lauren clung to the doorjamb. "I think I'm still drunk."

Dawson picked up Violet's little black backpack and slung it over his shoulder. "You can sleep in the car and again on the plane."

"How are you awake? You must have gotten about two hours of rest."

"I'm used to it. Come on."

Lucas bent to give her a kiss on the cheek. "Good luck, sweets. You'll knock 'em dead."

"Only with my breath. I've brushed my teeth twice, and my mouth still tastes like a toilet."

"You'll be fine. Just chew gum."

"Plus you could try tomato juice and green tea," Dawson suggested.

"What, together?"

Dawson never drank enough to suffer the consequences, but he'd had female housemates in the past. Ruby had sworn by green tea the morning after while Alexa chugged tomato juice on the rare occasions she overdid it. Not that she'd ever admitted to being hungover. Fuck, she shouldn't even have been drinking, but everyone had turned a blind eye. Those had been the good days. The times before everything turned to shit.

"No, separately."

"Do we even have those?"

Lucas brushed past them. "We don't have tomato juice, but there's green tea in the cupboard. I'll make it in a travel mug while you get into the car. Lauren, do you want some too?"

"Urgh, I hate green tea."

"Is that a yes?"

"Just a small cup."

Carl was back behind the wheel to drive them to the airport, and this time, Dawson sat in the back. Since Violet's state was partly his fault, he needed to do everything in his power to rectify the situation.

Like sitting stock-still while Violet fell asleep with her head on his shoulder. Like carrying both girls' luggage through the airport even though Lauren's case was pink. Like arranging a cab for Lauren, so all Violet had to do was hug her friend goodbye. Like running into a gas station for gum on the trip from LAX to Racino's office.

And when Violet went inside for her meeting, he waited in the lobby and did his best to block out the bottle blonde who offered him everything from a latte to her phone number. What if last night had messed up Violet's chances of landing the part? Dawson might not have given a shit about his own life anymore, but he found that he'd come to care about hers.

Finally, the door to the inner sanctum opened and she stumbled out, yawning.

Should he ask how it went? Or wouldn't she want to discuss it?

He thought back to his days with Bryony, even though it hurt. Yes, she'd always liked to talk no matter how bad things had gotten.

"How was the interview? Uh, the audition?" he asked once they were safely back in the car.

Violet surprised him by laughing. "Better than I thought. I

must have looked terrible, and I yawned in the middle of a scene, but Racino congratulated me on my method acting and said he wished more actresses would make that much of an effort to get into character."

Dawson chuckled, and Violet stared at him.

"What?" he asked.

"I haven't heard you laugh since…you know. You're not a cyborg after all."

Not unless cyborgs' dicks hardened when a pretty woman smiled at them.

"First time I've heard of going to work tired being a good thing. Does that mean you got the part?"

"I haven't heard yet. He said he'd make a decision within a few weeks. Lucas's agent is representing me, and she heard he has at least two more people left to see."

"He'd be crazy if he didn't pick you."

"Who are you and what have you done with Dawson?"

"I'm not allowed to be nice?"

"I guess it just confuses me."

Dawson's behaviour confused him too, but here in LA, without busybodies from the movie watching over them, the tension that normally plagued him like a thousand tiny fists squeezing every muscle eased a touch. He still had to be on the lookout—two fans approached Violet just on the way to the car—but as long as he buried his fear of commitment deep inside himself with all the other shit, he could enjoy this brief period alone with Violet.

Their driver had the car waiting at the kerb, and Violet stumbled as she climbed inside.

"I've got you."

"Thanks. I can barely put one foot in front of the other, and I still can't believe that today wasn't a total disaster. You know, when I was a little girl in Kansas, I used to pretend I was Dorothy from *The Wizard of Oz*, off on a big adventure." She smiled to herself as she fastened the seat belt. "Mom made me a blue-and-white checked dress, and after school, I'd borrow Trent's dog and skip along the path that ran through the backyard, looking for the Lion and the Tin Man."

"Not the Scarecrow?"

"No, he always freaked me out."

"*Trent's* dog?"

"We grew up together. My mom's been his parents' housekeeper for as long as I can remember. If I land this part, she'll be so freaking proud."

No mention of her father. Was he still around? "It's only you and your mom?"

"My dad died when I was twelve."

"Babe, I'm sorry."

Babe? What was he saying?

But Violet didn't seem to notice Dawson's slip of the tongue. "I've gotten used to it now, I guess. At least it was sudden. A heart attack. I walked in after school, and he was just lying there on the kitchen floor."

She said she'd gotten used to it, but she looked so utterly devastated that Dawson said to hell with it and shuffled across the seat to hug her. She clung to him, her curves moulded to his chest as if the two of them were pieces of the same jigsaw puzzle.

"I still miss him," she mumbled against Dawson's shoulder. "But not as much as Mom does. She still cries, even now."

"At least you have each other."

"If I do get the part, I'm gonna send her on a cruise. She's always wanted to go on one, but we've never had the money. One of those luxury trips around the Caribbean with an all-you-can-eat buffet and cabaret in the evenings. Have you ever been on a cruise, Dawson?"

Not exactly. "I've spent some time on boats."

"Boats? What kind of boats?"

"Big ones, little ones, all kinds. I was in the Navy."

She leaned back and looked at him. "Really?" A quiet giggle. "It's crazy—I've licked you while naked, but I know nothing about you. You're just Dawson, this mysterious guy who shows up in my hour of need. Do you even have a surname?"

"Masters. Dawson Masters."

"And what about your family? Where are you from?"

"Not much to tell there. I grew up in Buttfuck, Ohio, and my parents are divorced. My dad's an asshole, and now my mom's married to a different asshole."

"I guess I can understand why you didn't stick around. That's it? Any brothers or sisters?"

Shit. The question he didn't want to answer, or one of them at least. But Violet was Violet, and he didn't want to upset her by shutting the conversation down.

"I had a sister. Hannah."

"Had?" This time, it was Violet who hugged him. "I'm so sorry. Was it recent?"

"Four years, ten months, and twenty-four days ago, but it doesn't feel like that long."

She squeezed him harder, and dampness seeped into his shirt. Oh, hell. This was supposed to be a good day.

"Vi…" What should he say? He couldn't tell her things would be okay because they wouldn't. "Sometimes, it helps to let out the pain."

"You cry?"

"No, I hit things."

"Like a punching bag?"

"Yeah." And people, occasionally.

"The thing I regret most is not being able to say goodbye to my dad. Did you get to say goodbye to your sister?"

"She didn't want that." He swallowed the lump in his throat. "She took an overdose."

And left a damn note. Two words: *I'm sorry*. She'd known he was coming to visit after three hellish months in some fucked-up sandpit in the Middle East, and she'd downed sixty codeine pills and half a bottle of wine two hours before he found her on the couch. Even now, he was still angry at her, and hurt, and so fucking sad that she still blamed herself for what had happened eight months before. If only he'd caught an earlier flight. If only…

Violet sniffled, and Dawson kissed her hair. "I've got you, babe."

But how long could he hold onto her?

After five minutes, she listed to the side, and Dawson realised she'd fallen asleep. He shifted so she could use his thigh as a pillow. Silky brown hair flowed across his legs in a mahogany river, and he twirled the ends in his fingers. Violet didn't look anything like Bryony. His fiancée had been a slender blonde, almost as tall as him in heels, while Violet stood a foot shorter with full hips and breasts and a tiny, nipped-in waist. But they both had a sweet innocence about them, even naivety. Bryony had let people take advantage of her while Dawson was on deployment—nothing big, just neighbours who borrowed yard tools and didn't return them, old school friends who kept asking her to babysit, that sort of thing—because her heart was too big to say no. Violet put up with far more of Mikki's shit than she should, and more than once, he'd wanted to step in but held back because it wasn't in his job description.

For once, Dawson was glad for the crawling traffic as they inched toward the airport. Being cocooned in the back of a limo was better than trying to find a quiet spot to rest in the terminal. Violet was travelling economy, and therefore Dawson was too.

"Wake up, Violet," he whispered when they finally reached LAX.

Her eyelids flickered, then opened wide when she realised where she was lying.

"Sorry, I…"

"Time to go."

"Where are we?"

"The airport. Do you need a hand?"

"I'm so tired."

Oh, fuck it. He wrapped an arm around her waist and grabbed her bag, then nodded to the driver as they walked inside. Exhaustion caught up with her on the plane, no doubt fuelled by their emotional conversation and the stress of the audition. She woke up for long enough to walk to the car at the other end, but when they reached the beach house, she was dead to the world again.

"Must have been some day," Carl said as they pulled up outside.

"She didn't sleep well last night. Could you get the doors? I'll put her straight into bed."

Dawson had gotten the key to the pool house from Violet before they took off, and he'd also messaged Lucas and asked him to leave her essentials in there. She probably wouldn't thank either of them if she woke up near Mikki.

"Want me to stick around?" Carl asked once Vi was safely under the covers.

Dawson shook his head. "My car's parked down the road. Thanks, buddy."

"No problem."

Once the driver had disappeared, Dawson sat on the side of the bed and watched Violet sleeping. She looked so peaceful, her face so relaxed. He didn't want to leave, but he couldn't stay, no matter how tempting that empty space beside her looked.

When he bent to kiss her forehead, she didn't wake, but the corners of her mouth flickered a little.

And so did his.

CHAPTER 29

DAWSON

"Dawson? It's me. Violet."

As if he could ever mistake that breathy little voice for anybody else.

"What's wrong?"

Because if she was calling him at six a.m., something wasn't right.

"Uh, did you leave me a message last night?"

"What kind of a message?"

She couldn't be talking about that kiss, could she? No, he shouldn't have done it, but…

"On the mirror in the bathroom."

What the fuck?

"That wasn't me. What does it say?"

She began speaking faster, sounding panicked now that he'd confirmed her fears. "It says 'Did you miss me?' I didn't notice until I got out of the shower, but the mirror steamed up and there it was."

"Don't touch it. I'll be there in five minutes."

"Five minutes? Where are you?"

"I just walked out of the sea."

Since he couldn't sleep last night, he'd gotten up early and gone for a swim. When he left the Navy, he'd thought he wouldn't miss the water, but after months of flitting between cities and mountains and the desert, he'd started craving the wet stuff. And what better place for a dip than the public beach near Violet's temporary home? Not only were the tides good, but there was also a public shower block nearby, which saved him from driving back to Brax's apartment.

Except this morning, he bypassed the shower, pulled on a T-shirt, grabbed the duffel bag from the trunk of his car, and ran straight to the pool house.

Violet was pacing in the bedroom-slash-living room when he arrived, wearing a fucking towel.

"Give me strength," Dawson muttered to himself. How was he supposed to concentrate when one gentle tug would reveal that perfect body? In his swim shorts, there was little to hide his true feelings on the matter either.

Deep breaths.

"Can you show me the message?"

She looked him up and down. "You were really in the sea? I thought you were joking. You're… I've never seen you in anything but a suit before."

"Thought I'd try the casual look this morning." He checked her out too, concentrating on the mundane rather than lingering on the good parts. Violet might have been acting brave, but her hands were trembling and she kept biting that bottom lip. If she knew what that did to him… "The message? In the bathroom?"

She'd closed the door, and even though the steam had mostly dissipated, the words were still visible.

"This definitely wasn't here before? When did you last shower in here?"

"The day before the party, I think? No, no, I was too tired, so I just washed my face and put dry shampoo in my hair. Uh, it would have been the day before that. Last Wednesday."

Shit. Either someone was playing a particularly

unamusing prank, or Violet's stalker had paid a visit. Time to call the boss again.

Except when Dawson pulled the phone out of his bag, she grabbed his hand.

"Who are you calling?"

"David."

"No! I'm not meant to be sleeping in here."

"We have to tell him."

"Please?"

Dawson phoned Lucas instead, and five minutes later, there were three of them squashed into the tiny bathroom with the shower running. Lucas snapped a photo of the mirror.

"Vi, I'm with Dawson on this one. We have to tell David."

"But—"

He held up a hand. "Listen, we'll move your stuff out again and say you came for an early-morning swim, then because you're such a considerate roommate, you showered in here to avoid waking us with the noise."

"But what about the others? Will they go along with that?"

"Kane won't say anything, and if Mikki opens her big mouth, I'll let it slip that she was entertaining two men last night. All night." Lucas put his hands over his ears. "Ow, the noise."

"Two? Are you serious?"

"Deadly. Bet that would have gotten a few hits on the YouTube channel."

"Eeuww!"

"I barely slept."

Dawson held up the phone. "So, am I calling David now?"

"Okay, okay. You win. Just give me two minutes to tidy the place."

"Those words could have been left for anyone."

David stood in the bathroom doorway, hands on his hips, surveying the scene of the crime.

"Don't you think it's more than a coincidence?" Dawson asked. "When you add it to the plants and the fact that someone jacked off in Violet's damn trailer?"

That earned Dawson a glare, but he didn't give a shit. He'd already had an interrogation about why he was at the beach house wearing shorts and a T-shirt despite the fact he wasn't officially on duty yet, and David's keep-the-movie-on-track-at-all-costs attitude was grating on Dawson's last fucking nerve. How was the asshole supposed to film if his leading lady was terrified?

"Look, the chances are that it happened on the night of the party," David said. "Two hundred people had access. Do you want us to question them all?"

"That would be a good start."

The cop standing to the side cleared his throat. "We'll run fingerprints just in case, but Mr. Jackson's right. We don't know if this is connected."

"But what if it is?"

"If we had endless resources, then sure, we could question hundreds of partygoers, but budgets have been cut again, and we had a multiple homicide downtown last night." He turned to David. "How many people knew of the threats against Miss Miller?"

"Where do I begin? The cast, the crew, some studio employees, my office staff, your people, plus anyone else they might have mentioned it to. And as you're aware, Mikki Moretz also received a letter. She told a crowd of journalists about it, so most of the world knows."

"So this message could have been aimed at Ms. Moretz, and Ms. Miller just happened to find it?"

David shrugged. "That's entirely possible."

"Or Mikki wrote it herself," Lucas muttered under his breath.

"Sir?" the cop asked. "You think she might have done that?"

"I wouldn't put it past her." He looked at Violet and Dawson in turn. "Sorry, but she might have."

The cop snapped his notepad shut and held out a hand for David to shake.

"Well, I think I've seen all that I need to see here. Someone will be in touch regarding the fingerprints."

Once the officer had left, David tapped his watch. "Time's ticking, people. Dawson, I hope you brought a suit with you."

"Yes, I did."

The asshole appeared surprised. "Good, good. Violet's first scene is with Scott, and we don't want to keep him waiting."

David followed the cop out the door, and Violet sank onto the couch. She'd remained remarkably calm so far, and Dawson didn't know whether she hadn't realised the full implications of the message or if she was just becoming numb to the repeated threats. Neither option was good.

Because worst-case scenario, the writing on the mirror had been left for Violet. And if that was true, then whoever left it knew she slept in the pool house. And that meant they'd been creeping around the property at night, watching her. Fuck.

Judging by David's attitude this morning, he wouldn't willingly stump up for extra security, which meant Violet would have to start sleeping in the main house, preferably with a personal alarm in her hand and a gun under her pillow. Did she even know how to shoot a gun? Had Trent taught her anything useful back in Oakwood Falls?

Given the situation, Dawson thought it would be easy to convince Violet not to go near the pool house, but if there was one thing he'd learned about women, it was that they always surprised him.

And not necessarily in a good way.

"Yes, I'm staying in the pool house tonight," Violet told Dawson in the car on the way back from the studio.

"Vi, think about this for a minute."

"I've been thinking about it all day, and David's right. If that message was meant for me, it was probably Mikki messing around. Lucas asked her if she was involved."

"And? What did she say?"

"She denied everything, of course," Lucas said from his seat on the other side of Violet. "But she was really over the top."

"Mikki's always over the top," Dawson pointed out.

"And I also heard her inviting a couple more 'friends' over this evening." Lucas used his fingers to make little quotation marks around the "friends." "If my parents weren't in town this evening, I'd be joining Violet in the pool house."

"You're going out for dinner?" she asked.

"Yes, my dad wants Italian food."

"Just don't go to that weird place Debbie sent me to with Trent. My pizza was burned on the edges and soggy in the middle."

"Thanks for the tip."

"Guys," Dawson interrupted. "We were talking about the pool house?"

Violet sighed and closed her eyes. "I understand what you're saying, but the more I go over what happened, the more I think I overreacted this morning. It probably *was* someone's idea of a joke. None of us have seen anyone hanging around outside, have we?"

"No, we haven't," Lucas said. "I'll walk Violet down to the

pool house before I go out, and I'll check on her when I come back, okay?"

She smiled and laid a hand on Dawson's arm. "And I'll keep the door locked, I promise."

"Fine. Just be careful."

What could he do but pretend to acquiesce? He understood that Violet didn't want to believe she was in danger, but he'd seen the worst of human behaviour during his time in the Navy, and something about this situation left him twitchy. The packages he could write off as a cruel prank, but the cum on the couch? The guy had been close, too close. And if the message on the mirror was part of the same problem, then the night before last, he'd been even closer.

If Violet wouldn't take care of herself, then he'd just have to do it for her.

CHAPTER 30
VIOLET

I'd had some stupid ideas in my time, like moving to California in the first place, but this one took first prize. What on earth had possessed me to sleep in the pool house again?

Earlier, in daylight, I'd been determined not to give in to the fear. If I succumbed, it meant that whoever was stalking me had won. It had taken every acting skill I possessed to convince Lucas and Dawson that I'd be fine by myself, and now I regretted making the effort. Even listening to Mikki having an orgy in the next room would have been preferable to sitting alone in the dark, jumping at every shadow.

And there were a lot of shadows. A storm was passing overhead, lashing the roof with rain, and I could see the fronds on the palms by the pool whipping back and forth in the howling wind. Two o'clock in the morning, and I hadn't slept a wink.

A flash of lightning outside made me jump, and I rolled out of bed to check the doors again. First, the wooden door that opened from the kitchenette, then the French windows in the living room. Thunder rumbled as I slid the gauzy curtain back to watch nature's show of strength outside. Earlier, the weather forecaster had jabbered on about jet streams and areas of low pressure and climate change, but that didn't do this storm justice.

I only hoped the rain didn't get as far as Kansas. The forecaster said it should move northeast toward Wyoming, but sometimes they got it wrong.

Lightning flashed again, and I froze. No. *No, it couldn't be.* I'd imagined it. Just for a second, I thought I'd seen a face on the far side of the pool. My heart hammered as I pressed my nose to the glass, waiting for the sky to light up again.

There. Oh, hell! There *was* somebody out there, crouching under one of the palm trees. And he was watching me.

I stumbled on my way back to the bed, then fumbled for my phone on the nightstand. *Lucas, pick up!* But he didn't. His jokey voicemail invited me to "leave a message for the Blue Avenger. Current response time is four days and seventeen hours. If your call is urgent, try Aquaman."

Now what? My fingers quaked as I scrolled through the list to Dawson's name. What would he be able to do? Probably nothing, but at least if the freak outside broke in and murdered me, he could raise the alarm, and the cops would come and find my body.

"D-D-Dawson?"

The line was terrible. Crackly. The storm, probably.

"T-t-there's someone outside. Watching me."

"I know. It's me."

"What?"

"Babe, there's a crank targeting you."

"But, but… You can't sit out there in the rain!"

"Go back to sleep, Vi."

He hung up on me. He actually hung up on me. I tried calling back, but the phone rang and rang, and then went to voicemail. Not even a fun voicemail like Lucas's, just the generic greeting provided by the cell company.

Honestly, this was ridiculous. I glanced at my bed—my

nice, comfy bed—then out at the pool. The moon popped into view for a moment, and the rain falling in sheets made me shiver even though I was safely inside. How long had Dawson been out there? Since I went to bed? He must be freezing.

Oh, screw it. I fumbled with the lock, then yanked the door open, and even though I ran, I was still soaked to the skin by the time I reached him. He was leaning up against a tree trunk, huddled under a poncho.

"You're crazy! You can't stay here."

"Vi, just go back inside."

"What if you get hypothermia?"

"Believe me, I've spent the night in worse places."

Worse? What could possibly be worse than sitting in a puddle in the middle of a freaking hurricane? Then it hit me.

"Oh my gosh. You…you were homeless?"

He began laughing, which wasn't quite the reaction I'd expected.

"Fuck, no. I was a Navy SEAL."

"Huh?"

"A SEAL." He shouted over the storm, but I'd heard him the first time. "You know—sea, air, land. Assholes who crawl around in the jungle while other assholes shoot at us."

I knew what a SEAL was. Lauren had given me a whole calendar full of them for Christmas last year, although Dawson eclipsed even Mr. July, and he'd been my favourite. In casa Miller/Rossi, it had been July for three whole months. But I also knew that SEALs were supposed to be scary guys, and Dawson wasn't scary. Not to me, at least. Not anymore.

And whether he'd crawled around in the jungle or not, he still wasn't staying out in the rain all night. How could I make him come inside? I thought of trying to drag him, but I'd have had more luck moving Mount Denali.

So I sat down in front of him.

"What are you doing?"

"If you insist on staying out here, then I'm staying with you. When are you planning to sleep?"

"I'll catch a couple of hours while you're on set."

"Hmm, maybe I need a cushion. Is your tree comfortable?"

"Vi, this isn't funny."

"No, it's not."

Another flash of lightning, and Dawson's gaze dropped. "Your shirt's gone see-through."

I could feel his damn smirk, and I folded my arms, purposely propping up my boobs.

"Nothing you haven't seen before, right?"

Quicker than I thought possible, he jumped to his feet, and suddenly I was cradled in his arms.

"Hey! Put me down."

"I will. In bed."

He swore under his breath as he carried me across the pool deck, but I didn't care because I'd won. A point to me. With a little sideways thinking plus a touch of pigheadedness, I'd beaten Dawson at his own game. Yee-haw. Victory was sweet.

At least, I thought so until he dumped me on the bed and then headed for the door again.

"Wait!" I leapt up and grabbed his hand. "Stop."

He actually rolled his eyes at me.

"I'll just come outside again."

"How about I tie you to the bed?"

Okay, a new tactic was needed. I let go and smoothed my dripping hair, then puffed out my chest.

"Tie me up? Do you like that sort of thing, Mr. Grand?"

"Fuck me. I've created a monster."

"Your choice. If you refuse to go home, you're staying in here with me."

Although I didn't truly want him to go home. I'd been terrified on my own, and with Dawson here, I might get some desperately needed sleep. Thankfully, he felt the same way.

"You're one stubborn lady, Violet."

I took a bow. "Well, I'm not apologising for it. Are you staying?"

"I'll take the couch."

As well as allowing me to sleep at night, having Dawson sleep on the couch came with an unexpected bonus. He had to shower in the morning.

The sound of the water woke me just after six, and I rubbed the blurriness out of my eyes. A duffel bag had appeared from somewhere, and he'd hung his soggy clothes over the back of a chair. Shirt, jacket, pants, socks, boxers.

Then he walked out of the bathroom wearing nothing but a towel, and I didn't know where to look. His broad shoulders, his smooth pecs, or his washboard abs? The angel tattooed on his left side or the devil on his right? Dawson wasn't so much sculpted as chiselled out of granite, all hard lines and angles. He made Kane look like a sumo wrestler, and Kane worked out for an hour every morning.

"You're staring," he said. "I feel like a fuckin' zoo exhibit."

"It's only fair. You spent an entire night looking at me."

"Good comeback, Fawn. You got me there."

He bent over to get more clothes out of his bag, and I willed the towel to loosen, but my luck had run out. It stayed firmly fixed in place, and I let my head slump back onto the pillow as he disappeared to change. I needed a fan. Or dry ice. Or one of those industrial freezers. Would Dawson insist on staying with me again tonight? I kind of wanted him to, but I wasn't sure how much of his testosterone my libido could take. My vagina might as well have rolled out a welcome mat, which was all kinds of awkward when I was sharing a tiny house with Mr. I-Don't-Do-Relationships.

Hmm, did he do no-strings sex?

Violet! Stop it.

My alarm rang on the nightstand, reminding me that I did indeed have a job to do today, and I needed to stop drooling over my bodyguard and get on with it. Dawson and his magic cock were totally off-limits.

Oh, heck. I was in big trouble, wasn't I?

As soon as Dawson emerged from the bathroom, I scooted into it, and I didn't come out until I heard Lucas's voice in the living room. Safety in numbers, right?

"What's with the bag?" Lucas asked Dawson.

"I'm sleeping on the couch until this asshole gets caught."

Yup, my worst fears had just been realised. And my deepest fantasies.

"You don't think you're overreacting?"

Dawson shrugged. "I have a bad feeling about this."

"I suppose it's better to be cautious. Beers tonight? If I'm awake, that is."

"Not while I'm working, but I wouldn't say no to a soft drink. Mikki kept you up again?"

"I don't know where she gets all the men from. It wasn't even the same two last night. If she keeps it up, I'm strongly considering asking her for tips."

How could they act as if things were normal? Every time I thought my life was even a tiny bit under control, someone came along and pulled the rug out from under my feet. Right now, I didn't know whether to keep fighting or curl up and rock. Perhaps going back to Kansas wouldn't be such a bad idea after all?

CHAPTER 31
VIOLET

The new normal was anything but. Dawson was the perfect housemate—quiet, tidy, quick in the bathroom—and last night when I'd gotten sick of salad, he'd headed out and bought a pizza. But days of spending almost every minute with him had left me permanently on edge. In the battle of oestrogen versus testosterone, I was the loser.

Sure, I got some sleep, like five hours a night, but during the moments when I lay still in the dark, I heard Dawson tossing and turning. Occasionally, he'd mumble something, but I could never make out the words. Other times, when he was quiet, I suspected he was awake too, but he never spoke and neither did I.

Until the fifth night.

On the fifth night, I heard him calling out for a woman. Who was Bryony? And why did he sound so anguished? He didn't say anything more, but the squeak of skin on leather followed by a soft *whoomp* as his blanket hit the floor said he was having another nightmare. Ten minutes ticked by, twenty, then silence.

"Dawson? Are you awake?"

I thought I was mistaken, that he'd drifted off again, but after an age, a quiet, "Yes," came through the gloom.

"Are you okay?"

"As okay as I'll ever be."

"Who's Bryony?"

"Fuck."

I switched on the lamp next to the bed and padded across the room to kneel beside him. His cheeks glistened in the dim light, and my heart lurched. Was Dawson crying? This big, strong mountain of a man? I wiped a thumb across his cheek and found it was wet, but rather than talking, he turned away. What had happened to destroy him like this? I didn't know how to help, how to take the pain away, so I just held his hand and tried to offer comfort.

"Dawson, whatever happened, I'm so incredibly sorry that you're hurting this badly."

He gripped my hand tighter, and another five minutes passed. I watched the wall clock *tick-tick-tick* slowly while his pulse raced so fast that I felt it in his thumb. It matched my own.

"Bryony was my fiancée."

He whispered the words so softly I barely heard them, and I went rigid. Dawson had been engaged? This man who didn't do relationships had been engaged? I almost didn't dare to ask my next question.

"Was?"

"She died. On the tenth of October, five and a half years ago."

Tenth of October. Tenth of October… "The tattoo on your wrist?"

He nodded, his gaze fixed on the window in a thousand-yard stare as I processed this latest piece of information. He'd lost his fiancée as well as his sister? No wonder he was messed up.

"Do you want to talk about it?"

"No." A long pause. "But I will because this is…difficult. Being near you all the time, I mean. I like you, Vi, and I'm not stupid. I see the way you look at me. But I can't get involved, not with anyone. Not again."

I sat beside him, still holding his hand. I wanted to hug him, but it didn't feel as if that would be appropriate under the circumstances. His voice cracked as he began to speak.

"I met Bryony right after I finished BUD/S School. That's the first stage of SEAL training, and I came out of it wrecked, but I was still alive, and I passed. The last thing I was looking for was a relationship, and I thought love at first sight was just bullshit from chick flicks. Me and my swim buddy had gone out for beers, and she was drinking in the bar. Such a fucking cliché, right?"

"Who cares? If a person's right for you, it doesn't matter where you meet them."

"Try telling that to a bunch of SEALs. They thought it was damn funny at first, until they realised we were actually serious. I trained, I ate, I slept, and I spent every spare moment with her. She had this way of making me feel good about myself, you know? No matter how I fucked up, she always forgave me, even the time I fell asleep in the middle of her birthday dinner because I'd had five hours' sleep in the last four days."

"Not face down?"

"Sideways. Fell right off my chair. We were in some fancy restaurant, and the manager tried to kick us out because he thought I was drunk, but she kept a dead straight face and told him I had narcolepsy. Then she made up a story about me dropping off in the middle of a baseball game and missing a home run."

"And he didn't make you leave?"

"He brought us free desserts. Everybody who ever met Bryony adored her. She was too damn sweet. And we were happy together. When I was away, she'd call, but she'd also write these long, sappy letters, and she deliberately used pink paper and covered them in lipstick kisses because it made the other guys laugh."

"You didn't mind them laughing?"

He shook his head, smiling as he remembered. "Nah. Secretly, those assholes were all fuckin' jealous." His smile faded away. "Anyhow, we'd been together for a year when I got sent overseas for six months. We missed each other like crazy, but she always said that I was born to be a SEAL in the same way that she was born to be with me. A month into my deployment, she called me, and I knew something was wrong, except it turned out not to be wrong but very, very right, just bad timing."

"She was pregnant?" I guessed.

"Two and a half months. Puking everywhere. And the baby might not have been planned, but we both wanted it, and that was when I asked her to marry me. Fast forward four and a half months, and she had everything organised. I'd come home, we'd get married, and then we'd live happily ever after. But life is no fucking fairy tale."

He paused, just breathing. Steeling himself for what was to come. I stayed quiet because there wasn't anything I could do or say that would make this any better. Pain seeped out of his every pore. I felt it rolling over me in a heavy wave.

"A week before I was due to come back, she got stomach pains. My sister was staying with her to help with all the wedding shit, and she said she'd drive her to the hospital, only they never made it. Nobody knows what happened for sure—maybe an animal ran out, maybe they swerved to avoid another vehicle—but the car ended up wrapped around a tree."

Oh, screw it. Dawson needed a hug, whether he admitted it or not. I wrapped my arms around him, wishing I could take his heartache away.

"Dawson, I'm so, so sorry."

But he wasn't finished. "Our baby died in the accident, but the girls got out. Burned. They were both burned, but Bryony took the worst of it. I spent every dollar I had and more getting them treated, but Bryony never came out of her coma. And you already know about Hannah."

"She couldn't live with what happened?"

"She always blamed herself. Started drinking and missed most of her therapy appointments." He leaned down, elbows on his knees, and stared at the floor. "I didn't realise. Every time I spoke to her, she said she was okay, and then… I should have quit work. Gotten signed off or something, but training constantly was the only way I knew how to cope."

"The hurt never goes away, does it?"

"I got shot in Afghanistan, and I broke my leg in a bad parachute jump, but none of that pain even came close to the agony of losing three people I loved. I'm just a bitter, twisted old man now. Bitter and twisted with no fucking heart."

All the little pieces of Dawson-jigsaw started to slot into place. His determination, his closed-off demeanour, the way he'd rather sleep with a nameless girl in The Dark than get involved in a relationship. But he was lying about one thing. Dawson was no Tin Man.

"But you *do* care. You care enough to look after me every night."

"Because it's my job, Vi. My boss would have my balls if anything happened to you on my watch."

Ouch. I was just a job? That hurt, but I understood why he said it, and it also confirmed what I already knew. He *did* have a heart, and he had to protect it. The question was, would he ever let anyone past his defences?

Sitting there in the dark, I realised that I'd barely thought of Trent for days. Yes, I'd answered most of his messages, but not with the care I once would have, and when my phone buzzed, I no longer felt that little skip of joy in my chest.

Instead, my mind had been consumed with a very different man. I wanted to get through Dawson's walls. I wanted to scramble over them or kick them down or drive through them with one of those big-ass monster trucks. He might have been holding onto the past, but I was a very different person to the girl of six months ago, and part of that transformation was due to him.

Maybe I'd never get him to change, but I had to try. It would be challenging, and it wouldn't happen overnight, but I didn't want to see Dawson go through the rest of his life with that kind of ache locked up inside.

And while he might pretend I didn't matter to him, I refused to say the same.

"Well, *I* care. And there's nothing in your rules that says we can't be friends, is there? Like I'm friends with Lucas?"

"Like with Lucas. Right."

"Everybody needs friends. Even grumpy Navy SEALs who snore on my couch all night."

"I don't snore."

"Sure you do. Really loudly."

He looked at me, puzzled for a moment before I burst out laughing. "You believed me, didn't you?"

"Not for a second."

"Liar."

"You moan in your sleep. Cute little whimpers."

Dammit, I probably did, but only because I kept dreaming of that night we'd spent together in The Dark. With Dawson sleeping in the same room, I hadn't been able to take care of myself when I woke up, and the little ball of energy bouncing in my stomach left me uber-frustrated.

"You have an overactive imagination, Dawson Masters." I kissed him on the cheek and wriggled out of his arms. "But thank you for helping me to understand."

"We should get some sleep."

As if that was going to happen. But I climbed back into bed and tucked myself under the covers anyway, watching him until I turned the lamp off.

"Good night, Dawson."

"Night, Vi."

CHAPTER 32
VIOLET

"**D**id you have to bring the bodyguard?" Trent asked.

I glanced sideways to see whether Dawson had heard, but he was still in the kitchen, changing a washer on Mom's leaky faucet.

Trent had been waiting for me at Mom's house when I got to Oakwood Falls, and his scowl as I walked in with Dawson had made his feelings quite plain even before he asked the question. The question that, for some reason, irritated me to no end.

"In light of the threats against me, yes, I did have to bring Dawson. David Jackson insisted."

What David had actually said was, "I'm paying a flat rate for Masters's services, so you might as well take him with you, and he can shovel you into a cab after your party. Do me a favour and don't come back hungover. Bloodshot eyes aren't good from a continuity point of view."

Well, David clearly didn't understand the concept of an Oakwood Falls party. I was far more likely to suffer sugar overload from drinking too much iced tea. Mom and her cohorts loved the stuff super sweet.

"I'd hoped to take you out to lunch," Trent said.

"You still can."

"I meant just the two of us."

"Dawson can wait at the front, the same as last time."

"Still…"

"Where are you planning to go for lunch?"

"I thought I'd take you to a proper Italian restaurant, not a strange little place like the one we went to last time. The food at Oregano is top notch. I'll book us a table."

Perfect.

But it wasn't. Not anymore.

Trent hadn't been kidding about the food. Perfectly cooked pasta in a creamy sauce with melt-in-the-mouth prosciutto, and the piece of his pizza I tried was delicious too.

"Has this place been open for long?"

"Three months. The owner's a client of mine. You'll meet him at the party later."

"Who else is coming?"

"The usual crowd from high school, plus all the people Mom invited and a few clients. Did you ever meet Wayne Breski?"

"No. Who's he?"

"He moved here from California and married Ivy McLeod, must be a year ago now. I'm sure you'll have plenty to talk about. Oh, and I made an appointment at the beauty salon for you this afternoon."

"The beauty salon? Why? Is there something wrong with my hair?"

"No, no, not at all. But every woman wants to look their best, don't they?"

I actually just wanted to have two whole days without

someone fussing over me, but since Trent had gone to the effort, I nodded and plastered on a smile.

"I guess."

"And I figured you'd bring your own dress. The designers give out freebies to all you Hollywood people, don't they?"

A dress? Trent's parties had never been that formal, so I'd just brought jeans and a sparkly top. Now I had to find a whole new outfit?

"Designers pick and choose who they lend to, and it's mostly for awards shows."

"Oh. Well, I'm sure you've selected something stunning."

"What time is my appointment at the salon?"

"Four o'clock. I thought you could come and meet the people at the office beforehand."

"Sorry, but I promised Mom I'd give her a hand at home."

Trent chuckled and winked. "With my cake? Guess I'd better let you stay, then."

Mom was making his birthday cake? I must have missed that memo. Hopefully it was finished because I didn't have the time to mess around with frosting as well as go dress shopping. I glanced at my watch, and thankfully, Trent took the hint and asked for the check. When I got out my purse to pay my half, he waved the money away.

"Let me get this. After all, you flew here especially to see me."

"Thank you. That's very kind."

And it would have been kinder if he'd left more than a five-dollar tip for our waitress. Five dollars on an eighty-dollar meal? Didn't he understand how tipping worked? Or was he just really bad at math?

"A five-dollar tip?" I asked. "That's less than ten percent."

"They get wages too, don't forget."

"But those aren't very high."

"If waitstaff earned the same as doctors and lawyers, what would be the point in going to college?"

Wow. Didn't he remember that I'd worked as a waitress? Firstly, I knew what a tough job it was being on your feet all day, and secondly, my wages had been a fraction of what Trent undoubtedly earned. And if everyone decided to go be a lawyer, who would cook his fancy dinners?

I considered pointing that out, but Trent was already halfway to the door, so I saved my breath and tucked an extra twenty dollars under the pepper mill instead. On my way out, I couldn't help glancing across at Dawson's empty plate by the bar. He'd left ten bucks, and on the way out, he raised a hand in thanks to the bartender.

At least one of the men in my life wasn't a cheapskate.

"Where to now?" Dawson asked as he took up his place beside me. "Someplace else with Trent?"

"No, I need to go dress shopping."

His eyes widened. "Dress shopping?"

"It's an emergency, okay?"

"Babe, escaping from a burning building is an emergency. Running from a psycho with a gun is an emergency. Dress shopping is not an emergency."

Ahead, Trent turned to see where I was.

"Just coming," I called to him. "Please," I begged Dawson. "Don't tell Brax."

Thank goodness. "I promise I won't."

"What do you think of this one?"

Dawson raised an eyebrow. "I'm a bodyguard, not a fashion consultant."

"Yes, but you're a man. You must have some idea what looks good on a woman."

"Sure I do. Just lose the dress completely."

Heat crept up my cheeks, but luckily, Dawson had turned

toward the street. If he'd still been watching me with that intense gaze, I might have been tempted to do as he said. A moment later, Emma Rose, the owner of the only store in the whole of Oakwood Falls that sold evening gowns and cocktail dresses, was fluttering around me, tugging bits of fabric and lace while I turned this way and that in the mirror.

"It fits you well," she said.

"I look like a doily, don't I?"

"It might be a little old for you."

Darn it. So far, I'd tried on eight different dresses, and I was running out of options unless I wanted to channel a prom queen or Morticia Addams. All I needed was something simple and knee-length. Was that really too much to ask?

"Do you have anything plain? I could jazz it up with a necklace."

She crinkled her nose, and her pince-nez glasses fell off. I'd never met anyone else who wore them, but they suited her. Slightly odd. Offbeat.

"I do have one other dress. The wholesaler delivered it by accident, and they're dithering over taking it back, but I think it would suit you."

"Okay, bring it out."

"Just go in jeans," Dawson said. I'd explained the reason for my sudden shopping excursion on the way over. "If Trent has a problem with that, then maybe he should've filled you in on the dress code before you left."

"But I don't want to feel out of place."

"Babe, you'll be out of place anywhere you go since you're prettier than ninety-nine-point-nine percent of the female population."

Oh. I didn't really know what to say to that, but luckily, Emma Rose came back and saved me.

"Look, it matches your name," she giggled.

Yes, the dress was bright purple. As well as strapless, skintight, and decorated with sequins. Emma Rose zipped me into it and turned me to face the mirror. Holy smokes. Well, it fit. I just wasn't sure I'd dare to wear it out in public because it showed every single curve.

"It might be a bit too…"

"Risqué, honey?"

"Yes. Risqué."

"I have a perfect pashmina you can wear over the top. Hold on, I'll be right back."

I studied my reflection again. This sure was a beautiful dress for, say, attending the VMAs or perhaps going to an event hosted by *Vanity Fair*. But for Trent's birthday party?

"What do you think?" I asked Dawson.

"If it helps, I've gone hard just from looking at you."

I glanced down and found he wasn't kidding, and right there and then, I decided to buy the dress. For Trent, obviously. Emma Rose draped a black pashmina around my shoulders, and it took the outfit from lady-of-the-night to passable-for-a-twenty-eighth-birthday-party. Better than jeans, right?

"I'll take it."

"Wonderful. I'll wrap it up."

Dawson groaned, his lips close to my ear. "You're killing me."

"Aren't Navy SEALs famous for their discipline?"

"My swim buddy didn't have tits like yours."

"I'd be worried if he did. Who was your swim buddy? Do you see him anymore?"

"An asshole from Detroit named Shawn. Yeah, we still get together, but he's deployed overseas right now."

"You left the Navy and he didn't? Why?"

"Long story."

And one I didn't have time to hear because Emma Rose came back with my dress in a paper carrier bag, and I only had fifteen minutes to get to the beauty salon. Kathy had been running the place forever, and I secretly suspected she was a closet sadist. If she lived in the big city, she'd probably earn her money as a dominatrix instead.

"What are you getting done?" Dawson asked when I hesitated outside the door.

"As little as possible."

CHAPTER 33
VIOLET

"This is Violet Miller," Trent said to a portly man in cowboy boots and a string tie. "Violet, this is Clyde. He owns the Italian restaurant we ate in earlier."

"You don't look very Italian," I blurted.

"That doesn't matter, little lady. Business is business. I have six restaurants now, three Italian and three Chinese. People like all those exotic foreign foods nowadays, and as long as I hire the right staff, they practically run themselves. Say, I saw your picture on the internet the other day. Surfing, right? You looked quite the professional."

"It was actually the first time I'd tried it. I had no idea where to put my feet."

"I don't suppose many people were paying attention to your feet, darlin'."

His words were aimed at my chest, and I tugged the pashmina around myself a little tighter. Trent had smiled when he saw my dress, but most of the other guests just stared. Some nudged each other and whispered, and I wasn't sure whether that was because of my attire, my role in *Rules of*

Play, David's YouTube channel, or the trash they read on Celebgossip.com. I should have gone with the doily outfit.

Trent chuckled along with Clyde, even though Clyde's comment hadn't been funny at all, then tucked an arm around my waist. "Let's go and say hello to Matthew Gibson."

"Who?"

"He's hoping to build a mini-mall over in Oakwood Ridge."

"Another client?"

"Potential client. It's important that we make a good impression this evening."

And so it went on. This wasn't like the old Vickers family parties, where everyone ate and drank and laughed and somebody had to carry Maggie Morgan home at the end of the night. This was more of a corporate gathering. The only thing missing was the PowerPoint presentation. Sure, the usual crowd was still there—Trent's mom and her friends were drinking iced tea in the conservatory, and our high-school acquaintances were hanging out on the back deck with beer and potato chips, but when I tried to join them, Trent hustled me back inside to meet more of his clients.

"Violet, this is Reuben Lockie. He's in the process of buying a ranch on the outskirts of town. You know, the old Akram place. Reuben, this is Violet Miller."

"A pleasure to meet you, a real pleasure. I've seen all of your movies."

"I've only actually made one."

"And I'm a big fan."

Let go of my hand. I gave it a gentle tug, but Reuben didn't take the hint. Out of the corner of my eye, I saw Dawson glare at him and then whisper to a waitress. She veered in my direction, holding out a tray.

"More champagne, ma'am?"

Thank goodness. Reuben had to release me so I could take

a drink, and I shot Dawson a grateful smile while Trent blabbered on about property deeds and surveys. He'd changed too. Old Trent would have been playing pool in the games room or even beer pong if he'd had enough alcohol first. New Trent was more concerned with making small talk and showing me off like a trophy while I smiled and played the dutiful companion. Was this how life would be as Mrs. Trent Vickers? A constant cycle of stuffy parties where I always had to dress up and say the right thing? Because I wasn't so good at that.

Since I wasn't allowed to get a word in edgewise, I had plenty of time to think. For all these years, had I been in love with Trent, or just the idea of Trent? A handsome man who would take care of me and provide companionship? It was possible. And maybe, if I was honest, I'd also been blinded by the fact that Trent was the most eligible bachelor in Oakwood Falls. But Oakwood Falls was a tiny dot on the map, and there was a whole world out there for me to explore. Did I want to broaden my horizons and seize the new opportunities coming my way, or settle for a dream I was beginning to suspect I'd outgrown?

Even watching a trashy horror movie in the pump room at the beach house had been more fun than this, and that was because of the company. Lucas, Lauren, Jeanie, and Dawson. *Oh, Dawson.* I couldn't even begin to make sense of my thoughts about him. That first night in The Dark had made me feel like a woman rather than a girl for the first time in my life, and even though he was paid to be by my side, I still felt as though there was a connection between us. After all, David hadn't told him to sleep in the pool house, had he? That was Dawson's choice. He kept his distance, but at the same time, he liked to stay close. A paradox indeed. Such as tonight— when I'd suggested booking him a room at the Oakwood Falls Motel since Mom's house only had two bedrooms, he'd opted to sleep on the couch instead.

If I couldn't have Dawson, then maybe I could look for a partner more like him than Trent? A man who genuinely cared about other people rather than calculating what they could offer him, a man who didn't take his eyes off me the whole night, who made me feel safe, and who tipped the waitress more than five miserable bucks.

"Trent, I'm gonna head back to Mom's."

"What? But you haven't met Bruce Marlon yet, and he's one of my biggest clients."

"I'm sure I'll meet him another time. I have a long day tomorrow, and I need to get some sleep."

Bored to tears, I faked a yawn, but it quickly turned into a real one.

"Just another half hour, okay? I'll drive you back home myself, and I'll even drop the Neanderthal back at the motel. I assume that's where he's staying?"

Excuse me? The *Neanderthal*?

"I'm sorry?"

"I'll drive you home myself."

"No, what did you call Dawson?"

"A Neanderthal? I mean, if his knuckles got any lower, they'd drag on the ground."

"Good night, Trent."

"Wait, wait. It was a joke. Did you leave your sense of humour back in the Golden State?"

"New York changed you."

"Of course it did. And all for the better, trust me. What time do you want to get breakfast tomorrow?"

"Tomorrow, I'm planning to visit the horses at Delbert's ranch in the morning, and then I'm going to the diner for lunch. I already told you that when we were eating at Oregano."

"Did you? What time were you thinking for lunch? I have a catered client meeting from twelve until two, but I can meet you after that."

How could I have been so stupid, and for so long? Trent knew I was coming to visit, yet he'd still booked meetings for half of the time I was here.

"Sorry, but I have to leave for the airport at two."

I didn't, but suddenly three extra hours in the departure hall seemed preferable to eating fancy food while Trent attempted to brainwash me.

"Never mind. We can arrange for you to fly back for another visit soon, yes? Lester's drawn up the plans for the house, and I want you to take a look. I'm not sure about the layout for the kitchen. Do you prefer two sinks side by side or one in the island and another by the window? After all, it's you who'll be using them the most."

Sinks? Good grief. I knocked back the last of my champagne, cringed when Trent kissed me on the cheek, then backed away. He tried to follow, but a red-faced man wobbled up and asked a question about a power of attorney and I more or less shoved Dawson out the front door.

"I thought you'd be there until the end," he said once we got to the rental car.

"I changed my mind."

"About Trent? I thought you liked the guy."

"So did I, but it turns out I was mistaken." I took a deep breath. "He's not the same person I grew up with. While I've been in California, Trent's become this self-centred, work-obsessed… I can't even…"

"Should I be commiserating with you because he's changed or congratulating you on your escape? I'm not certain, but I'm bound to say the wrong thing."

"Right now, I just want to go home."

"Sorry he turned out to be a dick, babe." Dawson opened the car door for me, and I slumped into the passenger seat. "Home to California, or home to your mom's place?"

"Just to Mom's place. I already told Trent I'm busy tomorrow." Dawson started the engine, and we pulled out of

Trent's drive. "On second thought, can we stop for a drink on the way back? I don't feel ready to sleep."

I'd probably stay awake for hours, ruing the wasted years. Years when I could have been feeling the flutter of anticipation that perhaps I'd meet The One that evening, or possibly competing with Lauren to see who could go on the worst online date.

"Sure."

"And you can join me."

"I'm on—"

"You're *not* on duty. Nobody's threatened me in Oakwood Falls, and I didn't tell anyone apart from you and David and Lauren and Lucas that I was even coming here. One beer."

"Okay, one beer. Do you want to change into jeans first? Because if you bend over a pool table in that outfit, I'm not responsible for the consequences."

I batted my eyelashes. "What, you think a handsome cowboy might take advantage of me?"

"No, I think I might take advantage of you."

"In that case, I'll keep the dress on."

Dawson took me home to change. Spoilsport. But he put on a pair of jeans too, so it wasn't all bad. The soft, worn denim hugged his ass, and more than anything, I wanted to slip a hand into his back pocket. But I didn't think that would go down so well.

He'd put on a leather jacket too, more to hide his gun than because it was cold, and I liked this new, casual Dawson. I liked him too much.

"Are we walking?" he asked.

"The bar's only five minutes away on foot."

"The place with the neon Budweiser sign?"

"Yup. That's been there for as long as I can remember. I'm amazed it still lights up."

One beer turned into three, and despite Dawson's earlier

words and also the fact that I was the world's worst pool player, I decided to pick up a cue.

"One game?"

"Is this like your one beer?"

"Maybe." I wobbled a little on my way across the bar. "But if we play three games, then I get to stare at your butt three times, which is a really good thing. Oops…" I clapped both hands over my mouth. "I'm not supposed to say that."

Aw, I liked his playful smile, even if it was kinda fuzzy.

"As long as I get to stare at your ass too."

"Stare away." I tripped up a step, but Dawson caught me. "It's all yours."

"Fuck." He shook his head as he followed me. "You drive me crazy, woman."

Good. "This is fun. Aren't you having fun?"

He rolled his eyes, and I giggled harder. Mr. Oh-So-Serious needed to loosen up. I considered inviting him to join me on the tiny dance floor in the corner, a suggestion that he'd undoubtedly have said no to, but I wanted to see his lips do that flickery thing where he tried not to laugh again. Except before I could open my mouth, a voice called to me from the other end of the bar.

"Well, if it isn't Violet Miller. Decided to slum it with us mere mortals again?"

I turned to see Grady Hughes swaggering toward me. He'd been a jackass in high school, and judging by the cocky grin on his face, he hadn't changed.

"Oakwood Falls is my home. I came to visit Mom and Trent."

"Trent Vickers? Now, there's a man who thinks he's too good for this town." Grady rested one hand on my arm, and I felt rather than saw Dawson bristle behind me. Just a subtle change in the energy that seemed to radiate from him at all times. "Don't understand why he didn't stay in New York with the other stuck-up lawyers."

I shook Grady's hand away, but two seconds later, he put it back again. No, he definitely hadn't changed since high school. I still remembered Verity Thornberg throwing a glass of water in his face when he tried the same trick, but I only had beer and I didn't want to waste that.

I didn't need to.

One blink later, Dawson had Grady bent backward over the bar, his hand at Grady's throat. Grady tried to push him away, but Dawson didn't move an inch.

"Take the hint, buddy. She doesn't want you touching her."

"Who the fuck are you?" Grady choked out.

"A friend who's suggesting you leave."

A couple of men from Grady's crowd hovered in the background, but the moment Dawson turned his cold gaze on them, they both took a pace backward, and when he glanced at the door, they shuffled toward it.

"Do you understand?" he asked Grady.

"Y-y-yes."

As soon as Dawson let him up, Grady hightailed it after his group, and the barmaid pushed two more beers in our direction.

"Don't want trouble in here, but that needed to be said. Grady Hughes doesn't know how to take a hint."

Dawson nodded to her, then turned to me. "You okay?"

"You don't think that was a little drastic?"

"Where your safety is concerned? No. Vi, I'm here to protect you, and that includes keeping wandering hands away."

There was one set of hands I wouldn't mind wandering all over me, but even when I accidentally-on-purpose brushed against him, Dawson didn't catch on. Ah well, there was always beer. I picked up my bottle and took a swallow. With only one night away from San Francisco, I intended to make the most of my short-lived freedom and enjoy myself.

Or at least, that was the plan. Some time later, cool air puffed against my face, and I woke up on a bench in the nearly empty parking lot with Dawson rifling through my pockets.

"Wh-what's happening?"

"I'm looking for your keys, and then I'm taking you home."

"Did I finish my drink?"

"Babe, you finished *all* the drinks and then fell asleep on the pool table."

"No! I didn't! I never did that."

"Face down with the cue still in your hands."

I cupped his cheeks with both hands. "Can I please have one of those strawberry things with the little umbrella?"

"Pretty sure that place doesn't serve anything strawberry." He found my keys and straightened. "Can you walk? Or do you want me to carry you?"

"I think I can walk." Dawson pulled me to my feet, and the ground rippled alarmingly. "Actually…"

A strong arm wrapped around my waist, and I found myself plastered to Dawson's side. Oh, this was much better. I should get drunk more often.

"We'll go slowly. Hopefully you'll sober up on the way, or your mom's gonna kill me."

"She'll kill me too. We can share a cloud in heaven, so that'll be nice. And a harp too. And one of those… I don't know. I forget."

"One foot in front of the other, Vi. I've got you."

"Why did you let me drink so much?" I asked Dawson in the morning.

My head pounded, and he passed me a package of

painkillers and a glass of orange juice. I'd made it as far as the kitchen, but I was strongly considering crawling back to bed.

"You looked as though you were having fun. You even won ten bucks in a pool game."

"I did?"

"Yeah, and you spent it on more beer."

"Oh, cheese and rice. I'm never drinking again."

"I don't know… The way you kept squeezing my ass was kind of cute."

"I'm sorry. I'm so, so sorry."

"Don't—"

Footsteps sounded, and Mom appeared in the doorway. "How are you feeling, sweetheart? Trent said you'd gone home sick last night."

Sick of him, more like. "I still have a headache."

"How about I make you both scrambled eggs and grits before I go to work? Or pancakes with bacon?"

Not after I'd consumed an entire week's worth of calories in beer last night. The wardrobe lady would have a fit if none of my costumes did up.

"I'm gonna have oatmeal."

"But you've always hated oatmeal."

"I've been eating it in California, and I like it now."

Mom clearly didn't believe me, but she gave me that "I'll humour you because you're my daughter" look she'd perfected over the years.

"The oatmeal's in the cupboard beside the microwave. Dawson? Would you like eggs? A bowl of oatmeal isn't going to keep a man like you going all day."

"Eggs would be great, thanks, Mrs. Miller."

"Amy, please." She turned back to me. "I'm surprised you're not having breakfast with Trent this morning. Everyone said you made a lovely couple last night."

"We're not a couple."

"But I thought… Trent said…"

Mom looked so disappointed that I almost backpedalled, but there was no point in misleading her. She deserved to know the truth.

"Trent's a childhood friend, that's all. He's not my type."

"But his mom said he's building a house for the two of you in your favourite spot."

"I live in California, Mom."

"You're not moving back home?"

Darn it, I should have followed Trent's advice and called her more often, because now he'd filled her head with nonsense and I'd have to let her down.

"Not right now. I'm auditioning for a new movie, and even if I don't get that part, there'll be others." Mom's eyes glistened, and I gave her a hug. "Maybe one day I'll move back here, but not yet. This is my chance to make something of myself, and if I returned to Oakwood Falls now, I'd always be in Trent's shadow."

Mom threw her arms around me. "I'm so proud of you. I miss you, but I'm so proud. Your father would be too."

I sniffed back the tears that threatened. If I let them out, they'd never stop. "I'll visit more often, I promise. After *Hidden Intent* wraps, I'll have the time."

"Well, make sure that you do." She stepped away, her mouth set. "Or I'll have to come to California, and I'm not sure Hollywood and I would make good bedfellows."

"I will."

"And take care of yourself. I know you have this gentleman at the moment…" She nodded at Dawson. "But he won't always be around."

Logically, I knew Mom was right—of course I did—but my stomach still sank at her words. I glanced across at Dawson, but his face was unreadable.

"I'll take care of your daughter, Amy," he said. "You have my word on that."

CHAPTER 34
VIOLET

Aaaaand…. Back to reality. Or at least, reality TV.

Last night, I'd arrived at the beach house to be greeted by Lucas with the joyous news of a script reveal the next morning. What a time to give up drinking.

"How many more of these do you think we'll have?" I asked.

"We must be more than halfway."

"Scott scared the crap out of me in our scenes the other day. I know he was only acting, but the way he got all up in my face…" I shuddered. "I almost don't want him to come back."

"Think positive—this nightmare will soon be over, and we'll never have to eat breakfast with Mikki again. How was your trip home?"

Hmm, how did I describe it? "A mix of good and bad. Constructive, I guess."

"That sounds ominous."

"I've decided that Trent isn't the man for me."

"Really? But I thought he was Mr. Perfect?"

"Okay, so he paraded me around his clients like some sort

of prize, asked what type of sinks I'd prefer in the house he just assumed I'd move into with him, and he also called Dawson a Neanderthal."

"I'm with him on the Neanderthal thing."

"Lucas!"

I shoved him, but he was already laughing. "Your face! I love the way you get so defensive over Dawson."

"We're just friends, that's all."

Friends who'd spent the whole day together. After breakfast, he'd driven me to the ranch and watched from the fence while I rode one of Delbert's horses, and then he'd charmed the apron off Betty when we ate lunch at the diner. She even insisted on giving us a doggy bag full of donuts, which Dawson ate on the way to the airport because I needed to diet. And when we checked in, the lady at the desk had practically swooned over his moody smile and upgraded us both to business class. He made the perfect travel companion.

"Ah, but you want to be more than just friends."

"Shut up."

"Knew I was right."

Mikki swanned into the dining room, caked in make-up at seven o'clock in the morning. Whatever I tried, I looked awful in these videos, so today I'd given up after mascara. At least my grey pallor had faded following yesterday's hangover.

"Nice of you to join us again," she said, sickly sweet.

Lucas matched her saccharine smile. "I could say the same to you, but I'd be lying."

"Now, now…" David clapped his hands from the doorway. "Let's not behave like children, at least not before the cameras are rolling. Where's Kane?"

"Probably still screwing last night's blonde," Lucas muttered.

"Sorry, what was that?"

"I said, I haven't seen him this morning."

255

"Somebody needs to find him. Kristen, go and look for Kane."

Eventually, he sauntered in with the cat in his arms, not at all bothered that he'd kept everyone waiting. David gave him a dirty look, but Kane ignored him and snagged a Danish from the plate we weren't supposed to touch. Evidently, our leading man had gotten sick of jumping through hoops too.

I knew the moment David sat down that this was no ordinary script reveal. The sideways glance in my direction and the glint of excitement in his eyes, those were the giveaways. What horrors lurked in today's golden envelope?

It didn't take long for me to find out. The words jumped out at me as I flicked through the pages: *Kelvin tears off Veronica's clothes…naked…bedroom…sex…passion…cowgirl-style*. Oh, heck. I should have borrowed Mikki's bronzer because I felt the colour drain out of my face. Like, right down to my feet. My stomach contents travelled in the other direction, and I had to swallow hard to stop myself from throwing up all over the table.

"So, Violet," David asked. "What do you think of today's script?"

I glanced at Kane, and he was grinning. Asshole. He thought this was funny?

"It'll be an interesting challenge."

"When we first started filming, you found this type of scene difficult. What's changed between then and now?"

Mikki was watching me, smirking, and I felt an unbearable urge to wipe that expression right off her smug little face. So I gave a sugary smile.

"I just made sure to fit in plenty of rehearsals."

David choked on his orange juice while Lucas burst out laughing. Mikki's lost her smirk, and it transferred to Kane. Oh, tell me he wasn't taking the credit for my practice. He was, wasn't he? And because of David's earlier directive, I couldn't even correct the insinuation.

256

Good going, Violet.

Still, I had to think positive. Mikki's thunderous expression was oddly satisfying. Guess she didn't like losing the limelight. And after the cameras stopped, David was over the moon.

"That line, Vi. Brilliant! The whole world's gonna be speculating about you and Kane. They'll give you one of those couple names."

"Like what? Bliolet? Vane?"

"Hmm, yes… Neither of those really work, do they? I'll get Debbie to come up with something and post it on Twitter. Hey, I almost forgot—we're planning to film the four of you having dinner tonight. We thought we'd just give you a selection of mystery ingredients, and you can cook a meal yourselves."

Mystery ingredients? My guts heaved in anticipation.

"But Mikki's vegan this week, and Kane's on a paleo diet."

"Even better. Conflict means ratings, Violet."

And during dinner, it also meant Mikki shrieking because a piece of Kane's dead cow touched her salad. David chuckled from behind the camera as she stomped across the kitchen and stuffed the whole lot down the waste disposal, steak and all.

"That's my dinner!" Kane yelled at her.

"No, this here is karma. If you cared more about animals, it wouldn't have happened."

"I care about animals. I have a cat."

"And didn't you buy a new leather purse two days ago?" Lucas asked.

"Shut up!" she hissed.

Oh, for goodness' sake. Dawson was waiting in the pool house, and I just wanted to get out of there.

"Kane, you can have my steak. Mikki, sit down and I'll cut you up another head of lettuce."

"No dressing. It has egg in it."

"Fine, no dressing. Then can we eat? Some of us want to sleep tonight."

Three nods. Thank heavens for that. If the acting thing didn't work out, I could always become a kindergarten teacher.

The next day, a new career looked more and more appealing. Say, cleaning sewers or tasting dog food or working as a morgue attendant. Anything would be preferable to getting my clothes ripped off by Kane so the entire world could look at me naked. Okay, not *totally* naked. Shonda had stuck a little beige patch between my legs that left pretty much nothing to the imagination, and Kane apparently had a tiny baggie tied over his joystick and jellybeans.

"You okay?" Dawson asked.

He'd been so sweet last night, from bringing me a box of chow mein after the disastrous dinner to watching a movie with me when I couldn't sleep.

"No."

"It'll all be over in a few hours."

He gripped the back of my neck, rubbing the tension away with a thumb and forefinger. My stomach still kept churning, though.

"Is it too late to run away? Which countries don't have extradition treaties?"

"I hear Russia's nice this time of year."

A year ago, a trip to Moscow would have been a hard pass, but the new Russian president was hot in a sugar daddy kind of way, at least according to Lauren. Gennady Markovich had come to power via Hollywood. By accident, quite literally—a plane crash had wiped out his predecessor. Only time would tell whether President Markovich was able to run a country, but he'd had a reasonably successful acting career, starring in several movies before he landed the lead role in popular Russian cop show *Detektivy*. Maybe if I failed in showbiz, there was a place for me in Congress? Qualifications seemed optional in the world of politics.

"Can you pass the vodka?"

I'd snuck a bottle in with me this morning because there was no way I'd get through this scene sober.

"One shot, babe."

"I'll drink the rest when I'm done. You'll be here waiting?"

"Right here, I promise."

I didn't want Dawson to watch me with Kane. Even though acting was my job and Dawson knew I wasn't fond of my co-star, and officially, Dawson and I were just friends, getting it on with another man somehow felt like cheating. David had agreed to clear out all the hangers-on, so at least only twenty or so people would see me in the buff pre-edits.

My eyes prickled, and I reached for a tissue. Shonda would kill me if I smeared my make-up. When this was over, I'd only make horror movies. Or maybe sci-fi. I didn't mind getting eaten alive by zombies or devoured by alien life forms as long as I didn't have to kiss any of them.

"Vi, come here."

Dawson opened his arms, and I stepped into them for a hug. Yup, I'd definitely been friendzoned. Just when I thought today couldn't get any worse.

"When filming ends, can we do something fun together?" I asked. Begged. Whatever. "Go to an arcade or try hiking or visit a museum? I know your contract will be over, but…"

"We can do anything you want." He spun me toward the door. "Time to get this over with. And think positive—when I first started in the Navy, I had to run through the sea with a boat on my head for five fucking days, and the instructors rode in the boat and beat us with paddles. At least you won't end up with bruises."

"That really happened?"

"Yup. They called it Hell Week. We got four hours' sleep."

"Four hours each night?"

"No, for the whole period."

Wow. "This is my Hell Day."

"And you'll get through it. I have faith in you, beautiful."

CHAPTER 35
DAWSON

The jealousy was irrational. Dawson knew that, but heat still simmered in his veins, enticing him to do something stupid like haul Violet back inside, shove her up against the wall, and kiss the breath out of her.

But he hadn't spent years testing his willpower to make a mistake now, so he gave her a gentle push toward the door.

"Knock 'em dead, babe."

He lived in hope. Kane was a first-class asshole, and after the steak fiasco last night, Dawson had been tempted to go inside and tell him exactly that. But then he'd get fired, and he needed to stick around to take care of Violet. There hadn't been any new threats, but this wasn't over. He could feel it. That prickle at the back of his neck, the uneasiness in his gut… Someone was out there, watching, and it bothered him that he hadn't spotted them yet. Where were they hiding?

In the privacy of Violet's trailer, he took out his gun and popped the magazine free. Unloaded. Reloaded. Once, twice, three times, anything to keep his hands busy. But his mind still meandered, and the thought of that entitled, arrogant prick with his fake tan and designer teeth putting his grubby hands all over Dawson's girl made him clench his jaw so hard he regretted not having a dental plan.

Hold on…*his* girl?

No, she deserved better than a washed-up ex-SEAL who'd been dishonourably discharged because he'd done what every other man left alive on his team longed to do. Back then, he hadn't cared about losing his job, but now… Maybe he'd behave differently if he could turn back the clock.

But then he'd never have met Violet in the first place.

Fuck, this situation was impossible. Why hadn't he stuck with mercenary work? It paid better, and while he got shot at on occasion, at least his clients were ugly bastards. He lay on the couch and emptied his mind, but that only worked for a few minutes, and then he was back to thinking of the future. What would he do when this job ended? He'd agreed to go somewhere fun with Vi, and he never broke a promise, but what about after that? Should he accept another bodyguard contract? Or head out to the Middle East again? Africa, perhaps?

One thing was for sure—if he didn't get out of the trailer and grab a coffee, he was gonna start on that damned vodka. How much longer would this scene take? Vi and Kane been at it for three hours, and his sanity was holding on by a thread.

"Hey! Hey you, bodyguard!"

He turned to find Vi's useless assistant trying to jog toward him in high-heeled flip-flops.

"Can you do me a favour?"

"What?"

"Take this to Violet?" Kristen thrust something pink and silky at him. "I'd do it myself, but I need to help Jimmy find Mikki's Hermès scarf. It's gone missing, and she's throwing a *fit.*"

Before Dawson could say a word, she scurried off toward a guy driving a golf cart without so much as a thank you, leaving Dawson with… What was it? He shook out the

bundle and cursed under his breath. Fawn's robe from The
Dark? He held it up to his nose and breathed her scent in,
then hastily looked around to see if anyone had noticed.
Shit.

He didn't want to go near the set, but if this was meant for
Vi to wear after her scene with Kane, he could hardly leave
her naked, could he?

Okay, buddy, you can do this. He'd faced the Taliban, Daesh,
and too many other insurgents to name, but nothing made
him hesitate like the prospect of walking into that building
and seeing the woman he cared about screwing around with
another man.

He went anyway.

Dawson heard Violet before he saw her, that breathy
whimper he dreamed of every night. A little moan, a sigh,
and his dick went hard instantly.

Fuck, fuck, fuck.

This. *This* was why he should have stuck to shooting
people. He shifted the robe in front of his straining fly and
crept forward, even though his head told him to run in the
other direction.

And there she was, straddling Kane, hands on his thighs
and her head thrown back. Dawson knew they weren't
actually fucking, but she was a damn good actress, and he
didn't know whether to throw her over his shoulder,
caveman-style, or punch Kane's fucking veneers out. His fists
clenched, scrunching up the silken fabric, and he took half a
dozen steps to the side. Her eyes were closed, which meant
she couldn't see him in the shadows as he stared at those
perfect tits, bouncing in time to her movements. And her ass.
That ass was made for his hands.

Just leave the robe, Dawson. Leave it and walk out of here.

But he couldn't. His feet were stuck. A camera passed in
front of him, and he moved to get a clear view again,
torturing himself in the process. But that meant he was

looking right at her face, her lips, and if he hadn't been, he might have missed it.

"Grand," she cried.

Oh, hell. Did she even realise what she'd said? It seemed not because she didn't miss a beat until David yelled, "Cut!"

Her eyes popped open, and she stared in Dawson's direction, their gazes locking until David interrupted.

"Who's Grand?"

"Huh?"

"You called Kane 'Grand' instead of 'Kelvin.'"

"I-I-I don't know. I don't remember."

"We'll have to edit it out in post. Good job, anyway. I didn't think we'd do that final shot in one take."

Vi looked around frantically, and Dawson realised she was searching for her robe.

"Here. Kristen asked me to bring this."

"Thanks."

She shoved her arms in and cinched the belt tight, but she wouldn't meet his eyes. Dawson knew why. The blush was a dead giveaway. She was embarrassed, both by what he'd seen and what he'd heard. And worse, he couldn't even reassure her with all these people around.

"Do you have shoes?"

"Uh, somewhere."

"Has anyone seen Violet's shoes?"

A crew member handed him a pair of ballet pumps, and he set them on the floor in front of her.

"Feet, babe," he murmured, too quietly for anyone else to hear, and she obliged. "You want to go back to the trailer now?"

A tiny nod. "I want to get the feel of him off me."

That made two of them.

CHAPTER 36
VIOLET

Oh hell, oh hell, oh hell.

How much had Dawson seen? He hadn't been present when we started the final scene, that was for sure, but when I opened my eyes, there he was, holding the robe I'd kept as a memento of our night together, watching while I pretended to have sex with another man. And I'd called Kane by Dawson's freaking name! It was obvious who I'd been thinking of, and now Dawson looked pissed. Really pissed. His jaw was rigid.

Don't cry, Violet.

At least, not until I got into the trailer. I needed to shower because I was covered in Kane's sweat, and I needed to brush my teeth because he'd eaten blue cheese for lunch. But first, I needed to drink that vodka.

I practically sprinted off set with Dawson following, and I didn't even stop when I lost a ballet pump. Dawson stopped to pick it up, but I was no Cinderella. If Cinders had met Prince Charming wearing a souvenir from a sex club, that fairy tale would have had quite a different ending, of that I was sure.

"Vi, don't you want your shoe?"

No, I just wanted to be on my own. I tried to shut the door behind me, but Dawson wedged his foot in the gap and shouldered his way in.

"What's wrong?"

"Where's the vodka?" I ran into the living area and spied the bottle on the arm of the couch, but Dawson grabbed it and held it out of reach. "Please, I need that."

"Not until you talk to me."

The first tear escaped, and I swiped at it with my hand. Hell, I was a mess in every possible way.

"I didn't want you to see that, okay?"

"I didn't want to see it either, but I did." He ran one hand through his hair, tugging at it. "Fuck. I can't keep doing this."

"Doing what? Being my bodyguard?"

"No, I can't keep my fucking hands off you."

He dropped the bottle on the cushions and stalked toward me, pushing me backward until he'd pinned me against the closed door. Wow, was that…? I glanced down, and there was no mistaking the bulge in his pants.

"Yeah, I'm so hard it hurts. And guess whose fault that is?"

"Uh…"

Dawson brushed his lips over mine, then nipped at my earlobe with his teeth. "Answer the question, babe."

"I… I…"

"Do I have to give you clues?" He trailed his tongue along my jaw, and I shivered in his arms. "She's a dark-haired temptress who looks edible bent over a pool table and doesn't know how to hold her liquor."

I tried to kiss him, but he dodged and wrapped my hair around his hand, pulling my head back to give himself better access to my neck.

"Answer the question."

"Me," I whispered.

"Right. And every day I spend with you, I want you more. You bring me to my knees, Violet."

And then he dropped to them. One quick move and my robe fell open, leaving me pretty much naked in front of Dawson's hungry eyes. Only the tiny patch kept anything hidden, and I could already feel that loosening because I'd soaked it through.

Slowly, slowly, Dawson peeled it away, and I cringed as it landed on the floor with a squelch.

"Looks as if Mr. Grand really did it for you, babe."

"You know damn well he does."

He gripped my ass with both hands, arching me away from the door, closer to his mouth. Was he seriously going to…? Oh. Oh! He was. I shuddered under the first swipe of his tongue and tangled my fingers in his hair for balance as he sucked on the tiny little bud that throbbed between my legs. I'd hated every moment of today, but the horrors of Kane pressed against me were worth it if this was the result. Who knew a little jealousy would be the answer to my prayers?

Dawson paused to glance up at me, and my thighs tensed all of their own accord.

"Don't stop," I gasped. "Please don't stop."

"You taste delicious. Never gonna get enough of this."

I managed to point at where I wanted him, and he chuckled against me as he got on with the job once more, licking and sucking and swirling until my knees buckled and stars exploded behind my eyes. I'd have ended up in a quivering heap on the floor if Dawson hadn't held me up.

He shifted and pressed me up against the wall on my tiptoes, holding me there with his hips as he leaned his forehead against mine, but I wanted more. I wanted the hard cock that was digging into my stomach. I wanted it in my mouth, in my pussy, and between my breasts like the woman in one of those dodgy porn clips Lauren had sent me.

When Dawson didn't make a move, I squashed my hands

between us, fumbling for his belt buckle, but he shook his head.

"Not now."

"What? Why?"

"I fucked up." He shrugged sheepishly. "No condom. I didn't want to get tempted, but I should've known you'd wear me down. Now I'm kicking myself."

What was this? Just sex? I didn't think so. If Dawson merely wanted to shoot his load into a warm body, he could do that in The Dark, and there was a deeper connection between us. I didn't want anyone else, and I really hoped he felt the same way.

"Dawson, I take birth control pills. Not because I spend time with lots of men, just because I get heavy periods otherwise, and if this is more than a one-time thing for you…"

"It is. It will be. If I have you again, I'll never be able to give you up."

"Then…?"

"I'm clean. I swear I'm clean. I haven't gone bare since…since…"

He closed his eyes, and for a moment, I thought I'd lost him, but then he opened them again and looked right at me. In that unguarded moment, I saw all of him. The pain, the fear, the lust, and what I hoped might one day turn into love.

This time when I reached for his belt, he didn't stop me. No, he kissed me instead. Wait. "Kissed" was the wrong word. He devoured me. I took everything he gave, fumbling to get my prize at the same time.

Dawson groaned as I stroked his shaft, but he didn't break the connection, just lifted me higher so I could guide him inside. The last time this happened, I'd only had the use of four senses, but this time I could see him too. I could see the heat in those brown eyes as I took him deep, followed by the shock as the outside door opened.

"Violet?" Shonda called. "You in there?"

"I'm about to take a shower."

"Are you okay? David thought you looked kinda stressed."

Dawson muffled his laughter in the crook of my neck, but his shoulders were shaking.

"Shut up," I whispered in his ear. "This isn't funny."

"It's fucking hilarious."

"No, no, I'm fine," I told Shonda. "I just got a bit hot."

"Got that right," Dawson whispered, twitching inside me.

"And where's that fine bodyguard of yours? I could use me some eye candy."

Another whisper. "You can suck me any time, babe."

I glared at Dawson, but he just grinned back. I couldn't complain. That look made me melt.

"Uh, I asked Dawson to go and find me a package of mints. Kane ate smelly cheese for lunch."

"Imma go get you a donut, hun. Sounds as if you deserve one."

The door slammed, and I loosened my death grip on Dawson. Phew, that was close.

"We should be quick," I told him.

"Not sure I'll last long anyway. I'll make it up to you tonight."

Tonight. I held on as Dawson thrust, and when he came inside me, the full implications of what was happening hit me. I'd gotten the man I wanted. The handsome, mercurial, kind, strong Navy SEAL I'd grown to more than like. We weren't just friends anymore. This was uncharted territory, and although I couldn't wait to explore, a tremor of apprehension ran through me. Because anyone could see that Dawson was a man with secrets, and I suspected I hadn't even scratched the surface of his troubled mind.

CHAPTER 37

VIOLET

With no repeat of yesterday's dinner debacle, I ran through the next day's lines with Lucas and then escaped to the pool house. When he commented about my smile, I just said I was relieved the big love scene with Kane was over, and luckily, he bought it. Not that I wanted to keep secrets from Lucas, but this…this *thing* with Dawson was so new, and I wanted to get it straight in my own head before other people found out. After all, what was it? Not just sex, but was Dawson after a long-term relationship or something more casual? And what exactly did I want? So far, I only knew that I wanted him in my bed. I'd barely considered the future.

I was so distracted that I walked clean past the door and had to double back. Dawson, of course, watched me out of the window the whole time, and he was laughing by the time I got inside.

"Thought you were going for a swim," he said.

"It's not funny."

"Would it make you feel better if I told you I almost brushed my teeth with that stuff in the pink tube?"

"My hair removal cream?"

"Fuck. Is that what it was?"

"You can't think straight either?"

He shook his head. "The last thing I was looking for when I came to California was a relationship, but then I met you, and…yeah…" He gave me this funny little smile, part sweet, part shy. "You're bad for me, babe, in all the best ways."

My heart did a funny little jig, tap-dancing against my ribcage. "You want a relationship?"

"Don't you?"

"I think so. I mean, yes. But you know what a disaster my love life's been in the past."

"Well, I'm not gonna leave you stranded in a parking lot, we've already established I don't have a micro-penis, and I'm not gonna cheat on you. That's got to put me ahead, right?"

I quickly pulled the drapes closed, then stepped into his arms. "You're a long way ahead, Mr. Masters. The others are just tiny specks of dust in the distance."

This time when we kissed, it was slow and delicious rather than with the frantic desperation we'd shared earlier. And it really hit me how tall Dawson was. Even on tiptoes, I barely reached his lips, and that was with him bending his neck. At this rate, I'd need a box to stand on.

Or he could just pick me up. That worked too.

Six steps, and we were at the bed. He laid me down almost reverently, then propped his head up on one elbow beside me.

"Sorry for what happened earlier," he said. "I behaved like an animal."

"Well, I'm not sorry. It was exactly what I needed after that scene. Kane ate a cheese salad—the stinky cheese with the mould in it—right before the cameras rolled, and I felt like I was gonna puke most of the time."

"What happened to his paleo diet?"

"I expect it went the same way as Mikki's vegan fad when she ate a smoked-salmon-and-cream-cheese bagel for lunch."

"That pair should start dating. They'd be perfect for each other."

"I'm not sure Mikki could cope with someone who spends longer in the bathroom than she does. Which reminds me—I need a shower."

"Reckon I might join you."

"You mean…shower sex?"

"Why not?"

Why not, indeed? That night, Dawson was back in his Mr. Grand persona—sweet, funny, and a little bit adventurous. He even got me to put the blindfold on again at one point, and I didn't mind because the image of him as he came was already burned onto the inside of my eyelids. And after we'd finished exploring each other's bodies in the early hours of the morning, I curled up in his arms. He dropped off first— hardly surprising considering the amount of effort he'd put in today—and even in sleep, he held me tight. Twenty-five years old, and this was the first night I'd spent in bed with a man, but it was worth the wait. And tonight, I knew I'd made the right decision. Dawson treated me like a princess rather than an accessory, and while I had a feeling life wouldn't be plain sailing with him, we'd weather the storm together.

"What the hell is this?" David yelled the instant I walked into the kitchen in the morning.

Up until then, I'd been on cloud nine, but when I realised his anger was directed at me, I fell back to earth with a bump.

"What the hell is what?" I asked.

He threw a newspaper at me, some tabloid, and I scrambled to catch it. Oh. My. Goodness. It was open to the entertainment pages, and I was the headline.

Is Violet Miller cheating on Kane Sanders?

"I tried to call you," Lucas whispered as I collapsed onto a stool.

"I think my phone's still in my purse." In fact, I was certain of it, and it was also set to silent.

Below the headline, a reporter had gotten hold of a grainy picture of Dawson and me, stumbling home from the bar in Oakwood Falls. My "mystery man," they called him, and even though our journey had been more or less innocent, there was no denying that we looked totally wrapped up in each other. I squinted closer. Oh, crap. I had one hand in Dawson's back pocket, and I might even have been squeezing his ass.

"Nothing happened, I promise," I told David. "I just had a bit too much to drink."

"So you and Dawson didn't spend the night together at your childhood home?"

I scanned farther down the article. Who on earth had told them that? They knew we'd been out to visit Delbert and eaten lunch together at the diner too. Had one of my neighbours sold the story?

"We did, but Dawson slept on the couch."

"Do you realise how much effort Debbie's putting into every aspect of this publicity campaign? We need to keep you and Kane front and centre of every gossip site, not you and some muscle-bound meathead."

"I'm sorry; I'll be more careful."

"And there's nothing going on between the two of you?"

I hesitated. Too long. Long enough for Mikki to put down her fat-free, sugar-free, flavour-free yogurt and mutter, "Nothing? Yeah, right. That's why the pair of them sleep in the pool house every night."

I'd never seen a man explode before, and if the shrapnel wasn't flying in my direction, it would have been quite fascinating. David kind of shrank and turned red, then words and anger and spit flew out of him as he whirled his arms in every direction.

"They've been *what*?" He advanced, reminding me of one of those monsters out of Greek mythology. What was the one with all the heads? The hydra? "Violet, is this true?"

"He was sleeping on the couch. After the message on the mirror, I got scared."

"This is the set of a reality TV show, not a damn hotel. I paid him to give you peace of mind, not screw with my ratings. Which part of 'no guests' didn't you understand?"

Lucas dropped his spoon into his cereal bowl. "Violet isn't the only person who's had friends stay over. Mikki, are those two guys still in your room, or did you kick them out before David got here?"

"I don't know what you're talking about."

"Want me to refresh your memory?" Lucas gave a convincing groan. "'Harder, harder, Rylan. Deeper! Stick that big piece of meat in my mouth, hot stuff.' Did you forget the second dude's name?"

"Shut up! You just like Violet better than me. I bet *you're* screwing her too."

Lucas burst out laughing. "Stop slinging mud, Mikki. It won't stick because you're talking shit again."

Dawson chose that moment to walk in, face back to its usual impassive mask as he straightened his tie, and David turned on him immediately.

"Masters, which part of your contract made you think it was okay to spend the night with Violet?"

He glanced at me, but I didn't know what to say. I had no idea how to get us out of this new mess.

"The part that said I needed to protect my principal from danger. She received threats here."

"A plant through the mail and a message someone

probably wrote as a joke. Hey, maybe it was you? Did you use it as a way to get into her panties?"

"How dare you?" Now I was shouting, but I couldn't help it. "That's not how it was at all."

"Oh, really? Well, let me tell you how it's going to be from now on. Dawson's going to walk out of this door and call the accounts department for his last paycheck, and tonight, you're going to sleep in this house with everybody else."

"Are you crazy?"

"Do I have to remind you who's paying your fee?"

"Who cares? I quit."

"You can't quit. You signed a contract."

"What are you gonna do? Sue me? Because all I have is a shitty Honda and an overdraft."

"You'll never work in Hollywood again."

"At the moment, I don't see how that's a bad thing."

Lucas put a hand on my arm. I tried to push him away, but he held on, gentle yet insistent.

"Easy, Vi. I get that this is difficult, but arguing won't help."

"He can't fire Dawson."

"I can do whatever I damn well want," David yelled, waving his phone. "This article is a disaster."

Kane stepped in, and for once, I was glad of his presence. David didn't respect anybody else.

"Look, buddy. Let's all calm down. We need to get this movie finished, and who cares if Violet's fucking her bodyguard?"

"I care. The two of you are supposed to be going to an awards ceremony this weekend, as a couple. Nothing gets more publicity than a celebrity romance. Would anyone even know who Katie Holmes was if she'd never married Tom Cruise? Meghan Markle without Prince Harry? We need to fix this, and we need to fix it fast."

This time, it was Dawson who spoke.

"I apologise for everything. I'm the problem here, and I'm leaving."

He was what? "Please, no. I can't…"

"You can. Trust me, Violet. Do you trust me?"

As if I even had to think about that. "Yes."

"Then get this movie finished. I'll still be here when you're done."

"You promise?"

"I promise."

I sagged against Lucas as Dawson's soft footsteps disappeared into the hallway. How could today have gone from amazing to awful in less than five minutes? If I ever made another movie, I'd be putting so many extra clauses into my contract, the most important being that my personal life was totally off-limits.

David, meanwhile, was looking rather smug. Asshole.

I pointed a finger at him. "If you think I'm staying in here with that…that…" I glared at Mikki. "No way. I'm sleeping in the pool house, or I'm getting a hotel room."

"I thought you didn't have any money."

"Fine, I'll sleep in my car."

"David…" Kane's voice held a warning. "Compromise on this, okay? Let Violet use the pool house, and Mikki, do us all a favour and stop bringing men home. None of us can sleep, and I'm getting bags under my eyes."

She flicked her hair back and huffed. "You people are *so* boring. This is like being in prison."

"Give me strength," Lucas muttered.

I would have if I'd had any left myself, but after Dawson's departure, I felt like a chewed-up piece of string. Welcome to Hollywood, land of hopes and dreams.

CHAPTER 38
DAWSON

F uck. Dawson's whole day had turned to shit in less time than it took to inflate a RIB and only marginally longer than it took to unload the magazine on his AR-15. He'd known Mikki was trouble from the moment he met her. Always out to create drama, only ever worried about herself.

But he'd screwed up too. He'd given in to temptation and ruined the one woman he'd cared for since Bryony and Hannah died. Third time lucky, the old saying went, but it sure as hell hadn't turned out that way. And worse, he'd left Violet to shoulder the mess while he hightailed it out the door.

He had to fix this.

Somehow, he had to make this right again.

Dawson reached his car and slid behind the wheel, slamming the door behind him. What was that article David had been whining about? The one on his phone? Dawson had only glimpsed it, but he'd recognised the photo of Vi and himself in Oakwood Falls. A quick online search turned up a bunch of hits, all of them speculating about the man she was spending time with behind Kane's back. Dammit, this was her reputation they were trashing.

And tomorrow, if they found out who Dawson was, it would be his name in every gossip column, being dragged through the mud again. Third time lucky? More like unlucky, and this time, he wasn't sure he had the energy to dig himself out of the hole.

Dawson had wanted to tell Vi about his past, but he'd been afraid she wouldn't look at him in the same way. That she'd judge him like everyone else did. But he should have bitten the bullet because now she'd find out anyway, and he wouldn't even be there to set things straight. Tonight. He'd explain everything tonight, and in the meantime, he'd just have to pray that the media didn't put two and two together first.

Ten minutes had passed, and he bet Vi would be either on her own or with Lucas, so he decided to risk a message.

Dawson: Vi, I'm so sorry this happened.

Vi: I hate the movie industry.

Dawson: You okay?

Vi: No. I'm trying to talk myself out of ramming a stiletto heel down Mikki's throat.

A shoe? A steak knife would be more effective.

Dawson: Try not to get arrested. Orange isn't a great colour, and I prefer you in pink.

Vi: It's okay, I'm in the pool house with Lucas.

Dawson: Thought you weren't allowed in there?

Vi: I told David I'd sleep in my car before I'd share a house with Mikki again, and Kane talked him into letting me stay here.

Really? The man might have been a prick, but Dawson had to thank him for that one.

Dawson: Perfect. I'll come and see you later tonight.

Vi: There are reporters everywhere. You can sneak in?

Dawson: I was a SEAL, babe. Sneaking is what we do.

Vi: I can't wait. Should I bring dinner?

Dawson: No, eat first. I might be late if there are people around. You know the drill—get Lucas to walk you down, lock the door, and don't open it to anyone you don't know.

Vi: Got it. What will you do today?

Dawson: Hang out at Brax's place.

Probably he should have faced up to Jeff, but he needed a few hours to work out what to say. His old friend would be beyond pissed that Dawson had slept with a principal and risked the reputation of his business.

Vi: Is Brax back in town?

Dawson: Doubt it. He was still in New York yesterday. Woman trouble.

Vi: :- :-**

Nobody had sent Dawson kissy messages since Bryony, and a lump formed in his throat. He was getting in deep. He felt it in his gut, those little flutters in his chest, the way his pulse sped up when Violet was near. And his dick? Well, that had already been in deep, and it was pretty damn happy with the arrangement.

Dawson: <3

Cheesy, but he didn't care.

The engine started with a satisfying growl, and he peeled out of the parking lot toward Brax's apartment, taking his anger out on the asphalt. Vi would be okay today; he had to believe that. Lucas would keep an eye on her, and there were plenty of people on set. And in the whole time that Dawson had been acting as her bodyguard, he hadn't spotted anything that worried him apart from the obvious—the heart in the plant pot and the writing on the mirror. The heart had turned out to be from a deer, as he'd suspected. He hated to admit that David might be right because if being an asshole were an Olympic sport, the movie director would win gold, but the Venus flytrap had been delivered by USPS and the message could have been left by anyone for anyone. It might well have been a sick joke.

Dawson would still be there with her tonight, but right now, he didn't feel the same fear that had led him to sit outside in a thunderstorm, watching. No, today he'd catch up on sleep because he hadn't gotten much of that lately, see what food Brax had in his freezer, and watch bad TV until the time came to leave again. Who needed a job anyway?

Except it didn't quite work out as he'd planned. Five minutes after he lay on the couch with pizza and a glass of orange juice—because he drew the line at beer before lunchtime—the front door crashed into the wall and footsteps sounded on the tile. Leather-soled shoes by the sound of it.

"Carissa giving you trouble again?" Dawson called.

Brax appeared in the doorway, dressed in a tailored suit as usual.

"Is it that obvious?"

"How big is the crack in the wall?" Dawson held out his plate. "Pizza?"

"No, I need a beer. Or something stronger."

"It's eleven o'clock."

Brax glanced at his watch. "On the East Coast, it's two o'clock, and in my world, everyone drinks at lunch."

He headed for the drinks cabinet in the corner of the great room, home to an expensive collection of Scotch that Dawson had been avoiding since he arrived in San Francisco.

"Because the murky world of finance is stressful?"

"Because we all married high-maintenance women. Apparently, I'm a selfish asshole because I won't close down an entire restaurant on a Saturday night so one of Carissa's friends can hold a baby shower. That's an unreasonable request, right?"

"I'd say so."

"Sometimes, I start questioning myself. She's brainwashed me. Never get involved with a woman, buddy. Just stick with your hand and use the leftover millions to buy a sports car and a yacht."

"That's gonna give me a problem."

"Why? Did you get wrist strain?"

"I have three thousand bucks and a shitty car to my name." At least, he would assuming that David made good on his promise to pay Jeff. Otherwise, Dawson's bank account would be in the red. "And I might've met someone."

Brax paused mid-pour. "But the last time I saw you, you were very much single, and that was only a month ago."

"I know. You introduced us."

Whisky slopped out of the glass as Brax spun around. "Not the actress?"

"Yeah, Violet. Fawn."

Brax started laughing, and Dawson threw a cushion at him. Not that the couch missed it—Carissa had left hundreds of the damn things all over the apartment. The bed in the spare room he was using had fourteen fucking pillows.

"I guess I can see it… She has that sweet, innocent vibe you like so much. And if she visited The Dark, I guess she's adventurous too. A dangerous combination for you. When are you going ring shopping?"

"Shut up. This isn't funny. Have you seen the papers this morning?"

"No, why?" There was no need to answer because Brax already had his phone in his hand. He squinted at the tiny screen, and Dawson saw the moment recognition dawned. "Shit, that's you? She's playing you off against Kane Sanders?"

"Of course she fucking isn't. She doesn't even like him, but the press twists everything. Oh, and the movie director found out about the rumours and fired me."

"So, what? You're gonna sit around here and wallow in pizza and misery?"

"No, I'm gonna pay a visit to the shooting range, then sneak back into the beach house where Vi's staying with the rest of the cast once dinner's over. Maybe fit in some sleep first. What are your plans? Pity party for one?"

"I'll get lunch at the club and then put in a pair of earplugs at three o'clock. That way, when Carissa realises I've skipped our mediation session, she won't burst my eardrums. Take my advice, pal. If you ever get tempted to buy a ring, put your credit card through the waste disposal."

"Duly noted. Want to come to the range with me?"

"Can't. I have a conference call at three thirty."

"Still trying to take over the world?"

"Not the world, just a small mining company. Commodities have been volatile lately, but I believe they'll go up in the long term."

Long term. Two words that scared Dawson. Thinking of a future with Violet and the upheaval that would cause in his life made him nervous, but nothing worried him as much as losing her before they even began.

CHAPTER 39
VIOLET

S
even p.m., and Mikki was rooting through the refrigerator, throwing out anything that contained aspartame and seemingly oblivious to all the damage she'd caused earlier. If you opened up the dictionary on the word "self-absorbed," it would have a picture of Mikki next to it, probably carrying a designer purse and wearing an indecently short skirt.

"What time is Dawson coming back?" Lucas whispered.

"Late. I warned him that David threatened to drop by and check up on us."

"David might be a great director, but if I'd realised what a control freak he was, I'd have passed on this project."

"It wouldn't be so bad if Mikki wasn't here too."

She had a hedgehog of a personality—okay if you stroked it in the right direction, but one wrong move and you'd get spiked. And now she straightened.

"Where's my Protex Seven Skin Serum?"

"Your what?" Lucas asked.

"The very expensive skin serum that I had to import from Venezuela. It's filled with organic rokhaberries, extract of platinum, vergi mushrooms from the rainforest, and triple-strength guarana to reverse the ageing process."

She sounded like a freaking infomercial.

Kane glanced up from his iPad. "That pink bottle with the fruit on the label?"

"Yes, where is it?"

"I thought it was syrup, so I put it on my dessert. Didn't taste that great, though."

Mikki's shriek made my eardrums protest.

"That cost four hundred dollars!"

So about the same as my car.

Kane just shrugged. "I'll buy you a new one."

"There's a six-month waitlist. Don't you know how to read? The label clearly said it was a beauty product."

"It was in the refrigerator."

"You...you... I hate you. Where's the bottle? I'll have to scrape the last bits out."

"In the garbage."

Three seconds later, Mikki upended the trash can all over the floor. Something slimy trickled in my direction, and I pushed the remains of my dinner away, feeling sick. Was it too much to ask for just one evening to pass without drama?

"Want to escape to the pool house?" I whispered to Lucas. "We could share a bottle of wine. Goodness knows, I need it."

"I'll walk you out, but then I need to come back and call a friend."

"Or bring your phone with you? I don't mind."

His cheeks turned red. "Not that kind of friend, sweets."

"Oh." My eyes widened. "Oh!" I grabbed a chilled bottle of white from the pile Mikki had dumped on the counter and hurried after Lucas. "Did you meet someone?"

"Maybe. A guy on the internet, but he doesn't know who I really am."

"Are you going to tell him?"

"I don't know. It's difficult. How can I trust a man to keep my secret if I've never even met them?"

"You're right; that *is* difficult."

We reached the pool house, and I paused to look out at the night. David still hadn't removed the privacy screens, so I couldn't see the beach, but I heard the waves crashing onto the shore, the relentless power of the ocean. Stars shone from a clear sky, and something was in bloom because a hint of fragrance travelled on the breeze. Lilac, perhaps? Under any other circumstances, my surroundings would have been idyllic, but Mikki was right about it being a prison. A beautiful prison, but a prison nonetheless.

At least tonight, I'd have a cellmate.

"See you tomorrow," Lucas said, giving me a quick hug.

"Or come back later if your call doesn't take as long as you think."

"If I crash and burn, you mean?"

"I didn't—"

"Relax, I'm kidding." He gave me a kiss on the cheek. "Don't forget to lock the door."

Once he'd gone, I flopped onto the couch and listened to the near-silence. Only the softened sound of the water through the double glazing gave a hint of the world outside. Thinking about it, this was the first time I'd been alone for weeks. Dawson had been my shadow, and if he wasn't there, I'd been on set with the cast and crew buzzing around, or at the very least, Shonda. Maybe I could watch a movie while I waited for Dawson to sneak in? Or listen to music? Hmm. Or I could simply lie here because moving seemed like a lot of effort right now.

Then my phone pinged, quietly, but it still shattered the peace. An email from Lauren. She always did have a great sense of timing.

The subject line said *Have you seen this?????* Probably not, seeing as Lauren watched the news and read the papers and scrolled constantly through social media, and I didn't. So I opened the message.

Oh, hell.

They knew who Dawson was, and now we were both headlining the biggest gossip website out there.

He's doing more than guarding her body…

Sources say that the man Violet Miller was seen getting cosy with in her hometown of Oakwood Falls is none other than her bodyguard, Dawson Masters. And where have we heard that name before?

Our research reveals that Miller's new beau is the same Dawson Masters suspected of involvement in the Blackstone House murder in Washington, DC, eight years ago. Although landlord Levi Sykes was subsequently jailed for causing the death of Ruby Costello, there are still some who believe the Sykes family's claims that he was the victim of a conspiracy concocted by the other roommates.

If I hadn't been sitting down already, my knees would have given way. Dawson had been suspected of murder? Underneath the opening paragraphs, a photo of a younger Dawson was printed beside another of our drunken pictures from outside the bar, and there was no mistaking the fact that they were the same man. Boy, his hair had been much longer back then. A third photo showed a group of people smiling and laughing. Seven men, one woman. I squinted a little closer. Was that…? Yes, it was Braxton, and Zach Torres was standing next to him. The caption underneath read *Eight of the Blackstone House gang: Dawson Masters, Justin Norquist, Braxton Dupré, Zach Torres, Nolan de Luca, Greyson Meyer, Levi Sykes, and victim Ruby Costello in happier times. Two housemates, Jerry Knight and an unidentified minor, are missing. Was one of them the photographer?*

Underneath the pictures, the website had helpfully included more details of the Blackstone House story, and I felt sick as I read.

What really happened behind the closed doors of Blackstone House one Saturday evening almost a decade ago? Maybe we'll never know, but the story has fascinated many over the years.

Ruby Costello, a twenty-year-old sophomore at Georgetown University, had been living in the shared house in the small town of Blackstone Bluff for over two years before that fateful night. When she didn't appear at breakfast the following day, her housemates assumed she was staying with a friend, but one of them was hiding a terrible secret. Upstairs, Ruby was lying in her locked bedroom, stabbed and strangled, her limbs arranged in a cross and a pentagram carved into her chest. Two days would pass before her body was discovered. Evidence shows that nobody apart from her housemates entered or left the house during that time.

So, who killed her?

Out of the nine people she lived with, only one had a solid alibi. Greyson Meyer, also a student at Georgetown and now running for Congress in the tenth district of Virginia, was on vacation in Florida at the time. According to their statements, Masters and de Luca were playing pool in the basement all evening while Dupré and Torres watched a movie in the living room. The other housemates were in their bedrooms, except for Sykes, who claimed to be in his studio on the third floor, painting. But evidence soon started coming to light that cast doubt on his assertion. DNA evidence proved the two had engaged in sexual intercourse shortly before she died, and at his trial, the others testified that he and Costello had shared a tempestuous relationship, with Sykes being described as moody, unpredictable, and volatile. He also had an interest in the occult.

After just a day of deliberation, Sykes was convicted by a jury of his peers and sentenced to life imprisonment. Despite this, Sykes's mother, Mary, continued to protest her son's innocence until her death a year later, but to no avail. Levi Sykes is currently incarcerated at Redding's Gap, Virginia, with little hope of freedom on the horizon. Many believe he got what he deserved. However, there are some still convinced that the wrong man was convicted, although those voices have grown quieter over the years. With Dawson Masters back in the public eye, will Sykes's defenders once again rally to the cause?

As I read, the last of my happiness leached out through my pores, replaced by dread and no small amount of fear. The idea of Dawson being involved in a murder was ridiculous, right? I mean, he might have killed people when he was a Navy SEAL, but there was a difference between fighting for his country in a war and strangling somebody he lived with. Unless…unless he'd been angry. I thought back to the bar in Oakwood Falls, to the way Dawson's hand had wrapped around Grady Hughes's neck as cold fury radiated from his eyes. How well did I really know Dawson?

Or the others? Braxton and Zach had lived in Blackstone House too, and they'd obviously stuck together over the years. A lifelong friendship formed under challenging circumstances, or an unbreakable pact forged to cover up a murder?

And Dawson would be here soon. Just him and me, alone… What if…? What if…?

Violet! I was doing the very thing I hated—listening to the media and their lies rather than finding out the truth for myself. Yes, I'd only known Dawson for a few weeks, but in that time, I'd never once felt nervous in his presence. Quite the opposite—he made me feel safe, and even though he'd manhandled Grady, Dawson hadn't actually hurt him, plus he'd only been doing his job.

Okay, deep breaths. I needed a plan. First, I'd do a little research on this Blackstone House affair, and then I'd ask Dawson for his side of the story. He wouldn't hurt me. Deep down, I believed that. But before I spoke with him, I'd call Lauren. She'd soon let me know if I was being stupid.

"Hey, it's Lauren. You know what to do."

Darn it. Voicemail. Of course, it was her book group evening—a drinking club with a reading problem, she said—and she always turned her phone onto silent for that. Wine and words, her two favourite things. And I couldn't talk to Lucas because he was busy with his "friend," and hopefully having more fun than me. I started typing out an email to Lauren, but a soft knock at the door made me jump out of my skin, and I almost dropped the phone. Had Dawson arrived already?

No. But a familiar face peered through the glass, and I hurried to let him in.

"What's up? Why are you here? Is there a problem?"

"No problem, well, not a huge one. Dawson has several reporters following him, and it's not safe for him to come here tonight, so he asked me to pick you up."

"Really? He didn't tell me that. Maybe I should call him?"

"Sure, you can try, but he said he was heading into a meeting with his boss at the security company. An urgent matter—that's why he sent me instead. I'm supposed to take you to his friend Braxton's apartment, but if you'd rather stay here, it's fine. I'm sure he'll come tomorrow."

Braxton Vale? Who, it seemed, had once been called Braxton Dupré. Did I want to spend another day waiting? Another twenty-four hours bottling up all my questions about Blackstone House? My head was spinning, and I'd never sleep unless I got some answers.

"Okay, I'll come. But would you do me a favour?"

"What kind of a favour?"

"Could you wait outside Braxton's apartment while I talk to Dawson? I might need to come back here afterward."

"I guess so. You won't be long, will you? Only I haven't had dinner yet."

"I'll be quick, I promise."

I walked toward the door, but he paused. "You might want to wear a hat or something? In case there are reporters lurking on the beach?"

"Oh, good idea."

"Jolly Rancher?" He offered me a package of candy, and I took one.

"Thanks."

A minute later, I'd found the baseball cap that I started toting around after *Rules* took off and a photo of me with hideous hair appeared on a whole bunch of websites. Post-rainstorm frizz wasn't a good look on any girl. How long would it take to get to Braxton's apartment? Thirty minutes? Forty? Walking along the beach reminded me of the day I'd snuck out with Lucas on my way to The Dark to meet Mr. Grand. Both evenings, my insides had tied themselves in knots, but this time the tangle was caused by worry rather than anticipation.

"Which car is yours?" I asked my guide.

He pointed at a green Toyota. "Not as nice as your usual chariot, I'm afraid."

"It's still better than my own car."

"What do you drive?"

"A Honda."

"Those go on forever as long as you service them regularly."

We reached his car, and I patted my pockets. "Wait. I forgot my phone. Can we go back?"

Duh, I must have left it on the nightstand while I was looking for my hat. Mom always said I'd forget my own head if it wasn't screwed on. Trent's mom bought me a calendar for Christmas every year, and I forgot to fill that in too.

"Uh, I'm not sure… We got lucky with the reporters once…"

"It'll only take two minutes, and I didn't see anyone. Just wait here. I'll be quick."

A sting in my thigh startled me, and I looked down to see a syringe sticking out of my leg. What the…? I tried to look up. My neck didn't want to cooperate, but I forced it to move by sheer willpower. The man with me, the one I'd thought was an ally, stared with a strange expression, a mix of excitement and apology as my knees gave way.

"I didn't want to have to do that, Violet, but you left me no choice."

Thoughts scrolled through my mind, jumbled, out of order. Lucas warning me to keep the door locked, the strange gifts I'd received, the message on the mirror… Dawson. He didn't send this man, did he? This was my stalker, a man I thought I knew, and now I couldn't move. The ground came toward me fast, and I scrabbled in the dirt, trying to escape, but he grabbed my leg and pulled me backward. Strong… Stronger than he looked. Dawson… Where was Dawson? A fingernail broke off as I scratched at the ground, trying to leave a message in the only way my fuzzy brain could think of. Dawson… I needed him. Dawson…

CHAPTER 40
DAWSON

"Want me to order dinner?" Brax asked.

Dawson didn't have much of an appetite, but he'd told Vi to go ahead and eat, so he figured he should do the same. Brax would get the club to send food over in a cab the way he usually did.

"Is steak on the menu today?"

Brax picked up the phone. "Two tenderloins, one rare, one medium rare." A pause. "Scalloped potatoes. Thanks, Wendy." He turned back to Dawson. "Forty-five minutes, which gives me enough time to deal with the rest of these damned emails."

What time would things quiet down at the beach house? Dawson wouldn't be surprised if David hung around all evening to check everyone behaved, like some ratings-obsessed chaperone. The man might have been a creative genius, according to the mutterings on set, but he was also fucking nuts.

Normally, Dawson had endless patience. He'd spent enough time on tricky operations that the wait shouldn't have bothered him, but tonight, he felt restless. Antsy. And when he sent a message to Vi and she didn't reply, the niggling feeling that something was wrong only intensified.

"Reckon I might go over to Vi's place now," he said.

"Dinner will be here in five minutes."

"I'm not hungry anymore."

"You're always hungry. Remember how pissed Alexa used to get if you ate any of her goodies?"

"Don't remind me." Dawson glanced at his watch. Half past eight. "I'll take the food with me and eat it later."

"Whatever you want." Brax's phone vibrated, and when he checked the message, Dawson could tell by his scowl it wasn't good news. "Fuck. Have you seen this?"

"Seen what?"

Brax tossed the phone over. "The assholes in the press are raking over the Blackstone case again. You're there, I'm there, Zach's there, and he's gonna throw a fit if this bullshit overshadows his surfing."

Motherfucker. That minor niggle turned into full-on stress. What if Vi saw the article before Dawson had the chance to talk to her? Or worse, what if she'd seen it already? Was that why she hadn't replied to his message?

"I need to get to the beach house right now."

"Did you tell Violet about what happened?"

"What do you think?"

"I think that maybe you should have mentioned it if things are half as serious as you seem to believe they are."

"Thanks for the advice, Dr. Phil."

"Want me to come with you? If we both talk to her…"

"No, I should be the one to explain." It hadn't been this difficult with Bryony. The case was still fresh in people's minds when they met, including hers, and she'd come over to his table drunk to ask for his autograph. His fucking autograph. Instead, he'd driven her home after she collapsed at his feet, and the next day, he'd dropped by after training to deliver a lecture on personal safety and an invitation to dinner. On some levels, the two women were similar, but while Bryony had been sweet and crazy, Vi was sweet and vulnerable. Who knew how she'd take this news? "Might need that Scotch later."

"Good luck."

The phrase left unsaid? *You're gonna need it.*

Dawson moved silently up the beach, keeping to the shadows, pausing every so often to watch and listen and *feel*. But the place was deserted. With a chill in the air, the reporters had given up and gone back to their nice warm offices to file their garbage ready for the morning editions. Good. If they saw Dawson Masters sneaking around, they'd probably accuse him of being the *Hidden Intent* stalker.

The almost eerie stillness continued into the grounds of the beach house. Once Dawson had vaulted over the security fence that bordered the edge of the property, there were no signs of life apart from a glow in Lucas's window. Even the pool house was pitch black, and that sent a shiver down Dawson's spine. Was Violet sitting in there in the dark? Or had she decided not to come?

The door was locked, and he couldn't see her inside. Now what? One thing was for sure—he couldn't stand around by the door. Should he retreat to the foliage or let himself in? He carried a set of lock picks in his wallet for little emergencies like this, and two minutes later, the door swung open on squeaky hinges. Dawson settled onto the couch, uneasy, and messaged Lucas. No reply from him either. Had they gone out for dinner?

Just in case Violet had missed his first text, he typed out a few more words—*Hope you're okay, need to talk*—and pressed send before he could chicken out. Maybe David had come up with— Hold on, what was that? A soft *ping* sounded from the nightstand, and Dawson saw the screen of Vi's phone light up as his message came through. But if that was her phone, where was its owner? She always kept it with her unless she was filming.

Another notification caught Dawson's eye, a message from Lauren this time. *Did you get my email? Call me before Dawson arrives tonight! IMPORTANT!*

Oh, fuck. There was only one reason why Lauren would want to talk to Vi before she saw Dawson, and that was because she'd seen the news. And if Lauren's email said what he thought it did, that could explain why Vi had been upset enough to leave the pool house without her phone. If Lucas was also incommunicado, they were probably together. Part of Dawson wanted to barge into the house and find them, but that would hardly endear him to her, would it? No, he'd have to wait, no matter how excruciating that might be. Even if she didn't intend to sleep in the pool house, she'd come back sooner or later to pick up her phone.

Thirty minutes passed. An hour. Dawson forced himself into the meditative state he'd used in training when he had to stay underwater without air. He slowed his breathing and then his heart rate until his body barely existed anymore, only his mind.

And then he heard footsteps.

Violet?

No, Lucas. Had she sent him because she couldn't face talking to Dawson?

Then Lucas knocked. Odd. Why hadn't Vi given him the key?

"Have you come for her phone?" Dawson asked. A lump of lead had settled in his stomach, leaving him nauseous.

"Her phone? No, I came to see Violet. I didn't think you'd arrive until later."

"But I thought Vi was with you?"

"Mikki was on a rampage in the kitchen, so Violet beat a hasty retreat around…" Lucas checked his watch. "Around an hour and a half ago."

"I've been waiting for just over an hour, and she hasn't been here that whole time. I thought… There's some stuff about me in the news. Something happened a long time ago, and the gossipmongers are dredging it all up again."

"Well, she didn't say anything to me. She's mostly been avoiding the internet lately."

"Then where is she?"

"I don't know. My room's next to hers, and I didn't hear her come into the house."

The two men stared at each other, and Dawson's queasiness turned into full-on vomit-inducing fear. He hadn't felt that in years, not since he'd received the call about Bryony and Hannah. Sure, the Navy was dangerous, mercenary work too, but he'd been able to plan and manage the situations he got into. Now? Now, there were two possibilities. Either Violet had run off for some reason, or she'd gotten into trouble somehow. Neither scenario was within his control, and both sent panic spiralling through him.

"Okay, so what do we know?" Lucas asked. "You mentioned her phone?"

"It's on the nightstand."

"Well, she won't have gone far without it. What about her purse?"

"On the couch."

"Maybe she just needed some air?"

"For an hour and a half?"

Lucas pulled out his own phone and tapped away.

"What are you doing?" Dawson asked.

"Checking Celebgossip.com. They have a reporter camped opposite the front gate, so if Vi went out that way, there'd be pictures online… Hey, this is you. What's Blackstone House?"

"Brax never told you?"

"Told me what?"

"I guess that doesn't surprise me. Afterward, he changed his name and tried to forget the whole thing. But didn't you read the papers back then?"

"I've always tried my very best to avoid them. What the hell happened?"

"When I was nineteen, I moved from Ohio to northern Virginia for a construction job, and I shared this weird old house with nine other people. The guy who owned it won it in a poker game."

"You're kidding? He won a *house*?"

"The place was falling down. We rented rooms for fifty bucks a week, and the deal was that we'd help him to renovate. It was kind of…odd. We started off as strangers, but after we'd spent a year replacing floorboards and fixing holes in the roof and replumbing the whole damn place, we became friends. Or at least, I thought we did. Levi, the landlord, killed Ruby one night while I was playing pool in the basement. Left her in the house for days without saying a word."

"That's sick."

"Tell me about it. Even then, it might have passed without much attention, but Levi's parents tried to blame the murder on the rest of us. Said we'd gotten together to frame their son."

"And what happened to Levi?"

"He's rotting in prison, where he belongs."

Dawson closed his eyes, remembering the moment he'd discovered Ruby's body. Greyson Meyer's room had been next to hers on the third floor, but he'd been away visiting family on the evening of the murder, and nobody else had heard a thing. When Grey arrived home two days later and swore his room smelled funky, they'd all joked about his dirty underwear before Dawson found a ladder and climbed up to peer through Ruby's window. He'd never forget the sight of her naked, bloated remains lying there on the bed. The heat had been turned up high, blasting from the radiator he'd installed in her funny little turret room, and that had sped up the decomposition process, according to the cops. Poor, sweet Ruby.

As far as Dawson was concerned, Levi Sykes deserved every second of his sentence.

"And you're worried that…what? That Violet read the story and thought you were involved somehow?"

"There are still people out there who believe the conspiracy theory. Linus Sykes hired dozens of experts and raked through our pasts. Our childhoods, for fuck's sake. I used to shoot rabbits and squirrels to eat, and he told the world I'd mutilated animals for fun." Dawson shook his head. "If I hadn't learned how to make rabbit stew, me and my sister wouldn't have eaten."

Hell, he missed Hannah. He'd stayed in Ohio until she went to college, then moved away to earn the money to pay for her tuition. She'd been his rock through the court case, her support never wavering, and he'd never even contemplated that she might not be around one day.

"Relax, we'll find Violet. She can't have gone far." Lucas scrolled through the gossip website on his phone. "Nope, there are no pictures here of her leaving. So either she's in the yard somewhere, or she walked along the beach. The back gate unbolts from the inside, right? Was it open?"

"I came over the fence."

"What about her car? Is it still at the studio?"

"As far as I'm aware."

That meant she had to be on foot. Unless of course she'd taken a cab, but her purse was still on the couch. Dawson quickly checked the contents. Yes, she'd left her wallet behind.

"If only there was a way to check what she'd been looking at on her phone," he muttered. "Lauren sent a message saying they needed to talk. Something about me. It flashed up on Violet's notifications."

"You think Lauren saw the stories about Blackstone House and told her?"

"Yeah, I do. I don't suppose you know her PIN?" Why hadn't Dawson paid more attention when she tapped it in?

"Sorry. Want me to call Lauren?"

"You have her number?"

"She sends me memes every day. That girl really needs to get a cat."

"Call her. Please."

Dawson paced the room as Lucas dialled. If they could get an idea of Violet's frame of mind, perhaps they could work out where she'd gone. Or maybe she'd said something to Lauren?

Except Lucas shook his head. Several platitudes later, he promised to keep Lauren updated on the situation and hung up.

"She didn't speak to her?" Dawson asked.

"You're right; Lauren did see the story and sent an email and then a message, but Violet didn't reply."

"So we can't be certain whether she knows about the Blackstone mess?"

"No. Why don't we try guessing her PIN? Then we could see if she read the email or not."

"Because we'd only get ten chances, and then the phone would lock us out permanently."

"What we need is a teenage hacker with some time on their hands," Lucas kidded, but his joke fell flat. There was nothing funny about the problem, and besides, his comment hit too close to home.

Or what had once been home. Blackstone House and the grubby little waif who'd stolen Dawson's laptop from his pickup outside Walmart one freezing winter evening. She'd have gotten away with it too, if it hadn't been for the snow. But her cunning had needed work back then, and he'd followed her footprints all the way to a nearby church, where he found her and his missing computer hiding out in the damn crypt.

"Hey, let go of me!"

He could still hear her cry now, but it had mostly been bluster. She'd trembled in his grip when he grabbed her wrist.

"Sure, as soon as the cops get here."

Ouch. That kid could kick. She'd gotten a boot to his shin before he could pin her to the wall, and even when he'd immobilised her, she still glared at him with a hatred worrying in a child that age. But under the hatred lay fear. He could smell it rolling off her.

"Don't call the cops," she whispered. "Please. They'll send me back."

"Send you back where?"

Silence.

"Why'd you take my laptop?"

"Mine broke."

"So? You can't just go around stealing."

She tried to shrug, but her shoulders barely moved because Dawson had her hands pressed against the brick.

"Yeah, well, I need to eat."

"And how does a laptop help you to do that? Why didn't you take a donut from Walmart?"

The kid rolled her eyes as if he was the stupid one. Boy, did she have an attitude. "Because I use the laptop for work, and then I buy food with the money I earn."

"Work?" He snorted out a laugh. "How old are you? Thirteen? Fourteen?"

"Eighteen."

"Bullshit."

"Okay, fine, sixteen."

He stared at her.

"What, you want me to produce a birth certificate?"

She was a kid. And when Dawson took a few seconds to look around the tiny, dank room they were standing in, he realised that she wasn't just hiding there; she seemed to be living there too. A camping lantern lit the space, revealing the sleeping bag in one corner, a neat pile of folded clothes beside it, and packages of crackers plus half a dozen juice boxes sitting on top of a sarcophagus.

"You're homeless?"

"I've been staying here."

"For how long?"

"Couple of weeks. The pastor's too old to walk down the steps, and nobody else ever checks."

Shit. She was tiny, barely up to his shoulder, and now that she'd stopped struggling, she looked more like a wet kitten than a tiger. The bulky jacket she wore hid her body, but she felt like skin and bone.

"I'm gonna let go. If you run, you'd better believe I'll catch you."

She eyed up the door, and he quickly moved in front of it. Not because he wanted to hurt her, but because he found himself wanting to help her. In some ways, she reminded him of his sister.

"When did you last eat?"

"This morning." A quick glance at the crackers.

"I meant properly. A hot meal."

"Week before last." She folded her arms. "What's it matter to you?"

"There's a soup kitchen on Deighton Avenue."

"That place is full of freaks. I went there once, and some perv felt me up. Then one of the do-gooders tried to call Child Protective Services."

"Maybe you should have let them?"

"Oh, really?" She tugged off her jacket and pulled up one sleeve, revealing a row of faded greenish-yellow bruises.

"Because they never helped last time. Or the time before. Or the time before that."

"I'm sorry."

"Don't be. Just go back to your fancy house and your girlfriend and your dog."

"What makes you think I've got a fancy house and a girlfriend and a dog?"

"Blackstone House? Sounds like one of those McMansions."

A jolt of surprise ran through him. "How do you know where I live?"

"The address was on an envelope in your passenger seat, and the seat was covered in dog hair. You really should lock your truck, by the way."

"Right. And the girlfriend?"

"You looked in the mirror lately? I'm sixteen, not blind."

"Fourteen."

"Whatever."

"Blackstone House isn't a McMansion; it's a Queen Anne-style dump. I'm single, and the dog belongs to my boss. And right now, I'm buying you dinner, so put your jacket back on."

The girl's eyes narrowed. "Why?"

"Because it's cold outside."

"I meant, why are you buying me dinner? Whatever you're looking for, I'm not selling it."

Fuck. Surely she didn't think…? "I don't want anything from you, and definitely not that. But I do want my laptop back."

She gazed at it sitting on the sarcophagus, almost wistfully, it seemed. Why was the computer so important to her?

"Where do you want to go?" he asked. "Taco Bell? Pizza Hut? The diner down the street?"

After a full minute of silence, the prospect of a burger won out. "The diner."

Dawson stepped to the side and waved through the doorway. "After you."

He picked up his laptop and followed. She moved jerkily, checking behind herself every few seconds to see where he was. Twitchy. Not from drugs, he didn't think, just nerves. A strange kid. Smart, but not particularly streetwise yet. And hungry. When they slid into a booth, she ordered two cheeseburgers, fries, onion rings, and a strawberry milkshake.

"So," he started. "What happened to your laptop?"

Silence.

She lined up the salt and pepper shakers, then turned the ketchup bottle around so the logo was at the front. Squared up the menus.

"Hey… I don't even know your name?"

She pulled off her woolly hat and blonde hair fell out, long and greasy. Slim fingers tucked it behind her ears. How long since she'd taken a shower?

"Alexa."

"Your name's Alexa?"

A single nod.

"I'm Dawson. What happened to your laptop, Alexa?"

"I hit someone with it, and the screen broke."

"Why'd you hit someone?"

"Because…" Her bottom lip wobbled. "Because he tried to rape me."

A single tear ran down her cheek, but she didn't wipe it away. No, she just stared out the window at the gloomy parking lot.

Fuck. This girl shouldn't be living on the streets. "You said you used the computer for work?"

"I write code and sell it."

"You?" She looked as if she should be playing with dolls, not computers.

"And you're a bouncer in a nightclub, right? Or a wrestler? Wait, wait, you deal steroids in a gym."

Fourteen and precocious as hell. Okay, perhaps he shouldn't be so judgmental.

"I work construction. Where did you learn to code?"

"School. If I stayed in the computer lab at lunchtime, I didn't have to go outside. But I got expelled for hacking into the principal's records."

"You ever think you shouldn't have done that?"

"She took two thousand dollars the football team raised for charity and spent it on a long weekend in Florida. I reported it to the school board, and *I* was the one who got in trouble because they didn't believe me. She put the money back and said I'd made up the story to get attention."

By the time Alexa finished her meal, including the slice of apple pie and ice cream she ordered when Dawson asked if she was still hungry, he'd learned that she'd been fending for herself since her mom remarried two years ago. She wouldn't talk much about her stepfather, but he suspected the abuse ran deeper than the bruises.

In the daytime, she hung out anywhere she could find an electrical socket and a Wi-Fi signal—at the back of diners, quiet corners of the library, some dude's garage because he didn't lock it and she'd found out his password—and at night, she retreated to the church. Although she made a few bucks from unspecified coding—she told him he wouldn't understand the details anyway—most of it was in cryptocurrency, whatever the hell that was, and she had trouble converting it to cash because she didn't have an address and therefore couldn't get a bank account.

What Dawson should have done was take her to Child Protective Services and explain the situation, but he knew she'd only run away again. Alexa might have been delicate to look at, but now that she'd realised he wouldn't hurt her, her eyes shone with a determination he admired.

So he'd lost his fucking mind and texted Levi Sykes instead.

Dawson: Any chance a friend could stay in that small storage room next to mine until she gets back on her feet?

The nine bedrooms at Blackstone House were all occupied. Dawson had gotten the last one, large but dark since it was in a corner of the basement with only one window high up in the wall. But it was cheap, which meant he could send more money to Hannah at college.

Levi: Forty bucks a week, and he'll have to help out with the renovations.

Dawson: She. Her name's Alexa.

Levi: You'll have to clean out the room yourselves. Mom wants me at home most of this week.

Dawson had put the deal to Alexa, and she'd given him another of those suspicious looks. He got the impression that nobody had done anything nice for her in the past.

"All I need to do is help to fix up the house?"

"And pay forty bucks a week. Can you afford that if I help you to get a bank account?"

A quick nod. "And you won't call CPS?"

"No, but what about your parents?"

"Trust me, they won't even notice I'm gone."

Turned out she was right, and Dawson couldn't decide whether to be sad for her or happy that they left her alone. Alexa seemed content in her own strange way. She helped out by designing the security system and chipped in with whatever else was needed—painting, cleaning, electrical work, that sort of thing—but she spent the rest of the time in her gloomy little room in the basement, quiet as a mouse. Every week, she handed forty dollars to Levi, and those weeks turned into months.

A year on, and Dawson didn't know much more about Alexa Stone than the snippets divulged on that first night in the diner, but he'd noticed several subtle changes in her.

When she first moved in, she'd lived on ramen and potato chips, but as time passed, she started ordering more groceries, always delivered to the house because she rarely went out. Vegetables, fresh fish, organic meat. A bunch of pasta sauces from Italy. Macarons from France. And every time he caught a glimpse of the inside of her room, her collection of electronics seemed to have grown. Four laptops at the last count, plus a bunch of boxes that whirred away with blinking lights. Oh, and she'd convinced Justin to climb onto the roof and install her a satellite dish. A fucking satellite dish.

Dawson never asked what she was doing because, in all honesty, he didn't want to know. Alexa's moral compass had wobbled in her early teens, but he hadn't realised quite how far off course she'd gone until a year after Ruby's death. Fuckin' Alexa. He still shook his head at the memory of what she'd done, incredulous.

One thing was certain—she'd have gotten into Violet's emails in a heartbeat, and then Dawson wouldn't have been left wondering why the hell his woman had locked up the pool house and disappeared into the night without a word to anyone.

Too bad he hadn't spoken to Alexa since the night he'd helped her to escape from her foster home, over seven long years ago.

CHAPTER 41
DAWSON

"We need flashlights," Dawson told Lucas. "I have one in my car."

"We should probably check the house first. What if she snuck back inside and I didn't notice?"

"I guess."

Dawson's gut told him that if Vi was upset, she'd have steered clear of Mikki, but how well did he really know her? Perhaps not well enough.

In the beach house, Violet's bedroom door was closed. Lucas knocked once, but when there was no answer, he barged in anyway and found the room empty. A few clothes hung in the closet, but most of Vi's stuff was in the pool house. It didn't look as if she'd intended to move back in.

"Maybe she's downstairs?" Lucas said, although his tone suggested he didn't believe that for a second.

Why was it so tempting to clutch at straws? "Yeah, we'd better search properly."

The last place they checked was the living room, where Mikki was sitting with green shit all over her face, giving a running commentary as Kane attempted to watch a car show with the cat on his lap. Poor asshole. The cat, not Kane.

"That one doesn't even have a trunk. Where are you supposed to put your— Hey! You're not meant to be here. David banned you."

"Have you seen Violet?"

"She's probably hiding out in your little love nest."

"Kane?" Lucas asked.

"Not since Elphaba here destroyed the kitchen earlier."

"Did you just insult me?" Mikki asked.

"I sincerely hope so."

Seemed as though even Kane was done with the bitch.

"How dare you…?"

Kane ignored her. "Why? What's wrong?"

"We can't find Violet," Dawson told him. "She was meant to be in the pool house, but she left over an hour ago, and she didn't take her purse or her phone."

"And you have no idea why she left?"

"There's some shit about me on the internet. I'm worried she saw it and flipped out."

"What shit?"

But Dawson didn't have to answer because Mikki was already googling. "OMG! You killed a girl? Get the hell away from me!"

"My ex-roommate killed a friend of mine. I wasn't involved other than finding her body."

"That's not what it says on the internet."

"Oh, then it must be true," Lucas snapped. "Shut up, Mikki."

"Stop being so rude. Why does Violet always get to be the centre of attention, anyway?"

"Hello, pot, have you met kettle?"

An argument was precisely what they didn't need. "Does anyone have a spare flashlight?"

Kane and Mikki both shook their heads, but Kane at least offered to help search. Mikki just settled back into her pile of cushions and picked up the remote.

"David's gonna go mental if Violet looks tired in the morning," she said.

True, but Dawson had bigger worries than the director's frame of mind, and trying to search for Vi with one flashlight between the three of them was far from ideal. They needed help.

"Brax?" he said when his friend picked up. "Are you good to drive?"

"Why? Do you need a ride? Can't you take a cab?"

"Vi's gone missing, and I need help finding her."

A moment of silence. "You think she flipped out about Blackstone House?"

Dawson walked outside, out of earshot of Kane and, more importantly, Mikki. "I know a friend sent her an email with some of the details, but I don't know if she saw it." Dawson groaned. "Times like this, I miss Alexa. She'd find that shit out faster than she could eat a fucking Twinkie."

"You want me to ask her to look?"

What?

"You're still in touch with Alexa?"

"Sort of. I mean, I wasn't, but she emailed me out of the blue a few years ago." This time, it was Brax's turn to groan. "Told me my finance director had a gambling problem and he was stealing money from me to pay for it."

"You're kidding? How did she know?"

"When I asked, she just laughed."

"You spoke to her?"

"She called me, and no, I didn't give her my number either. But since she seemed to be good at ferreting out information, I've been paying her to do background checks on potential employees, so I have her email address."

"Why did you never mention this?"

"Because Alexa prefers to stay in the shadows, and I respected that."

"Do you trust her?"

"Alexa? About as far as I can throw her. But so far, she's been right on everything she's sent me."

"Okay, get in contact. We need all the help we can get." Dawson read out Violet's email address. "Lauren sent Vi a message tonight. I want to find out if Vi read it."

Dawson would deal with Alexa's reappearance later. Right now, he didn't have time to process that piece of information, and he still didn't know whether to kiss her or kill her for what she'd done seven years before. Brax had obviously made his decision and formed some sort of alliance, albeit an uneasy one.

"And…done. Anything else?" Brax asked.

"Yeah. Get over here and help us search. Bring flashlights."

Brax arrived half an hour later, having undoubtedly broken all the speed limits, but even with four of them combing the area, there was no sign of Violet. Surely if she heard them calling, if she heard the panic in Dawson's voice, she'd have come out if she were hiding? That left an escape along the beach as the most likely option seeing as the rear gate had been unbolted, but the sand was full of footprints, and there was no way of identifying hers. Nor did they know who'd unlocked the gate. Violet? Or had somebody else jumped the fence as Dawson had done?

Then Dawson's phone rang.

Withheld number.

"Violet?"

"Guess again."

Fuck. "Alexa? How did you get this number?"

"Your girlfriend needs to use a stronger password on her email account."

"You got into it?"

"Would I be calling if I hadn't?"

"Just tell me. Did she read the message about Blackstone House?"

"Yes, and she also started writing a reply. It's in her drafts folder."

Alexa sounded different, but she also sounded the same. Supremely confident, cocky even, while she talked about her favourite subject—computers—but Dawson bet if he changed the subject, she'd clam up the way she always did. But her voice had changed. The harsh New York accent had softened, and the pitch was lower. She was a woman now rather than a girl.

"What did the draft say?" Dawson asked.

"'Lauren, this is crazy. My whole life is crazy. I don't know why Dawson didn't tell me about this, but I'm sure he wouldn't have…'"

"Wouldn't have what?"

"That's it. She stopped mid-sentence."

"Like she got disturbed?"

"Maybe."

But there were no indications of a struggle, and the door had been locked. What had Violet seen?

"Sounds as if she was defending you," Alexa added quietly. "Brax didn't say much in his email. What happened? Obviously I've seen the news. I have alerts pinging all over the place."

"You know who Violet is?"

"Some actress? I don't watch TV unless I absolutely have to."

No changes there. Ruby had always liked the TV on in Blackstone House, Greyson too, and Alexa had bought herself a pair of custom-made earplugs.

"Yeah, she's an actress, and she was staying at a house on the beach. I was supposed to meet her there this evening, but when I arrived, she was missing."

"And you thought she flipped out over Blackstone?"

"I don't want to think of the other possibility."

"That she went out for a walk?"

"She's been receiving threats."

"Oh. Someone took her?"

"There are no signs of a struggle."

"So either they lured her out, or she knew the person."

Trust Alexa to put the thought Dawson didn't want to have into words. Bluntness always had been her forte.

"Fuck. I need to call the cops."

And David. Neither of those conversations would be easy.

"Good luck." Her voice dropped. "Let me know if there's anything else I can do, okay?"

"How do I get ahold of you?"

"Ask Brax for my email address."

Dawson knew he had to call the police, of course he did—Violet was missing—but an hour later, as some dick with a badge interrogated him, he wished there had been a way around it. At least Brax was still out searching.

"So, Mr. Masters, you were the last person to see Ms. Miller?"

"I already told you, I didn't see her. Lucas Collins was the last person to actually see her."

"We only have your word for that, and there are two witnesses who say Mr. Collins didn't leave the big house all night."

"When I got to the pool house, Violet was already gone."

"And yet you waited over an hour to raise the alarm?"

"I thought she was still in the main house."

"Why didn't you simply walk up there and check?"

"Because…" Fuck, why did this conversation get more awkward with each passing minute? "Because me and the director of the movie Violet's in don't see eye to eye, and he banned me from being here."

"I see. So technically, you're trespassing?"

"Violet invited me."

"Do you have any evidence to back that up?"

"She told Lucas I was coming. Look, while you're wasting your time questioning the wrong man, whoever took Violet is getting farther away."

Over five hours had passed already. Five minutes was too long.

"The trouble is, I just don't see any evidence of an abduction here. There's no indication of a struggle, no break-in. Maybe Ms. Miller decided she needed a break? Like… what's her name? Velvet Jones? The LAPD started a statewide manhunt for her, and it turned out she'd gone to 'find herself' in the Appalachian Mountains."

"There's a missing woman. Surely that's evidence in itself?"

"But she's an adult. She hasn't even been gone for twenty-four hours, and according to Mr. Jackson, she threatened to walk out yesterday."

David was furious about Dawson's presence and even angrier about Vi's disappearance. He seemed to take both as a personal insult. Dawson had thought the man was gonna take a swing at him, but then Debbie appeared and dragged him off to discuss the angle he should take on this for the media. Fucking reporters. They knew something was wrong; they just didn't know what yet.

And one thing was clear from talking to the cops: if Dawson kept pushing the kidnapping angle, he was going to find himself a suspect. Still, he had one more try.

"You realise Violet received several concerning messages, right?"

"Almost every famous person in California gets those. None of them threatened abduction, from what I understand?"

No, they were on their own in this, at least for now.

"You know what? Maybe you're right. The last two days have been difficult for everyone. Vi probably just wanted to clear her head."

Finally, the cop smiled. "I'm sure she'll walk right in tomorrow and wonder what all the fuss was about."

End of shift, no doubt.

"Let's hope so."

Five minutes later, the cops had disappeared back to the precinct, leaving only Dawson and the housemates plus David and Debbie. Why was that pair always together? Both wore wedding rings, but they seemed to spend more time with each other than was strictly necessary for work. But, hey, that was none of Dawson's business. What *was* his business was Violet and the need to find her.

Even when David refused to admit there was a problem.

"You just couldn't leave things alone, could you? First, you drove Violet to disappear, and now the reporters outside are asking all kinds of questions. I knew hiring you was a mistake."

"You're the one making the mistake. Something bad has happened to her."

"Bullshit. Even the cops think you're overreacting. All I can say is that she'd better be back by…" He checked his watch. "Hell, it's two o'clock in the morning. She'd better be back by eight because she has scenes to film."

"You're more worried about your shooting schedule than her life?"

"Get out! Just get out! I'm gonna hire proper security, professional guys, and if you set foot on this property again, you'll be the one getting arrested."

What choice did Dawson have but to leave? As he headed for the beach, he'd never wanted to be wrong about something more in his life. Because if David was right, then Violet was okay, and she'd be back once she'd mulled over whatever it was she needed to mull over.

But Dawson's gut didn't agree with the asshole. Instead, it churned with apprehension, the same way as it had in Afghanistan before he lost six of his men on a mission they should never have been sent on. Vi was in trouble.

CHAPTER 42

DAWSON

D awn broke over the small group gathered on the beach—Dawson, Brax, Lucas, and Kane, plus Alexa on the phone. Brax had emailed her right after David left, and boy, did they need the assistance.

"Right, what do we know?" Alexa asked. "Someone needs to fill me in here."

"We know that the cops won't help," Dawson said.

"Doesn't surprise me. Every time they ever got involved in my life, they fucked up. And did you ever hear of the Theresa Saldana case?"

"No. What happened?"

"She was an actress who got stabbed by her stalker. Before he did it, the cops told her that the threats she'd received were just a regular part of being in the entertainment industry. Nothing to worry about."

"That's exactly what a detective said to me last night."

"There's anti-stalker legislation now, but the authorities don't bother to enforce it. Unless there's a body getting cold and their PR's taking a beating, they'll put their resources on other cases. The Velvet Jones thing didn't help, of course. You heard about her dumb antics?"

"Yes."

"Alexa," Brax said. "Shut up. Telling us how useless the cops are isn't constructive."

"Fine. I've read their files, which are remarkably thin, so perhaps you could come up with a better idea?"

"How did you get their files?"

Silence.

Dawson had forgotten how anti-establishment Alexa was, and even if his views had shifted to align with hers over the years, Brax was right. They needed to concentrate on what they could do to find Violet, not what the cops wouldn't do.

"Let's start at the beginning. Violet received two odd gifts before I came on the scene. Lucas? Can you go over that?"

"First, a bunch of roses appeared in her trailer, but they had thorns all over them, and she cut herself. A guy brought them to the front gate, brown hair, average build, but he was never identified. Then somebody mailed a box of chocolates to the studio, and they turned out to be chocolate-covered locusts."

"A delicacy in Mexico. Crunchy," Alexa said.

"You've eaten them?"

"They don't taste as bad as they look. If you ever go to Brazil, Silveiras is worth a visit in October or November. They coat queen ants in chocolate, and those have a subtle mint flavour. You can't beat local produce."

Seemed as though little Alexa had gotten a passport in the time they'd been apart. What else had she been doing?

"You act as if eating bugs is normal," Lucas said.

"In some parts of the world, it is. Are you sure it wasn't just a gift from a genuine fan?"

"There was no note, and the tag said they were truffles."

"Okay, so that's slightly odd. What happened next?"

Dawson took over. "Another bunch of flowers arrived, white lilies this time. Only they were in a vase filled with blood, and they turned pink."

"Getting more sinister."

"And then someone jacked off on the couch in her trailer."

"That was the tipping point, right? When it went from a little hinky to totally fucked up."

"Exactly."

"Nothing from the DNA?"

"Last I heard, it was still stuck in a backlog at the lab."

"I can try to bump it up the line, but if they haven't started analysing the sample yet, it'll take a few days. Is there anything else?"

"A Venus flytrap mailed to the house. The pot had a deer's heart buried in it. Then there was a message on the mirror in the pool house. It said 'Did you miss me?' and showed up when she took a shower."

"Any fingerprints?"

"Whoever wrote it used gloves or a Q-tip. It appeared right after a party, so it could have been left as a joke. Either that or someone knew Violet was staying in the pool house, and she'd been keeping her sleeping arrangements quiet."

"I don't blame her for moving out. I watched ten minutes of the YouTube show, and the other assholes in that house would drive anyone to sleep elsewhere."

Dawson choked back his laugh at Kane's indignant expression. He might have forgotten to mention the man's presence to Alexa.

"Kane Sanders is right here."

"Really? Dude, stop acting so stuck up. Your shit stinks just like everyone else's."

Vintage Alexa. She might have travelled the world, but her filter was still as broken as it had always been. Dawson wasn't sure whether to send her virtual hugs or attempt a half-hearted apology to Kane because at least he seemed to be helping now.

"You've never even met—" Kane started.

Brax held up a hand. "Enough. Both of you. Alexa, Kane's

offering his assistance, and we need every pair of hands we can get. Kane, there's no point in arguing with her because you'll never, ever win."

Luckily, Lucas's ringing phone put an end to the discussion, and they all turned to watch as he stared at the screen with raised eyebrows.

"Who is it?" Dawson asked.

"Lauren." Without further discussion, Lucas answered. "Have you heard from her?"

The answer must have been no because Lucas's hopeful expression quickly faded.

"What do you mean, you're here? Where?" A groan. "Fine. Park your car, and I'll come to find you."

"Lauren's here?" Dawson asked the moment Lucas hung up.

"Apparently, she has a bad feeling about this, so she got in her car and started driving after we spoke last night. She's in the public parking lot by the beach."

"And she still hasn't heard anything from Vi?"

"Not a word."

"Who's Lauren?" Kane asked.

"Violet's friend," Lucas told him. "She was at the beach party."

"The blonde who looked at me like I was something she'd scraped off the bottom of her shoe?"

"After you called her chubby? Yes, that's her."

Kane shifted uncomfortably. "Great."

Dawson barely knew Lauren, but if she'd driven all the way to San Francisco overnight, then she clearly cared about Violet. He only hoped she'd prove to be an asset rather than a liability.

"I'll go and get her," he said. "Maybe while I'm gone, you could come up with some ideas about what to do next."

Because Dawson was floundering. In the Navy, he'd needed to plan on the fly, but he'd never been an investigator.

No, he might have seen the worst of human nature and acted on it, but he hadn't needed to search out those tiny clues that mere mortals missed. That took a special kind of skill he wasn't sure he possessed, but Vi was still depending on him.

The parking lot was deserted at that time in the morning. An old Ford with a flat tyre sat rusting in one corner, and the only other vehicle was a compact Toyota near the entrance. Dawson jogged over and knocked on the window.

"Hey."

Lauren opened the door right away. "Thank goodness. I know it's early, and I was gonna wait until seven o'clock, or six at least, but I've been here for an hour and the woman in that pink house over there keeps peering at me from behind her drapes. She thinks she's being subtle, but I've caught her four times now."

"What woman?"

Lauren pointed at a second-floor window, and sure enough, the drapes twitched.

"See? Some people have nothing better to do with their time. Wait! Where are you going?"

A nosy neighbour with nothing better to do could be exactly what they were looking for. Dawson didn't bother to open the gate, just vaulted the picket fence and ran right to the front door. A bell jangled somewhere deep in the house, and after what seemed like forever, he heard the shuffle-shuffle-shuffle of feet moving across a hard floor.

"Who is it?" The woman's voice was reedy but strong.

"My name's Dawson, ma'am. You were watching me in the parking lot."

"Well, I might have glanced out…"

The door cracked open, held in place by a security chain, and Dawson looked down two feet to the tiniest lady he'd ever seen. She'd teased her white hair up by at least three inches to give herself extra height, but she was fighting a losing battle there.

"Did you happen to glance into the parking lot yesterday evening?"

"Maybe once or twice. It's a free country, you know. I'm not one of those peeping Toms."

"I never thought for a moment that you were. It's just that my girlfriend disappeared last night, and we think she might have walked along the beach. She's been under a lot of stress lately, and I'm a little worried about her."

"What does she look like?"

"Five and a half feet tall with dark brown hair and a suntan."

"I saw a girl with dark hair, but she was wearing a cap, and she was with another man."

"What time?"

"Now, let me see… It was right before my sister phoned, and she always calls at eight thirty."

The time frame fit, and Vi kept a baseball cap in the pool house. Was it still there? Could they have found a witness?

"Where did the pair go?"

"They both climbed into a green car in the far corner of the parking lot, next to that hideous Ford. Someone abandoned it there months ago, and the police won't do a thing. Such an eyesore. Honestly, back in my day, people took pride in their neighbourhoods."

"She just got into the car? Willingly?"

"I don't think she was feeling well. It looked as if she fainted, and then the fella helped her into the passenger seat."

Fainted? Why would Vi have fainted? She'd promised to eat dinner before she went to the pool house, so her blood sugar should have been fine. Unless she'd had help… Could the man have drugged her?

"Did you see the licence number?"

"My sister keeps telling me I should wear my glasses, but the new pair pinches my ears. I have an appointment with the optometrist next week, but I'm not sure if he'll be able to fix them or—"

"That's a no?"

She seemed annoyed at being cut off mid-flow, and Dawson was treated to a thin-lipped glare.

"I apologise for interrupting, but if my girlfriend isn't feeling well, I should get her to a hospital. Can you describe the man who picked her up? He might have been one of her friends."

"He was wearing a cap too. And a black jacket. Or maybe dark blue. Or green."

"How tall was he?"

"Not as tall as you, but I don't suppose many men are."

"Taller than my girlfriend?"

"Just an inch or two."

"Was he fat? Thin?"

"Around average, I'd say."

Dammit, the best lead they had, and it wasn't taking them very far.

"How about the car? You said it was green?"

"Pale green. Something small, like the other girl's driving. Why has she been sitting there all morning? She's not one of those prostitutes, is she? I wasn't sure whether to call the police."

For fuck's sake… On her own? What did the woman think Lauren was doing? Jilling off for cash?

"She's my girl's best friend, and she came to help look for her."

"Then you should tell her not to sit out in a car by herself. There was a murder last year, not five miles away from here. Some poor girl walking her dog alone, and a hoodlum stabbed her right through the heart. It was on every news show for days."

"I'll tell her. Are you sure you don't recall anything else?"

"The car wasn't there for long, but I might have seen it

once or twice before. The fella would get out and go for a walk along the beach. I thought he was visiting a friend. I mean, nobody ever reported a trespasser. My neighbour Binkie's daughter works police dispatch, so I'd have heard."

That bastard. He'd been watching Violet, hadn't he? Probably Dawson too, but Dawson had been so distracted by Vi's sweet curves and sweeter heart that he hadn't been doing his job properly. And now she'd been abducted, and it was partly his fault.

He backed away from the door, trying to work out his next move.

"Thanks for your help."

The lady gave him a half-smile. "I hope your girlfriend feels better soon."

Back in the parking lot, Lauren was waiting by the car.

"What was all that about?" she asked.

"The lady who lives there saw a girl fitting Vi's description being helped into a car at around eight thirty last night."

"Helped?"

"She thought everything appeared normal until Vi fainted next to the car."

"Why would she faint?"

"I'm assuming she was drugged."

Dawson headed toward the white Ford, unsure what he was looking for but struggling to think. Vi had been snatched from right under his nose. If he'd left Brax's place half an hour earlier, maybe even twenty minutes, they could have been curled up together in bed right now. Instead, he didn't even want to think about where she might be. The prospect of a madman holding her captive made him feel sick to his stomach and incandescent with anger at the same time.

"It must have been here," Lauren said, snapping him out of his thoughts.

"What?"

"There are scuff marks. And… What's that? It says 'lollo.' What's lollo?"

No, not lollo. 10/10. The tenth of October. Dawson stared at his wrist, at the tattoo marking it. Vi was telling him the worst had happened in the only way she could.

"Fuck. It means something to me, and it means something to her. It's a call for help."

A tear rolled down Lauren's cheek, and Dawson put an arm around her shoulders.

"Hey, don't cry. We'll get her back."

"I guess I just didn't believe it until now. I thought… I thought she'd run away because I sent her that stupid email about you. You didn't do any of that stuff, right?"

"No, I didn't."

"I'm so sorry."

"Don't blame yourself. Someone was out here, watching her, and if he hadn't acted last night, he'd have tried again soon."

Lauren's knees buckled, and she sank into the dirt that had gathered in the quiet corner before Dawson could catch her. His reactions were slow today. Violet consumed his every thought.

"Yes, but… Ugh, yuck!" Lauren unstuck something from her knee and sniffed it. "What the hell is that?"

Dawson peered closer. "Is it candy?"

"Smells like watermelon."

Where had Dawson seen watermelon candy recently? Somebody had given him a piece, and recently too… He never bought that crap himself. But who? Somebody working on the movie… That kid who never tied his shoes properly… Mikki's assistant… Jimmy? Right, Jimmy. He was always eating candy on set, and he'd offered a piece to Dawson at the beach house after the Venus flytrap incident. And hadn't he been the one to bring in the first plant? Yeah, he had access. What was more, their only witness at the studio had described a brown-haired man leaving Vi's trailer, and guess what colour Jimmy's hair was? Once again, Dawson set off at a run, leaving Lauren stumbling along behind.

"Why do you keep doing this? Haven't you heard of walking?"

He glanced back but didn't slow down. "No time."

Not when Violet's life could depend on solving this mystery.

CHAPTER 43
DAWSON

Dawson skidded to a halt in front of the group assembled on the beach.

"I have an idea who it might be."

"Who?" Lucas asked.

"Mikki's assistant. Jimmy?"

"What? Why would you think that?"

Dawson recapped the clues Violet had left. "Vi hardly knows anyone here in San Francisco, but she must have seen him around often enough at the studio and here at the house. She probably trusted him."

"What, and she suddenly realised in the parking lot that he was the stalker?" Brax asked.

"Something happened there," Lauren told him. "There were scuff marks, as if Vi struggled."

But Lucas was shaking his head. "Jimmy? He's never shown any special interest in Violet, and he seems like a nice guy."

"I'm not certain about that..." Kane put in. "I went to a club with Mikki a few weeks ago, some new place downtown. Jimmy tagged along, and a girl slapped him on the dance floor."

"Why?"

Kane shrugged. "Who knows? I figured alcohol was involved. Plus he takes musical theatre classes—I overheard him telling my assistant that—so the nice-guy thing could be an act."

"From a fight in a club to kidnap? That's a big step. And what was his motive?"

Dawson didn't care about the man's damn motive. He only wanted to get Vi back. How long did a typical kidnapper hold onto their victim? Would there be a ransom demand? Or did the culprit have other plans for Violet? The prospect was enough to turn him murderous.

"We can worry about that later."

"But the motive might be important," Lucas said. "If Jimmy kidnapped Violet for money, that's a very different mindset to a psycho obsessed with a woman he can't have. I mean, if he wants a payoff, he's likely to take better care of her than— You're right. Let's discuss that later."

Dawson took a deep breath and pushed away all those dark thoughts. "Right now, we just need to find Jimmy. Does anyone know more about him? His full name? His address?"

"Kane?" Lucas asked.

"Sorry. But Mikki probably will."

Lauren put both hands on her hips, and her eyes took on a worrying glint. "Then let's ask her."

"She'll be asleep," Kane said. "You can't just walk into her bedroom."

"Watch me."

Lauren marched off along the beach, and Dawson shrugged. "Like the lady said—we'd better watch her."

"David won't be happy."

"David's never happy. Why are you even helping us? I thought the two of you were friends."

"Truthfully? I want this movie to get finished, and if Violet's gone, that means months of work and millions of dollars are wasted. Since David's burying his head in the sand, somebody has to look out for our investment." Kane shook his head. "At this rate, we'll end up with a half-made movie and a thousand clips of Mikki throwing tantrums."

"David's a dick for making you all live in a house together," Dawson said.

"Privately, I agree with you, okay? I've known David for a long time, but after he married his second wife, he changed. He never used to be this demanding. And I don't agree with the way he treated you and Violet either. Who cares what we do when the cameras aren't rolling?"

"Right. Ah fuck, Lauren's almost at the house."

Everyone took off after her, and by the time they caught up, she was rattling the back-door handle.

"It's locked."

"Of course it is," Lucas said. "We're trying to keep the place secure."

"Well? Can you open it?"

"Are you sure this is a good idea?"

"As opposed to what? We all sit around chatting while my best friend gets molested by some freak?" Lauren gulped back a sob. "Or worse."

"Unlock the door," Dawson ordered. "Or I'm going through it."

Lucas did as he was told.

Inside, Lauren sprinted up the stairs and barged straight into Mikki's room. Shit. Remind Dawson never to get on her bad side.

"Wakey-wakey."

She yanked the drapes open as Mikki rolled over in bed, yawning as she peeled off one of those frilly mask things women wore because they couldn't just close their damned eyes.

"Who the hell are you?"

"We need to ask you some questions about your assistant."

"Do you even know what time it is?" She blinked several times and spotted Dawson. "Hey! I already told you that you're not supposed to be here. I'm calling David."

Lauren didn't miss a beat, just batted the phone out of Mikki's hand. "Where does Jimmy live?"

Oh, if looks could kill… Mikki narrowed her eyes to tiny slits. "Why the hell should I care? He turns up, does his stuff, and goes home again. It's not as if I'm gonna visit."

"What's his surname?"

"Uh, Wilson? Wilkins? Williams? Why does it matter? What's all this about?"

"He might have kidnapped Violet."

Mikki burst out laughing, and Dawson shoved his hands into his pockets. Strangling a Hollywood actress wouldn't look good on his résumé.

"Jimmy? A *kidnapper*? Have you been smoking crack? Violet took off for a few days, for crying out loud. She just can't hack showbiz."

Lucas had a try. "We're really worried about her, Mikki. She received threats, after all, and it was Jimmy who delivered the first bunch of flowers."

"Yeah, but he didn't buy them."

"How can you be so sure?"

"Well, I guess he didn't. I mean, I just don't think he'd do a thing like that."

Dawson had come across enough liars in his time to know that Mikki was hiding something, and he suspected he knew what it was.

"But you would, wouldn't you?"

"What are you insinuating, you jumped-up little Boy Scout?"

Near the window, something twinkled in the early-morning sun, and it caught Lauren's eye too. She snatched up a pair of fancy crystal shoes and kicked open the door to Mikki's balcony.

"Talk!" she shouted. "Or these Louboutins are going in the swimming pool."

Mikki's gasp said the shoes were important. "You wouldn't dare. Those are limited edition."

"Watch me."

Lauren wound an arm back, and Mikki screamed. Fuck, the woman had a pair of lungs on her.

"Okay, okay. I sent the damn flowers. Put the shoes down!"

"And the chocolates?"

"It was a joke, okay?"

"The lilies in the blood?" Lauren asked. "That was supposed to be funny?"

"Those weren't me, just the roses and the candy. Whoever sent that dead thing in the plant was sick."

"And sending Violet dead things in chocolate wasn't sick?"

"I didn't think she'd be stupid enough to eat one."

"Why? Why did you do it?"

"She's such a goody-two-shoes, always so prim and perfect. Someone needed to teach her to loosen up."

"You're nuts."

"No, I just know what gets good ratings. Violet doesn't have a clue. She swanned in from Kansas and expected Hollywood to fall at her feet."

"That's not what she did at all."

"Really? She made one low-budget movie, and suddenly she has a casting with Racino. Some of us actually worked to get where we are."

"Violet worked. At least sixty hours a week, every freaking week."

"What, in a fast-food restaurant?"

"A bar. It was exhausting."

"Yeah, yeah. Save your whining for somebody who cares." Mikki held out her hands. "The shoes? You said you'd give them back."

"No, I said I wouldn't throw them into the swimming pool." Lauren marched into Mikki's en-suite, and Dawson heard the toilet flush. "There. You can have them back now."

"You bitch!"

Mikki's wails echoed behind them as they walked down the stairs, but Dawson struggled to give a shit. Mikki deserved everything she got for the way she'd treated Violet.

But her revelation about the roses threw Jimmy's involvement into doubt. Dawson didn't want to rule the man out completely, but with only a half-sucked candy to connect him to the abduction, the link was tenuous.

"What now?" Lucas asked once they'd reconvened in the kitchen. "Does anyone want coffee? What? Why are you all staring? I don't function well without caffeine."

Dawson pushed back the waves of tiredness, something he'd learned to do during his Navy years, but Lauren yawned.

"I suppose I could do with a cup."

"Lucas and I should go to the studio," Kane said. "We both have scenes to film, and David'll go insane if his production schedule gets even further behind."

The movie? Kane was worried about the damn movie? "I don't give a fuck about David's schedule."

"We can ask around while we're there. And think logically —if Jimmy *is* involved, then I bet he won't have shown up for work today, so if he's there, that most likely rules him out."

Dawson hated to admit it, but Kane had a point. And it wasn't as if he could ask the questions himself since David had declared him persona non grata. If Dawson set foot on the set, he'd be escorted off the property before he could blink.

The coffee machine hissed as Lucas coaxed an expresso

out of it. "Going to the studio isn't a terrible idea. If Kane and I distract David, he won't get in the way while the rest of you poke around here."

"Okay, go to the studio. Alexa? You still there?"

"Where else would I be? What else could I possibly have to do on this fine evening?"

"Evening? Where are you?"

"Somewhere far, far away, frantically having an associate shuffle my schedule around so I can dig your ass out of a hole."

She had associates? The old Alexa had been very much a lone wolf. New Alexa surprised him with every tiny revelation, and what she didn't say only intrigued Dawson more. Some things hadn't changed, though. She was lying. There was nothing frantic about her tone of voice.

"Could you dig into Jimmy too, just in case?"

"Get me a surname, and I'll take a look."

"Tell me you have news," Dawson said when Lucas called almost five hours later. "You took your time."

Dawson had worn a track in the carpet in Brax's great room by then, and Lauren had burst into tears twice, poured three glasses of wine, drunk one, and tipped two down the sink. Luckily, Brax had been on hand with tissues, although he was looking stressed himself because he'd ignored at least eight calls from Carissa.

They'd also spoken to half of the neighbours around the beach house—nobody had seen anything useful, and the others weren't home. They'd have to try again later.

"Guess who called in sick today?" Lucas sounded kind of excited. Did Dawson dare to hope for a lead?

"Jimmy?"

"No, Elton."

"The rent-a-cop who sits outside Vi's trailer?"

"Yup. And when we asked Jimmy, he said Elton gave him the bag of Jolly Ranchers he was eating the other week."

Holy fuck. Dawson ran through each of Violet's episodes in his head, and it fit. It all fit. With the first two gifts from Mikki discounted—those had arrived before Elton came on the scene—the man would have had the opportunity to leave the other surprises.

"He could have put the lilies in the trailer himself."

"And he was the only person who claimed to have seen someone walking away after the jacking-off incident."

"He knew the address of the beach house to mail the plant."

"And he was at the party the night our man left the message on the mirror."

Shit. He'd been right under their noses the whole time. Vi trusted him—after all, he'd been employed to help ensure her safety—so she'd probably have gone with him last night if he'd spun her a good enough story.

"Tell me you have more information on him."

"What do you think we've been doing all day?" Lucas asked. "The dragon who runs the studio's HR department refused to give us any information, so we had to wait for her to go out to lunch. I fluffed my lines over and over to buy Kane enough time to sweet-talk her assistant. Anyhow, Elton's full name is Elton Smith."

"Did you get anything else?"

"Oh, please. Give us a little credit."

"Spit it out. I'm really fucking worried about Vi, and with every minute that passes…" Dawson couldn't finish the sentence.

"We're all worried, okay? We have his résumé, copies of his timesheets, his social security number, and the mugshot they took for his security pass. I don't honestly want to know what Kane had to do for that lot, but he was smiling when he came out."

"Can you send the stuff over?"

"Kane's scanning it with his iPad as we speak."

The address. That was all Dawson wanted. Just the address, and then he was going to get Violet. In between wearing holes in Brax's floor, he'd stripped down both of his pistols half a dozen times each, cleaned them, and reassembled them. He could do it blindfolded. Literally. Back when he was in the SEALs, that had been one of the tricks he used to keep himself calm on operations, sitting in whatever hovel they'd called home at the time with a scarf tied around his face so he didn't get tempted to look.

Brax had his laptop ready and waiting, and it only took seconds to type the zip code into the search engine. Where was she? Where had that bastard taken her?

"What the…?"

Brax switched to image mode and peered closer. "It's an empty lot. I'll try his phone number." A moment passed while Brax dialled. "It's disconnected."

Dawson scanned down the remainder of the page. Date of birth, personal statement—Elton Smith was enthusiastic, dedicated, and totally focused on his goals. All the qualities a proficient stalker needed. In the past five years, he'd held three positions—two at shopping malls and one working the night shift in an office building. According to a brief biography at the bottom, he enjoyed DIY and spending time with his family.

"What about his reference?" Dawson asked. "Michael Gamboli, office manager at CGR Systems."

"I'll try it… No, that's out of service too."

"Why would he fake his entire résumé?"

Brax slumped forward on the couch, elbows resting on his knees.

"Isn't it obvious? Elton Smith didn't meet Violet and then fixate on her. He planned this all along."

"Alexa? I need help."

With every second that passed meaning a possible death sentence for Violet, Dawson turned to the only other person who could provide assistance. He'd considered calling the cops again, but after the way they'd dismissed his concerns last night, how likely was it that they'd suddenly change their minds? And even if they did believe him, they had procedures to follow and hoops to jump through, which meant even more delays.

"Finally. He admits it," Alexa said. She'd called him thirty seconds after he emailed.

"Dial back the snark for five minutes, would you? We found out who took Vi, but he's disappeared."

"Who was it?"

"After the first couple of malicious gifts, the studio employed a security guard to sit outside her trailer, and we think it was him." Dawson gave her a quick recap of their reasoning. "But the home address he gave to the studio doesn't exist."

"Okay, send over everything you found."

"On its way. We have a headshot, and he's about five feet ten with an average build."

"Accent?"

"There's a hint of a twang, but I'd say he hasn't lived in the South for a while. Any chance you can find out if he drives a light-green compact?"

"Leave it with me. Nobody can disappear completely, and unless he's living in the dark ages, he's left an electronic footprint."

"Thanks, Lex. And I know I should have said it before, but I'm glad we're back in touch."

A moment of silence before, "Yeah, me too."

Alexa hung up, and Dawson was glad she sounded confident because he sure didn't feel it. No, at that moment, he felt something that had been blessedly absent since those dark days when Bryony and Hannah died. Helplessness. The horrible knowledge that events were out of his control and in the hands of fate.

CHAPTER 44
VIOLET

I once spent four hours outside in the snow on Delbert's ranch back in Oakwood Falls, caring for a sick mare that had suffered a nasty coming together with a fence. By the time the veterinarian arrived and stitched up the wound so we could move her to a stall inside, my fingers were blue and I couldn't feel my feet. Until now, I'd never known such never-ending cold.

How long had I been in this freezing basement? Years, it seemed like, but since Elton had taken my watch along with every other scrap of clothing I'd been wearing, I truly had no idea. I didn't even know whether I was still in California. All I knew was that I'd woken up here in the pitch black with a chain padlocked around my waist, and when I'd followed it, hand over hand, I'd found it was shackled to a metal ring that had been attached to the brick wall. The shackle…it was lumpy. Someone had welded it closed.

Damp seeped into my prison, and when I tried to stand straight, my head hit wooden floorboards overhead. I couldn't even jump up and down or jog on the spot to keep warm. When I stayed still, all I could hear was the *drip, drip, drip* of distant water and the occasional creak from the building above—no traffic, no voices, no other signs of civilisation.

My prison was spacious, at least. Ten steps by twenty when I paced as far as the chain would let me reach, but the room was empty apart from a bucket in one corner. At first, I'd wondered why Elton had left it there, but as the fuzziness in my head cleared and my bladder grew heavier, I realised. And yes, I'd been forced to use it. Now the smell of urine permeated the musty air, and my mouth was dry and gummy because that assclown hadn't left me any water.

I'd explored my prison over the last hour or two, running my fingertips over the walls, the floor, the ceiling, but apart from a rusty nail in one of the beams that I couldn't free with my bare hands, there was nothing useful. The wooden stairs in one corner were rough and steep, and I could only reach the first two with my outstretched hand before the chain stopped me.

The dark started to mess with my head. It felt like a tangible thing, a shroud enveloping me to the point of suffocation. And the silence. The silence drove me mad. I'd just begun to think that there was nothing worse than frigid isolation when I realised that, in fact, there was.

Footsteps sounded on the floor above.

Clump. Clump. Clump.

Something metallic rattled at the top of the stairs, and I shrank back and tried to cover myself with my hands when a beam of light hit me in the face.

"There she is."

Elton's voice was different, almost singsong, tinged around the edges with insanity.

"Let me go!"

"You know I can't do that."

"I swear I won't tell anyone. I'll just go home and keep quiet, I promise. I *promise*."

My captor came closer, and I squinted into the light.

338

"It's taken me weeks to plan this. Honestly, I wasn't quite ready, but when I realised how close you were getting to that…that criminal… Somebody needed to save you, and fast. I risked everything for you, Violet. Even coming to fetch you in daylight with those reporters around. Boy, they're not as observant as they think they are."

"What are you talking about? What criminal?"

"Your so-called bodyguard."

"Dawson isn't a criminal."

"He was involved in a girl's death, Violet. I read the reports on the internet while I was at work yesterday."

"Another man was convicted for that. He's in prison."

"And yet there were gaps in the evidence. Legal loopholes. Did you realise that your boyfriend's knife was used to carve a pentagram into the dead girl's chest?"

"*What*?" I gasped. The newspaper article had never mentioned the weapon, but even if Elton's claim was true, there had to be a rational explanation. Right? "You're lying about Dawson."

"They found the knife in his room, covered in her blood, but it got suppressed due to a problem with the search warrant."

"No. He wouldn't have done it."

Of that much, I was certain. Yes, he'd been trained to kill, but there was no way Dawson would have murdered an innocent woman.

Elton snorted a laugh. "Check out Slide49.com. It reports all the things the deep state doesn't want you to hear. Ninety-nine percent of Americans have been brainwashed by the mainstream media, did you know that? They peddle their fake news every hour of every day because nobody wants to hear the truth. You think the police are on your side? They're agents of tyranny, and don't even get me started on the military. As for the so-called entertainment industry, it's nothing but a distraction. A ploy to keep the sheep quiet. But

I'm here to help you, Violet. Once the heat dies down, we can build ourselves a quiet little homestead to ride out the storm. The world's a dangerous place."

Sitting naked and chained in a basement, I could see his point on that last part.

"Okay, sure. I'll check out Slide49. Just bring me a phone, and I'll do it right now."

"*Tsk-tsk-tsk*. Do you think I'm stupid?"

"I think you're deranged."

The words just slipped out. Elton's eyes were two dark shadows, but I saw them narrow.

"No, Violet, I merely have foresight. If I hadn't rescued you, you'd have gotten sucked into the Hollywood nightmare and ended up like all the other freaks. Kane, Lucas… Those men are so rude. And do you really want to turn into Mikki?"

"Well, no, but—"

"And I've heard those stories about the casting couch. How many men did you have to fuck to get your part in *Hidden Intent*?"

"None! How dare you?"

"Really? I heard that David Jackson has paid three different actresses to keep quiet about the things he's done."

"*You're* the one who's locked me in a freaking cellar!" I was shouting now, and more than a little hysteria had crept in. "If you're so damn concerned about my well-being, then let me out."

"You don't understand, do you? It's fate, Violet. We're meant to be together. You need guidance, and I was asked to come and take care of you."

"Asked by who?"

"That doesn't matter."

"And how do you expect to take care of me? I'm chained to a damn wall."

He gave a heavy sigh. "I'd hoped for slightly less hostility."

Elton was insane. There was no other explanation for it. I rolled my eyes, then blinked as he shined the flashlight in them.

"See?" he said. "There's that unfortunate attitude again. I can see we'll need to take things slowly, so here's how it's going to work. I'll set you tasks, and for each one that you complete to my satisfaction, you'll earn privileges. Eventually, once you've gotten used to the rules, we can have a normal relationship."

A relationship? Did he mean…? Oh, hell. I caught the glimmer of a predatory smile in the dim light. The guy was sick. Out of his mind.

"What about your family? Your wife? Your little girl?"

"Oh, Violet…" He shook his head. "You're not the only one who can act."

"You made it all up?"

He gave the faintest chuckle, and the sound hit me like a hail of bullets. "Let's start, why don't we? At the top of the stairs, I have a bottle of water and a sandwich. If you want them, you'll need to drop your hands to your sides. There's no point in hiding yourself. We're going to be together for a long time, you and me."

"I'm freezing. I need clothes and a blanket. And a light."

He *tsk-tsk-tsk*ed at me again. "That all needs to be earned, Violet." His voice hardened. "Drop your hands."

"Go to hell."

Although Satan would probably turn him back at the gates. Nobody liked competition.

"As you wish. I'll be back later."

He headed for the steps, muttering, "Patience, Elmer. You knew this would take time."

Elmer? Elton wasn't even his real name? Once he'd gone, I slumped against the wall, shaking from cold and fear. How would the cops find me? They must know I was missing by now, surely? I'd left that message for Dawson, plus the half-sucked sweet so they could check for my DNA. Oh, hell, what if it had rained? I desperately tried to recall the weather forecast. Sunny with a chance of showers, I was almost sure of it. What if my clues had been washed away? Or worse, what if everyone thought I'd left on purpose after my comments to David? After all, hadn't Velvet Jones done a moonlight flit and wasted hours of police time only to turn up safe and well in a whole other state?

I was screwed, wasn't I?

Metaphorically and physically too, if Elton-slash-Elmer's comments meant what I thought they did.

A tear ran down my cheek, and I wiped it away, then pinched my eyes shut. I couldn't afford to waste a single drop of water, not when I had to earn food like a performing seal.

If I ever got out of this mess, I was never leaving Dawson's side again, not for a second. He couldn't have been involved in that girl's death, could he? Not the kind man who'd taken care of me, who'd curled up with his arms around me at night so I was safe even in sleep.

Not Dawson. Not Mr. Grand.

Not the man I'd fallen in crazy, hopeless love with.

CHAPTER 45
DAWSON

"Go to the webinar app on your laptop," Alexa told Brax, her voice crystal clear despite her being on the other side of the world. "That way, we can show each other documents."

"I don't have a webinar app."

"Yes, you do. I installed it earlier when you were in the shower. Then I patched your software to stop anyone else from hacking into your webcam. You still have that stupid tattoo? I thought you'd have gotten it removed by now."

Brax's only tattoo was on his ass cheek, Dawson knew that much, the result of a drunken night out with Jerry Knight during their Blackstone House days. The Chinese symbol was meant to say "strong," but later, Brax had found out that it actually said "asshole." He blamed the error on Jerry, and Jerry blamed it on the tattoo artist.

"You were spying on me? You little snake."

"Isn't that my line? I'm not so little now, Brax, and I *have* seen a man's ass before."

Fuckin' Alexa. "Can we keep this on track?"

"Sure. The webinar program?"

Lucas, Kane, and Lauren had joined them in Brax's

apartment to talk strategy. Not that they had much of a plan. While Lucas and Kane were finishing up at the studio, Dawson had gone to check out the empty lot where Elton claimed to live, just in case, and Brax had canvassed the rest of the neighbours around the beach house with Lauren. The lot was indeed empty, save for a broken shopping cart and a bunch of weeds, and nobody in the local area had seen anything.

That meant Dawson was pinning his hopes on a hacker with an ethics problem who was barely old enough to drink. In other words, they were fucked.

"Did you find Elton Smith?" he asked her.

The webinar program opened, and Dawson saw a box for a video feed. He leaned forward, curious to get his first look at Alexa in seven years, but instead of a live feed, an avatar of a fedora popped up, grey with a black-and-white striped band.

"What's with the picture?" he asked.

"White hat, black hat, grey hat. Sometimes I have an identity crisis, and I'm not the only one. Did you know that Elton Smith doesn't exist? Well, he did, but he died six years ago. Lung cancer, according to his obituary, and his wife and two children miss him terribly."

"He stole someone's identity?"

"It's not as if the other dude still needed it."

Alexa flashed a picture on the screen, and that guy definitely wasn't the Elton they knew. Not only was he Black, but he was also in a wheelchair with an oxygen cylinder strapped to the side.

"Shit. So we've got nothing?"

Dawson would have to go to the cops again, even if it meant getting questioned himself. And he had no alibi, which combined with his dubious history, meant he'd get the third degree. Still, if it gave them the slightest chance of finding Violet…

"I didn't say that. We have two phone numbers."

"But they're both disconnected."

"So? They still have a history."

"You found something?"

"Maybe. Here's where it gets interesting. Both phones were burners, and neither is registered. The one Elton claimed as his was bought at a mall in San Francisco, but the number he gave for his referee came from Oakwood Ridge, which is in—"

"Kansas," Dawson said. "Right next to Oakwood Falls."

"Are you a geography expert now?"

"Vi lives in Oakwood Falls. Someone from her hometown was involved?"

"Either that or we're dealing with a bloody great coincidence. Only one call ever came in to that number, from the HR office at the studio, and when it was answered, the phone was located near the cell tower in downtown Oakwood Falls."

"Can you narrow it further?"

"No further than that, I'm afraid. But a second call was made from the phone twenty minutes later. Somebody called an Italian restaurant named Oregano right before lunch. Maybe they got hungry?"

"I've been there."

"To the restaurant?"

"Yeah. Vi ate lunch at the place with some dick she knew growing up." And the bad news was, it had been busy. Bookings only for lunch and dinner. Half of the town probably ate there. "Can you get the date and time? We could ask if they keep records."

"Already tried that. Long story short, I know someone who knows someone who knows someone who's in the FBI, but the restaurant owner told the agent who visited that he needed a warrant. Faking those isn't so easy."

Dawson shook his head in disbelief. He'd spent years

working for Uncle Sam, complete with security clearances, and Alexa still had better contacts than he did. She was also correct—warrants weren't easy to get ahold of.

He thought back to his visit to the restaurant, to the barman-slash-maître d' he'd spent an hour chatting with and the old-fashioned paper ledger the man had used to meticulously allocate tables. If Dawson could get a look at that book, he might be able to obtain a list of the people who'd eaten there on the day in question. Of course, their suspect could have been booking ahead or phoning about something else entirely, but with no other leads, it was a chance they'd have to take.

"I might know a way around it, but I need to get to Kansas."

Brax already had his phone out. "Fastest flight to Wichita is… Shit. Six hours with a stop in Dallas."

Plus the trip to the airport, the wait for boarding, and the journey at the other end. In that time, Violet would most likely be going through hell.

"Does anyone know a pilot? Or could we charter a plane? I don't have the cash up front, but I could pay someone back in instalments."

Over, say, a decade or two.

"I might be able to borrow a Learjet," Brax said. "Could anyone get tickets to something as a sweetener? A movie premiere or a concert?"

Lucas and Kane both raised their hands.

"How fast can the plane get here?" Dawson asked.

"I'll check. The guy who owns it lives in New York. Otherwise, I'll call the charter companies and see what they can do."

"We need a backup plan," Lucas said. "Should I book the commercial flight anyway?"

"This lady means a lot to you, Dawson?" Alexa asked, her voice softer than usual.

Was that a rare show of empathy?

"Yeah, she does. She means everything."

"Okay." Alexa hesitated in the way she always used to when she needed to consider her next move. She might have been brash and snarky, but she was also incredibly smart. And kind, in her own strange way. "I have favours owing. Let me make a call."

An hour later, Dawson was ushered across Travis Air Force Base in the back of a military jeep, all the way to the tarmac. His escort pulled smoothly to a halt next to a drab green building and saluted.

"We're here, sir."

Dawson saluted back out of habit. Alexa had been worryingly vague on the details, just told Dawson to get his ass to the front gate and give his name. That had worked surprisingly well, leading to a much bigger question: who exactly was Alexa? And what the hell had she been doing for the past seven years?

But there was no time to search for those answers right now. A blonde dressed in a flight suit strode toward him, her back straight and confident. Before he met Vi, Dawson would have rated the newcomer as stunning, but since he'd lost his heart to a certain actress, all other women had faded to mediocre.

The blonde held out a hand. "Storm."

Storm… Storm…

"Not *the* Storm?"

"Whatever you've heard about me, it isn't true."

Rumours of the female fighter pilot had been circulating for years. How she'd flown a helicopter through a hail of gunfire to rescue a Delta Force team and three hostages who were pinned down by militants. The dogfight she'd engaged in over Libya that resulted in the destruction of four enemy jets. How she could fly anything with wings or rotors and had once stolen a MiG from an Israeli Air Force base just to prove it could be done.

"I'm not so sure about that. Dawson Masters." He shook hands with the lady.

"I know who you are. Congratulations on punching out Senator Presley."

A groan slipped from Dawson's mouth before he could stop it. Presley had deserved his broken nose, but six of Dawson's friends had died because of that asshole, and the aftermath had hardly been Dawson's finest hour.

"I got kicked out of the Navy for that."

"Sucked. We were all rooting for you." She waved toward a fast jet sitting on the tarmac. "We're going to Wichita, right?"

"Right. But why are *you* taking me? Won't the powers-that-be get pissed? You know, abuse of government funds, yada yada yada?"

Not to mention the fact that Dawson was no longer welcome in the hallowed halls he'd once called home.

"Don't worry about the little things. Just understand that I'm not here, this plane doesn't exist, and this flight never happened."

Okay, he could live with that. "How do you know Alexa?"

"Alexa? Who's Alexa?"

Storm wasn't kidding. Her tone said she genuinely didn't know. And at that moment, Dawson realised he didn't know Alexa either, not even a little bit.

"Never mind."

Once a Navy man, always a Navy man, and Louie the bartender had served three years as a sailor before he got married and moved back to Oakwood Falls. One pizza and two soft drinks later, they'd reminisced over the good old days on the water, and Dawson had spun a story about visiting Oregano with Vi on the date the phone call was made. They'd talked to a guy at the next table, Dawson said, a retired engineer, and it was really bugging him that he'd promised to look the guy up on social media, and now he couldn't remember the name. Jack? Joe? James? He should have written it down. Was there any chance he could take a look at the seating allocations in case it jogged his memory?

No problem.

Ten minutes and a hefty tip later, Dawson strode outside with two weeks' worth of bookings safely photographed and stored in his phone, but where to next?

"Did you get it?" Storm asked, now dressed in civvies. Jeans, a T-shirt, and a pair of aviators.

He'd assumed she'd fly right back to California, but she'd surprised him by picking up the keys to a borrowed Ford and driving him to Oakwood Falls. A favour for a friend of a friend, she said. Officially, she was on leave, and they had two days to find the person who'd provided Elton's reference.

But at this moment, they only had names, not addresses, and Dawson didn't know the town at all. Should he try Violet's mom? The last thing he wanted to do was alarm her, but he needed help.

"Hey, I recognise you. Where's Violet?" a voice asked from behind him.

Great. Dawson hadn't warmed to Trent on his last visit, mainly because it was clear that the man wanted to get into Violet's panties, and the last thing he felt like doing was making small talk with the enemy.

"She's in San Francisco."

"Then why are you here? And who's this lovely lady?"

Storm's bland expression said she didn't find Trent as charming as Vi did, but she put on a vague smile and stuck out her hand.

"I'm Storm."

"Storm? An interesting name. And what brings you to our little town?"

Dawson and Storm looked at each other. They hadn't talked much on the flight due to the noise, and in the car, they'd decided to concentrate on getting the list first, then wing the rest. Should he tell Trent about Violet's disappearance? Much as Dawson disliked the man, he was a close friend of hers. Perhaps they could turn that to their advantage?

"Violet's gone missing. We're worried something's happened to her."

"Missing?" Trent paled a shade. "What do you mean, missing?"

Dawson gave a quick precis of her disappearance from the pool house, and by the end of it, Trent looked like Dawson felt. Scared.

"You really think this security guard took her? This Elton?"

"Yeah, and the motherfucker's a ghost. Our only connection is a phone call made by his possible accomplice over a month ago."

"To Oregano?"

"That's right. We need to work out who in this town would have provided Elton with a false reference and why." Dawson pulled the fake Elton Smith's mugshot up on his phone. "Do you recognise this man?"

Trent peered at the photo, eyes narrowed. "No, I don't. And apart from a few years spent in New York, I've lived around here my whole life."

"Well, somebody knows him. Can you help us to go

through the restaurant bookings for the week and eliminate anyone unlikely from the list?"

"Anyone unlikely? Based on what?"

A good question. They really hadn't thought far enough ahead. "At this moment, I'm not sure."

"I'll do anything to help Violet, of course. Why don't we go to my office and think this through? I can at least tell you a little more about each person whose name I recognise."

When Dawson glanced sideways at Storm, she shrugged. Well, it wasn't as if either of them had a better idea.

CHAPTER 46
VIOLET

I gulped down the entire bottle of water, almost without stopping. I'd had to give in, even though revealing myself to Elton made me want to vomit. Probably I would have if my stomach hadn't been empty.

His beady eyes perused my naked body while I ate my sandwich in big, barely chewed bites, half-blinded by the bright flashlight he wore strapped to his forehead like a futuristic Cyclops. His gaze burned into me, and I wanted to curl up into a tiny ball, but I was too afraid that he'd take the food away.

As it was, the dry bread and cheese landed like a rock, and my guts churned in protest.

"See? You're learning."

He sounded extraordinarily pleased with himself, no doubt because his horrible plan was working. And what choice did I have but to play along? Even if someone was looking for me, they'd never find me down here.

"Can I have more to eat?"

"Please. You have to say please."

"Can I have more to eat, please?"

"Not now. Later."

Asshole.

"What do I have to do to get a blanket?"

"Okay, so you have to kneel in front of me each time I come in. And put your hands on your thighs."

Had this man watched *Fifty Shades of Grey*? Or was the idea to treat me like a pet dog a product of his own warped mind? I was still trembling, but now a smidgen of the fear gave way to anger. How dare this lunatic lock me up in a freaking cellar? For the first time in my life, I wondered how it would feel to hurt somebody. Really hurt them.

But all I had were my fists, and they were no match for a man bigger than me.

I dropped to my knees.

"Good girl. Now your hands… Yes, just like that. As long as you assume that position every time you hear my footsteps, I'll bring you a blanket."

"Can I have the blanket now? Please? I'm freezing."

"No, when I come back. I have to go out for a while."

"Where?" I scrambled to my feet. "Why?"

"Don't you worry your pretty little head about that, Violet."

"What if something happens to you while you're gone? Like you have a traffic accident or fall down a flight of stairs? Then who would feed me?"

"Hmm…"

Oh, sugar. He hadn't thought this through, had he?

"You'd leave me down here to die?"

"Okay, how about this? I'll leave you extra water and food, but it's your breakfast and lunch for tomorrow, right? So if you eat it all now, you'll have to go hungry in the morning."

"And a blanket?"

"No!"

I shrank away from his yell. One step forward, two steps

back. My knees quaked, but I refused to give in and sit again before he left.

"I'm sorry." I hated to apologise, *hated* it, but if I was going to survive this ordeal, I needed to build some kind of rapport with the monster. "I didn't mean to upset you."

"This isn't easy for me either, you know. I've never done this before. But the moment I saw you, I knew I had to have you, and then that ogre arrived and messed up my plans."

That ogre? "Do you mean Dawson?"

"How could you let him push you around the way he did? Violet, do this, Violet, do that… He was so demanding."

Said the man who'd tied me up in his cellar and ordered me to kneel.

"Because I trusted him to keep me safe."

"And yet he didn't do a very good job, did he? I promise I won't let you down in the same way. With me, you can stay pure, not get corrupted by Hollywood hotshots like David Jackson and Debbie. They're vultures who only want to exploit you for their own gain."

Did he even understand what he was saying?

I'd signed a freaking contract to get exploited by David and Debbie, maybe a little stupidly, but I certainly hadn't signed up for *this*. And what was Elton's endgame? Did he plan to keep me down here forever, or would he let me out to play the dutiful girlfriend or whatever once he'd moulded me into his ideal woman?

Right now, I had no choice but to play along and find out.

CHAPTER 47
DAWSON

"I think we can discount Penny-Sue Jameson," Trent said. "And Brady Marks. Penny-Sue suffers from dementia, and Brady hates talking to strangers. He has a stutter, you see, and he's always been sensitive about it."

They were in the conference room at Vickers & Vickers, surrounded by a sea of coloured sticky notes with names written on them. Pink for the women, blue for the men, green for the folks Trent didn't know.

The number of "plus ones" on the list was concerning, but for now, they were working on the assumption that if somebody had called Oregano to book a table, they'd have done so in their own name.

After a brief discussion, Dawson, Storm, and Trent decided to work through the bookings for the whole week after the phone call. In a town the size of Oakwood Falls, Trent suggested people wouldn't make a reservation any further ahead. Fifteen tables in the restaurant, seven days, lunch and dinner. Almost two hundred names. Some people had eaten there twice, which reduced the numbers slightly, but even so... There were too many damn suspects. They'd only managed to eliminate twenty-three people so far. Trent had stuck seven others into a "quite possible" pile of dubious characters, which still left them with a fuck ton of names and less than two days for three people to sift through them all.

Dawson couldn't think straight. Or eat, or drink, and as for sleep... Yeah, right. Trent seemed more focused, but Dawson saw the other man's hands tremble every so often and stuffed his own into his pockets to keep them from doing the same.

At least they had Storm to keep them on track. Since she'd never met Vi, she could stay detached, or perhaps that cool façade was just her normal demeanour. Who knew?

"Marie Pickles," Trent said. "Rumour has it she supplied a false alibi for her husband several years ago."

Storm shook her head. "If Violet was kidnapped for ransom, I could see a woman being involved, but there haven't been any demands, so that feels wrong. This was a man she knew, a man who'd been obsessing over her and most likely toying with her for weeks."

"What about cases where a wife or partner has been complicit? Think of the Jaycee Lee Dugard case."

"How often does that happen?"

"Rarely, I'll admit, but what if we discount the one person who can lead us to Violet?"

"So, what do you propose? That we check every single person? Do you know how much time we don't have?"

"Whoever provided the reference might just have thought they were assisting Smith to land a job. Maybe they weren't involved in the kidnapping at all?"

"Then why the secrecy? Burner phones for a simple fake reference? Really?"

Dawson rubbed his temples. He'd rather walk across a minefield in clogs than try to solve this damn case.

"You're both right, okay? Trent, we need to consider everybody, but Storm has a point. We need to prioritise. The longer Elton Smith has Vi, the less hope she has of getting out of this in good shape."

"Fine." Trent clenched his teeth. "I'll ask Virginia to bring more coffee."

Sure, and they could line it up next to all the other beverages they hadn't drunk. Trent seemed to take a coffee break every time he got stressed, which struck Dawson as odd for a man who made his living by arguing. Perhaps he wasn't much of a lawyer?

"And I'm going to use the bathroom," Storm announced.

Left on his own, Dawson slumped into a seat. This was impossible.

Alexa was running through the list herself, of course, while Lucas, Kane, Brax, and Lauren kept asking questions in San Francisco, but even with their help, Dawson had never felt so alone. Usually when he worked in a team, they were trained for the task and had a coherent plan. He wasn't cut out to be a private detective.

Okay. Think. If Smith had asked an acquaintance to vouch for him, it would need to be someone he trusted. And also someone he trusted not to spill the beans. A parent might help with a reference for a job, but would they enable their child to commit a serious crime? Unlikely. Dawson tried to put himself in Smith's shoes. If he needed backup of a sketchy nature himself, he'd go to one of his former housemates— Brax, Zach, Justin, maybe even Nolan—or an old Navy buddy, although those guys tended to have a more rigid moral code.

Using that logic, they'd be looking for an old friend of Smith's, or possibly a work colleague, most probably around the same age. Had he genuinely worked as a security guard in the past? Or was that a lie too? Was the false reference necessary because of a lack of experience or because he'd had an issue in a previous job?

With Trent's help, they identified twenty-four men in their

late twenties or early thirties, including one who used to work as a mall cop in Wichita and another who'd been employed as a security guard at the bank before he got fired for persistent lateness. They'd try them first.

"Are we going to split the list between us?" Storm asked.

Trent shook his head. "People around here aren't keen on strangers."

"They seemed friendly enough the last time I visited," Dawson said.

"That's because you were with Violet. We should go together."

Storm's turn to disagree. "There's no time for that, and these are men. Believe me, I'll convince them to talk."

Looking at her sky-blue eyes, high cheekbones, and full pink lips, Dawson did believe her. Any red-blooded male without a ring on his finger would tell her anything she wanted to know and probably buy her dinner too.

"Let's visit the two likely candidates together and then divide up the others. We only have a few hours left today, and a number of our targets might not even be at home."

"Fine," Trent said. "And what story are we telling people? The truth? Because if the news gets out and word reaches the kidnapper, he might panic. One of the cases I studied in law school involved—"

"We'll make something up," Dawson interrupted. He didn't want to hear any kidnapping horror stories, not today when he was already struggling to stay positive. "Never give up" had been his mantra in the Navy, but not once had he experienced this feeling of utter helplessness at work.

"How about we tell them I'm looking for Elton Smith for one of my cases? That's plausible."

"For you, maybe." Storm shrugged. "I'll just say he's an ex who ran off with a bunch of my stuff, and he talked about having a friend here."

If Storm said Smith was an alien sent to abduct the town's

firstborn children, most men would have nodded and agreed as long as she showed cleavage. Certainly Trent would— Dawson hadn't missed the way the lawyer looked at her. If Storm hadn't become a fighter pilot, she could have been a model.

"Can we get on with this?" Dawson checked his watch. Seven thirty, and Vi had been missing for almost twenty-four hours now.

Trent took a bunch of keys out of his desk drawer. "I'll just fetch my car."

"Let's hope today's more productive."

The following morning, Storm ate a slice of toast while Dawson forced down a glass of orange juice. At least she looked as if she'd gotten some rest. Dawson hadn't slept a wink.

"It has to be," he said.

After all of their efforts of yesterday, the evening had been something of an anticlimax. The mall cop had shown them the photos from his vacation in Cancun, taken at the time the call had been made, and the bank guard had spent that week in the hospital with appendicitis.

Of the other nine men they'd attempted to visit, two had been out, and none of the other seven admitted to knowing Smith. Dawson didn't think any of the four he'd spoken to with Trent were lying, and Storm said the same about her three. She'd arrived back at Trent's place with two phone numbers, a box of candy, and the offer of a shooting lesson from the president of the local hunting club.

Dawson very much suspected a shooting lesson would be wasted on Storm.

Trent had offered them a bed for the night, and although

Dawson still didn't like him, he had to admit the man had been helpful, including clearing his schedule so he could tackle the rest of the shortlist with them today. He'd even offered to assist with the less promising candidates after Storm left if they had no luck.

A prospect that didn't bear thinking about.

Footsteps sounded in the hallway, and when Trent walked in, he headed straight for the espresso machine. His unkempt hair and the dark smudges under his eyes said he'd gotten as little sleep as Dawson.

"Ready to go in five minutes?" he asked. "Billy Barker always gets up before sunrise."

"We're ready right now."

Billy Barker lived on a ranch just outside the town limits, and the rickety gates at the end of the driveway suggested it had seen better days. According to Trent, Billy bred horses and had made a decent living until he started betting on them too. Dawson figured Billy also spent a good portion of his cash on alcohol. Even at that hour of the morning, he reeked of whisky.

"What do you want?" he asked, glaring at Trent.

Fortunately, Storm jumped in. "Mr. Vickers is helping me to locate my ex-boyfriend. We split up, but when I was going through the things he left behind, I realised I had his grandma's ring, and I know it's important to him. I'm hoping to give it back."

"Why'd you split up?"

"I wanted to move to Alaska, and he didn't. Quite honestly, I'm having second thoughts."

"What makes you think I can help?"

"He used to live around here, and you're the same age. I'm hoping to find an old buddy who might have a forwarding address. Or maybe a relative?"

"What's his name?"

"Elton Smith."

"Nope, don't know him."

"I think he might have gone by a different name before I met him." Storm lowered her voice. "Between you and me, he had a gambling problem, and he needed a fresh start."

Billy nodded, understanding. "You got a picture?"

"Sure."

He squinted at Elton's mugshot, and Dawson expected to draw another blank, but instead, Billy scratched his chin thoughtfully.

"There a reward?"

"A reward?"

"For information."

"I'm sure I could find a few bucks." Storm pulled a wallet out of her pocket and produced a fifty. Billy tried to grab it, but she held it just out of reach.

"Information first."

"Reckon I might have seen him around."

"Really? Where?"

"Not in this town. Over in Oakwood Ridge."

"Whereabouts in Oakwood Ridge?"

"A bar. I forget which one, but he had longer hair back then."

"Back when?"

"A few months ago."

Dawson didn't need to look at Storm's face to know what she was thinking. How reliable was this drunkard?

"Are you sure it was him?"

"Mebbe ninety percent? I always had a gift for remembering faces. Wish I had a gift for makin' money instead." He chuckled at his own joke.

"Which bar?"

"You got me there. Try AJ's Bar and Grill or Green Seventeen. That's where I go most often. Or the Draft Club on Main Street if you strike out at the first two."

"Did you talk to him?"

"Only about the game."

Storm handed over the cash, and for the first time since Vi disappeared, Dawson felt a flutter of hope in his chest. They had a lead. A tenuous one, but a lead nonetheless.

"Thanks for your help," Storm told Billy.

"Say, if you plan on sticking around, how about I take you for a burger tomorrow night?"

"Sorry. I've booked a two-month cycling tour of Europe, and it starts next Monday."

"Cycling?"

"Yup. Sixteen women travelling through eight countries to find ourselves. It promises to be a spiritual experience."

She said all that with a straight face, and at the mention of spirituality, Billy backed into his ramshackle house. Time to move on.

"Do you think he was telling the truth?" Trent asked. "Or was he just after the cash?"

"I'd say he was being truthful," Storm said. "He was after a date, and lying wouldn't have been a good way to impress me."

"Neither was extorting cash."

"Information has its price, the same as everything else."

"Okay." Trent blew out a long breath. "So, what do we do now?"

"What time do the bars in Oakwood Ridge open?"

"Noon, most of them, ready for lunch. A little earlier on Sundays to catch the folks leaving the early church services."

Irrelevant seeing as it was Friday. "Then we'll carry on working through the list of names until then. Someone else might have seen Smith too."

"Fine. But first, I need to swing by the office and speak with one of my colleagues." Trent waved his phone. "Virginia messaged me—we have a client emergency."

"And this isn't an emergency?"

"It'll just take two minutes."
"Hurry. We'll wait in the car."

CHAPTER 48

VIOLET

K neeling for Elton had earned me a tiny, thin blanket, and last night, I'd gotten a couple of hours of fitful sleep curled up in one corner of the cellar. Before Elton went out, he'd kept his word and brought me a paper grocery sack with a package of crackers, two tubs of yogurt, and half a dozen bottles of water. The blanket had arrived when he came back several hours later. Freezing, I'd dropped to my knees as soon as I heard footsteps, and when the flashlight beam hit me, he'd let out a long exhale.

"Good girl. I thought you might have forgotten."

Oh, sure, because I had so many other things going on in my life right now.

This morning—at least, I assumed it was morning, I really had no idea—Elton's breathing quickened as he watched me in silence, and I imagined all the things I wanted to do to him. *Shut his foot in a bear trap. Run a cheese grater over his skin. Shove him headfirst into a pit of boiling tar.* But as the flashlight beam played over the rest of the room, no doubt to check I was behaving myself, I caught a glimpse of his groin. Bile rose as the implications hit me. That bulge in the front of his pants right at my eye level—it could only mean one thing. This turned him on. Me naked, his prisoner, forced to obey if I wanted to survive. While he hadn't touched me yet, it would only be a matter of time.

I had to get out of this freaking cellar. But how?

"Okay, today's lesson. We need to work on your smile. Nobody likes a misery guts."

A bubble of laughter popped out. I couldn't help it. I was locked up like an animal, and this asshole wanted me to smile? If I'd ever had any last, lingering doubts over his sanity, he'd just erased them.

"My smile?"

"That's right."

"And what do I get out of that?"

"Well, firstly, you'll please me…" As if I cared about that. "And secondly…" He reached behind himself to the stairs. "You'll get shoes."

He held them up, a pair of pale-pink fleece-lined moccasins, similar to the ones my mom wore around the house. I'd never seen anything so beautiful in my life.

You're an actress, Violet. You can do this.

I forced a saccharine grin onto my face, the same sickly expression used by beauty pageant contestants the world over. There wasn't a hint of substance behind it, but it still seemed to please Elton. It was the power, I realised. He only cared about having control over me. About moulding me to his will.

"Very good. If you manage it again at lunchtime, then you can have these."

That…that asshole! Now he was just playing.

"Why not now? What difference does it make to you?"

"Women like something to look forward to."

"Yes, if it's a vacation or a trip to the theatre or dinner with friends. Trust me, women don't enjoy spending five extra hours with ice-cold feet."

For a moment, he stilled. Considering my point?

"No, I think we'll do this my way. My game, my rules."

This was a game to him? In spite of the fact that I was on the verge of hypothermia, a trickle of sweat ran down my spine. If I didn't get out of this dungeon soon, I'd be trapped for weeks, months, maybe even forever because I'd lose the little strength I had left. Unless Elton-slash-Elmer got bored and killed me, of course. He could bury me right here under the dirt floor, and nobody would ever find my body. Dawson would always wonder if I'd hightailed it out of town because of him, and Mom would be left with a thousand unanswered questions and no daughter. Would Trent comfort her? I liked to think so. I missed him too, even if I didn't adore him with the same passion I'd once felt.

The thought of dying just as I'd found love, just as I'd started to make something of my life, caused me to choke up, but given the choice between that and living the remainder of my life as a madman's prisoner, choking might actually be the better option. Unless I could pull off a miracle and escape. But how?

I glared at Elton, letting my smile turn into a frown. That didn't make him happy. I could hear the disappointment in his tone.

"Eat your breakfast, Violet. Your defiance is disappointing, but I can see we've still got a ways to go. Bob Marley was right when he said that women who are worth it aren't easy."

I was pretty sure Bob Marley hadn't been talking about kidnapping when he came up with the quote, but pointing that out to Elton wouldn't help the situation. Instead, I kept quiet and looked at the dusty floor, refusing to lift my gaze until he'd climbed all the way up the stairs and closed the door. A muffled *click* told me he'd locked it from the outside.

Think, Violet. Think!

My brain had turned to mush, but my stomach grumbled. At least one part of me still functioned correctly. I rummaged in the grocery sack at my feet. Would Elton bring more snacks for dinner, or did two tubs of yogurt and a package of crackers have to last the whole day? After careful consideration, I decided to eat half the food and drink one bottle of water.

Once I'd finished, the chain dug into my waist. That was my biggest problem. Even if I somehow managed to incapacitate Elton, I'd still be stuck in the damn cellar, and the chain was so tight that I'd never be able to force it over my hips. Dawson said he loved my curves, but at this particular moment, I saw the benefits of a more athletic figure. Could I wiggle the chain over my head? No, it got stuck on my boobs. Dammit!

What if I could get the other end undone? I crawled toward the wall, feeling my way along the links, and ran my hands over the metal ring. Four screws held it to the brick, and I'd never remove those without a screwdriver. If only I'd been wearing a bobby pin, I could have tried to pick open the padlock, but when I was off duty, I either wore my hair totally loose or scraped it back into a ponytail.

Damp clung to my fingertips, and I wiped my hands on the blanket. Although I hadn't seen the outside of the house, it felt old. Decrepit. Maybe even abandoned. The kind of place that needed either a bunch of TLC or to be put out of its misery, much like me. Back in Oakwood Falls, Trent's parents had an old garage similar to this in their backyard, a dank, cloying cave of a building. I used to play in it as a child, pretending to be Cinderella waiting for my prince, but then I'd gotten banned from going near it because the crumbling masonry made it unsafe.

Hmm. Crumbling masonry?

I thought back to the layers of brick that had chipped away when Trent kicked a soccer ball against the outside. Age and water damage…

What if…?

I grabbed the metal teaspoon I'd used to eat my yogurt

and attacked the brick with it, barely able to contain my whoop of joy when a tiny piece broke off in my hand. If I could chip the ring away from the wall, I'd be halfway out of here.

A new energy buzzed through me, and Kane's third rule for surviving Hollywood popped into my head: never give up.

CHAPTER 49
DAWSON

"Why does Trent always do that?" Storm asked.

"Do what?"

She and Dawson sat on the low wall outside Trent's office, waiting to make the trip to Oakwood Ridge. Storm's fingers twitched as if she'd rather be holding a cigarette between them.

"Every time we make progress, he stalls."

"You mean the way he constantly drinks coffee and then goes to take a leak?"

"Unless he has a bladder problem, he's not taking a leak every time. He's calling someone."

"A client?"

"Possibly. He seems nervous."

"So? I'm fucking nervous. We're all nervous. You used to smoke?"

"Quit a decade ago, but…yeah, I still get the urge."

Her phone rang, a rock song, but she ignored it.

"Aren't you gonna answer that?"

"It's my ex. Never date a lawyer." She jerked her head toward the shingle outside Trent's office. "Maybe that's why I dislike them so much."

Dawson checked his phone again, but there was nothing from Alexa. Last night, she'd called to say she'd checked half of the list and found no red flags, and she'd sounded as exhausted as he felt.

"The guy's in love with Violet. He wants her to move back here and play happy families."

"But she's hung up on you?"

"Yeah."

At least, she had been until the Blackstone House affair reared its ugly head.

Storm raised both eyebrows. "Awkward."

"Doesn't even begin to cover it."

"I thought Trent was just an old friend."

"They've known each other since they were kids, but he only began paying attention after her first movie hit the big time. Now he wants her to give up her career and become his secretary."

Storm's disgusted look mirrored Dawson's thoughts.

"But if he's so into Violet, why is a client meeting taking priority over finding her? He knows the clock's ticking."

Yeah, he did. Dawson was ready to head into the office and drag the asshole and his overblown ego outside when Trent finally walked through the front door, tucking his phone into his pocket.

"I've been in touch with an acquaintance in Oakwood Ridge," Trent said. "He's going to show Smith's picture around to help us out. Ready to go?"

"We've been ready for a half hour," Storm muttered under her breath. Two steps later, she tripped over and clutched at Trent to stay upright. "Sorry. Not a morning person."

"You want me to grab you a coffee?"

"No, I want to get a move on." As they reached the car, Storm tossed the keys to Dawson. "Your turn to drive."

On any other day, that would have been a good thing because Dawson would ignore every speed limit in his quest to find Vi, but today? Trent led the way, and he drove his Mercedes with the urgency of a man heading to his own funeral. Dawson was stuck behind him, squashed and uncomfortable in Storm's borrowed Ford compact as the miles ticked slowly by. Two nights, Violet had been gone, and if she was still alive, she was suffering. Dawson had broken his promise to keep her safe, and guilt ate away inside him.

But Storm was smiling, and when they cleared the town limits, she pulled something out of her pocket.

"Okay, let's take a look at this."

Dawson glanced across at her. "Fuck, you lifted Trent's phone?"

"Just curious."

"Isn't it locked?"

"I watched his reflection in the window when he typed in the PIN yesterday."

"Are you a pilot or a spy?"

A shrug, and Storm fell silent for a moment, scrolling. "Who's Elmer?"

"Elmer? I've never heard Trent mention that name. Maybe it's the guy in Oakwood Ridge he said he spoke to?"

"Nope. Trent's dialled Elmer fifty-three times this week, but none of the calls have connected. And he hasn't tried anyone else this morning, not on this phone at least."

"He could've used the office phone."

But even as the words left his mouth, Dawson wasn't convinced. Why hadn't Trent called his contact from the car to save time? From the moment they met, he hadn't liked the man, his competitor for Vi's affections, but he'd convinced himself it was just jealousy on his part and buried that animosity for the sake of finding her. What if his gut had been right all along? While he'd never crossed paths with Storm before yesterday, he got the impression that she lived by her instincts too, and now alarm bells started clanging.

"Drop back a bit, will you?" she said. "I'll try calling Elmer from my phone instead."

The sound of ringing filled the cabin, followed by a man's voice.

"Hello?"

"Hi, my name's Tiffany, and I'm calling from SmartPlus Mobile about the savings you can make on our new all-inclusive plan."

"I'm not interested."

"We guarantee to beat any of our competitors on price, plus we've partnered with Netflix to offer six months on their premium plan absolutely free."

"Really? And how long am I tied in after that?"

Fuck. That was Elton; Dawson was sure of it. He mouthed as much to Storm, then swerved back onto the right side of the road before they hit an oncoming truck.

"Only another six months after that. We also use AT&T as our network provider for improved coverage."

"My service *has* been patchy lately…"

"Who are you with currently?"

"GoTech."

"Figures. They haven't been investing in their infrastructure. How's about I go through the details with you?"

"I'm kind of busy right now."

"Would you like me to mail you more information? The first thousand customers to sign up for the new plan also get a fifty-dollar Apple voucher."

"I'm in temporary accommodation at the moment."

"Aw, landlord problems? I've had awful trouble with mine."

"Just travelling around. I wanted to see the West Coast."

"Really? Me and my girlfriends were talking about a road trip. Anywhere you'd recommend?"

"Spend some time in San Francisco. Everyone should drive over the Golden Gate Bridge at least once in their life."

"Any other suggestions?"

"Save up. Everything in California's overpriced." Voices sounded in the background. "Sorry, I gotta go."

"Shall I put you down for a callback? In, say, a month?"

"Sure, you do that."

The line went dead, and Storm dropped the phone into her lap. "Gotcha."

"I'll kill him."

"Elmer or Trent?"

"Both."

"Calm your itchy trigger finger until we've gotten enough information out of Trent, okay? Look, there's a rest area ahead."

She reached over to honk the horn and turn on the blinker. Luckily, Trent got the message and slowed. Glad for yet another delay? Dawson realised now that Trent hadn't wanted them to find Elton, Elmer, whatever his name was at all. No, he'd wanted to keep his secrets.

The rest area beside the highway was little more than a gravelled patch with a handful of picnic benches and an overflowing trash can, the spot half-hidden by trees and long grass. It was also empty. Perfect. As they drew to a halt, Dawson forced himself into the cold, calculating headspace he'd used as a SEAL. Much as he wanted to strangle Trent with his bare hands, Storm was right. They needed answers first.

"Do we have a plan?" Storm asked.

"Yeah. I'm gonna ask Trent nicely what the fuck he thinks he's playing at."

"Want me to do that? Good cop, bad cop?"

"Go for it."

Trent was already out of his car, striding toward them, the

arrogant bastard. He still thought he'd gotten away with his deception.

At least until Storm met him halfway, holding up his phone.

"You dropped this."

"I did?" He patted his pockets. "Oh, thanks."

Trent reached for it, but Storm moved her hand out of reach. "Who's Elmer?"

All the colour drained from Trent's face, but even then, he didn't come clean. "Elmer who?"

"That's what we're asking you. He must be real important if you've called him so many times."

"Oh, *that* Elmer. I thought he might be able to give us a lead on Elton Smith. Wait a second… How did you access my call log?"

"Why?"

"Why what?"

"Why did you think Elmer could give us a lead?"

"Because he's a private investigator."

Trent didn't have time to take another breath before Dawson slammed him against his Mercedes so hard the window cracked.

"Don't lie to us."

"Get your hands off me, you knuckle-dragging Neanderthal!"

"Tell the fucking truth for once."

"I *am* telling the truth. Elmer freelanced for me as an investigator, working on legal matters."

"Was that before or after he started moonlighting as Elton Smith?"

"You think…" Trent's laugh was forced. "You actually think Elmer is Elton? No, no, no. The idea's preposterous."

"We just spoke with him. I recognised his voice, asshole."

Trent's shoulders dropped, and he sagged back against the car as the last ounce of bluster left his scrawny body.

"He answered the phone?"

Storm nodded. "To me, he did."

"None of this was supposed to happen," Trent whispered.

"Why was Elmer there? Why was he in San Francisco with Violet?"

"I sent him to keep an eye on her. When she first talked with me about making the movie, she sounded on edge. Distinctly unenthusiastic. I've heard the stories of powerful men—casting directors, producers, agents—taking advantage of young actresses, and I didn't want the same to happen to her."

Dawson took a step forward, getting into Trent's space. "He sent her gifts. Flowers steeped in blood. An animal's heart." No reaction. "He jacked off in her fucking trailer." Ah, now Trent looked startled. "You knew about the first two, didn't you? Why didn't you warn her? Tell Vi he was sprung?"

"I didn't realise that at the time."

"And why the secrecy?" Storm asked. "If you were truly worried about Violet, why didn't you tell her you'd sent an acquaintance to lend a hand?"

Another piece slotted into place in Dawson's mind. "You had another agenda, didn't you? Those gifts were your idea, not Elmer's. After Vi told you about the first bunch of flowers and the candy, and you heard how nervous she was, you wanted to scare her back to Oakwood Falls."

Trent's clenched jaw told Dawson that was exactly what had happened.

"Why'd you do it?" Silence. "Answer me, motherfucker."

"You met Violet five minutes ago, and you think you understand her? You don't. She isn't cut out for the showbiz lifestyle. Before she moved to California, she was a good girl. Pure. Innocent. If she stays in Hollywood with those backstabbing prima donnas and sleazy douchebags, it'll destroy her."

"Well, you got your wish. She's not in Hollywood anymore, is she? Where did Elmer take her?"

"I don't know. I swear! That's why I was trying to call him, but he won't answer."

"And rather than telling us this, you decided to waste time by leading us on a merry dance all over two fucking towns, looking for a man we'd never find. You gave Elmer the false reference, didn't you?"

"I've known Elmer for two years, and he never showed any indication of—"

"*Didn't you*?"

"It wasn't entirely false. He *did* do work for me."

"You really are a selfish fuck, aren't you?"

"I had good intentions."

"Violet could die because of your stupidity."

"Oh, that's rich coming from the man who's suspected of killing his own roommate."

"Bullshit. Another man was found guilty. You need to stop trying to justify what you did and give us every scrap of information you have on the monster you unleashed."

"It wasn't all my fault. *You're* the bodyguard. Why didn't you do your job properly?"

"Let's start with his full name."

"Are you even qualified to be a bodyguard? Or did you bluff your way into the position?"

Dawson balled up his fists, but before he could introduce Trent to his knuckles, Storm got him in the groin with her knee. The duplicitous prick doubled up in agony, coughing.

"I thought you were the good cop?" Dawson said.

Storm flashed a grin. "I was born to be bad."

When Trent had swallowed his balls back down, he began talking. Elmer Schmidt was an unlicensed investigator specialising in off-the-record research. Committing a few minor felonies in the course of his job didn't seem to bother him, which was why Trent had thought of the man when he needed assistance in convincing Vi to come back home. His desperation to take Vi back from Dawson meant that neither of them had her now.

"Are you going to tell her about this?" Trent asked when he'd finished his confession.

"Too damn right I am."

"But she and I have been friends for years."

"Friends don't fuck with each other's lives the way you did."

"I'm sorry, okay? I only wanted what was best for her."

"No, you wanted what was best for you."

"Says the washed-up soldier after her money."

In the past, Dawson had gotten little pleasure out of breaking bones, instead viewing violence as a means to an end, a necessity. Today, he made an exception for Trent's nose. They left the man bleeding by the side of the road as they piled back into the car, Storm driving this time.

"Well, we have the name," she said. "Now what?"

"Now I need to call a friend." He was already messaging Alexa. "I'm hoping we can track his phone."

"The plane's available for the rest of the day. Just let me know where you want to go."

"Why are you doing this?"

"Because in my world, favours are a currency."

"But you don't owe me any favours. We've never met."

"A friend asked me to help out."

"What friend?"

"If she wants you to know, then she'll tell you."

She? It wasn't Alexa, they'd already established that much, but Dawson was at a loss for other possibilities. And he didn't have time to think about that conundrum right now because Alexa was calling.

"You got something?" she asked.

"Trent Vickers sent our suspect to terrorise Violet."

"Trent Vickers? He was on the booking list for Oregano

twice that week. I tracked him to New York, but he got fired from a fancy law firm when he cheated on his fiancée. His fiancée whose father happened to be a senior partner. I mean, what a dumb-ass. She caught him in bed with an intern, by all accounts."

Trent had been engaged? Dawson would bet everything he owned—which admittedly wasn't much—that Violet was blissfully aware of that snippet of information.

"He also wanted Vi to play happy families with him in Oakwood Falls, so he sent a man to encourage her back home. Elmer Schmidt. We have his number, and the phone was turned on twenty minutes ago. Can you trace it? His service provider is GoTech."

"Easy. What's the number?"

Dawson read it out, and Alexa repeated it back to him. Easy, she said. He had a feeling that extricating Violet from the man's clutches would be anything but.

CHAPTER 50
DAWSON

"**S**acramento," Alexa said. "Schmidt answered the call in downtown Sacramento. That's the good news."

Another half hour had passed, and Storm was back in her flight suit, looking far more relaxed now that she was near something mechanical with wings. While she did the pre-flight checks, Dawson paced beside the hangar, still furious with Trent. How could a man do that to the woman he claimed to care for?

"Dare I ask about the bad news?"

"He's turned the phone off."

"Fuck. So we can't track him?"

"Not right now. Do you want the other bad news?"

There was more? "Not really."

"I can't find any connections between Schmidt and that area. Usually, there's a thread. But his credit card shows no activity since last week when he used it to buy gas in San Francisco, and the only relative I can find is his mom."

"And where is she?"

"A retirement facility in Oklahoma."

"No grandparents?"

"Died a decade ago in Bristow."

"What about the car Schmidt was driving?"

"The only vehicle registered to him is an RV, so he either stole the car or bought it off-the-books. There might be a security camera at the gas station he used."

"An RV? If he stocked up on supplies, he could stay right off the grid."

"Yup. And if he's only turning his phone on when he's in town, he's not stupid either. You got lucky and called him at just the right time."

Lucky? Lucky would be if Vi wasn't missing in the first place. If they'd avoided being photographed the night of Trent's party in Oakwood Falls. If he were still working as her bodyguard and they'd had plans to sneak off to some out-of-the-way restaurant for dinner. If she'd leaned into him and promised they had a future when this fucking movie was over.

Speaking to her abductor wasn't lucky.

It fucking sucked.

"Can you monitor the phone?" he asked Alexa.

"I'll check on it every hour, but I have to be careful because I'm not exactly supposed to be in GoTech's system."

"What about his bank account? He'll need cash."

"He withdrew five thousand dollars before he left San Francisco. Five hundred bucks a day for ten days running, and nothing since."

"Fuck."

"Much as I hate to admit it, there are some occasions when human intelligence is better than electronic eyes. I'd try visiting the mother. In the meantime, I'll dig deeper into Schmidt's background. Something might pop."

When Dawson hung up, Storm met his gaze and raised an eyebrow. "What now?"

"How much time do you have left?"

"Why?"

"Feel like testing out your acting skills in Oklahoma?"

Dawson's stomach was roiling by the time they landed at Tinker Air Force Base, and not just because of Violet. When pushed, Storm had admitted she was logging their activities as test flights, and that meant she had to do some actual testing.

They quite literally needed to go under the radar.

"This jet's had a few tiny modifications. If we need to eject, the handle's between your legs."

Gee, that was comforting. Yet tempting when Storm flew the damn jet above the plains at…well, Dawson didn't know how many feet exactly because he'd closed his eyes. At one point, they'd been level with the treetops. But by a miracle, he survived the trip, and the nausea was worth it because she got them to Oklahoma City faster than fucking sound.

"Not bad," she said, patting the plane's fuselage as she hopped to the ground beside the hangar. "What did you think?"

"I think you have a death wish."

And nerves of fucking steel.

"Aw, you don't like flying?"

Even as a child, Dawson hadn't been fond of heights, and when he joined the SEALs, he'd preferred to keep his feet on the ground whenever possible. He learned to parachute because he had to, but he'd never enjoyed skydiving, and he never would. As for air travel, he didn't mind commercial jets as long as he got enough legroom, but military transport? No thanks.

"The only thing worse than being in an airplane is jumping out of one. Being stuck in a metal tube at twenty thousand feet isn't my idea of fun."

"How about the parts when we were at fifty feet? Did you enjoy those?"

"No."

The bitch just laughed as she went to change her clothes. This time, she swapped her flight suit for jeans and a frilly blouse, high-heeled pumps too, and the shoes put her eyes level with Dawson's chin. She gave him a twirl.

"Well? Do I look like girlfriend material?"

"Your knife is sticking out of your pocket."

"Oops." She tucked it away and then smoothed down the ruffles. "Better?"

"Yeah." He pinched the bridge of his nose. "I can't believe this is happening. I keep thinking I'm gonna wake up soon."

Storm laid a hand on his arm. "Don't worry. We're getting closer, and we'll get Violet back. Let's go meet Momma Schmidt."

"Mrs. Schmidt?" Storm asked.

The grey-haired lady looked up from her seat by the window in the communal living room and adjusted a pair of wire-framed glasses, although judging by the way she squinted, they didn't help her eyesight much.

"Yes. Yes, I am. But who are you?"

"I'm a friend of Elmer's. More than a friend, actually."

"Elmer? Where is he? Who's this man?"

"This is my brother. Elmer's…well, I was hoping you'd be able to tell me where he is. We had a fight a few days ago, and he said he needed some space, but now he's not answering his phone, and…and…" Storm gave a convincing sniffle. "I don't know where he is, and I'm getting a little concerned. He told me all about you, and I just thought…"

Mrs. Schmidt's expression softened. "Then you must be Violet?"

Dawson jolted as if he'd been Tasered, but Storm didn't flinch.

"Yeah, that's right, I'm Violet. He mentioned me?"

"Oh, yes, the last time he called. And don't you worry about Elmer. He's always been a flighty one, but he said you were the love of his life and you'd be together forever. His girl, he called you. I'm sure that whatever you fought over, it was only a silly quarrel. Elmer's father and I, we used to argue all the time, God rest his soul, but it was just our way of showing we cared. My Clayton had a real Italian temper on him, even though he was third-generation American."

Elmer had spoken with his mom about Vi? The freak was delusional. Insane. Vi had barely noticed the man until he'd kidnapped her.

Storm clutched her hands over her heart. "That's a relief to hear. But I'm still so worried that I haven't heard from him. It's been nearly three days."

Mrs. Schmidt peeled away one of Storm's hands and clutched it in both of hers, papery skin stretched thin over dark veins.

"My Elmer knows how to take care of himself. Why don't you join me for a nice glass of iced tea? They have the best iced tea here. Not too sweet and plenty of flavour." She called out to a young brunette in a pale pink uniform. "Kayleigh, could you please bring us some of that iced tea?"

Dawson didn't want iced tea. He wanted fucking answers, but he knew they had to play the game. Grudgingly, he took a seat beside Storm while Mrs. Schmidt reminisced about Elmer's childhood. The upbringing of a crackpot. What had gone wrong?

"He always was fussy about his food. Getting him to eat vegetables was an ongoing battle. His grandma used to give him candy, and he'd eat junk all afternoon."

"Couldn't you have asked her to stop? Or switch to fruit?"

"Oh, Elmer had her wrapped around his little finger." She

gave Storm a nudge. "Always had a way with the ladies, so he did."

Because drugging them and shoving them into a car was a sure way to guarantee a long-lasting relationship.

"I only wish I could talk to him," Storm said, getting the conversation back on track. "He drove off awful fast and even left his laptop behind. When I looked at the screen, it had a map of Sacramento, but he never mentioned knowing anybody in Sacramento."

"That'll be his godmother. She lives out near Clarksburg."

"I don't suppose you have her number? If I could just find out that Elmer's okay, I'd sleep better tonight."

"I'm sure I have it back in my room. Once we've drunk our tea, I'll go and hunt it out for you. When you talk to him, would you remind him to send the money for my new mattress? It seems to have slipped his mind, which doesn't surprise me if he's been busy with you. You're a pretty thing."

"Uh, thanks?"

"Would you like a cookie?"

"I'm on a diet."

"Really?" Then her eyes lit up. "It's not because you need to wear a special dress soon, is it?"

"I actually prefer pants."

"Because I always hoped Elmer would get married while I was still around to see it. You'll make a beautiful bride. Are you having a summer wedding?"

Okay, now Dawson saw where Elmer got his penchant for delusion from: it was genetic.

Storm just smiled, and honestly, the woman deserved an Oscar. "We don't want to rush into anything."

"Then one cookie won't hurt. Kayleigh! Could you bring a plate of cookies?"

CHAPTER 51
DAWSON

Back at Travis Air Force Base, Brax was waiting by the front gate, his Porsche Cayenne gleaming under the streetlights. Storm pulled their borrowed jeep in behind it.

"I thought we'd never escape," she muttered. "And those cookies were like dusty leather."

"At least it wasn't only me who hated them." Food had tasted of nothing to Dawson since Vi disappeared. "I'm not sure what to say. Just…thank you."

"Hey, it made a change from flying all day, every day. Let me know when you find Violet?"

"Yeah, I will." Dawson appreciated her confidence in him. "Give me your number?"

"It's already saved in your phone."

She grinned and climbed back into the jeep, and before he could say a proper goodbye, she'd disappeared back onto the base. Which left him with another female sidekick. Lauren climbed out of the front seat of Brax's SUV and into the back, skirting puddles from the recent rainfall. Dawson swallowed a groan.

"I thought I told you to come alone," he muttered to Brax.

"You try arguing with her. She's worse than Carissa. Ditching her would have taken a monumental effort, and besides, she might come in useful. She helped with Mikki."

"You know exactly why I didn't want company." Dawson lowered his voice. "Did you bring the other gun?"

"It's under the passenger seat. And I booked us into a hotel on the outskirts of Sacramento for the night, but they only had two rooms left."

"A waste of money. I won't sleep."

"Guys," Lauren complained. "Can we get this show on the road?"

As soon as they reached the highway, Dawson emailed Alexa, and she called right back. He'd sent her the godmother's phone number when they got it from Mrs. Schmidt, and since Alexa seemed to be tapped into every damn database in the United States, he'd have been shocked if she hadn't found the records.

Of course she'd found the records.

Dawson's phone pinged, and their grey-hatted hacker had ferreted out not only an address but Betty Crandall's call history, her last credit card statement, and a satellite photo of her house.

"She spends half of her social security on knitting supplies," Alexa said. "Elmer never calls her. Not much of a godson, is he?"

"He kidnaps women in his spare time, Alexa."

"And stalks them. He got kicked out of Wichita State for paying one woman slightly too much attention, but it all got hushed up because the governing board didn't want a scandal."

"Shit."

"Funny you should say that because she found him naked in her bathroom one evening."

"He didn't write on the mirror, did he?"

"No, he invited her to take a shower with him, then acted surprised when she ran out screaming."

"Okay, enough with the horror stories. Did you find anything else useful?"

"Brax visited the gas station and found the car's licence plate details. It's a Toyota Corolla, and Elmer bought it for cash six weeks ago. The former owner is a housewife from Walnut Creek, and I can't see any other connection between them. When I called her, she said he got her number from an ad on Craigslist."

"No sign of the RV?"

"Not a whisper. But Elmer's a registered independent, he shops at Walmart, likes country and western music, and last July, he made a purchase from Century Guns in Topeka. Watch your backs."

Lauren's gasp from the back seat made Dawson wish that Brax was better at arguing. The last thing he wanted to do was wade into a gunfight with a cocktail waitress in tow.

"How about you stay at the hotel when we visit Betty?" he suggested. "We can pick you up on the way back. Or drop you off at the airport? You could fly home."

"No way. Besides, I got fired for missing two shifts running, and I'm already late with the rent. I can hardly afford gas, let alone an airplane ticket."

"How much is your rent?" Brax asked.

"Eight hundred dollars."

He pulled a handful of bills from his wallet and held them out to her. "Here you go."

"Don't you dare try to buy me."

"I'm not. I'm just trying to be nice. You know, do the right thing?"

"Sure. Right. I'm still not going home."

Brax sighed. "It was worth a shot."

"How long until we're there?"

Alexa let out a peal of laughter. "Lauren, take the money. Trust me, Brax can afford it."

"Have you been looking at my bank account?" he asked.

"I plead the Fifth."

After snatching a couple of hours' sleep in the hotel room he was sharing with Brax, which was at the nicer end of the market since Brax had expensive tastes, Dawson borrowed his friend's iPad and enlarged the image of the house Alexa had sent. Elmer's godmother lived in a small ranch-style home, and even from the aerial picture, Dawson could see it was in poor shape. Overgrown trees dominated the yard as the forest did its best to encroach, a contrast to the patchy lawn at the front. The oil-stained driveway was empty.

"No vehicles," he muttered to Alexa through the phone. "When was this picture taken?"

"Last week."

While Elmer was still in San Francisco. Was he keeping Violet in the RV? Hard to see him holding her in the house if the godmother was living there too. Dawson took a deep breath and forced himself to plan. They'd need to do a drive-by first to see who was around, and then he'd move in closer. Thanks to Betty's lack of horticultural prowess, he had plenty of cover to sneak up to the house. Then he'd have a choice to make—hit the place hard right away, or wait for the best moment. Option one carried a greater risk of unexpected surprises, but waiting had its own downsides. Dawson didn't want Elmer alone with Vi for a moment longer than necessary.

"Brax, can you drop me off near Betty's place? I want to take a look in person."

"Now?"

"Yes."

"It's three o'clock in the morning."

"Says the man who's made a living from hanging out in the dark."

"I'll grab the car key."

A trickle of adrenaline ran through Dawson's veins. Years ago on his first overseas operation, a mission in Afghanistan where death was a very real possibility, his mind had flickered like a movie reel, every scenario flying through his head one after another, each more horrifying than the last. In the dappled moonlight, the loudest sound had been his own breathing, amplified in his head as though Darth Vader were standing behind him. When he'd looked down, his knuckles were white where he gripped his weapon, and every movement had sent another jolt through his frazzled nerves. Then the gunfire had started, and his training kicked in. He'd drilled a hundred times for that moment. And he'd come back alive—all of his team had—and from that day onward, the job had gotten easier. He'd learned to channel the sense of hyper-awareness and use it to his advantage, and experience had dulled the edges of his fear. But it never quite went away. If it had, he'd have ended up dead.

Today, that fear was back—not for himself, but for Violet.

"This is the road," Brax said. "Should be half a mile ahead."

Dawson slouched in his seat and pulled the Dodgers cap he'd found in the footwell next to a pile of discarded fast-food wrappers low over his eyes. He didn't want to risk being recognised, even at this hour. That could ruin everything. Luckily, Elmer had never seen Brax, or Lauren, who'd insisted on coming too.

The Porsche slowed as they got closer, and the house came into view. Number 3023, according to the yellow stickers on the sides of the mailbox—definitely the right place, but there was no RV and no Corolla. Fuck. Where was he?

"Place looks deserted," Brax said.

"Mailbox is empty, though." The front hung open, askew. "Nothing, not even junk mail."

"Want to take a closer look?"

"Too damn right I do." Because if they were wrong about this, then… No, Dawson didn't even want to consider it. "Let me out by that stand of trees, then wait farther along the road. I'll double back and check the rear."

The lots were spread far apart, surrounded by trees. Betty's nearest neighbour was a quarter mile away. Did she get lonely out here on her own? According to Alexa, she'd lived in the same home for fifty years, first with her husband and for the last decade on her own. Maybe she didn't want to leave the memories behind?

Dawson had already tucked a gun into his waistband, not his usual piece but an old Ruger P95 with the serial number filed off. It had been lounging in Brax's safe for the past three months. When Dawson bought a rifle from an old buddy a few years back, the guy had tossed the handgun in as a freebie, "for those little emergencies," and today certainly qualified.

The trees rustled in a gentle breeze as Dawson watched the house, waiting, controlling his breathing as he stayed alert for movement. An hour passed, then two, and the sun slowly came up. Nothing stirred, and he slipped closer, keeping his steps slow so that he didn't attract attention. Somebody was an early riser. The faint sound of laughter drifted from the house—not the genuine kind but the canned laughter that came with sitcoms—and Dawson risked peeping through the nearest window. A bedroom. Neat as a pin but dusty, and there was no sign of a man's belongings. Next came the bathroom, and although the glass was frosted, Dawson didn't see any signs of life, so he moved on. Dated furniture filled Betty's bedroom, old but still functional—a dressing table stacked with lotions and potions, a chunky chest of drawers, a bed covered in a handmade quilt. Photos of a couple were arranged neatly on the nightstand, some in colour, some black and white. Betty and her late husband?

In the living room, a grey-haired lady sat in front of the TV, occasionally smiling as knitting needles flashed in her hands. She barely looked at the bright red sweater in her lap, her attention focused on the show. Betty certainly didn't look like a woman harbouring a fugitive and a kidnap victim. And when Dawson checked the final room, the kitchen, that was empty too.

Where the hell was Elmer?

Brax had messaged to say he was waiting farther along the road with Lauren, and Dawson skulked back to the car, deflated. He recounted what he'd seen to the others.

"How about I knock on the door?" Lauren suggested. "Betty might talk to me the way Mrs. Schmidt talked to Storm."

"What if Elmer comes back?" Brax asked.

Then their luck would finally have turned. "I'll go with Lauren. Elmer won't get anywhere near her, trust me."

"It's only eight a.m."

"And Betty's been awake since six."

"Come on, Brax," Lauren coaxed. "Let us do this."

"Just be careful, okay?"

Five minutes later, Lauren pasted on a smile and knocked on the door with Dawson at her elbow. Another minute passed, and then Dawson heard the shuffle, *tap*, shuffle, *tap*, shuffle, *tap* of Betty moving toward them with a cane.

"Who is it?" came a shaky voice.

Lauren did the talking. "You don't know me, but I'm looking for Elmer. Your godson?"

"Violet?"

Did everybody know who she was?

"Uh, that's right."

"Edna Schmidt told me you'd be coming." The door

cracked open. "Boy, you made good time. What did you do? Fly? Come in, come in. I have iced tea and cookies."

More cookies? Great.

Betty gave the impression that she didn't get many visitors, and Dawson felt kind of sorry for her as she fussed around with plates and glasses and even a fucking doily. But he wanted to get some answers and then get the hell out of there. They didn't have a moment to waste. A quick prod to Lauren's arm, and she got the message.

"Have you seen Elmer recently?" she asked.

"Sorry, honey pie. The last time he dropped by was a month ago. Could you pass me that tray?"

"Really? Because when I mentioned Sacramento, Edna said you were the only person he knew here."

"That's what I thought too, and he never mentioned having any friends in the city. Elmer always was a loner. Maybe he just wanted to see the outdoors? When he was a boy, he used to love exploring the area. Hours, he'd spend out there. He went hiking with my Albert on Stevens Trail, and they used to explore Loch Leven Lakes too. The two of them walked for miles, and that boy could eat like a horse and never put on weight."

"When you last saw him, did he mention coming back to the area?"

"He didn't give me a date or anything, just said that he'd see me soon. I know you're worried, but Elmer's gone on trips before, and he always shows up again. How sweet do you like your tea?"

Betty headed for the kitchen, and Lauren sucked in a breath.

"I hate iced tea," she mouthed to Dawson, then pasted on a smile. "However it comes. I'm sure it's delicious."

English hadn't been Dawson's strongest subject at school. Mrs. Lenahan next door used to tell him to keep his words sweet in case he had to eat them someday, but that was a crock of shit. You couldn't eat words. And when it came to putting food on the table, Dawson had better things to do than read. But today, the words from one poem came back to him.

> 'Tis better to have loved and lost,
> Than never to have loved at all.

Such a lie.

There was nothing good about the ache in Dawson's chest. His insides had been scraped out by half a pound of C-4. People feared guns, but love was the most dangerous weapon of all.

He opened the back door of the Porsche for Lauren and waited for her to climb inside. They were out of leads, and any hope of finding Vi quickly was starting to fade. She'd been missing for four days now, and he worried that she was losing hope too. If only there were a way to let her know he was searching, that he'd be coming just as soon as he could. She had to realise he wouldn't abandon her, right?

"What now?" Brax asked. "I genuinely thought Betty would've given us a lead."

"So did I. Dammit, we know Elmer was in Sacramento. Why else would he come here? What's the connection?"

"He has a friend we don't know about?"

"Alexa hasn't found any evidence of that."

"An RV park?"

"He wouldn't risk keeping Vi near other people."

"A quiet campground?"

"Maybe." Dawson tried to put himself in the mind of a fugitive. If he needed to hide himself and his victim, he wouldn't risk leaving a paper trail. Nor would he park the RV where it could be seen from the road. The campgrounds near Loch Leven Lakes would be too crowded. Although the police weren't looking for Violet, Elmer didn't know that, and he was an investigator, for fuck's sake. No, if Dawson was on the run, he'd look for somewhere he wouldn't be disturbed. Such as a…

He snatched up his phone and emailed. Two seconds later, it rang.

"Alexa? Find me all the unoccupied properties around here. Not townhouses and apartments. Farms, ranches, barns, anything secluded."

"You think he's squatting?"

"I think it's a possibility. He knows the area from his visits to Betty, and he needs to stay away from prying eyes."

"Okay. Two minutes…" The wait was interminable. "I'm tracking your phone, and there are two places nearby. Brax, take the next left."

The first farm was a washout. The gates had dropped off their hinges, so overgrown with brambles and ivy that they were barely recognisable. Nobody had been through them for years.

"Could there be another way in?" Lauren asked.

"Doesn't look like it," Brax said as they trundled along the fence line. "Don't forget, Schmidt's in an RV. He won't be able to drive across a rutted pasture."

Dawson nodded his agreement. "Try the next place."

Potholes dotted the driveway at the Hickory Hill Ranch, half-filled with water from yesterday's storm. There wasn't a hill or a hickory tree in sight. The worst of the weather had blown over before Dawson arrived, but Brax and Lauren had driven through the tail end of the downpour on their way across from San Francisco. Today, the grey clouds gathered in Dawson's head.

Were there any fresh tyre tracks? Impossible to tell in the wet.

A crumbling house loomed ahead, more of an oversized log cabin, really. Nobody had lived there for years, that much was clear. The roof had collapsed at one end, charred around the edges. Had there been a fire? A lightning strike?

A wooden sign hung on two chains outside the front door, welcoming them as it *squeak-squeak-squeak*ed in the light breeze.

"I can't see an RV," Brax said.

"Stay in the car."

Dawson climbed out, gun in hand, and made a careful circuit of the building, checking each window. The only movement was a spider the size of a fist that skittered over his hand when he tried the back door. Locked. The gesture seemed pointless, given that when Dawson rounded the corner, he found a man-sized hole in the wall.

Another avenue exhausted. When he returned to the car, Lauren was heading for a clump of nearby bushes.

"I thought I told you to stay in the car?"

She waved a package of tissues at him. "A lady's gotta do what a lady's gotta do."

Brax climbed out too, stretching his arms up and bending from side to side. "I shouldn't have gone for the sport seats. They're too hard." His spine cracked. "Better. Alexa found another place a few miles farther away. I've already programmed it into the satnav."

"Lauren, hurry up."

"I can't pee any faster."

Finally, she finished, and they bumped along the driveway. The Porsche might have been an SUV, but it sure wasn't designed to go off-road. Low-profile tyres, stiff suspension…

"Wait!"

"What?" Brax asked.

A glint had caught Dawson's eye, sunlight on metal or glass.

"Back up."

"Did you see something important?"

Dawson wasn't certain. But that glint had been out of place, an anomaly among the undergrowth. And in the SEALs, he'd learned to trust his gut.

"Maybe."

CHAPTER 52
VIOLET

Ouch! The nail slipped and scored across my left hand, leaving a fiery trail in its wake. When I touched my tongue to my palm, I tasted the metallic tang of blood. But the ring I was chained to was loosening. I couldn't afford to give up. Desperation made me attack the mortar with renewed vigour, scraping and chipping at my only hope of escape.

I'd started off digging with the teaspoon, but the handle soon bent. So I'd wrapped the paper bag around the nail in the old wooden beam and pulled and swung and wiggled until the ageing wood finally loosened its grip. How long had I been at this task? It seemed like days, and every time I heard the rattle of the key in the lock above me, I had to stop and hide the evidence.

Four visits, Elton had made. I'd finally gotten my moccasins, and on his last appearance, he'd given me a hairbrush. A freaking hairbrush! That man seriously needed to re-evaluate his priorities.

Although if I had anything to do with it, I wouldn't be in his grip for much longer. A minute ago, I could have sworn the brick moved, and now, as I gave it another tug, I felt it give again. Only a fraction of an inch, but it wasn't solidly attached to the rest of the wall anymore. I grew frantic, rocking the ring from side to side with such desperation that I almost missed Elton's footsteps outside the door.

Shit!

The brick was still sticking halfway out of the wall, and I didn't have time to push it home before he ran down the wooden stairs. All I could do was spring back a few feet, tugging the blanket around myself to hide the nail in my hand. Why was he in such a hurry? Usually, his movements were slow and measured, and his gaze lingered in the vile way that made my skin crawl.

Today, he didn't hesitate, just stepped behind me and covered my mouth with his hand. His other arm wrapped around my chest, holding me against him. He hadn't taken a shower in days, and the smell made me gag.

"Shhh."

Why? What was happening? Why was Elton acting weird? Okay, weirder… Was somebody nearby?

I tried to jerk my head away, but Elton's grip tightened, vice-like, his nails digging into my cheeks. He might have been wiry, but underneath his ill-fitting clothes, he hid a strength I'd never suspected that first day I saw him sitting outside my trailer.

Elton didn't say anything more, and I realised he was listening. We had visitors, didn't we? The police? Dawson? Or just a poor lost soul who'd stumbled across this tiny corner of hell?

Time ticked by. The only sounds were our rasping breaths and the distant *drip, drip, drip* that had been my soundtrack for days. How long did we stand there in our perverted embrace? Five minutes? Ten? No noise came from above, and I began to think I was mistaken. That there was nobody upstairs, and Elton's paranoia had finally turned into full-on delusion. I shifted surreptitiously from foot to foot, testing his hold on me, but his arm stayed firm. With him standing behind me, I couldn't even knee him where it hurt.

Then I heard it. A car engine, powerful by the sound of it, and the throaty purr grew fainter as I strained my ears. It was leaving. Whoever had been outside was leaving, and I was still trapped here.

An animal instinct buried deep inside me took over, clawing its way to the surface. As the noise of the car receded, Elton relaxed a little, and I twisted and swung my fist at him with the nail sticking out of the end. I was going for his eye, but he turned at the last moment and I got his cheek instead. His roar wasn't human.

And neither was I. One almighty yank and the brick came free, hurtling toward me on the end of its chain. I scrambled for it on the dirt floor, and when my hand closed around the ring, I swung the makeshift club with all my might at Elton's head. I didn't score a direct hit, but when he stumbled and dropped to his knees, I sprinted for the stairs. The sting of splinters didn't slow me down as I hauled the door open. *Oh, hell.* Where was the key? *Where was the key?* Elton must have put it in his pocket, but I couldn't go back for it, not when he was still conscious. I heard his foot on the bottom step. The door would have to stay unlocked.

Run, Violet. Run!

I was in a barn of some kind. A narrow shaft of light cut between two tall doors at one end, and I skirted a white RV and ran toward freedom. *Get out, get out, get out.*

The right-hand door creaked as I pushed it, the rotting wood scraping along the ground as it opened slowly, oh so slowly. Sunlight burned into my eyes, and for a moment, I couldn't see a thing. Being locked in the dark for days had ruined my vision. Shapes blurred—a rusted vehicle, a wood pile, trees. I ran toward the forest surrounding the clearing. If I reached the undergrowth, I could hide, but the chain hindered me, dragging behind and swinging around my legs. I tried to gather it up, but it kept slithering out of my hands.

"Help! Help me!"

There was no answer and no sign of the vehicle I'd heard earlier. Where were we? Was there a road nearby? My ankle cried out in pain as I twisted it in a hole, and I struggled to stay upright. Trees. I needed to get to the trees. We were surrounded by a wall of evergreens, and if I could just make it to the safety of their sweeping branches…

"Stop!"

A loud *bang* made me jump out of my skin, and I felt—I freaking *felt*—the bullet whizz past my ear. I stopped.

"Violet, Violet, Violet…" Elton didn't bother to hurry. He didn't need to. Since he had a gun in his hand, I wasn't going anywhere. "Why did you have to do that?"

"I'm s-s-sorry."

Or maybe I should *try to run?* At least if I were dead, I'd be nothing. Gone. Merciful darkness would be better than the living death that awaited me back in the cellar.

"We talked about this. About how you need to earn your privileges, and now we'll have to start right at the beginning again." He jerked the gun in my direction. "Get back inside."

"Shoot me."

"What?"

"Just shoot me, okay?"

"You're not thinking straight. I understand that this might be stress—"

He never finished the sentence because his head disappeared. Blood splattered the scrubby grass behind him, and he stayed standing for a second, swaying, before he crumpled to the ground.

Then I was in Dawson's arms and he was squeezing me and kissing my hair and whispering that it would be okay but how could it be because I was trapped in the middle of a nightmare and nothing made sense anymore.

"I've got you. Vi, I'm so sorry."

Was he real? He felt real.

A shriek came from behind me, a sound I'd heard many times before when we found spiders in our apartment.

"Lauren?"

She sprinted across the clearing and squeezed the breath out of me, leaving me sandwiched between her and Dawson. And I wanted to stay there when I looked to the side and saw Braxton, because I was naked and a mess and shaking and my legs wouldn't hold me up.

"Brax, find a blanket," Dawson instructed.

"Fuck. Is she okay?"

"Just get a damn blanket."

"I'm okay." It came out as a croak, and I tried again. "I'm okay."

"Did he touch you?"

I knew what Dawson was asking.

"Not…not yet."

Lauren picked up the chain, which was still dangling around my waist.

"He locked you up?" Her expression was a mix of fury and horror.

"In the dark. A cellar." The tears came, splashing over my cheeks and down my chest, leaving grubby tracks on my skin because I was filthy.

She peered over at the remains of Elton, then let me go and walked over to him. One not-so-dainty tennis shoe connected with his cold, dead balls.

"He's gone, Lauren," Dawson told her.

"I know, but he still deserved that."

Then she walked to the nearest bush and puked.

Dawson stripped off his jacket and tucked it around my shoulders. The leather was heavy and stiff but also warm, and it smelled of him, the comforting mix of man and cologne that told me I was safe. He wrapped me up in his arms and kissed my greasy hair, but I was too drained to apologise for the state of it.

Twigs cracked, and Braxton returned with a fleecy blanket, a luxury after Elton's rough woollen offering. Lauren helped me to wrap it around myself and tuck the edge in like a towel, and her kindness only made me bawl harder.

"There's a barn back there, hidden in the trees," Braxton said. "The RV's inside."

Dawson cursed under his breath. "How the hell did we miss that?"

"The track's hidden behind a tangle of bushes. If only Lauren had peed on the other side of the yard, we'd have stumbled across it."

"Shit."

"Please, can we stop talking about bodily functions?" Lauren begged.

A laugh burst out of my throat. I was safe, and Lauren was...embarrassed? "But y-y-you usually like talking about bodily functions."

"Not *that* type of bodily functions."

"Let's put you in the car." Dawson picked me up bridal-style. "Fuck, your feet are a mess."

I clung to his neck, scared that I'd wake up and be back in the cellar again, waiting for a monster to toss me a package of Frosted freaking Flakes.

"What about him? What about Elton?"

"The police can deal with the details. I only care about getting you somewhere comfortable."

"I can't believe you found me."

"I was never gonna stop looking, babe. I'm only sorry I didn't keep you safe in the first place."

"It was out of your hands. I was the one who opened the door that evening. He said you'd sent him."

"Motherfucker. If I could kill him again..."

Dawson followed Braxton along a narrow track, barely big

enough to fit Elton's RV. Overhead, I could see where he'd scraped the low-hanging branches driving it through. The track curved to the left in an upside-down J-shape, and we emerged into a clearing near a rotting house. A vehicle was parked outside, a big grey thing that probably cost more than I'd earned in my entire life, and Dawson slid me into the back seat.

"Lauren, can you take care of her? Put her in some of your clothes?"

"Of course."

I glanced down at myself, and anger bubbled up when I saw the damn chain again, trailing out of the car door.

"Can you get this off?" The tears welled up again. "I just want it off me."

"Give me a minute, babe. I'll look for the key."

"I think… I think Elton has it."

"Then I'll find it."

I reached out to touch Dawson's face, to ground myself. He hadn't shaved for days. Even with the rough stubble under my palm, I still struggled to believe I wasn't dreaming. That I'd never have to kneel for Elton again. That this man I'd fallen so hard for had found me and set me free.

"Dawson?"

"Yeah?"

"I love you."

And I did. Whatever was happening between us might have been new, but alone in the dark, I'd had plenty of time to think things through, and I needed him to know how I felt. I only hoped the mess I was in wouldn't put him off me for good.

But I needn't have worried. Dawson wrapped me up in those strong arms, and when they tightened, it felt as if he was pressing all the broken parts back together. Making me whole again.

"I love you too, Vi."

Within thirty minutes, the entire clearing was filled with police cars and ambulances and even a fire truck, their red-and-blue lights bouncing off the surrounding foliage. I'd been transferred to a stretcher and poked and prodded until Dawson growled at the medics to stop.

At least the chain was gone. Dawson had kept his word and found the key in Elton's pocket. And now, dressed in a pair of Lauren's yoga pants and a baggy sweater, I began to feel a little more human and a little less like an animal. *Elton had caged me like a freaking pet.* Gradually my heart rate dropped, as evidenced by the incessant beeping of whatever machine the EMTs had hooked me up to.

"Can you turn that off? That beeping?"

"It's monitoring your vital signs," the female EMT told me.

"But I'm awake. Can't I just tell you if I feel unwell?"

"You've been under stress."

"And you're putting her under more stress." Lauren solved the problem by pulling off the sticky pads and dropping them into the woman's hand. "We're good here."

The EMT glared, but at least she backed off.

"I just want to get away from this place," I whispered to Lauren. "It's worse than being on a movie set."

The only thing missing was Debbie, snapping photos for her Instagram or her TikTok or whatever.

"The cops have questions."

"Can we get some food first? I've barely eaten for days. How long was I missing?"

"You don't know?"

"I've literally been in the dark. I didn't even know whether it was day or night until I escaped."

"This is day four."

"It feels like so much longer."

"Tell me about it. We were all so freaking terrified, but Dawson wouldn't give up."

"I thought you'd left. Elton was in the cellar with me, and I heard the car drive off."

"Yeah, we were about to go, but then Dawson spotted a wireless camera hidden in a bush as we were approaching the gate. Elmer must've been watching for visitors."

"Elmer? Is that his name? He called himself that once, but I didn't dare to ask questions." I shivered, partly from the cold but mostly from memories of the dungeon. "I just want to go home. *Home*. I don't even know where that is now. Oakwood Falls, I guess? Oh, heck. Mom must be real worried, Trent too. I need to call them."

Lauren shifted uncomfortably. "Uh, why don't you wait for a little while?"

"Wait? Why would I wait?"

"Nobody told your mom you were missing. The cops wouldn't take our report seriously, and we didn't want to scare her."

"And Trent?"

"Yeah, so it turned out he already knew."

"Huh?"

"Let's talk about this later. Like next week or something."

What was Lauren hiding? "No, I think we should talk about this now."

I felt rather than saw Dawson behind me. He gave off vibes, not just the pheromones, but a ripple of reassurance that enveloped me like a safety net. I wriggled into a sitting position so I could wrap an arm around him.

"Talk about what now?" he asked.

Lauren made the same "oops" face as she had that time she'd been bitching on WhatsApp about a waitress at work, only to realise that she'd accidentally included the girl in our group chat.

"Uh, Trent?" she said.

"Fuck."

What was going on? "Is Trent okay?"

"Mostly."

"Mostly? Dawson, what happened?"

"He had to have his nose reset."

"Ohmigosh! How did it get broken? Was there an accident? Wait, was he helping to find Elton? Elmer?"

"Not exactly."

Braxton walked over. "Dawson punched Trent."

Just when I thought the worst was over, another chill ran through me. I tried to push Dawson away, but he wouldn't budge.

"Why the heck did you hit Trent?"

Again, Braxton answered. "Trent was the one who sent Elmer, sweetheart."

"He *what*?"

"He hired somebody to keep an eye on you so you didn't —and I quote—get taken advantage of. Except Elmer went rogue."

A little of the shock dissipated. "So Trent was only trying to help?"

Yes, that made sense. Trent had worried about me from afar, and he'd wanted me to stay safe. He cared. Obviously, I'd have preferred if he'd discussed his plans with me first, but his motive had been pure. And yes, he should have vetted Elmer better, but Elmer had fooled everyone. The fact that he'd turned out to be a raving lunatic wasn't entirely Trent's fault.

"At first, maybe he was trying to help," Dawson said, tucking loose strands of hair behind my ear. "But then he asked Elmer to send the lilies and the Venus flytrap."

What?

"Why on earth would he do that?"

"Because he wanted to scare you into going back to

Oakwood Falls, and he realised how nervous you were after Mikki sent the first two gifts."

"Mikki sent the roses and those disgusting chocolates?"

"She admitted it," Lauren said. "And then I flushed her Louboutins down the toilet."

Lauren turned to give Braxton a high five, but I was still processing, my brain creaking under the strain. Trent had instigated all this? No, there must have been a mistake. Crossed wires somewhere. Trent was my oldest friend. We'd grown up together. He was building us a freaking house.

"Can I borrow a phone?"

"Why?" Dawson asked.

"I need to call Trent."

"That's not a good idea, babe."

"I've just spent four hellish days chained up in a hole, and you're telling me one of my closest friends is responsible? I have to speak with him."

As the words left my mouth, I saw the hurt flicker in Dawson's eyes. Hurt that I didn't believe him. And I felt guilty for that, but this was *Trent*. If I could just ask him for his side of the story, he'd…he'd… What? What would he do? Would he even tell me the truth? The Trent I'd once known had changed, I knew that, and weren't lawyers trained to deflect?

Dawson held out his phone, and I realised that if I took it, the trust between us would be broken. And I did trust him. He'd never lied to me, he'd done everything he could to protect me, and today, he'd played detective and gone on a crazy manhunt to the middle of nowhere, then killed a man to save me. If Trent *did* care, where was he? Lauren was here and so was Braxton Vale, a man I barely even knew.

Trent was conspicuous by his absence.

"How did Trent know Elmer?" I whispered.

Dawson's tight expression loosened infinitesimally. "From

the law firm. He worked as a freelance investigator on some of Trent's cases."

An investigator…

A memory flittered back, an image of a message Trent had accidentally sent to me instead of Virginia—his father's secretary—because our names were next to each other in his phone.

Call Schmidt about the Maxwell investigation. I need the report by Monday.

"What's Elmer's surname?"

"Schmidt. Elmer Schmidt."

It was true. It was all true. Trent had betrayed me, and I'd almost died.

I pushed Dawson's phone away. I didn't need to call Trent. In fact, I never wanted to speak to him again.

"You okay, babe?"

"You should have done more than break his nose." Dawson smiled, and I knew then that we'd be okay. He was my anchor, my rock, and he'd hold me steady as I healed. "Can we go home?"

"Where's home?"

Not Oakwood Falls. Beyond that, I didn't know, and I didn't really care anymore. Who gave a hoot about places? People were what mattered.

"Home is wherever you are."

CHAPTER 53
VIOLET

"**A**nd stay away from me!"

I slammed the door and sagged back against Dawson, listening first to silence, then to the *slap, slap, slap* of Trent's leather-soled shoes walking toward the elevator.

"Remind me never to get on your bad side, babe."

"I'm shaking." I held up a hand, watching as it trembled. Anger didn't come naturally. "I can't believe he had the nerve to show his face here."

Worse, he'd hired another freaking investigator to find me. Had he learned nothing the first time?

"Some people never change." Dawson steered me over to the couch. "Why don't you sit down while I clean up the mess?"

Two dozen long-stemmed red roses lay scattered across the tiled hallway, shards of the vase they came in twinkling under the chandelier. After all that he'd put me through, Trent had tried to give me flowers, and then he'd acted surprised when I hurled them back at him. At least this time, they'd come in water rather than blood.

A faint *ding* sounded from outside as the elevator arrived, and I shed a silent tear for the death of my old life. There would be no more quiet, malleable Violet. If Elmer had taught me one thing, it was that I needed to stand up for myself. Dawson was right—some people never changed, but I was determined to learn from my mistakes.

I pressed my lips against his because he was anything but a mistake. "I love you."

"Love you too, Vi."

Eight days had passed since I'd escaped from Elmer's clutches, and with Trent's departure, I hoped things would finally begin to settle.

Filming was due to start again tomorrow, but changes had been made. To start with, I'd been excused from staying at the beach house. Even David could understand that I didn't want to go near the scene of my abduction, a place that held so many bad memories. Debbie had suggested renting a different house, but Kane had shot that idea down pretty quickly.

Yes, Kane. Dawson said he'd been unexpectedly helpful during the search, even if his ulterior motive was to get the movie finished. And I no longer had to fear the kissing scenes either. Yesterday, Lauren, who had less tact than me, had presented him with an economy-sized box of Tic Tacs and suggested he might want to eat one or ten. He didn't even get mad. I got the impression that he kind of liked her, even if the feeling wasn't reciprocated.

David didn't seem worried about me moving out, not with all the extra publicity my kidnapping had garnered. I'd faithfully mentioned my role in *Hidden Intent* to every reporter I'd spoken to, plus posted on social media about how thrilled I was to be completing the movie. A small lie, but I just wanted life to get back to normal, and it never would if I kept hiding out in Braxton's apartment.

Mikki, on the other hand, hadn't taken the news of my abduction well. With Lucas and Kane having played their part in my rescue, she'd been relegated to a distant fourth in the publicity stakes, a position she'd attempted to rectify by getting arrested for DUI last night. Thankfully, she hadn't killed anything but her reputation. Plus she'd spent the night in jail, so we'd had ten whole hours of blessed peace.

Perhaps the most painful part of this whole ordeal, even worse than those horrible moments after I escaped from Elmer's dungeon, was having to visit my mom and tell her what had happened. She'd seen the news, of course, and the sensationalised footage only scared her more. The first two days after I'd been rescued were taken up with hospital visits and police interviews and running the gauntlet of paparazzi outside every exit. Dawson had been officially cleared of any crime for shooting Elmer, but the media were still raking over his past. The rest of the Blackstone Nine too, although since Braxton had been summoned back to New York right after my return, Dawson was bearing the brunt of it.

We still hadn't discussed what happened at Blackstone House, and as I pushed—no, shoved—my time in the cellar as far toward the back of my mind as it would go, curiosity took over. What would Dawson say if I asked him about his past? I'd secretly read everything I could find on the case, mostly on my phone while I was in the bathroom, which would have worked out fine if Lauren wasn't staying in the apartment with us. Ever the caring bestie, she'd bought me a package of laxatives and a giant carton of prune juice "just to help out." Dawson, of course, had walked in right as she was reading me an article on how stress caused constipation, and I'd been forced to stuff an entire blueberry muffin into her mouth.

But visiting Mom was a hundred times worse.

The problem wasn't just my near-death experience, the tears, the "what ifs," and the whispered proclamation that no parent should outlive their child. No, the problem was that Mom worked for Trent's family, and if I hacked off his testicles with nail scissors the way I wanted to, that could put her employment in a precarious position.

Salvation had come in an unlikely form as we walked up the steps into the plane that Braxton had arranged to fly us to Kansas. A private freaking jet. Inside, it was furnished in pale grey leather with a plush cream carpet and gold bits on everything. It even had cashmere blankets. And hors d'oeuvres. And a giant flat-screen TV. Anyhow, I digress. My phone rang as I reached the top of the steps, and I almost dropped the darn thing because my hands were shaking so much.

"Violet? It's Donna."

Lucas's agent, and now my agent too. I'd barely spoken with her, and auditioning for parts was the furthest thing from my mind.

"Now isn't a great—"

"I know this isn't a great time, hun. I saw the papers. And I'm sorry, but this won't wait."

"What is it?"

"Racino's come back with an offer."

"He has?" I stopped dead, and Dawson nearly walked into me. "The role I read for?"

"Filming starts in twelve weeks. He came in at a million, I countered with a million five, and we settled halfway."

"Sorry, for a moment there, I thought you said he'd offered me a million dollars."

"A million and a quarter. Plus he's agreed to a no-nudity clause, and he'll write into the contract that Dawson Masters will be your bodyguard. I spoke with Lucas, and he filled me in. How does that sound?"

"It sounds…"

Unbelievable. I checked around for hidden cameras in case I was on one of those prank shows—David's next project, maybe?

"Everything okay?" Dawson whispered.

I muted the phone. "How would you like to be my bodyguard again?"

"I'll always be your bodyguard."

"I mean paid. Remember that movie role I auditioned for in LA?"

"You got it?"

"Apparently. Pinch me, would you?"

He kissed me instead, soft and chaste, just a touch of his lips. "No, I won't pinch you. You work damn hard, and you deserve everything you get. Yes, of course I'll look after you, but if we could avoid living with another Mikki, I'd be a happy man."

"No Mikki. We can rent a nice apartment. They're offering over a million dollars." Even after Donna took her ten percent, I'd be left with a fortune.

Dawson's eyes widened. "Fuck."

"Wild, isn't it?" We could have a pool with actual water in it. "I'm gonna tell them yes. I'll have almost two months off after we wrap *Hidden Intent*, so we can take a vacation too."

"Perfect."

Yes, he was. Donna was waiting patiently when I picked the phone up again, and I told her yes. A definite yes.

"I thought you'd say that." She somehow managed to sound fierce and happy at the same time. "Email me an address where I can courier the contract, would you? I'll have my lawyer check it over first."

"Thank you."

"I also have other offers. Two movies, a role as brand ambassador for a cosmetics company, clothing endorsements... Oh, and a resort in Hawaii is offering a luxury suite for two weeks if you'll post six appropriately tagged photos on Instagram. But I can put all of those folks off until you feel better."

I finally made it onto the plane, dazed, and then the biggest implication of the phone call hit me. I'd be able to take care of my mom. Screw the roof—I could buy her a whole new house. And if working for Trent's family became uncomfortable, she could quit and use Racino's money to become a lady of leisure. A weight lifted from my shoulders.

The angry part of me, the part that remembered the fear I'd felt when I'd received Trent and Elmer's sick gifts, still wanted to toss my so-called friend off the edge of the elephant mountain. Roses. He'd brought me more freaking *roses*, but no number of flowers could make up for the fact that he was so two-faced he was basically twins. He'd lied about his return from New York too. Mom told me his dad had mild angina, not a life-threatening heart condition, and an associate of Dawson's had sent us a photo of Trent and his ex, complete with a bottle of champagne and a sparkling diamond engagement ring. She'd gone on quite the tirade on Facebook after catching him in bed with his intern in their luxury apartment. Yes, they'd even been living together.

But the fragile part of me didn't want to see Trent at all. Not now, not ever. Broken Violet wanted to sneak into Oakwood Falls, cry onto my mom's shoulder, and leave without speaking to another soul.

And that was what I did. Mom sobbed, I sobbed, and Dawson promised to look after me. He looked somewhat alarmed when Mom wrapped him up in a fierce hug, surprised almost, and I wondered if his mom had ever given him affection that way. Hadn't he said they weren't close? I might have lost my dad, but after he died, Mom had showered me with enough love for two people, so I didn't miss out. I'd have to do the same with Dawson.

When I told Mom what Trent had done, her horrified expression broke my heart because with it came guilt.

"I encouraged Trent," she whispered. "I thought you liked him. And *I* liked him."

"I did like him once. But he was selfish, and he thought he could change me into something I'm not."

An accessory. A tchotchke he could take to parties and show off to his friends and clients. *Hey, Mr. Local Restaurant Owner, meet Violet. She made a couple of movies before she decided she loved me more than Hollywood.*

"What should I do? Mr. and Mrs. Vickers have always been good to me, but now…"

"If you like working for them, then carry on. Trent won't want his part in the story getting out. But if it becomes awkward, just quit." I told her about Racino's offer. "I'll look after you; I promise. And in the meantime, I'm going to get some repairs done on this place—the roof and the porch to begin with. No more buckets when it rains."

"Oh, Violet. Really?"

"Billy Johnson's dad agreed to start the work next week."

Cue a flood of tears. I also promised to call more often, and Mom said she'd visit me in California, although I had my doubts about that. She'd only left Oakwood Falls a handful of times in her life, and to her, the big, wide world was something that played out on TV like a soap opera, not a place to be lived in and explored.

And then we were back on board the plane, and I curled up beside Dawson for the trip in this flying palace. I traced his lips with one finger, pondering what to do next. We'd slept together every night since the kidnapping, but that was all. We'd only slept. No sex. Just Dawson, me, and an ocean of guilt, guilt because he tossed and turned every night, and I was at least partially responsible for that.

I needed to get something important off my chest.

"Dawson, I'm sorry."

"Vi, we've been through this. None of it was your fault. Elmer was responsible for his own actions, with Trent as the catalyst."

"I mean for what happened at the end. For putting you in a position where you had to kill a man. It can't be easy to live with, and I know you're losing sleep over it."

He surprised me by laughing. "You think that's why I can't sleep? Babe, after what Schmidt did, I was always gonna kill him. You just saved me from burying a body in the middle of the night."

"*What*?"

"Does that shock you?" Dawson asked.

Well, yes. That Dawson would have risked his own freedom to avenge my suffering made my chest swell. Would a cold-blooded execution have upset me? Honestly? While I was tied up in that cellar, I'd dreamed of Elmer's death. If I'd had the means and the ability, I'd have killed him myself and taken pleasure in it, and if he'd lived to stand trial, I'd have wished for the death penalty. Why? Because if things had been different, he'd have kept me in that dungeon until I broke completely or died, whichever came first. I'd seen it in his eyes.

No, I couldn't get too cut up over his fate.

And Dawson's fierceness in protecting me made my heart do a little trippy dance.

"Yes, it shocks me, but it doesn't upset me. So why can't you sleep if it's not because of Elmer?"

"Because I have a naked goddess lying next to me, and I'm fantasising about all the things I want to do to her."

Oh. Oh!

Warmth spread through me, pooling between my legs. My libido might have taken a short vacation, but now it was back with a vengeance.

"Ever joined the mile-high club, Mr. Grand?"

Now his smile turned filthy, and I loved it.

"Can't say I ever have, Miss Fawn. What did you have in mind?"

I straddled him in the plush leather seat, pausing to kiss him before I reached for his zipper.

"Close your eyes and find out."

CHAPTER 54
VIOLET

"I'm free!"

In my head, I ran screaming from the studio, but in reality, I walked out between Kane and Lucas amid a hail of flashbulbs. Filming for *Hidden Intent* was finally over.

The last few weeks had been intense, not least because we'd fallen behind schedule due to my unexpected absence. For much of the time, we'd been out on location, all the better to avoid memories of Elton sitting outside my trailer at the studio, watching me with a gaze I'd once thought was conscientious but now knew to be predatory.

I'd never set foot inside that trailer again. Instead, I shared with Lucas, although that had gotten interesting when we received the final chunk of script.

"Freaking heck! It was you? *You* stabbed Del Swanson?"

"Says here that he killed my girlfriend in a hit and run."

And in a neat twist, Kelvin James, the main suspect, shoved Veronica's abusive boyfriend down the stairs. Scott Lowes died convincingly, Veronica provided Kelvin's alibi, and then Lance found out and blackmailed her into giving him an alibi too. Although Veronica and Kelvin moved to

Hawaii to live by the beach, the three of them would forever be bound by their murderous secret.

Would it come back to bite them in the ass? The producers were already whispering about a sequel, but if I was going to be involved, big changes would need to be made. Huge. No beach house and no Mikki, to begin with.

But I wanted to work with Lucas again, and I'd cope with Kane as long as he kept up his breath-mint habit. He ate them all the time now, but I guess there were worse addictions to have. *Hollywood actor in Tic Tac scandal* was hardly a compelling headline. And Kane's last photoshoot had been a spread for *Your Cat* magazine with Lady Fluffingham. He'd surprised me by taking life as a pet owner seriously, and he'd gained a whole new legion of female fans because of it. Fluffy had her own Instagram page now, and I didn't even care that she had more followers than me.

"Later, Violet."

Kane gave me a kiss on the cheek and headed for his limo, but Lucas hugged me tight.

"Hey, hey! I ate way too much for that."

With no more bikini scenes for the foreseeable future, I'd pigged out at the celebratory buffet. Boy, had I missed cake.

"Gonna miss you."

"We're meeting up for dinner next week."

Lucas had invited us over to his home in the Hollywood Hills for a cookout, which appealed far more than eating in a fancy restaurant. Perhaps we'd return the favour in the future?

Not yet, because the house we'd just bought was a total mess, but someday.

Yes, you heard that right. We'd bought a house. Well, more of a cottage—an elderly lady had used it as her vacation home—but it was all ours.

Originally, we'd planned to rent a place, but with both of us stuck in San Francisco while I finished filming, we'd delegated apartment hunting to Lauren, who had more free time now that Braxton had found her a job with better hours. Five nights a week, she waitressed in the restaurant at Nyx in LA, which, according to Lauren, might have had a sex club in the basement but involved significantly less groping than she'd endured at the crappy sports bar we'd both worked in before. And it paid a heck of a lot more money too.

Anyhow, my brief of a "two-bedroom apartment with parking and maybe a pool" translated into "but it's such a cute house, plus it has plenty of yard space for your future kids."

"It needs a new roof," Dawson had pointed out.

"Yes, but the owner reduced the price for that."

"That kitchen came out of the seventies."

"Which is totally fashionable again."

"What's that building at the back?"

"A carriage house. The owner's father was an artist, and he used it as a studio. But look, guys, you said you wanted a pool, and it has one."

I scrolled through the photos. "The water's green."

"It's on a two-acre lot surrounded by trees. Think of the privacy."

I did. I also thought of the wraparound porch, and the cosy rooms, and the view of the ocean. And after that, I thought about the contracts I'd signed over the past week. Another movie to follow on after *The Thing*, the "stay healthy" campaign I'd agreed to front for a vitamin manufacturer, the luxury car ad I'd be co-starring in with Lucas.

If I wanted to buy the cottage, I could afford it.

Meanwhile, Dawson groaned. "She likes it."

Lauren squealed with glee. "I knew it! Violet's never really been an apartment person."

"Security could be a problem, especially if we're away working on Vi's movies."

"You're looking at your number-one house-sitter right here."

"I always swore I'd never renovate another wreck." Dawson was talking about Blackstone House, wasn't he? "Ever lived without electricity for a month?"

"We could get builders in," I said. "Stay in a hotel for a while."

"Are you serious about this?"

"Couldn't we at least take a look?"

One visit, and I'd fallen in love for the second time in my life. Dawson and Mulberry Cottage. I didn't count Trent—that was more of a misplaced infatuation.

The place was ours.

And Lauren was coming too. In the week since we'd signed the contract, an acquaintance of Dawson's had installed a top-spec security system, and Lauren would be staying in the carriage house to watch the place while we were away. We all knew the first few months would be like camping, but Lucas had offered us two guest rooms if the urge for a proper shower got too strong.

And of course he'd invited us over for dinner too, any time we wanted.

Now he gave me one last squeeze as we stood outside the studio. "I know I'll see you next week, but that's not the point. Who else am I gonna bitch about Mikki and her kind with?"

"Lauren?"

His phone buzzed, and he glanced at the screen. "Speak of the devil. Lauren informs me that according to Celebgossip.com, I'm dating Peyton Royce."

"Do you even know her?"

"I vaguely recall saying hello to her once."

Dawson leaned in to shake his hand. "Best of luck, buddy. I hope you have a long and happy life together. Ready to go, Vi? We have wallpaper to strip."

So he said, but first, I planned on stripping something else.

A month later, we had a roof with no holes, central heating, and wiring that wasn't a fire hazard. Next, we needed to tackle the lack of appliances in the kitchen, but I'd learned how to light a grill, and Braxton had sent us a camping stove as a housewarming gift.

Mom had a roof with no holes too. And a new smartphone. She'd always sworn she'd never use one of those confusing little gadgets because what was wrong with good old buttons? But now she'd joined Instagram, and I got to see pictures of my hometown every day. Plus she called me at least three times a week, usually with the phone on speaker as she was making dinner. She was still working for Mr. and Mrs. Vickers, and although they knew that Trent and I had fallen out, they didn't know why, and Trent wasn't going to tell them, was he? A part of me wished that he'd suffered the consequences for his dirty tricks, but when Dawson and I had spoken about it, he'd pointed out that Trent wouldn't have gotten a jail sentence for having Elmer send me a plant or candy, no matter how underhanded his intentions had been. My best revenge was happiness.

And besides, karma was kicking Trent's butt right now. Last week, he'd travelled to Dodge City to present a segment on "Tips for Young Lawyers" at a conference held by the Kansas Bar Association, and he'd been in full flow when a picture of him naked had popped up with the caption "Always practise safe sex—do it alone." His hand had been around his dick, and he'd talked on for a full thirty seconds before he realised what was on the screen behind him. Apparently, the really graphic part had been obscured by a very tiny smiley face, so disciplinary action was unlikely, but

I was certain Trent wouldn't be asked to speak at any more Bar Association events. And after the news had reached Oakwood Falls, he'd been disinvited from future church luncheons as well.

I needed to buy karma a drink. If revenge was happiness, then I'd certainly gotten my own back.

This evening, I curled up on the porch swing with my iPad while Dawson took a shower. The Blackstone House murder fascinated me, and I couldn't get it out of my head. The dynamics between the housemates, the murder itself, the conspiracy theories that followed... Ruby Costello had been found in a locked room, killed in what some sources claimed was a satanic ritual, dead at the hands of a man she'd considered a friend. What had made him snap like that? Theories ranged from paranoid schizophrenia to a rare alignment of planets causing a shift in negative cosmic energy.

Had anybody in the house suspected Levi Sykes? Seen through his mask to his true character? With Elmer, I'd witnessed firsthand how a man could appear perfectly normal on the outside while having the soul of Satan, and I wanted to understand why. Call it morbid curiosity, call it closure, call it a need to assign blame. In my darker moments, I couldn't help wondering whether I'd done anything to lead Elmer on, whether I'd given off some sort of signal that he'd misinterpreted to make him feel that I needed—in his words —to be saved.

"What's that?"

Dawson's voice over my shoulder startled me, and I tried to close the page on Slide49.com, the website that, ironically, Elmer himself had referred me to. But I wasn't fast enough.

As I twisted to face Dawson, his expression hardened. "Why are you reading that shit?"

"I just... I just want to know what happened."

He knelt in front of me, still unsmiling. "Vi, I swear I had nothing to do with Ruby's death."

Good heavens, that was what he was worried about? "I never thought for a moment that you were involved. I'm more interested in the person who did kill her. Like, what made him tick? The same with Elmer. I know the two cases are different—I mean, I was held prisoner while poor Ruby died in her bedroom—but why did Levi Sykes turn on her like that? Did he seem normal before?"

"Do we have to talk about this?"

"I guess not. I realise it sounds gruesome, but knowing that I'm not the only person who suffered at the hands of a madman helps me to straighten things out in my head." Hesitantly, I opened up my e-reader app and showed Dawson the true crime books I'd been studying. "And it makes me wonder whether all these psychos have something in common."

Dawson sighed as he settled beside me. The padded seat swung gently back and forth, pushed by a light breeze.

"Levi had problems, babe."

"What kind of problems?"

"I don't know, exactly, and he always refused to go into the details, but he took a lot of pills for a man with nothing wrong with him."

"He was sick?"

"In his head, I think. He had crazy-bad mood swings, and once or twice, he locked himself in his room for days. But other times, he'd be grinning like an idiot and buying everyone beer. So who knows? Maybe he forgot his meds?"

"Did he ever get angry?"

"Yeah, but never with the girls. The only time I saw him really blow up, the guy deserved it."

"What happened?"

"When I first moved into Blackstone House, there was a guy named Joey in Grey's room. A salesman who worked on commission, so he had either wads of money or no money, plus he was a sleaze. One of the bathrooms had a broken lock, so Ruby made a little sign to hang over the door handle. Pooping or not pooping, it said." Dawson smiled at the memory. "Always did make me laugh. Anyhow, Joey walked in on her showering and swore she hadn't turned the sign around, but Ruby always turned the damn sign around. And then it happened again, and she got mad at him."

"I would have too, if he'd done it deliberately. Do you think he did?"

"Yeah, I do. And so did Levi because he told Joey to get out of the fucking house, pronto."

"He left?"

"Not voluntarily. He tried to brush the shower thing off as a joke, but Levi called bullshit and started pushing him."

"They had a fight?"

"It didn't get that far. I helped Levi to pick Joey up, and we dumped him outside. His stuff too. Never saw him again."

"So Levi stuck up for Ruby?"

"Yeah."

"He liked her?"

"Yeah."

"But the newspapers said they used to fight."

"They didn't *fight*, fight. Levi's lawyers twisted our words in court. We all used to bicker from time to time, but mostly about dumb stuff. The temperature on the thermostat, what to watch on TV, whose turn it was to water the plants."

"Then why did he kill her?"

"Who the hell knows?"

"Is it… Is it true they found the knife that killed her in your bedroom?"

"Where the fuck did you hear that?"

Oh, crap. "Uh, Elmer told me."

"That's bullshit, babe. The knife…" Dawson took a deep breath. "The knife was in her chest."

"Did you ever think it might have been another of your roommates? Not Levi?"

"Truthfully? No. But I didn't think it was Levi either, not until the evidence began piling up. I know for certain it wasn't Nolan or Alexa because we were together in the basement on the evening Ruby died. Well, Alexa was in her room, but she didn't come out."

"Alexa?"

"Otherwise known as the unidentified minor."

"Wait… You don't mean the same Alexa who helped to search for me?"

"The one and only."

"Wow." All these little pieces of Dawson's past—they were fascinating. "What about Braxton and Zach?"

"What about them?"

"You stayed friends."

"Brax's fault. He's better at keeping in touch than I am."

"Did the cops rule them out right away?"

"They were watching TV together. Either neither of them did it, or they both did it. Brax can be shady, but can I see him strangling a girl? No way. He treats women like princesses, even his wife."

Dawson's shake of the head let me know exactly what he thought of *her*.

"And Zach? What about him?"

"Zach can't even kill a spider. I'm serious. Alexa had to catch them. Vi, if I had any concerns, I wouldn't have let you on a surfboard with him."

"Couldn't anyone else have broken in? The stories mentioned security cameras?"

"Alexa and her paranoia. She positioned cameras above the front, back, and side doors, and nobody but the ten of us came and went. Grey wasn't even there that day."

"What about the windows?"

"They were all locked from the inside. I installed the locks myself." Dawson sighed again. "Nothing good comes from dredging up the past. Trust me, I know. Every time I think of Bryony and Hannah, it's like being punched in the chest."

I squeezed Dawson's hand. "I'm so sorry you lost them."

"Can't change history, Vi."

"But don't you want to know what made Levi flip?"

"Even if we found out, what difference would it make? Ruby would still be dead, and we can't pretend the trial from hell didn't happen. If Levi was the devil, then his mom was a fire-breathing demon and their lawyer was Cerberus."

I'd gotten that from the news stories. Mrs. Sykes had never missed a chance to badmouth everyone but her son, and the lawyer had made the unidentified minor—Alexa—cry in court. Even poor Ruby hadn't been allowed to rest in peace. No, she'd been painted as a whore, a woman of loose morals who slept with any man who bought her a drink.

"Do you still see much of the others?"

"Apart from Brax and Zach? Not really. I speak to Justin, but he still lives in Virginia, so we don't get together often. After Ruby died, I changed my life. Until then, I'd worked evenings as a bartender and days on a construction site, but I wanted more. A career, not just a job. So I joined the Navy and shipped out overseas. Grey distanced himself from the whole mess, and Nolan's running a vineyard out here somewhere."

"Do you regret losing touch with Grey?"

"Sometimes. We were all close back in those days."

"What about…" Who was the tenth housemate? "Uh, Jerry?"

"Jerry disappeared." Dawson checked his watch, and there was nothing subtle about that move. "Should I make us dinner? You want burgers again? Steak? Chicken wings?"

Conversation: over. While I found it therapeutic to talk

over what had happened to me, to pick events apart and analyse what went wrong, Dawson, it seemed, felt the opposite. And I'd live with that because I loved him.

"Chicken wings. Want me to make a salad?"

"With sweetcorn?"

I'd discovered that Dawson loved the darn stuff. "With plenty of sweetcorn."

Soon, the smell of smoke and cooking meat drifted into the kitchen, and my stomach grumbled. But even as I chopped carrots and shredded lettuce, I couldn't get rid of the niggle at the base of my spine. Without closure, nothing ended.

And I had a horrible feeling that the demons of Blackstone House weren't dead, only sleeping.

A FEW WORDS FROM ALEXA...

If you're curious about what Alexa has to say, I've jotted down a few of her thoughts for members of my reader group...

Download the bonus chapter here:
www.elise-noble.com/a13xa

WHAT'S NEXT?

My next book will be the second in the Blackstone House series, *Hard Tide...*

Private investigator Ari Danner is out of money and out of luck in Las Vegas when she's offered the biggest contract of her life. The first problem? The job is in California. The second problem? She'll have to go undercover as a beach babe and she can't even swim. But the money is too good to pass up, and she'll do anything to secure her daughter's future, even cosy up to pro surfer Zach Torres as she gathers evidence of his role in a sports betting scam.

Zach doesn't usually pick up women by giving them CPR on his surfboard, but right from the start, he knew Ari was different. Smart, easy to talk to, interested in more than his billboard-worthy abs. But secrets can tear love apart, and Zach soon finds that there's more than his relationship at risk.

For more details:
www.elise-noble.com/hard-tide

WHAT'S NEXT?

If you enjoyed *Hard Lines*, please consider leaving a review.

For an author, every review is incredibly important. Not only do they make us feel warm and fuzzy inside, readers consider them when making their decision whether or not to buy a book. Even a line saying you enjoyed the book or what your favourite part was helps a lot.

WANT TO STALK ME?

For updates on my new releases, giveaways, and other random stuff, you can sign up for my newsletter on my website:
www.elise-noble.com

If you're on Facebook, you might also like to join Team Blackwood for exclusive giveaways, sneak previews, and book-related chat. Be the first to find out about new stories, and you might even see your name or one of your suggestions make it into print!

And if you'd like to read my books for FREE, you can also find details of how to join my advance review team.

Would you like to join Team Blackwood?

www.elise-noble.com/team-blackwood

facebook.com/EliseNobleAuthor
twitter.com/EliseANoble
instagram.com/elise_noble

END-OF-BOOK STUFF

I'm so happy that this book has finally seen the light of day! I wrote it several years ago, and it sat on my hard drive until I had enough spoons to tackle the rest of the series. Nine very different roommates, thrown together by circumstances, bound together by the past. Back when I originally plotted the Blackstone House mystery, I thought that maybe it would be a bit farfetched, but with everything that's gone on in the world since I first started drafting the big plot, the storyline seems perfectly plausible, lol.

Did you spot the Blackwood connection in *Hard Lines*? It's set in the same world, and there'll be a bit more crossover in the future. Maybe Emmy will even make an appearance at some point? I haven't decided yet, mwahaha. Anyhow, I hope you enjoyed the first instalment :) Next up, Zach's story… And then I'll skip back to a novella for Lauren. I finished writing it on the plane on the way back from Egypt last week, and I need to read it through this weekend because the ending may or may not be coherent. If you've read *Into the Black*, my experience at Sharm el Sheikh airport was on a par with Emmy's (thank goodness I took my own loo roll), so alcohol was a necessity on the flight home. Rewrites might be required. Wish me luck!

Until next time,

Elise

ALSO BY ELISE NOBLE

Blackwood Security

For the Love of Animals (Nate & Carmen - Prequel)

Black is My Heart (Diamond & Snow - Prequel)

Pitch Black

Into the Black

Forever Black

Gold Rush

Gray is My Heart

Neon (novella)

Out of the Blue

Ultraviolet

Glitter (novella)

Red Alert

White Hot

Sphere (novella)

The Scarlet Affair

Spirit (novella)

Quicksilver

The Girl with the Emerald Ring

Red After Dark

When the Shadows Fall

Pretties in Pink

Chimera

Secret Weapon (Crossover with Baldwin's Shore)

The Devil and the Deep Blue Sea (2023)

Blackwood Elements

Oxygen

Lithium

Carbon

Rhodium

Platinum

Lead

Copper

Bronze

Nickel

Hydrogen

Blackwood UK

Joker in the Pack

Cherry on Top

Roses are Dead

Shallow Graves

Indigo Rain

Pass the Parcel (TBA)

Blackwood Casefiles

Stolen Hearts

Burning Love (TBA)

Baldwin's Shore

Dirty Little Secrets

Secrets, Lies, and Family Ties

Buried Secrets

Secret Weapon (Crossover with Blackwood Security)

A Secret to Die For (2023)

Blackstone House

Hard Lines (2022)

Blurred Lines (novella)

Hard Tide (2023)

Hard Limits (2023)

The Electi

Cursed

Spooked

Possessed

Demented

Judged

The Planes

A Vampire in Vegas

A Devil in the Dark (TBA)

The Trouble Series

Trouble in Paradise

Nothing but Trouble

24 Hours of Trouble

Standalone

Life

Coco du Ciel

A Very Happy Christmas (novella)

Twisted (short stories)

Books with clean versions available (no swearing and no on-the-page sex)

Pitch Black

Into the Black

Forever Black

Gold Rush

Gray is My Heart

Audiobooks

Black is My Heart (Diamond & Snow - Prequel)

Pitch Black

Into the Black

Forever Black

Gold Rush

Gray is My Heart

Neon (novella)

Printed in Great Britain
by Amazon

87073712R00253